"DENSE AND POLITICALLY PROVOCA-
TIVE."—*New York Times Book Review*

"A compelling blend of solid mystery and well-
realized police background spiced with Maggie's
feisty personality."—*MLB News*

"Intriguing and refreshing.... [Hornsby's] thoroughly modern Maggie is a superb narrator who
is as likeable as she is understandable."
—*Deadly Pleasures*

"Wendy Hornsby is one of the most talented and
versatile authors today.... A tightly woven and
expertly constructed riveting mystery that seems
real and feels emotionally explosive."
—*Affaire de Coeur*

"Fascinating ... an exciting, thoroughly captivating
read."—*Booklist* (starred)

"In addition to writing with suspense and style,
Hornsby shows an enormous humanity."
—*Cleveland Plain Dealer*

"[Hornsby] knows her milieu and her characters
come alive."—*Fresno Bee*

THE MAGGIE MACGOWEN MYSTERY SERIES
BY WENDY HORNSBY

77th Street Requiem

A Maggie MacGowen Mystery

WENDY HORNSBY

AN ONYX BOOK

ONYX
Published by the Penguin Group
Penguin Books USA Inc., 375 Hudson Street,
New York, New York 10014, U.S.A.
Penguin Books Ltd, 27 Wrights Lane,
London W8 5TZ, England
Penguin Books Australia Ltd, Ringwood,
Victoria, Australia
Penguin Books Canada Ltd, 10 Alcorn Avenue,
Toronto, Ontario, Canada M4V 3B2
Penguin Books (N.Z.) Ltd, 182–190 Wairau Road,
Auckland 10, New Zealand

Penguin Books Ltd, Registered Offices:
Harmondsworth, Middlesex, England

Published by Onyx, an imprint of Dutton Signet,
a division of Penguin Books USA Inc.
Previously appeared in a Dutton edition.

First Onyx Printing, October, 1996
10 9 8 7 6 5 4 3 2 1

To He Who Shall Remain Nameless
You know who you are. Thank you.

CHAPTER

1

Fahizah taught me the perils of hesitation—to shoot first and make sure the pig is dead before splitting.

—Patricia Hearst, eulogy to Nancy Ling Perry,
June 8, 1974

May 10, 1974. I see the scene filmed in high-contrast black and white, like an old news photo. Roy Frady is, after all, old news. Old grief, too. Now that he is my film subject, that's how I will shoot him, in high-contrast black and white.

I never met Roy Frady. When he died, an L.A. cop with four years, nine months on the job, I was a kid in high school preparing for a summer in Europe. If our paths ever crossed, I doubt whether either of us would have paid the other any attention. He was a Vietnam vet with one marriage and two kids behind him. I was the daughter of a Berkeley physics professor, with braces still on my teeth. It may be difficult to explain how, twenty-some years after his murder, Roy Frady moved out of my documentary in progress and into my life.

Frady was to be the first project I produced under contract with one of the big three TV networks, a contract that wanted two documentaries a year aimed at a demographic audience about halfway between "Hard Copy" and PBS. I loved researching Frady, and it was nice to know that for a change I would be free from grubbing around for facilities and resources. But I had been an independent filmmaker for too long to accede graciously to network oversight: "Black and white? There's no color in black and white."

A contract of another sort had brought my daughter and me to Los Angeles, one that had clauses for either "from this day forward" or *adiós amigo* attached. Until I decided which, I needed to pay my share of the rent in one of the more expensive cities in the world, keep my daughter in tutus, and help with my sister's endless medical expenses. Working on Frady within the network framework was the price I paid for the price I was paid.

It was a daily battle with the brass, but I managed to at least begin the Frady film in black and white.

May 10, 1974, was a clear, warm Friday, a typical Southern California spring day. Roy Frady worked day watch out of LAPD's Seventy-seventh Street station, putting in his last day assigned to CRASH, the gang detail, working in the Watts area. He was confident of a commendation landing in his jacket for his success in creating a powerful police presence wherever gang members showed themselves; a commanding figure in his crisp uniform, he had ambition.

Frady had vacation time coming that he planned to spend in Long Beach with his girlfriend, helping her recover from the boob job his overtime had paid for. After his thirty days off, he would go back where he felt most comfortable, working street patrol out of

Seventy-seventh Street Division in the city's southeastern section.

At around 5:30, Roy Frady left the station wearing pressed chinos, soft-suede chukka boots, and a plaid flannel shirt with the tail hanging out to cover the .38-caliber, two-inch Smith & Wesson Airweight revolver tucked, not holstered, under his belt. He headed north on the Harbor freeway, driving his own car, to meet three of his coworkers for drinks at the police academy bar.

Officially, the four men were celebrating the reunion at Seventy-seventh Street of the Four Horsemen—Frady, Mike Flint, Doug Senecal, Hector Melendez. I say officially because wives and girlfriends had to be given some sort of excuse when all the men had in mind, probably, was getting drunk and getting laid.

I'm not sure what Frady's state of mind was at that point, or what he expected to get out of the evening. My sense is that he was full of cocky good humor: his work on CRASH moved him closer to a promotion, he had a steady girlfriend who loved him, and an estranged wife who still slept with him, and had, according to the evidence in his underwear, slept with him that very morning. He didn't go straight home after a few drinks, and I don't know why.

On Friday nights the Embers Room, the police academy bar, was always crowded, as it still is: cops out of uniform, brass off the high horse, and women looking for midnight blue dick. It was Frady's milieu.

When he walked into the bar, Frady spotted Mike Flint first—couldn't miss him, tall, skinny, sandy brown hair already beginning to recede at the temples, the wire-rim glasses that earned Flint his Conan the Librarian nickname; Flint only joined up after the department relaxed its vision standards. When Roy Frady set his course toward Mike Flint's baritone laugh and crossed the room to join his friends, it was six o'clock. Hector Melendez remembered checking his watch.

Doug Senecal's face was already flushed from drink when he moved over to give Frady the seat between him and Mike Flint. Senecal, handsome, muscular, dimples like exclamation points for the ends of his dark mustache, suffering through the breakup of marriage number three, seemed unaware of the women around him who did everything but back flips to get his attention.

Senecal slugged back a V.O. and water, chased it with beer, and signaled for another round: shooters for himself and Mike, Coors for Frady—always Coors—and Bacardi and Coke for Hector.

Hector leaned on the bar to see around Mike. "So, Frady, I'm driving past the Most Worshipful Mount Nebo Lodge last night around midwatch." Hector slurred his words some. "And what do I see spray-painted all over the front door?"

"It said, Fuck you, Melendez?" Frady shifted the revolver under his belt when he sat down.

"It didn't say fuck me." Hector laughed. "It said, Kill Roy Frady, then it was signed with some gang bejoobie. Getting to be a real nuisance in the division, Frady, all your little gangster buddies announcing their love for you on the streets like that. Good thing you're off CRASH or we'd be repainting the whole goddamn division."

Frady had seen the Kill Frady graffiti, too, all over the south end of the city. He was almost proud of it, meant he had gotten to someone. He swaggered. "Good thing for the Crips and the Brims I'm off CRASH. Took a lot of trial and error, but I found the spot at the back of their thick skulls, I hit it just right with my flashlight, pops 'em open like a ripe melon. Gangster brains all over the goddamn street."

"You need another drink, Frady," Senecal said. "Shrink that head of yours down to normal size. Talk about a ripe melon."

Mike had to contribute his own gibe. "A week in Seventy-seventh, we'll have him straightened around again. Right, Hector?"

Hector was distracted by a sweet young thing at a nearby table. His three friends watched him and exchanged lewd leers. Though Hector was the toughest street brawler in the division, and the hardest drinker, his dark curly hair and big brown eyes gave him a deceptive, teddy bear quality. Women wouldn't leave him alone. This one thrust out her chest when Hector smiled at her, smoothed the seat of her tight miniskirt over her baby-fat bottom.

"Jailbait, Hec." Frady grabbed Hec's shoulder and pulled him in close, with Mike trapped between them. "Be sure you ID her first. Or get a note from her mommy saying she can be out past ten."

"Just looking." Hector blushed behind his tan. "No charge for looking. Anyway, I gotta save myself for my date later."

"Your date have a friend for me?" Mike pushed them both away. "Make it a party?"

"Maybe. But only if you call home first, Conan,"

Hector scolded Flint. "I don't want your wife calling my wife anymore, looking for you. Gets me in the doghouse every time, you dumb shit."

"Conan, you're a bad boy." Frady grinned; so much shared history among them. The Four Whoresmen, the lieutenant called them. He gave them all a two-day suspension when he caught them dirty with some topless dancers from a bar out in Southgate, busted their little party in Flint's camper parked behind the club.

Mike punched Frady's arm. "Admit it, Frady. You missed us."

"Maybe." Frady looked sidelong at Mike, something defensive in the cock of his head. "But I had a good time in CRASH, developed some good street contacts, brought in better than my share of the little creeps, terrorized the 'hood. Captain said I have an affinity for the job."

"Yeah?" Senecal asked. "But can you spell affinity?"

"If I have to, I'll look it up."

"Sounds like you have a plan." Like an owl behind his big glasses, Mike studied Frady. "You moving on, Roy?"

"We're all moving on, Conan. Senecal's thinking about Metro. I know you'll go to detectives, and Hector's probably going to follow you because following you is what Hector does best." Frady grew serious, seemed a little sad. "I signed up for the next sergeant's exam. I want to stay on the street, work some more on gang suppression. Just promise you'll keep in touch when you're downtown running the head shed."

"One thing's for damn sure," Mike said, scowling.

"I'm never going into administration. Another thing, I'm never going to leave you out there alone."

"What is this, a wake?" Senecal nudged Mike. "Conan, tell Frady about your bust."

Mike shrugged him off. "Forget it." He concentrated on his glass. "We could get our asses fired on that one, so keep a lid on it, will you?"

"The stick caper?" Hector signaled another round because he was already half in the bag and wasn't keeping track; he'd only taken two hits from the drink in front of him. "I don't think we'd draw more than maybe a two-month suspension. Anyway, if you don't tell Frady, I will. It's my bust, too."

Senecal laughed. "You never tell a story right, Hec. You don't have the gift."

"So, tell it yourself, Senecal, you think you have the gift."

"Not me. Conan, tell Frady."

"I told you to shut up," Mike muttered.

Frady reached up to wrap an arm around Mike's neck. "No one but family here, Conan. Every person in this room but me has probably heard all about it by now. Why don't you tell me so I'll get it right?"

"No big deal," Mike shrugged. "But if I take the beef, I expect you three to make my house payment."

"Sure, partner," Frady said. "Better than that, we'll all draw two months suspension together, charter a boat and go down to Baja, do some serious fishing."

"Uh-huh," Senecal said. "Draw two months, find a couple more part-time security jobs to cover my alimony. Tell the goddamn story, Flint."

Mike shifted his rangy six-foot-two like a saddle-sore cowboy settling in for the long ride. "Started maybe a week ago, wasn't it, Hec?"

"About a week ago." Hector grinned in anticipation.

"Asshole breaks into this woman's apartment, beats her, rapes her, ransacks her house. Ugly scene. By the time she calls in and we get over there, he's long gone. She's in bad shape—about what you expect. We take her over to Morningside Hospital, get her patched up, take her report. She gives us a pretty good description of the guy, we get a good sketch, put out a Teletype by the end of watch. But we don't pull him in."

"Old boyfriend?" Frady asked, starting on his second Coors.

"Not this one," Hector said. "Complete stranger. "

Senecal glanced at Frady. "That nurse you're doing, JoAnn, she still working Morningside?"

"Yeah. I moved in with her."

Flint pushed aside his drink, leaned closer to Frady. "Hec and I drive by the victim's place at the start of the next watch, check on the woman—she's pretty shook up—thinking chances are it was so easy for the asshole, he'll be back—he promised her he would. And back he comes, but not until just about the time me and Hec are on the freeway headed for home. He puts her through it again, only worse: sodomizes her, breaks her nose, trashes what little she has left after the first time. She's living in this crappy little studio over a garage, working her ass off to keep it. It may not be much, I'm thinking, but it's all she has, and he comes in and destroys everything. Just because he can do it, because he can overpower her. And us."

Frady smiled in anticipation. "What'd you do?"

"Went looking for him. Every car in the division is looking for him. Sergeant has someone drive by the place every half hour or so. I think that if it gets tight enough for him, the asshole will go torment someone else, leave this one alone. He knows we're out there. He gets off on fooling with us, waits till we go by and then he hits her door again. He's inside there beating on her at the same time we're cruising by. This time, he doesn't even bother to rape her, he just settles for a quick pounding, and then he's gone."

Hector chimed in, "Moron don't know better than to tug on Superman's cape. You should have heard Mike when he gets the call."

"Who's telling this?" Mike glared at Hector. "There's no way he'll leave her alone until we catch him—the game is like an obsession or something. So, me and Hec get the sergeant's okay to set up a stakeout. For two days, we hardly even piss, we watch that damn place so close."

"But the asshole waits for an opening—we go for coffee—and he's in again," Hector said. "That's when you should have heard Mike."

"We've all heard Mike," Senecal said, taking over Mike's drink, downing it.

"You telling this?" Mike asked, eyes narrowed.

"Go on," Frady said. "I have places to go, so get on with it."

"So," Mike said, "he was in there with her while we were out front watching for him. Maybe we didn't see him go in, but we sure saw him come out. Butt first out the bathroom window, came sliding down the drainpipe right into the sights of my roscoe. I let him run a little, just so we could fool with him."

"You beat the dog shit out of him?" Frady asked.

"Nah. Just laid him on the ground and cuffed him, sorry son of a bitch. Then he gets froggy with me. 'I'll be out on bail in the morning,' he says. 'I'll be back.' We all know it's true. Hec gets the woman to come downstairs and ID him. She goes absolutely hysterical when she sees the guy, and he feeds on it, tells her what he's going to come back and do to her. Meantime, we have him cuffed to the car door, patting him down."

"So much noise, we're drawing a crowd," Hector said. "Whole damn neighborhood's out there, mouthing off, talking street justice."

Mike nodded. "I want to get out of there before the crowd moves in. I ask the victim if she's ready to press charges, but she's too scared to do it. Then that poor misguided *detainee* starts bad-mouthing me, too, kicking the side of the car, kicking at me, calling me every name his mother ever called him. I take out my stick, act like I'm going to sting him across the legs, try to settle him down. But he's just getting started. Everything he says, he's terrorizing this woman and he's loving it. He's got everything but a hard-on."

Hector said, "I'm thinking it's gonna get ugly when we try to get him in the car. And I'm thinking the folks around us are gonna barbecue him for supper before we get to that point."

"The victim's bawling, ready to come apart on us," Flint said. "She's screaming, 'Make him stop!' Gives me an idea. So, I go over to her, give her my stick. 'Hit him,' I say. She thinks I'm kidding, but I see the light come on in her. I walk her over to the car, I say it again, 'Go ahead and hit him.' "

Hector was the Greek chorus. "Crowd starts chant-ing 'Hit him! Hit him!'"

"She takes a little more persuading, but she taps him one, hits him on the legs, but too soft to do any good.",

Hector again: "People in the 'hood are all yellin', 'Hit him bitch! Hit the nigger harder!'"

"He starts howling police abuse," Mike said.

"Hold it," Frady said. "How come you didn't want to tell me about this caper, but the whole neighbor-hood knows about it?"

"They're not going to snitch me off," Flint said. "We're tight. Hell, I've arrested half their kids. Be-sides, they do anything, they know I'll come back on them."

Senecal gave him a nudge. "Get on with it."

"I am." Flint nudged back. "So I take the victim over to the telephone pole, show her how to use the stick, tell her to hit the damn pole as hard as she can. Takes her maybe three whacks before she decides she's going to get behind the swing. That fourth whack, she really made the old wood sing. So I walk her back to the car and I tell her to go to it, just don't hit him on the face or the head."

Mike got into it, too, demonstrating with an imagi-nary stick, making the sound of wood hitting flesh, "Bap, bap, bap. Better than a hundred years of ther-apy the way she took control and lit into him. I let her get in some good licks, let him see she wasn't going to take any more off him. She didn't really hurt him, but, shit, did she scare the son of a bitch. By the time I took my stick back, he was practically begging us to take him in and book him. Sorry-ass piece of crap."

"Crowd's going crazy." Hector gestured with both hands. "Everyone wants a shot at him. If we'd just turned our backs, they would have killed him for sure."

"Good story," Frady said, but he checked his watch as if he had someplace else to be right then. "Wish I'd been there."

"Where you shoulda' been is court." Hector, forgetting caution, pushed away Mike's restraining hand and grabbed Frady's sleeve. "We go to the arraignment, and the asshole's public defender starts whining about police brutality, says that Mike cuffed his client and told the alleged victim to beat him with his stick. The judge turns to Mike, says, 'Officer Flint, can this allegation be true?' And Mike says. . ." Hector started to laugh and couldn't go on, but laughing at the wrong time was why Hector never could tell a story right. Senecal prodded him until he caught his breath. "So, the judge asks Mike if he gave his stick to the victim. And Mike turns and gives the judge that innocent librarian look, and he says, 'Your Honor, does that story sound reasonable to you?' "

By then, they had gathered an audience; good story-telling always does. While the other three men attracted women with their good looks, Mike's asset was personality. A couple of the women started cheering about the rapist taking his medicine, draped their perfumed arms around Mike, and wanted more details. Wanted him. Someone bought Mike a drink. He blushed, dropped his head, laughed into his chest.

"Good thing we're all family," he said.

According to Hector, Frady seemed distracted. At 8:30 on Hector's watch, Frady told the others he had to call his girlfriend. Telephone company records show that the call was placed at 8:34 and lasted ten minutes, thirty-three seconds. The girlfriend corroborated the records.

Hector remembered Frady excusing himself to make a second call at around 9:15. There are no records of a second call. Any number of things could have happened: the number he dialed was busy, or he changed his mind and didn't call at all. Maybe he ran into someone on the way to the telephone and stopped to talk in the corridor beyond the bar.

There is a possibility that Frady needed a private conversation with someone who was there that night, and they stepped outside into the rock garden. His girlfriend's ex-lover, who also worked out of Seventy-seventh Street, was in the bar at some point in the evening. No one seems to remember when the ex, a cop named Ridgeway, arrived, only that he was shit-faced when he left at ten o'clock. When questioned, Ridgeway said he was so drunk that he blacked out the entire night, couldn't remember anything.

It is also possible that Hector, after his fifth beer, was simply wrong about a second call. There were a lot of people in the Embers Room by 9:15, a lot of coming and going and table-hopping. Who could keep track of anyone?

There is a consensus that at 10:40 Frady said he was late for a date in Long Beach. After his good-byes, he left the academy, alone, driving his own two-year-old gold Pinto station wagon. At that point he had been drinking for over four hours. Mike Flint didn't remember Frady as being drunk when he gave him a farewell handshake. But by 10:40 Flint wasn't in very good shape to judge anyone's sobriety.

Roy Frady might as well have driven his car out of the academy lot and into the stratosphere for all anyone has been able to find out.

Frady never showed up in Long Beach. There has been a lot of speculation about where he might have gone, or who he might have met. Speculation, but no answers.

After being missing all night, Frady reappeared in the jurisdiction of Seventy-seventh Street Division at 8:30 Saturday morning.

Mrs. Ella Turner was out of milk that Saturday morning. She had planned to make a special pancake breakfast as a farewell meal for her nephew, who had been visiting for a few weeks. So she sent her fifteen-year-old son, Matthew, and her eighteen-year-old nephew, Walter, to walk to the market two blocks away on Main Street.

Mrs. Turner specifically reminded the boys not to shortcut through the alley behind Eighty-ninth Street, because everyone in the neighborhood knew that a house on the alley had been burned down after a bad drug deal, and that the people in the house next door ran a bookie operation and car-theft scam. But who can tell teenage boys anything?

Cutting through the alley behind Eighty-ninth Street, Matthew Turner and his cousin Walter saw Roy Frady lying on the floor of what had been a bedroom in that burned-out house. At first they thought he was a bum sleeping it off and they picked up some gravel to peg him with. But his clothes—pressed chinos, chukka boots, a plaid Pendleton shirt—looked too good for a bum. So they decided he was sick or drunk and might have stumbled in the dark the night before and hurt himself.

Mrs. Turner's lectures on Christian charity apparently had some belated effect. The two boys went into the forbidden ruins to help the man. But they stopped when they realized that the Pendleton shirt was wrapped around the man's head, and that the dark smear they originally thought was vomit was instead the man's blood and brains leaking through the flannel.

The burned-out house was rebuilt years ago. Roy Frady's two young children have children of their own, and do not remember him. In the foyer of the Seventy-seventh Street Division an enlarged and faded black-and-white portrait of Frady hung among the portraits of six other officers killed in the line of duty until the spring of 1995, when the Seventy-seventh Street station was demolished and the portrait was sent to a government warehouse. But don't construe this to mean that Roy Frady has been forgotten.

Frady's murder is still an open case, never solved. The investigation is kept active by one senior homicide detective, who has Frady's murder book on his desk at Parker Center, the police administration building. Witnesses move, change their stories, die, and all of it is carefully entered into the record.

Police regularly update a special bulletin asking all law-enforcement agencies to test-fire every 9-mm weapon that is booked in, hoping one day to discover one with characteristics that match the Browning cartridge cases and bullets taken from Frady's body and found at the scene: 9-mm parabellum, six lands and grooves, right-hand twist, lands .085.

Even though I am not authorized to see them, I have read the frayed reports in Frady's murder book. They tell a good story. Good enough that they sold my network on Frady as a subject.

Roy Frady may have been a bad boy, but he was also one hell of a nice guy. The angle to his story that I found irresistible from the beginning, and the angle that cinched the project, was that there seemed to be a lot of people who wanted Frady dead, and even more who claimed to have done the deed.

I have the senior detective's full cooperation on the project. He knows that there is someone out there who knows what happened to Roy Frady between 10:40 Friday night and 8:30 Saturday morning. Publicity can only help find them.

The detective is due to retire from the department in May. Last night he told me that before he empties his desk drawers into a cardboard box and turns his back on the city forever, Frady's murder book will be shelved among the closed cases. After he told me that, the detective turned over and went to sleep.

CHAPTER

2

Mike Flint cried out in his sleep and wakened me. The bedside light was on—had been on the last three nights. I leaned over him, watched the nightmare contort the features of his craggy face, wondered which version of the terror was playing this time. The soft light behind his white hair gave Mike an off-center halo, made the sweat on his face all shiny.

You don't wake up sleepwalkers, but what are you supposed to do for someone in the middle of a three-night nightmare? Do you let him sleep, hoping he forgets about it in the morning? Or do you rescue him?

I wiped Mike's face with a corner of the sheet, then went on to dry his neck and chest. He woke up with a gasp like a drowning man reaching the surface. He grabbed my arm. "Maggie?"

"You okay?"

"Hector was here," he said, his voice loud in the quiet house. He raised up on one elbow to look around the room for Hector. "Hec sat right here on the bed between us. He talked to me."

"You were dreaming, Mike."

"Jesus, Maggie, it was so real."

"What did he say?"

"Usual bullshit about the old days." Mike dropped back against the pillow. "So damn real. We were talking. Then he got up and walked over to the window. Talking all the time—you know how Hector talks— he climbed up on the sill and he jumped. He didn't say good-bye or anything, he just floated away."

"You were crying."

"No. I felt like I couldn't breathe, that's all."

"Do you want a drink?"

He shook his head, splaying damp tendrils of his fine hair on the pillow. "It's easier to believe Hector can fly than to imagine he's gone. Hector in a box. Jesus Christ, Maggie. He survives almost twenty-five years working the streets, kicking ass, taking names, buying his own share of lumps. I've seen him take on three of the biggest, badass scumbags all at once all by himself, and he gets nothing more than a scuff on his spit shine. So how is it he goes over to help out a neighbor, and now he's in a box?"

"The neighbor had a gun. You always tell me domestic calls are the riskiest."

"So, why did he go in there? He's on his day off. He's not obligated to do anything. Why did he go talk to the guy? Asshole wants to die, why interfere just because some old lady comes crying, 'My boy's going to jump.' He was supposed to say, 'So, lady, call nine-one-one and keep off the sidewalk till it's over.' This is what I'm going to say in the eulogy: Hec, you big dumb fuck, don't you remember anything you learned out there?"

"I didn't know Hector all that well until we started looking into Roy Frady's murder," I said. "I'll miss him. The interviews he did for me with people who remember Frady are amazingly good, but I can hardly watch them without coming apart. How did he find all those people after so much time, and how did he persuade them to talk to a camera?"

"Hec was the smartest detective who ever worked this city. The best partner I ever had." Mike let out a quavery breath. "Jesus Christ, Hector."

Mike had tears on his cheeks. He's one of those throwbacks who thinks he's too tough to cry and too tough to need any help. I'm forever waiting him out, looking for the back way in. If he's difficult, he's also worth the effort. I got up on my knees with my back to him and started detangling the sheets so he could finish what he needed to do without a witness.

He put a hand on my arm when I bent over him to free the sheet caught under his hip. I kissed his flat abdomen, rubbed my cheek against the long muscle of his marathoner thigh.

"Please," he said, and caressed my shoulder. When I stroked him, though, he stayed soft. When I went down on him, I could feel his deep sighs, but they were the sighs of grief and not of passion. The sort of comfort he thought he wanted, his body would not give him.

I sat up, took him by the shoulders, and pulled him up eye-to-eye with me. "Let's run."

"In the middle of the night?" He put on his glasses

to look at the clock. "It's three-thirty. The neighbors will call the cops."

"You are the cops." I got out of bed. "Come on. Get dressed."

The night was clear, cold for October. We warmed up in the backyard of the rented house we shared in South Pasadena. Mike's nearly grown son, Michael, lived in the small guesthouse at the bottom of the yard. Tuition alone at Michael's private college was a stretch on Mike's detective salary; there wasn't enough left for campus housing. Mike stopped at the guest-house on his way to the alley gate, listened at his son's door, and checked the lock. It's a reflex. I had looked in on my teenage daughter, Casey, before we came downstairs.

The dog followed us out of the house. He loves to run with us, but Mike stopped him at the gate and told him to stay, leaving him standing sentinel over the yard.

Off in the distance I could hear the freeway, a sound like rushing waves. But around us there was the profound silence of a neighborhood asleep. Even the mange-eaten poodle at the corner didn't bother to come out and bark at us when we passed his fence.

We ran at an easy pace down the middle of the street, a luxury of open space, our shoes a soft pat-pat on the asphalt. Mike is by far the better runner in range and speed and generally looking cool than I am, but he stayed close beside me. For social reasons, I thought.

Halloween was less than a week away. Some of the bare sycamore trees on our block were hung with big plastic pumpkins, as they would be hung with plastic

Christmas bulbs in another month. A few families had done their best to make spooky yard displays: bed-sheet ghosts, stuffed-blue-jean scare-crows, witches draped with polyester cobwebs. By day they were funny, but in the shadows of night they were eerie, like prowlers lurking under dark windows.

We passed a yard lined with cardboard headstones. I smiled as I read the handwritten inscriptions, recognizing the names of the kids whose balls kept finding their way over our fence: Here Lies Chris, Died for a Kiss. Poor Hannah, Tripped on a Banana. Final Resting Placey, Our Ugly Sister Tracey.

"Seven months to retirement," Mike said, reading the headstones as we passed by. "The four of us, we went through so much together, we were always going to go out together. Frady's gone, now Hector's gone. Just me and Doug left."

"The Four Horsemen," I said.

He bumped my shoulder. "That was a long time ago. A very long time ago."

"What are you going to say in the eulogy?"

"That we've been cheated out of one hell of a retirement party."

Mike picked up the pace, challenging me to keep up. We crossed Fair Oaks at Mission Street and began to sprint when the park was in view. I dropped back when he entered the park: the grass was uneven, like hammered silver in the pale moonlight. Instead of running on ahead, Mike began to tease me, egging me into playing follow the leader. He ran into the children's sandlot, then vaulted through a swing, making sure I was behind him. He pounded up one side of the teeter-totter and rode it down the other. On the slide ladder he touched only two rungs on his way to the top; I hit every two. There was no way I could keep up with him when he turned it on, so he ran in circles around me, made me mad.

In the picnic area, Mike jumped onto the bench attached to a picnic table, stepped up onto the table, then in a long leap, hit the ground on the far side. He vaulted three tables the same way. I pumped as hard as I could, skipped the third table, and reached the fourth one right on his heels. I was on top of the table when he touched down on the grass and started to sprint.

I pushed myself into the air, flew into his back, brought him down flat on his belly. Sitting on his legs, I yanked down the back of his shorts, smooched his round, white ass—a shiny full moon against the darker turf—and then I was gone before he had his pants back up and had found his feet.

I ran as fast as I could, but in four steps he caught me around the legs, spun me, dropped me, hard, onto my back, pinned my arms over my head, and straddled me.

"When will you learn?" he said, whiskering my neck. "Tug on Superman's cape, you have to pay."

"Kissing your sweet butt is all the pay I need." I struggled under him just so it wouldn't be too easy, all the time trying not to laugh. Inside his shorts, where he pressed against me, he was hard. I lay still and looked up into his Bogart face, watched his smile finally break wide.

"Mike."

"You can't get away from me."

"I don't want to get away. Do me now."

CHAPTER

3

Doug Senecal dropped in for breakfast. To check on Mike he said, but it was Doug who looked in need of cheering. He set a place for himself at the table next to Michael, Mike's college sophomore son, and dropped an English muffin into the toaster. Michael filled him in: school was fine, his mother was fine, his girlfriend was still his girlfriend, and yes, it was nice to have Casey and me cluttering up the house after baching for so long with his dad.

"I ever tell you about the day I first met Mike?" Doug asked Michael as he poured his second cup of coffee.

"I don't think so." Michael, a more handsome version of his father, winked at me—we had all heard the story. "Tell me about it."

"I was still a probationer, fresh out of the academy. Right off, they assigned me to Seventy-seventh, toughest division in the city. We're talking war zone. Seventy-seventh is where the real cops were, the old-time gun-

slingers, legends. Street brawlers, guys'd as soon shoot
'em as book 'em. I was just a sweet young thing back
then. And just a tad nervous."

Mike laughed. "Trust me, you were never a sweet
young thing, Doug. And you weren't a little nervous,
you were all but shitting your pants."

Doug leaned back in his chair and smiled at Michael, woebegone no more. "I report to roll call, find
my name on the assignment sheet, partnered with
P-three Flint, my training officer. I start checking
name tags. Room's full of bad-looking guys, big and
mean-looking guys. I'm thinking, I'm going to go out
there and learn to be a real policeman with one of
these cowboys. I'm getting excited. Then I spot the
name I'm looking for, Flint, and the guy looks like a
librarian. I think, fuck, I'm doomed. I'll get killed out
there, riding Tonto to a scholar when I need the
Lone Ranger."

Doug and Mike both laughed, a male-bonding thing.
Michael got up and refilled my cup and his, patted my
back when he sat again; we were outsiders together.

I said, "But, as it turned out, Mike was the baddest
guy in the division."

"Yeah." Doug looked at Mike with pure love.
"Taught me everything I know about police work. If
it wasn't for Mike, I'd be a captain now." He slathered
marmalade on his second muffin. "We sure had fun.
God, I wouldn't trade those years for anything."

"Partners seven years, shop eighteen A ninety-
seven—drove the wheels off that car. With Roy and
Hector out there as backup. We were good. Got a lot
of criminals off the street." Mike pushed his plate
away and sighed. "They don't keep partners together

that long anymore. You ride with a new man every rotation, you're never sure you can rely on him or not."

"Maybe it's a good thing." I began picking up dishes. "Even kindergarten teachers know to separate the troublemakers."

Michael stacked his father's cereal bowl on his own in the sink. "Maggie, sorry I can't wait till Casey gets up. Do you want me to take her bags out to the car?"

"That would be a help," I said. "Thanks."

"Gotta go." He leaned over his dad and gave him a quick, manly hug. Then he reached his hand to Doug. "Nice to see you. Good story."

"Will you be home for dinner?" Mike asked him.

"Probably not. But if it's good, leave me something."

Mike caught my hand as I set off to follow Michael out. "What time is Casey's flight?"

"Eight."

"Do you want to meet us downtown after? Doug and I are going over the funeral plans with the brass. Maybe we can break for lunch."

"Sorry, I can't today." I kissed the top of his head. "I have a meeting with the senior producer and some New York types. And we're filming the Frady murder house today."

"Guido can take care of the filming stuff."

"He can. The network moved up my deadline—they want to broadcast the Frady film during February ratings sweeps—so I have to crack the whip a little. And there's an interview I'm trying to get." I glanced at Doug. "Hector found Barry Ridgeway for me.

Ridgeway doesn't want to talk, but I'm going to work on him."

Doug thought over that bit of news about his old Seventy-seventh Street colleague, one of the original suspects in Frady's death, and didn't seem very happy about it. "I thought Ridgeway was in the slam."

"He's been out for years," I said. "He served eight years for vehicular manslaughter, driving under the influence, went back in for six months on a parole violation, caught with an open container. When he got out, he went through rehab, and word is, he's clean."

Doug shook his head. "He left the department on a bad-checks charge, big-time gambling debts. Word on the street is he's done some mob hits to pay off his debts."

"There's no mob in L.A.," said Mike, the authoritarian.

"Vegas mob," Doug added.

"Could be." Mike thought it over, watching me put breakfast things away. He narrowed his eyes, something he does when he's going to offer a gem of criticism. "You're going to talk to Ridgeway dressed like that?"

I wore my usual jeans and an oxford cloth shirt, generic work clothes; add a blazer, I can do lunch.

"He won't talk to you," Mike said. "Not dressed like that."

"Why not?"

Doug chuckled, watched Mike with great expectation.

"You know the story about the farmer and the mule?" Mike said. "Farmer says he never has to beat his mule to make it go when it balks, all he has to do is get its attention and ask politely and the mule goes every time. But now and then he has to whack the mule over the head with a two-by-four to get its attention."

"And?" I said.

"An old cop is a lot like an old mule. Sometimes you gotta hit him over the head to get his attention. And, honey, those jeans won't do the job."

"What do you suggest, Mike?"

"A skirt. Short enough so he knows you have legs, but not so short I have to go down there and kill him for looking."

"You want me to hit him over the head with some leg?"

"You want him to talk to you? Trust me, a short skirt works better with an old cowboy like Ridgeway than a good vocabulary and serious intent."

He got up from the table and began to fill the dishwasher. He talked with Doug about work, a case entering the trial phase and another evolving—an ugly torture murder involving six teenage suspects. Doug said something about hiring a bagpiper to play at Hector's funeral. I reminded Mike he had promised to come along on an interview that night.

When I saw them off, Mike seemed all right, except that his suit pants irritated the rash he had got rolling around in the grass at the park. At least I knew he would be thinking about me all day.

The last thing Mike said was, "Give Casey a kiss for me."

All morning I felt a low buzz in my head; not enough sleep the night before, too much real world filling the day ahead. Every time I stopped moving, the same thought pushed to the surface, the same thought that kept pulling Mike down: Hector is dead.

I made some calls to my production staff before I went up and changed into a suit with a short skirt, and went in to waken my daughter. My day's schedule was full of freeway time, beginning with a trip to the L.A. airport that I did not want to make, segueing into a meeting, then trying to collar Ridgeway, and a full day shooting the house where Roy Frady's body was found, followed by an interview down in the southern suburbs. It was good to stay busy, but I was in no hurry to get started.

Savoring the last quiet moment, I stood at the foot of Casey's bed and watched her sleep, feeling sad that I might never be able to watch her this way again. The dog, Bowser, disengaged himself from his nest behind her skinny legs and low-crawled over for a head scratch. He seemed wistful, as he always did when there were packed suitcases going out the door.

Because there was no way of avoiding the inevitable, I shook Casey's foot and started to sing "Hit the Road, Jack."

"Please, Mom." She looked up at me through her mass of brown hair, her gray eyes narrowed and sleepy. "Don't sing."

"It's six-thirty. Your flight leaves at eight. If I don't see your sweet face downstairs in fifteen minutes, I am coming back and I will be in full voice—three verses, a cappella and off-key."

I turned and left the room, heard her stretch and yawn as she got out of bed, heard her shuffle around packing last-minute things into her carry-on. I kept walking, down the hall, down the stairs, when what I really wanted to do was take her on my lap and hold her one last time before she left. The lap scene was difficult to visualize: At sixteen, Casey was six feet tall. In my mind she was still, and always, a babe in arms.

I set out juice and a bagel for Casey to grab on her way through the kitchen, and then went out to make sure that Michael hadn't missed any of her bags. He was long gone—he ran in the hills before his early classes at Occidental College—but he had left a note for Casey on the windshield. Seeing it didn't make me feel any happier: a picture of a baby bird in a tutu flying from the nest. Was this premature event something to celebrate?

When Casey came out of the house she was radiant with excitement, fairly dancing as she made her way across the lawn toward the garage. She was so ready for the adventure ahead that I refused to dampen her spirits with my own qualms. In less than two hours she would be on her way to Houston for a year to study ballet at a top-notch academy. And from there?

I had to take a few deep breaths. If all went well in Houston, at the end of the year Casey could sign with a ballet company and go on tour. Maybe she was flying from my nest forever.

Bowser followed Casey with his tail between his legs. Before she was even in the car, he set up a howl.

"What a spoiled baby he is," Casey said. I saw the mist in her eyes as she turned to fasten her seat belt.

"Call me as soon as you get to Houston." I backed into the alley and headed for the street. "You have Guido's pager number, and Mike's voice mail number. Remember, if you have any sort of problem, call Rollie at the network's Houston affiliate. He owes me; he'll leap through fire for you."

"Chill, Mom. Dad's meeting me at the airport. He'll be with me for a whole week." She pulled down the mirror on her sun visor and began to put on her makeup—a quick brushing of blusher and mascara. "Did I tell you? Dad says that this case he's working on keeps him in Houston so much that he's rented an apartment. Two bedrooms. Any time he's in town, I can stay with him if I want to."

"Good." I didn't know what else to say. For Casey, after so many years of occasional weekend visits, having her father around might be good. I confess to having a twinge that felt like jealousy. Ever since the divorce, certainly ever since Scotty's remarriage and his move to Denver, I hadn't been called upon to share Casey very often. I wondered how Scotty's wife felt about sharing him with another woman.

"I'm going to be fine," she said. "But what about you?"

"I'll miss you. From Halloween to Christmas is a long time not to see your face."

"Oh great." She scooted up closer to the mirror so that she could see her face. "I knew it. Volcano zit."

It was a good diversion, but I caught her dab at her eyes.

At the departure gate, I managed not to cry or otherwise humiliate my daughter when I kissed her goodbye. But when she was gone, I needed a few minutes to compose myself before I walked away. It was nearly 8:30 when I made my way back to the freeway, certain by then that at least her plane had cleared the runway.

It was Wednesday. We had begun filming on Monday and already I had the film technicians' union on my back (they wanted more security because of the neighborhood where we were shooting), a network accountant was demanding ass-kissing, and an interviewee was threatening to sue if I aired what she had told me, even though I had her signed release on file.

Network protocol and all its attendant bother—union rules, Cal/OSHA, accounting, accounting, accounting—reminded me hourly why I had quit a network job years ago to go independent. And why falling back into a network contract, even if it was only for seven more months until Mike retired from the LAPD, had been such a personal capitulation.

The very worst part of being connected to a major media empire was meetings. Staff meetings, division meetings, meetings to plan meetings, and horror of horrors, every month or two the network sent someone out from New York to check on things. Normally, Lana Howard, my senior producer, and I did the verbal equivalent of jerking them off so they would go away mollified. But I resented having to go through the motions, especially when it kept me from the work I was hired to do.

Though I make documentary films for a living, the technical aspects of filming are not my forte. My assistant, Guido Patrini, an old pal from my days in the trenches, oversees the setup and camera work, and doesn't suffer fools gently. I had left the chore of setting up at the day's film site to Guido. When I called him from the car, he told me everything was under control, and that it was fine with him if I took my meeting with the New Yorkers without him.

We gathered in Lana's posh office with its view of

Hollywood under the smog, facing off over opposite sides of the vast conference table: me and Lana against Gaylord Smith, he of the olive-drab silk suit and loafers without socks—a bad sign—and Steven Roybal, his bun boy. Their combined age was less than fifty.

Under the gaze of New York scrutiny, I felt uncomfortable in my short-skirted suit. If I had known the nature of the meeting when Lana called, I would have skipped the stupid skirt for my usual jeans and added a field jacket as a reminder to Gaylord that my roots were in the news division and not Movie of the Week. And that I was no pushover. Gaylord wanted me to drop some dramatization into my documentary, and I had, so far, resisted.

Lana started the meeting by dropping in a little business. I thought her timing of this small gem was meant as a message to the boys. She handed me the business card of a freelance journalist named Jack Newquist. "*Rolling Stone* wants to do a piece on you. This Jack wants to follow you around. He'll meet you at the Ninetieth Street shoot. Any problem with that?"

I said, "No," and tucked the card into my planner. I had a feeling *Rolling Stone* was more interested in the Patty Hearst-Symbionese Liberation Army angle to my story than in me, but I saw the significant glance pass between Steven and Gaylord and said nothing more. In fact, the thought crossed my mind that Lana was making up the journalist to impress these men.

She opened her agenda by saying, "Our Maggie is certainly on the ascendance. We're making shelf space for Emmy."

"Love your work, Maggie," Gaylord said, his equivalent of giving me a hand job. "At network we're proud we brought you aboard."

"Nice to hear," I said. "When network sends some big guns out, compliments are not what one expects."

Still grinning his smarmy grin, he edged into the reason he had made the trip. "We want to reassure you that our only purpose in being here is to get a little progress update, offer the services a big company like ours can offer. You're not an independent on a shoestring anymore, Maggie. Take advantage of the available resources."

"I won't do staged reenactments," I said. "I don't work with actors."

"Has it occurred to you that network audiences might expect more. . ." Gaylord looked at Steven.

"Production value," Steven supplied.

Gaylord nodded. "Network audiences expect more pizzazz in programming than your PBS viewers did; they just won't sit still as long. You can't get around the demographics, Maggie. Black and white may say fine art to you, but to Bubba down in Dumbfuckville, whose greatest treasure is the big-screen he bought at the Wal-Mart, black and white says something's wrong with his set."

"Cinema verité," Lana said, just to let us all know she had gone to film school. "Maggie's strong suit is giving her viewer the hard edge of reality."

"The hard edge of reality is my only suit," I said, grateful for Lana's support, but worried how far it would go once my back was turned.

Gaylord's smile had frozen in place. "Sometimes reality falls short of good storytelling."

"I have content control," I said. "You put a long line of zeros behind the dollar sign in my contract just for the privilege of attaching the network logo to my films. Someone upstairs must have thought I knew what I was doing."

"Absolutely." Gaylord fiddled with his ponytail. "Maggie, darling, we have only the highest regard for your work. But now you're a team player. Use the talent."

"I have the real participants. I won't phony up their story with actors." I got up from the table and walked over to the wall of windows, felt the sun's warmth through the glass. I had enough union hassle managing a production crew. Who needed actors and SAG? Don't get me wrong, I'm union to the core. It's just that, from a management standpoint, the union is the biggest pain going.

Lana brought me a glass of fresh-squeezed orange juice and leaned against the window close beside me while I sipped it. "Trust me," she whispered, eyes front. "Tell them what they want to hear, throw them one small bone, and they'll go away. Save the project, Maggie. Give them color, toss in some dramatization. What will it cost you?"

"Save the project?" I turned toward Gaylord, caught him yawning. Caught Steven measuring my legs. "This meeting is about a whole lot more than adding a little color to make Bubba happy, isn't it?"

Steven, whose job seemed to be taking all the scut work, looked so uncomfortable that he reminded me of the doctor who had told me that my sister would never have any more brain function than a carrot.

After a deep, noisy breath, Steven said, "The thing

is, Maggie, cop stories don't cut it. Not since Rodney King. Read the demographics."

I expected Lana to jump in and explain how wrong he was, but I found her watching me, waiting for me, the same way Gaylord and Steven were. Sometimes I had to remind myself that Lana got where she was by playing the system, not bucking it.

"We had final project approval six months ago," I said. "We're into primary filming and we have a slot in the schedule. Isn't your concern a little late?"

"We have a new head of department."

That was all Gaylord needed to say to make the situation perfectly clear. A new man's job is to shake things up. And it looked as if I was marked for the tumble.

"Fine." I walked back over to the table and picked up my notes and production schedules and accounting sheets. "The termination clause in my contract will more than finance the completion of the film. I'll have my agent and my lawyer get to work on the papers."

I was reaching for the door when Gaylord finally gasped, "You're walking?"

"My schedule's tight. I don't have time for bullshit, not if I have to go find a new buyer."

Gaylord was aghast. "Lana?"

"She means it, Gaylord. Once they've gone independent, you can't tell them to clean their rooms anymore." Lana dropped down into her chair, stretched her long legs out front, and grinned evilly at the company boy. "I think the problem here is you don't have an idea in hell what she's working on. Roy Frady was a cop, sure. But I wouldn't describe Maggie's project as a cop story. Maggie, why don't you come back over here and pitch the story to Gaylord."

I let go of the doorknob. "Late in the game for a pitch, isn't it?"

"You can't walk, Maggie," she said. "Who would I do lunch with on Fridays?"

I turned to Gaylord and waited for him to say something. It was Steven who finally spoke. "There's a lot of chaos when a new person comes aboard. Mistakes get made. Talk to us. Are we wrong?"

I went back across the room, stood at the head of the table, and studied Gaylord and Steven long enough to make them uncomfortable. Casey's tuition at the ballet academy was outrageous, I tithed my salary to my sister's nursing home, and I had recently decided it was time to sock something away in case I lived long enough to retire. Then there were my share of the rent and other incidentals like power and water and food. If I walked out on my contract, if I missed even one of my checks, my dam against debt would burst and I would be swept under. But I wasn't planning to mention any of that.

Lana nudged my pump with the toe of her boot. "Sing it, baby."

I looked at Gaylord. I looked at Steven. I had their attention, so I began.

"Fade in, urban scene shot in high-contrast black and white." I smiled. "It's 1974. Even to folks in Dumbfuckville, who I believe you underestimate, 1974 was a dangerous time. Vietnam was collapsing, falling to the Communist menace Bubba was raised to fear, maybe had gone off to fight. The OPEC countries had cut off America's supply of cheap oil, and everyone who drove a car was waiting hours in line for the privilege of being gouged for another tankful; we all had to consider giving up our beloved, muscular, American-made cars for tiny Japanese shit, and it scared us.

"The president of the United States was waiting for Congress to hand down his orders of impeachment. We were in a recession that wouldn't end, prices rose a percent every month. Police had become 'pigs,' and youth was running wild in the streets, talking about revolution.

"In the Seventy-seventh Street Division neighborhood where Officer Roy Frady patrolled, where after work he was in the habit of stopping for a six-pack, the Symbionese Liberation Army had moved into a new safe house. Now and then some of these middle-class, white-bread radicals went to the market, or, if you believe rumor, walked the streets to earn a little easy money on their backs for the revolution.

"Roy Frady noticed women, would certainly have looked closely at any white girls he saw in South Central. He and everybody else in the country were looking for the SLA and their star boarder, kidnapped heiress Patty Hearst. Did Frady make a fatal connection between the faces on the street and the FBI wanted posters hanging in his squad room? Or did he just give in to an offer for a backseat blowfest with a pretty young woman?

"Less than a week after Frady died, the SLA went down in flames. Anyone over thirty, Gaylord, will remember the SLA shoot-out. Bubba sure as hell does. You want action? You got it. More gunfire than most Vietnam vets heard in-country. A six-pack of bodies turned to ash by the SWAT team. When that safe house started burning you could see it all over this country, because the news was there.

"One news hen, with SWAT teams all around her, gunfire coming from inside the house, walked right up and knocked on the front door: 'Are you really the SLA? Can I talk to Patty Hearst?' Why do you want cheap reenactment when I have the real thing on film?"

I watched Steven type "SLA" on his electric notebook.

"The newswoman's name is Christine Lund," Lana said. "Don't forget that. Still anchors the news on a rival network."

Steven smiled as he typed.

"Also in the general area, at that general time," I said, "there was a brilliant guy, an honor student who lucked into the E ticket ride out of the projects—a full scholarship to a private college up north. But he didn't fit in up there, he couldn't cut it socially, got bounced for roughing up a female student. So he came home, bitter and full of rage. He acted out his rage by blowing away college students and luring police officers to their death. By May tenth, 1974, he had killed or wounded at least five police officers and four students. He knew Roy Frady."

Steven typed that, too.

"Then there were the gang bangers. Frady had just finished working a gang detail, and the homeboys had put a price on his head." I waited for Steven to finish his memo.

"I told you Frady was easy with women, and he didn't care if they were married or otherwise attached.

It is possible that he was in the wrong bed when daddy came home. The killer could easily have been someone he knew: another cop, an old lover, someone with a score to settle.

"Frady had a wife and two kids who were barely making it on their share of his salary. Every month, Mrs. Frady paid the premium on hubby's life insurance."

I put down my notes and looked at Gaylord. "Roy Frady's story is so rich, I will not phony it up with a lot of crummy production value."

"Miniseries," Gaylord said, with a glaze over his eyes.

CHAPTER

4

When Roy Frady died, he was living with another officer's ex-girlfriend. The cuckolded officer was Barry Ridgeway. I thought he might offer me a different police perspective on Frady than the one I was getting from Mike and his friends. After what Doug had said about rumors that Ridgeway was into big-time mischief, I was even more interested in talking with him.

Guido promised me that things at the shooting site were still under control, so I stopped on my way there for a little conversation with former officer Barry Ridgeway.

Finding Ridgeway had been a coup for Hector. Shortly after Frady's murder, Ridgeway was forced out of the LAPD for bad debts, for writing rubber checks. He resigned before the department could fire him. At that point he was already a blackout drinker. Two months later he went down on a vehicular manslaughter charge—driving under the influence—and spent eight years in state prison for it. After he got out, alcohol got him into more trouble. Finally, he got sober, and then he dropped out of sight.

Hector made dozens of calls among the alumni of the Seventy-seventh Street station, class of 1974, before he got a line on Ridgeway. A week ago, Ridgeway's old sergeant spotted him going into Victory Outreach, a rehab center on Broadway south of downtown, and called Hector.

According to Hector, Ridgeway didn't want to talk to me. Out of jail, off parole, he had started over and he wanted shadows from the past to leave him alone.

So, I wondered, if Ridgeway wanted to start over, what was he doing in the neighborhood where he got into trouble in the first place? Victory Outreach was inside the boundaries of the Seventy-seventh Street police division, and only a few blocks from the house where Roy Frady died.

I drove off the freeway at Manchester, went east one block to the corner of Broadway. Before the Watts riots, the area around Broadway and Manchester had been a busy shopping area for a large blue-collar neighborhood; Lockheed, Hughes, and Mattel were nearby.

After Watts, the population moved south from downtown in layers, Hispanics displacing blacks, blacks displacing whites. The hope of them all was to find something better. The reality was always someone else's leftovers.

Broadway and Manchester was in the path of that moving rainbow. As chain stores fled to the malls, ma 'n' pa operations moved in. Ten times as many failed as made it, leaving behind a patchwork of sad-looking, barricaded storefronts and a lot of vacant space.

I parked in front of Jimmy's Smokey Pit—Jesus Is Real and We Deliver painted on the side—and crossed Manchester to Victory Outreach.

I had every expectation that Ridgeway would tell me to go to hell. My only opening wedge was that damned short skirt. I found him in a small back room at the center, counting freshly laundered white sheets and towels. I watched him through the open door for a moment before I approached.

Ridgeway was around Mike's age, late forties, though he looked a hundred; face like a beat-up road map of hard drinking, hard living, tough luck. While he looked a wreck, I got the impression that the damage was old. There was firm flesh on his bones, and his raisin-colored eyes were clear. In contrast to the other men in the center, most of whom wore thrift shop togs, Ridgeway sported a crisply ironed Hawaiian shirt over dark blue slacks with a crease, and his black loafers had a spit shine. His graying hair was short enough to pass police muster.

When he heard my heels on the linoleum, he looked up, ogled me, smiled.

"You from the county?" he asked, coming toward me to be helpful. "Women's home is upstairs. I'll show you."

"Barry Ridgeway?"

He flinched the way a man with a guilty conscience flinches when he hears a stranger say his name.

"We have some mutual friends," I said, offering my hand.

With an elaborate survey of my assets, he raised his brows like a gourmet before the buffet. "Any friend of yours has gotta be a friend of mine."

That was enough exploitation of the slut factor for me; Ridgeway was not a balky mule. I handed him my card with the network logo. "I'm Maggie MacGowen."

I half expected to get bounced. But after he gave me a new appraisal, Ridgeway pleated his beat-up face into a dazzling smile.

"So, you ain't Christine Lund," he said.

"Sorry," I said.

"Hell, don't apologize. Never could stand that broad. Remember the SLA shoot-out? Half of L.A.'s finest getting ready to shoot it out with six asshole kids—urban guerrillas, my butt—had more ammo in that house than Gadhafi. This Lund babe walks right up to the door and knocks. Molotov cocktails flying out the window."

"I remember," I said.

Ridgeway slipped my card into his breast pocket. "Hector Melendez came by the other day, told me some newsperson wanted to talk to me about Frady. We still had the black bands on our badges for Frady when the SLA went down. That's what made me think of Lund."

He wasn't the first to put Frady and the SLA into the same memory cell. He said, "I told Hector I didn't want to talk to you, so why are you here? Where's your film crew? Every TV newsie I ever met came with a film crew. Even Christine Lund don't misbehave without a film crew."

"I'm not a newsie, exactly, but my film crew's up on Eighty-ninth Street. I'm sure Hector told you I'm working on a film about Frady. Will you talk to me about your history with Frady?"

"I got questioned after he was found." Ridgeway became busy with his towels again. "Maybe I should call my attorney. Maybe you should go away."

"Whatever makes you happy." I looked at the bundles he was assembling: a sheet, a towel, a tiny bar of soap, a New Testament in each one. "Do you live here?"

He shook his head. "I have my own place. Way back when I got out of the joint, condition of my parole was putting in a year of community service here. Couldn't wait to get finished with it and get the hell out of town. But when I came back, this place looked more like home to me than anywhere else did. Can you feature that?" He frowned. "It's something to do, I guess. I come in every morning for the church service, then I stay and help out. I do grunt work, security now and then—can get pretty rough sometimes, guys in rehab kicking, come in seeing snakes and spiders, takes a pro to bring 'em down. Then around noon I walk a group from the women's home over to the AA meeting at Mother of Sorrows on Main, make sure they get past the liquor store on the corner and get home again." He gave me his dazzling smile; his teeth were false. "It's a rich life."

"You weren't easy to find. How long have you been back in town?"

"Three, four months. Don't know how long I'll stick this time. Can't seem to get into the old groove. Everything's different."

He seemed to have forgotten he didn't want to talk to me. I asked, "Feel like going for a walk around the old neighborhood?"

"Depends on what you have in mind," he said, dusting off some buried charm, openly flirting with me now.

"I need to check on the mischief my crew is into. Eighty-ninth Street is only a few blocks from here. I thought maybe you'd walk me up, talk about the old days on the way."

I saw him pale, saw his eyes grow hard. "I had nothing to do with the Frady shooting."

"Fine. But who knows the area better than you do? How long were you on patrol duty out of Seventy-seventh Street?"

"Six years." Ridgeway didn't seem unwilling, just cautious. He spent some time fussing with his stacks of sheets and towels, marking a tally in a notebook before he got around to saying anything more.

"This wasn't a good neighborhood when Frady got it," he said finally. "In twenty years, things haven't gotten any better. Sweet thing like you shouldn't hang around down here."

"Can't you get time off?"

"I make my own hours." He studied me with a wry grin on his face. Then, with his head cocked to the side, he asked, "If they was shooting all around you, would you go up to the door and knock, like her?"

"If I thought someone would talk to me, sure I would."

He smoothed the front of his shirt. "Guess I'm in for a ride, huh? Let's go out the back way."

We headed south on Broadway on foot. Sun had finally broken through the morning fog, leaving behind a gray haze that gave everything a silvery patina. By afternoon, when the air temp would climb into the low eighties, that cool haze would mix with the day's emissions to become a pall of choking smog. October is the worst month in L.A. for creatures who breathe.

Cops talk. That's just the way they are. Must be a test for it when they apply for the academy—the BQ, Bullshit Quotient—and Ridgeway must have scored high. I listened to him rattle on about the way things were and the way things ought to be. It was a performance. I realized early on that he was intensely lonely and if talking about something as touchy as the death of Frady was the price he had to pay to have my company, anyone's company, then he was willing to pay it. Loneliness can be a dangerous affliction, and I felt bad for him.

Ridgeway walked on the curb side of me. "Who else you been talking to?"

"Friends and family. Mike Flint, Doug Senecal, Hector."

"God, I can't believe the way Hector went down."

I could only nod because all my words suddenly jammed up in my throat.

Ridgeway said, "All I heard, he was being a hero, saving some kid or something."

"The kid was almost thirty, lived upstairs from Hector," I said. "He had a long history of mental problems and suicide attempts. When he threatened to jump, his mother went looking for Hector because she knew he was a cop. But she forgot to tell Hec one little detail: the son was armed. He shot Hector coming through the bedroom door, then he shot himself."

Ridgeway shook his head. "Hector made a mistake."

"That's what Mike Flint says, too."

"Flint. Haven't seen him in twenty years. Haven't

missed him, either." He set his jaw. "Frady, Flint, Senecal, and Melendez: the Four Whoresmen. Those guys were tight. Wouldn't let anybody get inside."

"Did you feel excluded?"

He shrugged. "We hung together. All the guys used to go end of watch to that liquor store on the next corner, Manchester and Main, get a six-pack, stand around, cool down before we went home to the old ball and chain. You know, like divers go through decompression. We had to get civilized again. Sometimes we'd go on down to Alphy's for breakfast, or over to the topless places on Florence. Unless we picked up a girl first."

"In the parking lot?"

"They'd be waiting for us." The charm again. "Lot of women like uniforms."

"Did Frady pick up girls?"

"Not on the street. Not like Flint and Hector. And me. Frady had regulars he serviced, nurses over at Morningside Hospital—that's where we both met JoAnn, in the ER—and a black chick he met on a disturbance call, couple others. But he didn't go in much for the groupies, if you want to call them that."

"You said, 'Not like Flint and Hector.' "

"Those two, Jesus. They couldn't beat the chicks off." He sniffed. "Not that they tried."

So Mike had been a slut. This wasn't new information. He was young in 1974, unhappily married to an in-your-face shrew, moonlighting three part-time jobs, hearing "pig" every time he got out of his patrol car and "bum" every time he pulled into his driveway. I was sure there was some cause and effect working here, because Leslie wasn't married to Mike anymore and she wasn't a shrew anymore. I wouldn't want to be a young cop's wife. Truth is, I was fighting off the pressure to become an old cop's wife. Or even, as Mike phrased it, to fucking come in for a landing.

Maybe it was the smog, but my chest felt heavy, as if there were a black hole inside that sucked up all the good air. Wasn't the first time the mention of Mike Flint and other women opened up that hole, consumed all the air around me. I trusted Mike, and I'm not by nature jealous. But I had been married for a long time to a womanizer, a good-looking world-class liar, and the experience had left me scarred and gun-shy.

We were directly under the approach path to LAX. Even though I calculated that Casey was somewhere in the air over western Texas, I kept watching the sky for flaming aircraft.

I took a big breath. "Tell me about JoAnn Chin."

"I shouldn't have brought her up," he hissed out the side of his mouth. "When Frady got it, JoAnn was the first question the department asked me. Tell you this, if I ever thought of killing anyone—and I didn't— I would have done her, not him."

"You weren't jealous when Frady moved in with her?"

"Jealous over JoAnn?" His denial had enough melodrama in it that it sent up a flag: methinks thou dost protest. . . "She was a gorgeous girl. Flat, but otherwise real built. And a world-class fuck—ask any of the guys. But she wasn't worth losing my family for. And she sure as hell wasn't worth killing Frady for."

"She broke up your marriage, and she didn't help Frady's any," I said.

"Don't give her too much credit. When my wife

called her and asked what was going on, JoAnn snitched me off, and I hated her for that. But she didn't break us up. It's just, I got caught dirty one time too many, I got drunk one time too many, and I mailed the house payment to my bookie. I can't blame JoAnn, and I sure as hell can't blame Roy Frady. And another thing, her and me were ancient history before she took up with Roy."

Ridgeway was having trouble breathing, too. And his face was red.

The neighborhood grew seedier the further south we walked from Manchester Boulevard. The original houses in the area were small, prewar frame bungalows. Fifty years ago, when the war came and defense plants opened nearby, little rental units sprang up like victory gardens in front yards, backyards, side yards—anywhere a bedroom, kitchenette, and bath could be planted. They were never what you would call nice, and fifty years of tenants and hard wear had turned them into stepchildren of the slums.

We crossed Broadway at Eighty-ninth and walked straight into what looked like a neighborhood carnival. Film trucks, Winnebagos for the crew, and a vast array of equipment filled the narrow street and provided entertainment for everyone for blocks around. We usually have two security guards on a shoot of that size. I counted five, and they were very busy with crowd control.

Ridgeway nudged my shoulder with his. "What the hell?"

"You wanted a film crew, you got it."

"You making *Gone With the Wind* or something? You need that many people?"

"All I need is a cameraman, but this is a major studio production. I don't know half the people here or what they're supposed to be doing—we hire according to union protocol."

We had hardly entered the block before I heard angry voices coming toward us and saw Brady, my gaffer—the head electrician—striding with a purpose down the sidewalk, aimed toward me. He scowled. Monica, one of the lighting technicians, followed him, scowling her own scowl. But she stopped two houses away when Brady came right up to meet me. She leaned against a scrawny tree and began to weep.

I counted to ten before I asked Brady, "Is there a problem?"

"No problem. Just wanted to inform you that I have to make a four o'clock flight to Sacramento."

"We have a full shooting schedule today. We'll be hustling all day to finish before we lose the light. Sunset's at six-forty."

"I can't get a later flight."

On the cusp of overload, I smiled at him instead of decking him only because I didn't want to be bothered with a union grievance. I said, "It's going to be hot today. Can you rig some decent ventilation for the people stuck by the truck outtakes?"

"If I'm gonna make my flight, I gotta leave here by three," Brady persisted. "And that's pushing it."

Try another diversion. "What's with Monica?"

"She's all bent. She made reservations for us at some effing hotel cuz my wife is out of town. But my kid's gonna be starting goalie in a tournament in Sacramento and the wife says I gotta be there."

At the mention of hotel plans, Ridgeway suddenly looked at Monica as if she might have potential.

I told Brady, "If you had enough time to make airline reservations, you had enough time to notify us to get a replacement."

He started unfurling excuses. "I called in, they musta lost the message."

"Do whatever makes you happy," I said, looking up into Brady's flushed, bearded face. "By all means, leave the shoot in plenty of time to get your flight if that's what you want. But I need a gaffer all day today. You're a key man. Union rules say I can replace you permanently if you walk off the job during filming. Keep that in mind when you make your decision."

Brady tried again, warming up with a "But . . ." that got no further.

He was a pro. He knew that I meant what I said, so the whining shouldn't have gone even that far. But Brady was first of all a southern-bred, forty-eight-year-old hunk of Nam vet who still sometimes called me sweetheart. His persistence now and then nudged us into the no-man's-land between his machismo and my authority. It was clear from his huffing and puffing that one wrong word from me and Brady would self-destruct.

I did the safe thing, and wheeled on Monica. "Let's get back to work." Then, cooler, I challenged Brady: "So?"

"Nice legs," he said, leering, and shambled back toward the trucks.

Monica, triumphant over having won back custody of Brady, at least until he got a replacement, led us up the sidewalk. Brady lagged, pouting, for maybe ten yards. Then his native resilience, or Monica's hard young ass, won back his good humor. He caught up to her, tickled her, nuzzled her until they were both laughing and teasing. It was like being led by jesters.

I didn't give a damn what the two of them did on their own time as long as it didn't affect their work. So I don't know why all of a sudden I thought about Brady's wife, unless it was that black hole again. The wife was nice, looked a little like Monica, but with a few more years on her and after three babies her ass wasn't as hard. I wondered whether she knew her marriage was in the toilet. Or whether she cared.

"Is it always like this?" Ridgeway chuckled. "You sound like the counselor at summer camp."

"Sometimes I feel like one, too."

When he laughed, I almost liked him.

Ahead of us, Monica reached out and put a possessive hand on Brady's sleeve, but he did not acknowledge it. He never seemed to fully acknowledge her. She just seemed to be happy breathing in whatever he exhaled.

Ridgeway was watching them now with a sort of longing in his eyes.

I asked him, "What makes her love a guy like that?"

"You're asking me?"

"Yes, I am. What does she get from holding the short side of the eternal triangle? How can that be enough for her? She's laughing now, but she always seems so sad."

"You speaking from experience?"

"I had a husband who taught me a lot about triangles."

"Husband, past tense?" Ridgeway asked, looking at me through his lashes.

"Past tense."

"No more triangles for you?"

"Nope." I didn't bother to say anything about the cupcake named Olga that I peeled off Mike's lap one night in a cop bar. And who now and then leaves messages for Mike.

I took out the 35-mm camera I always carry in my bag and snapped a few frames of the pair in front of us. Sometimes I need to see something on film before I can sort it out.

Monica fell into that black hole we were talking about. Was this adoring and adorable female creature—cute from the top of her curly head to the tips of her pointy-toed boots—somehow necessary to Brady and Mike and all the rest of them?

Guido had cameras and lights set up all over the narrow concrete-paved yard of 122 West Eighty-ninth. He acknowledged my arrival with a shout of something I could not hear but was sure was obscene. He had very little room to work in, and far too many spectators walking into his field of vision to satisfy his perfectionism.

In 1974 when Frady was found in the backmost apartment, 122 was a burned-out shell. It had been rebuilt sometime later, a long, narrow shaft of white stucco containing three small apartments; Frady had died in 122½. Unless you count the straight bars on all the windows, there was absolutely no ornamentation, nothing beyond building code minimum in evidence.

The house faced due west. We didn't have very much time left to shoot the front before the sun hit that long expanse of white and concrete and washed it out with light. That's what I was thinking about when Ridgeway spoke.

"Neighbors call it the ghost house," he said. "On account of Roy. Lot of people won't come past here. Same situation uptown where the SLA went down; landlady won't rebuild up there, says she hears screaming coming from the vacant lot."

"Did you ever hear the screaming?"

"All the time. Saw snakes and spiders for a while, too." He squinted against the hazy sun. "I've been sober six years."

"I heard you had a problem." I turned my back on the yard and studied Ridgeway for a moment. He had been very straightforward with me, so I just plunged in, said, "You were drinking at the academy the night Frady died."

"That's what they tell me." The topic didn't seem to bother him. "But if I was, I don't remember. Blacked out a good portion of that time. Drown myself in Rio de Jack Daniel's."

"Do you remember talking to Frady that night?"

He shook his head. "Nothing."

"Could you have left with Frady, or followed Frady?"

He looked grim. "You want to know if, drunk off my ass, did I follow Frady, ambush him, cuff him, bring him down here, shoot him, drive his car six or eight miles away, wipe it clean, walk back home? I think I would remember some of that."

"Where did you wake up?"

"Backseat of a patrol car, halfway through my shift. I guess I went down to Seventy-seventh to sleep it off. My partner got me dressed and into the car, covered for me at roll call. Didn't want me to get into trouble."

I knew the story, and knew who his partner was that rotation. I said, "Hector was a good friend."

He flinched again.

The one good perk that came with the network contract was Fergie, my personal tweenie. She came out of one of the Winnebagos waving a sheaf of notes in one hand and a Diet Coke in the other. She handed me both the notes and the Coke. "Your ex called, the main squeeze called, Lana wants you to take a follow-up meeting in her office at two. And your mom called. She sounded upset but she said no emergency."

"My mother?" I leafed through the messages, looking for my mother's, while Fergie waited for instructions. Mother had called from my sister's hospital room. "She said no emergency?"

"No emergency."

"I'll call her later. Fergie, this is Barry Ridgeway. Give him three reasons why he should sign a waiver and do an on-camera interview for us."

"One," she said, taking the Coke from me and handing it to him, "if you say no, Maggie will hound you to death. You might as well just skip the fuss and agree to it."

He touched my arm. "Your mother didn't teach you to say please?"

"Please is a question," I said. "Ask a question, you might not like the answer."

He laughed. Ridgeway had been looking around at all the activity and I thought he was enjoying it. I knew he would say yes just for an excuse to hang around. For something more interesting to do than counting sheets and towels.

I asked Fergie, "Any sign of a guy from *Rolling Stone*?"

"He's over there hanging out with Guido."

The Winnebago door flew open and Fergie ducked in front of us, groaning, "Oh God. Thea."

I had met Thea D'Angelo, certified public accountant, only the week before and already wanted to ditch her. She saw me as she bounced down the steps, squealed a greeting, and headed straight for me. Thea's mass of graying hair was a crown worthy of Medusa.

"Maggie's here," Thea sang out, as if any of the crew, A, hadn't already noticed, or, B, gave a damn. Thea had to be forty-something, but there was a childish dopiness about her that made her seem much younger. Like a lunkish adolescent, she towered over me.

Thea said, "Hi!" to Ridgeway with too much familiarity to someone she hadn't met as she presented me with a stiff brown balance-sheet binder. And then she waited for me to maybe pat her unruly head or otherwise gush in appreciation. I had told her twice already that account sheets should be delivered directly to Lana, but she insisted on showing them to me first— no matter where I was.

Thea was bright, competent, and didn't smell bad. The quality that repelled us all was, I believe, her endless neediness. I wished, like Fergie, that I had someone to duck behind every time I saw her.

I thumbed through the pages of figures while Thea

waited, expectant. "Thanks, Thea. Looks great. Now, I'd really appreciate it if you'd get them right up to Lana."

"Now?" Thea seemed crestfallen. "But we're still shooting."

I put my hand on her shoulder. "Lana needs them right away."

"All right, you're the boss." She winked at Ridgeway and then, ever chipper, she jogged off toward her ancient VW and folded her bulk inside.

"Thanks," Fergie said, watching Thea to make sure she was going. "She drives me crazy. Underfoot all the time."

Guido called out my name and I started toward him.

Somewhere behind me there was a pop and a fizzle, then instantly the low, cumulative hum of the generators, the air-conditioning running in the film trucks and crew trailers, the buzzing of lights and recorders and fans, and all the conversation disappeared. I had not been aware how much noise there was around us until it all stopped. Pop! then silence.

I yelled, "Brady!" just as he came out of the electrical truck at a run with Monica right behind him. He grabbed a fire extinguisher from among the black equipment cases stowed in the side yard, with me and Fergie close on his heels as he sped toward the source of the sound.

A slender gray plume of smoke rose from a big diesel generator built into the back of the electrical truck. Brady got there first, yanked open a service hatch, and aimed the extinguisher on the insides. There was no fire, only bad-smelling smoke.

"Overload," he said. "She blew."

"Can you fix it, or is there a backup?" I asked. The others crushed in behind us, breathing hard. Fergie leaned against me.

Brady poked around. "We can get a replacement. But the problem's gonna be if there was a surge, coulda messed up a lot of things, especially anything with computer components. We can't just turn the power back on until we get everything that's vulnerable checked out. Gonna take time. Maybe a day or two."

"When is that flight?" I caught his eye, stared him down until he looked away. "Any replacements we need—equipment or personnel—I can get within the hour. We better order an autopsy on this baby, find out what happened so it doesn't happen again."

Guido swore. "In an hour the light's fucked. Lost. A whole day shot."

Fergie pulled my arm. I looked down to see her rubbing her left leg. She said, "I think I sprained something."

I knelt, peeled down her sock, and saw a purple, golf ball–size lump rising over the slender ankle. Ridgeway saw it, too, and offered his substantial bulk as support. He said, "Should be looked at."

Fergie was in pain. I was in extremis. Brady was sweating more than I thought the heat of the day warranted. He said, focus somewhere beyond my left ear, "Overloads happen all the time."

CHAPTER
5

While Fergie was getting her ankle wrapped and iced so that Guido could take her to the emergency room, Barry Ridgeway wandered off to talk with Monica. I wanted to set up an interview appointment before he got away, but Jack Newquist, the *Rolling Stone* man, attached himself to me.

"I want to follow you around," he said. "I want to be the fly on your wall. You okay with it?"

"As long as you don't follow me home, I'm okay with it," I said. "Do you know what we're working on?"

"Lana Howard gave me background, and Guido pretty much filled me in."

He seemed innocuous enough, an average-size, middle-aged man with a three-day growth on his chin and the freelancer's uniform: cowboy boots, faded Levi's, blue work shirt with sleeves rolled up to the elbow, battered backpack. My first thought when Lana told me he would be hanging around was that he would be a pain in the butt. My second thought was that I would palm him off on Guido. But then Fergie got hurt, and I reconsidered the man's potentially leechlike presence. I needed to cover Fergie's afternoon agenda, and that meant going into some places where it wasn't real smart to go alone.

And Guido, every woman's favorite rent-a-guy, was otherwise engaged.

Thinking Newquist would do as a surrogate ride-along, I held the door of Guido's Jeep and invited Jack to climb into the backseat with me. Guido dropped us off at Jimmy's Smokey Pit, where I had left my car, then sped away to the emergency room with Fergie.

I was happy to get out of the Jeep and be spared Guido fuming anymore about Brady's screwup and how it had ruined his window of perfect light— "Shooting in black and white, there's no margin. The light is everything." I wasn't in the mood to stroke him.

Fergie didn't seem to mind. Truth is, everything Guido said sounded to her like God talking.

I transferred Jack to my car. As he buckled his seat belt, he said, "Fergie doesn't seem to be in a lot of pain."

"Going to the emergency room spares her from making a nasty follow-up visit to a hard case named Sal Ypolito, proprietor, Hot-Cha Club." I started the car. "You'll like the place."

"Hot-Cha Club?" Jack said, sounding dubious.

"Girls! Girls! Beautiful All Topless Girls!" I said, quoting Sal's billboards. "Sweet little dive over on Florence."

He smirked. "I was afraid this assignment would be a snore. Guess I was wrong."

"Could be." I found an opening in traffic and eased away from the curb. "We have some time before the appointment with Sal, thanks to Brady. Want a neighborhood tour?"

"Anything you want to do, I'm your slave." He popped a fresh cassette into his recorder.

I turned onto Manchester and began to narrate. "If you drew a circle from Jimmy's Smokey Pit, a half-mile radius would encompass the Seventy-seventh Street police station, the Frady murder house, the Symbionese Liberation Army safe house, and Frady's favorite liquor store. I want the film to convey the geographical relationship among those four sites. That feat is as crucial to the discussion of Frady's last night as it is tricky to pull off on a TV screen. We're going to try using a helicopter, see if an aerial overview works."

"You're all business, aren't you?" Jack said, grinning at me.

"When I'm at work I am."

He chuckled a little. "Where are we going?"

"Scouting," I said. "I want another look at the house where the SLA hid out before they moved uptown."

Jack patted his shirt pocket. "Mind if I smoke?"

"Actually, I do. It's tough enough to breathe in this city."

He didn't say anything. He just dropped his hand from his pocket and stared out the window.

From Jimmy's Manchester corner, I drove four blocks over to Eighty-fourth Street and parked in front of the little freestanding house at 833 West. Cramped quarters for nine people, I thought.

Sometime after the SLA moved across town and met their fiery deaths in another borrowed shack, and after the FBI raid and the press blitz, the little house on Eighty-fourth Street changed hands. The original wood siding had been crudely stuccoed over, so the place now looked like a badly frosted lemon cake. None of the corners seemed quite square and the tiny enclosed porch sagged so precariously that it looked as if, on a very hot day, it just might melt right off.

I rolled down my window. "This is where the SLA lived the night Roy Frady was shot."

He studied the house, then he studied me. "The SLA killed Roy Frady? Don't you think that's a stretch?"

"I think it's a real possibility," I said. "From the beginning of my research, the SLA angle to the death of Roy Frady intrigued me because of its dramatic potential. Much wilder than a jealous lover story or a gang banger beef or an obsessed cop-hater or a jilted wife with insurance-dollar plums dancing in her head. Besides, the SLA is a topic near and dear to me. And has been from the day Patty Hearst was kidnapped in January of 1974."

"Cop killings aren't my thing." Jack shrugged dismissively. "I usually cover rock groups."

"I didn't ask you to be here, Jack. You came to me. Where's your car? I'll be happy to drop you off. Want me to write a note to your editor: artistic differences? Get you off the hook?"

"No way." He backed off. "Sorry. I guess that came out wrong. I'm committed to do this story."

When I say "committed" the way he did, it usually means I've already spent my advance.

Jack opened his backpack and pulled out a nice Nikon. "I'd like to get some shots of the house. Do we have a minute?"

"Sure," I said. Did they pay him extra for pictures? "We have five or ten minutes. Go ahead."

We both got out of the car. While Jack walked around, playing with the angles, I leaned across the car trunk, itching to get a look inside that house. There was no way I would cave in and do dramatization, but, say I did; I thought I would recreate Patty Hearst walking out the door of the yellow shack with her teammates, William and Emily Harris—the three survivors who might be able to tell me what happened to Roy Frady that night.

I was beginning to worry that the whole project was too personal to me. That I had lost my objectivity.

When Patty Hearst was a student at the University of California, Berkeley, in 1974, my father was a teacher there. As a kid, I spent a lot of time in the campus grove named for Patty's great-grandmother, Phoebe Apperson Hearst, grande dame of the millionaire Hearsts, mother of William Randolph, founder of the university. Everyone knew about the Hearsts, but most of us had never heard of Patty until she was kidnapped in her underwear by the Symbionese Liberation Army.

The ersatz army that took her was no more than a handful of middle-class kids playing at revolution, led by an escaped con who played them for suckers. The name on the con's rap sheet was Donald DeFreeze, but he called himself Cinque after a slave rebel, and gave the others revolutionary monikers, too. He taught his recruits how to swear and how to shoot, gave them a politically correct front man for an uprising.

The group were not nice kids led astray or seduced by a pied piper. Though they were college graduates and came from *nice* families—the offspring of a doctor, a minister, a rich merchant, some teachers, an engineer—for the most part they were alienated, unlovable loners or otherwise members of the clueless fringe who never quite get it unless someone shows them the way.

Take Nancy Ling Perry, a rich kid who dropped out, turned on, and danced topless, sold her skinny body, and shoplifted to support a failed musician husband and twin heroin habits. The SLA got her off heavy drugs and into heavy crime, made her a leader for the first time in her life, unless you count being a high school cheerleader.

From what I've learned, Perry found a lot of humor in mayhem, laughed when she blasted the superintendent of Oakland public schools, Marcus Foster, into heaven, laughed when she pistol-whipped Patty Hearst's lover during the kidnapping.

Minutes after neighbors heard the six shots that killed Roy Frady, a 1968 or '69 green Buick Riviera with three or four people inside sped down the alley behind the death house. Neighbors remembered hearing someone inside the car laughing as it passed by.

Patty Hearst was only a few years older than me when she was snatched at gunpoint from the condo she shared with her lover. She and I shared a zip code at the time. I was at once terrified and fascinated by what happened to her: innocent girl stolen from her home by terrorists. Her parents agonized and forgot they had ever fussed about her living in sin. When she publicly joined her captors in a fatal bank robbery a few months later, I felt as if I'd been hit by lightning. She robbed a bank, for chrissake, when I still had to be in by midnight.

The kidnapping coincided with the moment I reached the full flower of my requisite adolescent rebellion. Though I never seriously considered joining any of the wannabe people's armies floating around my hometown—I remember that late phase of radicals as being a grubby, hairy, argumentative bunch of stoners—there was still, in my young mind, because of my older, charismatic sister's radicalism, a certain romance attached to those who went underground to reshape the world. Patty Hearst, the beautiful young woman seduced into terrorism, was, in my mind, the most romantic radical of them all.

For another thing: while my parents never let up on me, Patty's parents never gave up on her.

By May of 1974, the accumulated charges against the SLA included murder, arson, armed bank robbery, kidnapping, and at least three pages of illegal weapons allegations. After the Hibernia Bank robbery, the search for the SLA heated up. When I was on the dean's list, Patty and company were on J. Edgar Hoover's wanted list.

For a while, the nine core members of the SLA holed up in a roach-infested apartment in San Francisco. When it got too hot, and too uncomfortable—not enough food, dirty clothes, nosy neighbors—they decamped and came to Los Angeles, where Cinque had spent some of his youth as a criminal.

They drove all day, and, late on the night of May 9, 1974, Nancy Ling Perry found this shack at 833 West Eighty-fourth Street and the SLA nine moved in: two rooms, seventy dollars a month, no electricity, and no questions. When they moved in, they brought with them nearly two dozen guns and six thousand rounds of ammunition, nine sets of handcuffs, as well as the material to make pipe bombs, one of their signature toys.

Which brings us to the problem of laundry, the SLA, and Roy Frady.

So what I was thinking about as I leaned against my car was what this group of middle-class youth would do on their first day in a new house with the pressure off for the first time in a month. To me, it was obvious: the market, the laundry.

An old woman stopped on the sidewalk beside the car and stared first at Jack, and then at me; gave us the death stare. When she got around to talking, she said, "No white people supposed to be in this neighborhood."

I straightened up, took a step toward her. "Have you lived here a long time?"

She folded her arms across her ample chest and challenged me. "What you want?"

"Just looking at that house," I said. "White people once lived in that house. Do you remember them?"

"And ain't they all dead?" she said. "You best get to steppin'."

"Then you do remember them," I said. "Did you live here back then? Did you ever see them?"

She frowned and glanced back at the yellow shack. "They brought the police. Couldn't hardly walk out the door without some police stopping you, asking you questions about your own business."

"Before the police came, did you know who they were? Did you ever meet them?"

"Who are you, askin' me so many questions?"

I took out my card and reached it toward her. She pinched it between two fingers as if it might be toxic, studied it before she shook her head. "I never saw nothin'," she said, slipping the card into her handbag. The death stare again: "I said, you best get to steppin'."

I wished her a good day, watched her walk up to a small pink-stucco house. Jack was red in the face again, deeply chagrined and very nervous. Under his breath, he said, "Let's split."

"She didn't mean anything," I said. "That's just her way of looking after the neighborhood."

"I saw hatred in her face, like she thought I was the fuzz or something."

"The poh-lice," I said, mimicking the woman's accent. "No one says fuzz anymore except on 'Dragnet' reruns. Jack, honey, you just have to spend more time on the street. Where have you been?"

His color deepened. "Covering rock bands."

"I want to go up and knock on that door, but I don't have time. Like the lady says, we best get to steppin'."

On the outside, the Hot-Cha Club on Florence looked like a dive on a street pockmarked by dives. In place of front windows, there were garish cheesecake posters of exaggerated female forms, posed in the distorted hips-back, bosom-up pose of the genre. A sagging, faded red satin curtain hung in the open door. The owner was obviously vigilant about painting over new graffiti eruptions to keep his place from becoming a gang newspaper. His exterior was a patchwork of shades of brown made by his paint roller.

I parked in the side lot and got out.

"What is it you need to do here?" Jack asked.

"Talk to the owner about a filming date mix-up."

He was patting his shirt pocket again, feeling for his cigarettes. "I'll catch up to you."

My thought as I crossed the lot was that Jack should stick to covering rock bands because he just did not seem to have the pit bull instinct needed for investigative reporting. One thing I knew for sure, he would never go knock on a door in a hail of bullets. Hell, he wouldn't even follow me into a topless bar—a dud as an escort. I was afraid that if he didn't start doing some footwork, I was going to come off looking like a rock band.

I walked in alone.

A banner hanging from the low eaves of the Hot-Cha offered a businessman's buffet lunch special and lingerie modeling. It was noon and the place was packed with a clientele that looked like construction workers and salesmen. They weren't a rowdy lot, and seemed, frankly, to be as interested in the all-you-can-eat chicken wings and pizza as they were in the dancers bumping and grinding on the raised circular stage in the middle of the big room.

The air was blue with smoke and the music was tinny and loud, but, overall, the place wasn't as sleazy as I had expected it to be. The four dancers, even in their bizarre peekaboo lingerie, were beautiful. And young. With USC in the neighborhood and UCLA just up the freeway, I wondered what sort of scholarship program Sal Ypolito might be running.

An old relic of a man in a starched dress shirt and white towel apron stopped me at the door.

"Something I can do for you, sugar?" he asked, looking me over, ducking around to catch a glimpse of my rear.

"I need to see Sal Ypolito," I said.

He turned, aimed his voice at the man setting out fresh pizza on the buffet table, and yelled, "Sal! Lady to see ya."

Sal glanced up long enough to say, "We ain't hirin'."

I walked over to him and handed him my card. "I'm Maggie MacGowen. We seem to be having a misunderstanding."

"You, maybe. But not me." He hacked the pizza into a dozen narrow slices with a cleaver. "I understand perfect. I don't need you guys screwing around in here. Ain't good for business."

Fergie had warned me: Sal was a caricature of himself, a short, round, balding old geek with a heavy Jersey accent and the stub of a wet cigar plugged into the corner of his mouth. Fergie was a cream puff and he had walked all over her, taken advantage of her, made promises to let us film inside his place that he never intended to keep. He cashed our deposit against possible damages, and backed out. I needed to show him that I wasn't as easy as Fergie.

I said, "When I get a signature on a deal, I expect it to be respected. You gave my staff permission to film an interview in your establishment before opening, and now I hear you're trying to renege."

" 'Renege?' " he scoffed. "Is that a racial word?"

"You cashed the check we sent you, Mr. Ypolito. You can talk to me, or you can talk to the network lawyers."

"They as pretty as you, sweetcakes?"

"No. They are not. And they aren't as reasonable, either."

"Eh? Fuck 'em. There's lotsa places on the avenue just as pho-to-graph-ic as the Hot-Cha. Not as nice, sure, but you can fix them up with all the stuff you do. I been on the studio tour. I know you can fix up any place."

"I don't want any place. I want the Hot-Cha. I'm filming an interview with one of your former dancers, and I want to film it here, just like it says on the agreement you signed."

He turned up the cigar corner of his mouth, went off on a tangent as a diversion. "Michelle. She was one good-lookin' broad. Stacked up to here." He tapped the bottom of his double chins. "Not much of a dancer, but she brought in the customers. Course, I don't know why you want to take her picture now. She don't look so good no more."

"I haven't seen her yet, but looking good isn't the point." I surveyed the room and knew exactly where I was going to put Michelle—sitting on the edge of the stage, right next to the stainless poles one of the dancers was making love to, with the rotating pink lights behind her. Maybe we'd even use Sal's sound track, turned low, in the background.

"I did her," Sal said. Then he shrugged. "But who didn't?"

Since he was smiling, I asked him, "Do you remember Roy Frady coming in here?"

"Oh sure." The cigar twitched. "Came in here. Nice, clean-cut boy. That kind comes in lookin' for somethin' they never had before, you know?" He jabbed me with a flash of elbow and winked lewdly. "Somethin' a little bit different."

"Did he come in frequently?"

"Two, three times a week. I gave the boys in blue a little discount. It don't hurt business none when they come by. Put everyone on their good behavior, so to speak. Pour a few drinks in an off-duty cop, he don't mind breaking a few heads for you."

"Did Roy do that for you?"

"Now and then." He said it dismissively, as if any head breaking Roy might have done was inconsequential. "Lot of the boys came in back then. He was just one of them. I only remember him because of the way he went down." He paused. "And because the dicks was in here every day asking questions till I almost locked the doors and went home. To Paramus."

"Do the police still come in?"

"Not unless I call nine-one-one. These kids is different nowadays. Buncha' bodybuilders. They eat more yogurt than pussy."

When the little troll winked at me again, I backed up. I said, "So, what about our deal?"

"Maybe I should talk to your boss."

"I am the boss, Mr. Ypolito."

"Little thing like you?"

At five-seven, I was three inches taller than he was. "It's me or F. Lee Bailey. Take your pick."

"What did you want to do again?"

"Film a conversation with Michelle Tarbett on the stage where she used to work. We have her scheduled at nine o'clock tomorrow morning, before you open for the day. Read the contract," I said. And added, "Think of the publicity."

He turned toward the stage, where two women were simulating sex with each other. "Yeah. Okay. But only because I already spent the check."

"Smart decision, Sal." With a last look around, I left.

Outside in the smog, I drew in some deep breaths to get the smell of the place out of my lungs.

Jack was sitting in my car. "Everything go okay?" he asked as I opened my door.

"Just peachy." I thought I remembered locking the car. But maybe not. "Where shall I drop you?"

"I was hoping to tag along for a while," he said.

"Right now you can't come where I'm going," I said, pulling out onto Florence. "The shoot is shut down for the day, so your best bet is to go over to the studio and talk with Lana Howard, catch up with Guido there. Guido will give you the technical scoop."

Had I been in Jack's place, I would have pissed and moaned until my subject gave in and let me stay attached. But Jack told me where he had parked, down on Eighty-ninth, and I dropped him off with a promise to call.

I was back on the freeway five minutes later. I had an appointment with the FBI in Westwood to talk about the SLA's laundry.

On the freeway north, I returned calls. I got my ex's answering machine, a good sign because he should have been at the Houston airport waiting for Casey.

My mother answered in my sister's Berkeley hospital room.

"Emily had another grand mal seizure," Mother said. She sounded composed, but I heard the tension in her voice. "It passed. She's stable now."

"Do you want me to fly up?"

There was a pause before she said, "No. Your uncle Max is driving in tonight from the desert. If you came, too, it would alarm your father."

"I'll try to get up over the weekend," I said.

"Really, there's no need. Better you spend the time with Mike. Emily won't know you're here." She said that last sentence with a catch in her voice. Even after two years, the truth about Emily was incomprehensible.

Before she took a 9-mm round through her right temporal lobe in a Los Angeles alley, my sister Emily was a scrapper: brilliant, six feet tall, a powerhouse. Now, after two years in a coma, she looked like a poster child for the starving in Somalia, a rack of flesh and bone curled into a fetal position. When her eyes occasionally opened, they opened into a vacant house.

Ever since the shooting, Emily had managed to take care of the crucial functions all by herself: to breathe, to keep her heart beating. Then, a month ago, out of nowhere, she started having seizures. No one could tell us where they came from or what they portended. Or what legal provisions we should be talking about. And how we should begin to let her go.

Mother and I talked about Casey for a few minutes.

By the time we said good-bye, she sounded stronger and I felt better—the telephonic equivalent of sitting on Mom's lap.

I called Scotty's number in Houston again and told the machine I needed to talk to Casey right away. It was true; I *needed* to talk to Casey.

At the federal building, I passed through the metal detector without setting off anything, and managed to find my way through the FBI maze to the office of Agent Chuck Kellenberger, the resident expert on the SLA.

Kellenberger was in his fifties, gray hair, gray suit, gray office walls, a belly that said desk jockey. He had the reserve of a man whose job is finding information, not giving it out. Mike Flint had pulled some strings to get me this far, but it was clear that, on my own, this interview would be a difficult one.

"I'm not sure I know what you want," Kellenberger said, looking at me over the top of his reading glasses. "I know what the Freedom of Information form says you want. But I don't get it."

"You remember the SLA?" I asked.

He gave me a crooked, know-it-all smile. "I worked the SLA case. I was there."

"Early on the morning of the shoot-out, the SLA abandoned a house on Eighty-fourth Street and moved uptown to Fifty-fourth. After they left, the FBI raided Eighty-fourth Street. All I want is to see your inventory of the contents of that house."

Kellenberger had his hands folded on top of a manila file folder, as if protecting the file from me. "You filed a formal request. If there is a document, and if it is available for public access, we'll mail it to you."

"I believe Detective Flint explained that time is of the essence."

"Uh-huh." He was being a hard-ass and getting off on it. I knew the file I wanted was under his hands, and that after he had finished his shtick I was going to get a look at it. We just had to play this little scene through to its end.

I smiled. "Can you tell me what type of underwear was worn by the men in the SLA?"

He frowned to keep from smiling, to keep from telling me to get lost. "Detective Flint said something about a movie. What kind of movie is it?"

"Documentary." I took a notebook out of my bag and flipped it open. Scene one, act two. "Unsolved local cop killing, Officer Roy Frady. You familiar with it?"

He waffled his hand, meaning either he sort of remembered or the case was no big deal.

I said, "I believe the killing had many of the earmarks of an SLA caper. Frady was shot around midnight on May tenth. You worked the SLA case, you know the possible significance of the date." When I told him the address where Frady was shot, I got some reaction, a nod of recognition, so I continued.

"When Roy Frady was found, his head was wrapped in a freshly laundered pair of size thirty-six blue boxer shorts. Then his flannel shirt was tied around his head to hold the shorts in place."

He lifted the file and opened it.

I said, "According to the officers who shared the Seventy-seventh Street locker room with him, and the many women who might have firsthand knowledge,

Roy Frady never wore blue boxers, rarely wore anything except size thirty-two white jockeys."

Kellenberger leafed through the documents in the file.

"So," I said. "Other than cartridge cases and bullets from a nine-millimeter Browning semiautomatic, those boxer shorts are the only physical connection between Frady and his killers. All I want to know is this: did any of the three men in the SLA house wear size thirty-six boxer shorts?"

He took off his glasses. "The SLA already had enough heat on them. Why would they do something as asinine as shooting a cop?"

"At her bank robbery trial, Patty Hearst said that when the SLA moved to the Los Angeles ghetto, Cinque trained them constantly for search and destroys, which she defined as going out every night, stealing a car, destroying a cop, hiding out. In her eulogy to her dead comrades, she said—even though I believe she was fed the words—that Nancy Ling Perry taught her to shoot first and make sure the pig was dead before splitting. I think that describes what happened to Roy Frady in a very clear way."

"Yeah?" Another smug smile. "For instance."

"Besides motive and opportunity? The MO." I sat forward, met his eyes. "Precise planning. The killer took Frady's service weapon, and it has never been found. His car was commandeered, dumped down in the South Bay, by Ascot Raceway. Wiped clean of prints."

"Boxer shorts?" he said, pulling out a single sheet of paper, which he handed to me. My palms began to sweat, my heart pounded. My thought was, what a great gift to take home to Mike, the solution of the Frady murder. What a great promotional hook for the film.

The sheet was a fuzzy photocopy of the original Eighty-fourth Street inventory. I scanned the lines: groceries, dishes, mattresses, furniture. And this: "Two cardboard cartons, various items, men's and women's clothing. One suitcase, various items, men's and women's clothing." No details.

I handed it back to Kellenberger. "Where is this stuff now?"

He pointed to a notation at the bottom. Everything had been destroyed years ago. Kellenberger began to rise as a sign, I believe, that the interview was over. I stayed in my seat.

"You said you worked the case. Tell me what it was like inside that house."

"All I remember is trash. Nine people spend the better part of a week in two rooms, they generate a lot of trash."

"What about the autopsy reports?" I asked. "Anything about clothes?"

"Clothes?" He sneered. "After the fire there was hardly enough bone left for the coroner to identify. Clothes? Forget it. I think maybe you're out of luck on this one unless the three survivors want to talk to you."

"Not likely they'd say anything that might tie them to a murder. I know the FBI had a mole planted with the SLA. I don't suppose you'd tell me anything about him. Or her."

He shrugged. "Guess you're at a dead end."

"Maybe," I said, and turned to a new page of my

notebook. "The son of our next-door neighbor was kidnapped by the SLA the night Patty Hearst was taken. He was overpowered at gunpoint by Nancy Ling Perry as he got into his car in front of his mother's house. Perry blindfolded him with his own shirt, made him lie on the floor of the backseat under a blanket. He was still on the floor when the kidnappers dumped Patty, also blindfolded, into the trunk of his car and drove off with both of them.

"In Oakland, Patty was transferred to another commandeered car; the kid was thanked for his service to the revolution and abandoned. There wasn't a single fingerprint in that car when the SLA walked away. They were very consistent."

He said, "You think this is new information to us? You think we didn't go over every angle?"

"I'm sure you did. That's why I came to you."

He folded his hands across his paunch and studied me for an uncomfortable moment before he asked, "Where do you get your information?"

"Same place you do: police, witnesses, the press."

"I thought so." He sat up straight. "Because your information isn't very good."

"Where am I wrong?"

"The gun," he said. "Frady's gun showed up in a Las Vegas junkyard. Your police friends should have known that."

"When?"

"Couple years after the shooting."

"In Vegas?" It made a small mental click. Doug had mentioned Vegas that morning. "How did it get to the junkyard?"

"The lead's a dead end. Won't get you anywhere."

Kellenberger handed me the file of xeroxed reports. "They're still around, you know."

"Who is?"

"There were more lunatics in the SLA than the group that came to L.A. They all didn't die in the fire." He stood up and offered me his hand. "If anything turns up, give me a call."

"Sure," I said. "You, too."

CHAPTER

6

One of my best resource people is an old college friend, Darl Incledon. Darl can find anything. For the last six or eight years she has worked for a construction consortium, recovering heavy equipment that gets stolen from construction sites. She travels all over the country, matching serial numbers to skip loaders and road graders parked at construction sites. When she hits one on her hot-equipment list, she climbs in, this itty-bitty brunette in her demure little suits and prim little pumps, and drives it away. No one dares to challenge her.

When I got to the studio, I called Darl.

"I need you to find a gun for me, a thirty-eight-caliber Smith and Wesson Airweight, two-inch barrel, blue steel, five-shot revolver, serial number three two eight three one four."

"Where am I going to start looking?" she asked.

"Las Vegas. It was recovered from a junkyard after May of 1974, maybe a couple of years after."

"Twenty years ago?" Darl laughed. "No sweat, honey. I'll just pick it up on my way home from work. You expecting me to bring you this very gun?"

"That would be nice. But I would be happy if you could find out who found it and where it was found. And when."

"I'll make some calls."

"What I want is the route the gun took from Los Angeles. Any names you can attach to it." I gave her some background on Roy Frady and she seemed, as Darl usually seems, excited to be on the hunt, positive about the prospects for success.

"If I find it," she said, "you owe me lunch."

"Even if you don't find it, I owe you lunch. Bill me for expenses."

I was in the cutting room logging in film footage for the editor, hiding out from Thea D'Angelo, when Mike called from Parker Center.

"Talk to me," he said. "I have my bank shooter on the other line. Won't hurt to make him sweat a little. Let him hang on hold. So, what's new?"

"Your murderer called you?"

"I called him. He gave me his pager number after the first heist. We've been talking off and on all week."

"Tell him to turn himself in right now because your main squeeze is getting cranky about all the overtime he's causing."

"I'll give you his pager number and you can tell him yourself."

"Gladly," I said. "How are you?"

"My backside itches, but otherwise I'm fine."

"I'll put something on your back when you get home."

"What something?"

"Me."

He laughed.

I asked, "What's your schedule tonight?"

"Depends. I have a meeting on this bank case, people from every department where they've hit—I think they've done banks in five cities all told—and the Feds. We're trying to put everything we have together, get the big picture."

"I thought you didn't work bank robberies," I said.

"I don't. I told you, the bank shooters like me. He calls me all the time, she sends me little love notes. They want me on this case, I'm on it. I have a feeling the man is someone I busted or testified against, and they have some hard feelings. Whatever, they sure have the hots for me."

"I don't like it," I said. "What do the notes say?"

"Why?" He chuckled. "Jealous?"

"Not hardly. I can't see you running off with a woman half of the witnesses describe as an ugly man. Unless maybe you have a kinky thing for women who shoot old ladies in banks. There's a lot I don't know about you, Mike."

"We'll keep it that way." He ruffled some papers. "The notes say things like, they aren't stealing money out of banks, they are merely redistributing the wealth. And when they tell people to hit the floor, they mean it, so they don't feel responsible for the two people they've knocked off."

"Do you have a profile yet?"

"A profile?" Mike snorted. "I don't need some egghead to tell me how these assholes were emotionally neglected children who are acting out their aggression against authority figures by knocking off banks, because this is all I need to know: they're losers."

"You talk so tough," I said.

"Yeah?" There was a heh-heh in there. "I am tough."

"Not where it counts. Not where the sun don't shine," I said. "You coming home for dinner?"

"Hell yes. I need something on my backside."

"Happy to oblige. Did you find a bagpiper?"

"Yeah." He paused. "Something funny came up. Got the reports from the Santa Monica PD about Hector. The guy who shot him? His mother said he wasn't armed. Because of his mental history, she never allowed a gun in the house. She said she didn't know where the murder weapon came from."

"So, where did it come from?"

"Nowhere. It was reported stolen in a residential burglary fifteen years ago. Looks to me like a throwaway gun."

"What's a throwaway?"

"Sometimes you go out on a call or you pull someone over and you have to take a gun off a guy. If you don't make an arrest, it's just too much hassle to do all the paperwork to book the gun in. Some of the guys keep 'em for insurance in case they get in a shooting that goes down bad—asshole goes to his waistband, so you drop him. But when you turn him over, there's no gun. You cover yourself, kick a throwaway under the body."

I try not to sound shocked by what Mike says sometimes. I never worked the streets, I can't always make judgments. "Did you ever do that, Mike?"

"Not with a gun, but maybe a knife once or twice. When I picked up guns I used to toss them into the flood control on my way in. Saved a lot of paperwork."

"Maybe Hector took the gun in with him. Maybe it was one of his throwaways."

"I asked that question. When the neighbor woman went looking for him, Hec was just coming in from the beach with some friends. All he had on was running shorts and a jock. No place to hide a gun. And even if he was packing, he wouldn't let some lunatic get it away from him."

"You would have said the same thing about Roy Frady," I said.

"Maybe."

"Mike, you never told me Frady's gun turned up." There was a long pause. "Who says?"

"The FBI."

"There's no recovery notation in the department files," he said.

"Doesn't mean it isn't true. FBI says the gun turned up in Vegas."

"Oh, Jesus. Don't go looking for a mob tie-in."

"I wasn't thinking about the mob at all," I said. "There are all sorts of people in Las Vegas. Retirees from the Snowbelt, for instance."

"What brought that up?"

"I started thinking about Vegas this morning when Doug said Ridgeway had some Vegas tie."

"Gambling?"

"Don't be a cop for just a minute, and listen to

me," I said. "About a month after the big L.A. shoot-out, the three SLA survivors, Bill and Emily Harris and Patty Hearst, were taken east by this radical sportswriter."

"Oh yeah. What was his name? Hooked up with that long-haired basketball player." Mike hummed while he thought. "Bill Walton."

"Never mind the basketball player. This sportswriter's parents lived in Vegas, managed a little motel; snowbirds in retirement."

"Uh-huh" sounded like a challenge with the timer running.

"Patty Hearst and Bill Harris passed through that Vegas motel in June of 1974 on their way east to hide out, and again in September when they'd worn out their eastern welcome and had to trek back to Berkeley. Hell, the sportswriter's parents drove Patty all the way to New York. Sweet old white-haired people." I paused, gave him some considering time. "The SLA three started out with their usual duffle bag of guns. The sportswriter made them leave all weapons behind."

"They left the guns in Vegas?"

"I don't know. The important thing is, there's a connection."

"If you believe the FBI," Mike said.

"Will you make some calls for me?"

"Hmm," was all he said. Followed by, "What's for dinner?" Before I went upstairs for my two o'clock meeting with Lana, I stopped by my office cubicle, read through my stack of menus, and faxed a dinner order to the restaurant delivery service. Guido came in before I got out the door.

"Where's *Rolling Stone*?" I asked.

"Thea volunteered to give him a tour," Guido said. "Maggie, we have a problem."

"On a scale of one to ten..."

"The dancer isn't being very cooperative," he said. "Fergie said she couldn't get her to confirm an interview time and I want to shoot her tomorrow morning before we go back to the house. We're all set up with the Hot-Cha Club again, but the dancer's balking. Did she call you?"

"No," I said. "Hold on a minute, I'll try her." I loaded my computer's Rolodex, scrolled to Michelle Tarbett's number, and pushed Dial. I got Michelle on the third ring, and she agreed to talk with me that afternoon, no cameras. I hung up and turned back to Guido. "She'll be okay. We'll get her there in the morning."

"Cold feet?" he said.

"Camera shy; she's feeling fat. What do you want to do right now?"

"I left Fergie waiting for X rays," he said. "I want to go get her."

"Go. We'll schedule Michelle. No big loss if we don't. She isn't the only girlfriend Frady had."

"This day has a jinx."

"Take Fergie home and make her comfortable," I said. "Don't forget, we have a tentative date tonight. Eightish."

"Jack coming along?"

I said, "No."

Lana was alone when I walked into her office. She barely looked up from the balance sheets in front of her. "The accounting is beautiful. That kink-headed giant is a genius with this shit. Where'd you find her?"

"Thea? You assigned her from the staff pool."

"She's an odd one, but she's good."

When I sat down, Lana glanced up as if surprised. "Did I forget to call you? We don't need a meeting; you sold Gaylord. Just remember he has a short memory. By the time he gets back to New York, he may have reconsidered."

"So, we'll sell him all over."

"Won't be so easy next time. I suggest you think about what he said, Maggie. Think hard."

"Which part?"

"All of it."

I thought about it. Working around L.A. means driving the freeways, plenty of time to think about a lot of things.

I was back on the freeway in early rush hour, headed south toward the suburban town of Lakewood. A couple of fender benders held traffic to a crawl, the usual mess. Plenty of time for thinking about how long seven months can be.

You live in Southern California for a while, you learn to calculate a trip in time rather than distance. It isn't an exact science. The trick is factoring possible mishaps against the likelihood of a clear roadway. Sometimes you arrive too late, sometimes too early. It's a bitch either way. I was five minutes early for my appointment with Roy Frady's widow: one fender bender, one stray dog on the right shoulder.

Mary Helen Frady Rich lived in a neat green bungalow on a street lined with established shade trees and similar neat pastel bungalows. Before I was out of the car, she came out a side gate, a slender middle-aged woman. Mike had told me she was beautiful when he knew her, when she was still married to Roy Frady. At forty-four, she was attractive under her heavy makeup and frothy, permed hairdo. Even in gardening clothes, jeans, and a work shirt tied at the waist, she would turn heads.

"Miss MacGowen?" Mary Helen took off a cotton gardening glove and offered me her hand. She seemed intensely interested in me, giving me an evaluation as if she were casting me for a part. I began to feel uncomfortable under her scrutiny.

"Thank you for seeing me," I said. "I know the topic is difficult for you."

"It's been a long time. When you called, I hadn't even thought about Roy for weeks. Happens after a while; you forget to remember someone. For the life of me, I can't imagine why you'd want to make a movie about Roy."

"The film is as much about the craziness of the mid-seventies as it is about Roy. Society on the verge of a nervous breakdown."

She smiled sardonically. "Hell, and I thought it was just me. What do you think I can tell you?"

"Everyone who knew him had a different angle on Roy. I need to hear yours."

"Whatever. I'll help you as much as I can, as long as you get Tommy Lee Jones to play Roy in the movie and you put in a big sex scene—and believe me, honey, if you're doing a story about Roy Frady you know you'll have a big sex scene. Tommy Lee is one man I would like to see naked."

"So would I, but I'm not making that kind of a movie."

She frowned.

"We're doing the story as a documentary. I'll be filming you talking about Roy."

"Me?" She blushed, but she laughed. "Okay, then you write me into that sex scene with Tommy Lee Jones. Come on around back. I made us some coffee."

She led me through the side gate and into a Japanese garden fantasy: surreal bonsai woods, a Shinto shrine, a cherry-wood bridge over a pebble stream, a small teahouse. Mary Helen caught me staring.

"My neighbors think I'm crazy." She ushered me into the teahouse, where she had mugs and a carafe of coffee set out on a low table. "But, hell, my kids are grown, don't have a husband anymore, and I only go in to work four days a week. I have to have something to do with my time."

I set up my tape recorder while she poured coffee. She put Asahi beer coasters under everything.

"Today, all I want to do is talk in generalities," I told her. "Later, we'll bring a film crew, powder our noses, and do it all again in more depth for the cameras. That okay with you?"

"I don't mind." She pinched the extra flesh under her chin. "I have time for a little tuck job?"

When I laughed she leaned closer to me, watching my face. She said, "You aren't what I expected."

"I keep hearing that."

"You don't look like you'd put up with any fooling around."

"Me?"

"You look like a smart girl. What are you doing

with a cop?" I turned off the tape and studied her more closely. Sometimes we forget to take beautiful people seriously. I said, "I thought I was going to ask the questions."

"I knew who you were when you called the other day. I still talk to Leslie now and then—you know, Mike's number-one ex? She told me about you and Mike a couple of years ago. We went out one night, rented some of your movies, and got bombed together watching them. Cried our eyes out. They're good, but don't you ever do comedy?"

"There's more money in social outrage."

"Too bad." She stirred her coffee. "Are you going to Hector's funeral?"

"Yes. Mike's giving the eulogy."

"Poor Hector." She shook her head slowly. "He finally gets his life straightened around, gets sober, and that happens."

"I never knew Hector when he was drinking."

"You're lucky. He wasn't a pretty drunk." She tasted her coffee. "I'll look for you at the funeral. There'll be plenty of people there who can talk about Roy. I don't know about all the things he did. And I don't want to know. But I'll be happy to point out some of the old-timers who know chapter and verse."

"Thanks," I said. "I was afraid you wouldn't want to talk about him."

"I don't much. But the thing is, my kids keep asking me about their dad—they barely remember him at all. Now I have grandkids and it's starting all over. I'd appreciate having someone besides me tell them about Roy. I'm tired of lying."

"Lying?" I had the tape running again.

"My kids grew up without a daddy. I remarried when they were in high school, but my second husband was more a pal to my kids, not a father. They feel they missed out on something. I always told them their dad loved them and he was the best dad a kid could have, but the truth is, he was too busy working and screwing around to pay much attention to them. If he'd lived they probably would have hated him for abandoning us. Instead, he died, so he gets to be a hero."

"Do you resent that?"

"Damn right I do. In their minds he's always as perfect as a plaster Jesus. But I'm not. I'm too real. I was there every day, making them eat their vegetables and clean their rooms and do their homework. They love me, but their father is way up there on a pedestal. It's too late for me to change my story now. I want you to tell them the truth for me."

"What is the truth?"

From the heat I was hearing in Mary Helen's voice, I expected invective to flow. Instead, she gave me that sardonic grin again. "Roy Frady had the biggest, brownest puppy dog eyes you ever saw."

"Is that what got him into trouble?"

"That's how it started. He was good with girls. They'd look at him and he'd act kind of shy, make the girls be the aggressor. It worked on me, and I'm no pushover." She leaned in to whisper. "He was the best I ever had. If he could have sold it, he'd have been a millionaire."

"You loved him?"

She frowned. "Hard to separate good sex from love. Leslie said the same thing about Mike. We never denied them, never wanted to. So why did they have to go out looking for it?"

I didn't want to hear about Mike anymore. I needed to believe that Mike had finished with all that. Like faith, sometimes that belief defied logic, but I still clung to it.

I said, "According to the police report, you slept with Roy the day he died."

"I was his last." Pride snapped in her eyes. "He left me for this bimbette who worked in the emergency room. But he cheated on her with me, and I was his last. That's rich, isn't it?"

"You had a bad time after he died. Talked about leaving your kids with Roy's parents and joining the Peace Corps."

"Yeah, well." She waved it off. "Two kids, no job; it was too much to deal with. What I wanted was, out. Peace Corps wouldn't have me. Hell, even the army wouldn't take me because of the kids."

"How did you get through that period?"

"Mike and Leslie, Doug and whoever his wife was that month, Hector and what's-her-name. They'd take me out or come and sit with the kids. Mike made sure our pension benefits got through the system, took care of the hassle with Social Security. As soon as the insurance money came, well, I knew we wouldn't be on the street."

Mary Helen gazed off into the bonsai woods. "It's such a shock at first. All that day he died, I'm thinking my husband and I might get back together; I made him come twice in a row and he said he loved me. Then, out of nowhere, he's dead. It's too much to take in at once. With some help, you work through it. But those first weeks are a killer."

"Can we talk about Roy's insurance?"

"I got asked plenty about the insurance. Did I kill him for the money? Hardly. Roy had a twenty-one-thousand-dollar policy, double jeopardy for accidental death. Forty-two thousand dollars looked like a lot of money back then, but it wasn't when you break it down. I made a down payment on this house—hardly a castle, but the way prices were going up back then, you had to get into something or you'd get eaten alive. I set up college funds, bought us a car. The insurance gave us a little cushion in the bank. Social Security gave the kids something—less than Roy's support checks did—and I started getting Roy's pension, but I still had to work. Trust me, I wasn't a rich widow. But I'll tell you this, people were a whole lot nicer to me when I was a widow than when I was the estranged wife."

All I said was, "Hmm," but she read volumes into it.

"Divorced?" she asked, and poured more coffee. "If women knew how lonely divorce is, more of them would arrange to become widows."

"I hope not."

"I heard my divorced friends tell stories, but I didn't believe them until I went through it myself. People I thought would be my friends for the rest of my life dumped me like the plague." Now there was heat in her voice.

I said, "Hanging on to some fair-weather friends is hardly grounds for murder."

"If you're desperate enough, anything can be grounds for murder."

I felt a chill. I turned away from Mary Helen to pull out my notes.

She reached for my hand and gave it a gentle pat. "Don't worry, Maggie. Sometimes they settle down. Doug did. It took him three wives before he found the right one, but do you know anyone happier now? Maybe Mike is at that point. I don't talk to him, so I wouldn't know. If Roy had lived long enough, he would have found whatever it was that made him so itchy all the time and he would have given it a good scratch and been done with it. Looking for that itch is what got both him and Hector killed."

"That isn't how Hector died."

"Sure it is. He wouldn't have been in that apartment to take the shot if it wasn't for the whore lieutenant, Gloria Marcuse. Hec left his wife to move in with Gloria, you know. He hadn't even finished unpacking when she dumps him for some sheriff she met over on Catalina, leaves Hec with the lease. Ask Mike about her."

"I've met her," I said. "The four of us went out together a few times."

"Then you know."

From that point, the conversation drifted from the life and death of Roy Frady to the loves of Mike Flint, Hector Melendez, and Doug Senecal. My purpose in coming had been to establish some contact, to put her at ease. We had accomplished that with "Hello." We made progress; I felt I understood Frady better and maybe I had gained some insight into Mike.

I could happily have stayed all evening, talking to

Mary Helen. But I needed to go sweet-talk Michelle Tarbett. We promised to look for each other at the funeral and said goodbye.

Straight up the Long Beach Freeway, going against rush-hour traffic, the trip to East L.A. wasn't nearly as bad as I had expected.

Michelle Tarbett was more than just another of Roy Frady's women. In 1974 Roy took some heat for seeing her, because she also had a rap sheet for solicitation and possession. Association with her made Frady vulnerable to all sorts of suspicions. His sergeant had warned him off, but he kept seeing her.

I had seen Michelle's twenty-year-old cheesecake pictures and had spoken to her on the phone. But the babe in the pictures and the middle-aged voice on the phone didn't seem to belong together, so I did not know what to expect.

When I first asked Michelle to participate in the film, she jumped at it, talked about her experience in the "business" and how nice it would be to be back before the camera—according to Mike, her film experience had been making porno flicks for her customers. When she changed her mind, I was more than curious to know why.

Michelle greeted me on the porch of the old yellow bungalow off Brooklyn Street she shared with her sister Flora and various other relatives. Michelle was a bosomy, hippy, older version of the tiny, birdlike, no-nonsense Flora. Both women ran businesses out of the living room, Flora doing piecework for a bridal shop and Michelle booking services for senior citizens confined to retirement homes.

I felt suffocated in the small, hot house. Flora's sewing machine never stopped droning, and it was difficult to talk over the noise. Everywhere, there were billows of seafoam green chiffon ruffles; Flora was making the gowns for a *quinceañera,* the elaborate fifteenth-birthday celebration Mexican families give their daughters. Michelle's scarred desk was stacked with bolts of the fabric, leaving her hardly any room for her telephone and schedule book.

Michelle came back from the kitchen with a can of cold beer for each of us.

I took the beer she offered and opened it. "Can we go somewhere quieter to talk? My tape recorder is picking up the sewing machine."

"I have to hear my phone. But we can go sit out on the porch." Michelle opened the window, and we sat on old folding chairs in front of it, so it was only marginally more quiet outside.

Her looks were gone. Michelle was in her mid-forties but looked fifty-something. Chain smoking, hard drinking, and coke sniffing take a toll. But she still had something about her, attitude I suppose. It was attitude that carried her in the old posters I had seen from the Hot-Cha Club: big seventies hairdo, more dark eyeliner than a raccoon to draw attention away from a heavy chin and small, close-set eyes. She'd had a great figure—long gone now—but had never been pretty. In Michelle's old line of work, maybe the face doesn't count for that much. And I believe she didn't know she wasn't beautiful.

I started the interview by lying to her. "You look great, Michelle. You shouldn't worry about the cameras. But come early tomorrow. Our makeup people are the best. They'll make sure everything is perfect. And, I promise, head shot only. It'll be fun."

She made some girlie faces that meant she was sold but wanted more coaxing.

"Nine o'clock tomorrow morning still work for you?" I asked. "My stud muffin cameraman, Guido, will take good care of you."

"Stud muffin?" She got up to answer the telephone. I overheard the conversation through the window. "I can see you at six, Mr. Reynolds. Anything special tonight? Okay, hon, see you."

When she came back out she had another beer.

I turned on my tape recorder and started over. "Tell me about your business."

"It isn't much," she sniffed. "Old people in retirement places can't get out much, they call me, tell me what they need and I get it to them."

"Could be interesting," I said.

She apparently didn't think so. She drank from her beer, touched her full lips with the back of her hand and covered a little belch. "It isn't like the old days, you know, with customers all the time making a fuss over you. Back then, they was real nice guys—businessmen, cops, college kids. Quality, you know? They treat you real good, give you tips, take you out after to some nice place. They pay attention to you like you're somebody."

"What you're doing now is safer."

"I liked dancing a whole lot better than I like taking care of stinky old men." She sighed. "But you can't do that line of work forever. I always thought I'd get me a club like the Hot-Cha—it was a real classy place—but it's hard for a woman. There's a lot more to it than booking acts and serving drinks. A lot more."

Flora came out on the porch, stretched her back, and yawned noisily.

I asked Michelle, "You knew Roy Frady?"

"Oh, sure." She fluttered a layer of her Pic 'n Save eyelashes. "He was a real cutey, that one. And good. Mmm-hmm. Not real hung, you know, but he knew how to please a woman. I was real broke up when I heard he died. I think we coulda' gone places together."

Flora sneered. "He was married."

"He was separated," Michelle snapped back, reflex born of long-term bickering. "He told me as soon as he straightened out some things, took care of his kids, we could date out in the open, be a couple."

"Funny, ain't it," Flora mused, "how when a man comes, his memory of all that mush he said just flows right out the end of his dick. How many guys told you that same thing, Chelle?"

Michelle got huffy. "Roy was different."

"I don't remember you ever saying you was getting together with this Roy till after he was dead. What about them others?"

Michelle's riposte: "How many dresses you have to finish by five o'clock?"

"Twelve. Give me a hand, will you?"

"Bring 'em out here."

Flora went back inside, eased the screen door shut so it wouldn't slam.

Michelle leaned in close to me, smelling of beer and sweat and supermarket cologne. "Don't listen to her. She never had a real career like me, so she gets a little jealous when I talk about the old days. Flora jumped into that husband, kids routine right off. She never had a good time in her whole life, now she's too old to start."

"Did you ever marry?" I asked.

"Couple times. Never amounted to much. Men get too possessive when you tie the knot. Want you to earn money, don't like it when you do." She drained her can and sat back. "You married, Maggie?"

"Not anymore."

"You're better off on your own."

Flora came out with her arms filled with clouds of those seafoam green ruffles. She spread a white sheet on the porch and piled the gowns on top of it. Then she gave Michelle thread, needles, hooks, and eyes. "One at the neck," she ordered, and went back inside.

Michelle picked up the top cloud and found the top of the zipper among the neck fluff.

"Ain't this ridiculous?" She threaded a needle, bit off the end of the thread. "These little girls turn fifteen, their families go into debt to give them this big party, dresses for all their friends just like a big wedding. Caterer, bands, hundreds of guests, ceremony in the church with the priest—all on a loan they can't pay back. And you know what's sad?"

"What?" I said, on cue.

"At fifteen, that's the best it's ever going to get for these girls." With practiced hand, she started sewing a hook on the neck facing. "Their parents give the party because there's nothing else for their girls to celebrate after. They don't finish school, most of them. They take up with some *vato* and he gets her pregnant. If there's a wedding, it's done with just the priest because she's shamed. Then it's babies and beatings and working her ass off. See? At fifteen, that's the end for her."

"Surely not for all of them."

She made a knot and bit off the thread again. "It wasn't good enough for me. That isn't the life I wanted. I turned fifteen, I ran away. Went up north, got my first dancing job, did real well up there in some of the big clubs. Lied about my age, worked North Beach where the tourists come. Big tippers. I only came back to L.A. because my mother was sick and I wanted to be near her."

"Michelle, do you remember when you last saw Roy?"

"Oh, yeah. I remember like it was last night." She stitched with expert fingers. "Night before he died, he came to see me at the club. I hadn't seen him for a while 'cause he was working somewhere else for a while. So he came in before work just to say hello."

"Did you go out with him that night?"

"Couldn't get off. He came in the middle of my set. He had a drink, talked to some friends, stayed to watch me." She chuckled. "And I watched him. An old friend of mine from North Beach dropped in on me that same night. I have manners, so I had to introduce them. But I sure as hell didn't want them to get something going. She was a real good-looking woman when she fixed herself up."

"They didn't go out?"

"Not that I saw."

"I wonder if I could talk to her. Maybe he told her something about what his plans were for the next night."

"Can't." Michelle bent her head over her sewing. "She died."

The telephone rang and she jumped up, taking the dress with her. I overheard her end of the conversation: "I can't get to you until eight o'clock, Mr. Jacobs. You'll just have to stay awake till I get there. Tell me what you want."

She listened, made a note, told him it would cost him twenty-five dollars.

CHAPTER

7

The house was dark and quiet when I got home. Even though we had lived there for nearly a year, I still felt like an intruder; it was someone else's house. It was beautiful, an old South Pasadena mansion. And the landlord, a policeman friend of Mike's who inherited the place from his grandmother, gave us a break on the rent in exchange for work restoring its faded magnificence. Still, as beautiful as the house was, I couldn't make an emotional investment in it. We were interlopers, transients, dug in only until Mike had his walking papers. In the meantime, my own house in San Francisco had its own rent-paying squatters.

I went into my downstairs workroom and took messages off the machine. Mike was going over funeral arrangements and would be home late. Michael had a calculus tutorial at school. Jack Newquist wanted to know where to meet me in the morning. My sister was fine, my daughter was in Houston, my tenant had bailed on the rent, Fergie would be on crutches for two weeks, Thea had some questions about calculating overtime, the generator had been replaced. Lana fired Brady.

With Casey gone, the big house felt oppressively lonely. Even the dog was forlorn. Old Bowser, who can be best described as a fifty-pound genetic misadventure, lay by the patio doors with his muzzle resting on his leash, his muddy brown eyes drooping. He was so pathetic that I changed into running clothes—shorts, one of Mike's cast-off police academy T-shirts, Nikes—and took him out for a run through the neighborhood and down to the park. Just to be out.

The day had grown sticky and hot. As soon as the sun slipped below the rooflines the air cooled and smelled fresher. I was tired, so I took it easy on myself, set off at a gentle pace struggling through the first mile. Bowser, leash between his teeth, loped along beside me keeping pace.

At about mile two I found my stride, my head cleared, my breathing was easy. I began to push it around mile three, took an uphill street, heard Mike's voice in my ear all the way up, "You'll never make it, kiddo. You've got no speed on the upgrade, baby. Where shall I send the remains? Uh-oh, dial two-two-six, she's breathing hard." He could dial 226 for himself, because I didn't need the coroner. Every time I ran through that litany, I got madder, ran harder, felt clearer. I made it to the top of the grade and back around through the park and home in good time.

Some of us, as horses do, need a little burr under the saddle now and then to perform well. Mike Flint always obliged by providing a little burr.

Bowser, happy again, dropped his leash on the patio

and sauntered over to his water dish for a drink, then plopped down with his belly on the cool mulch under the huge avocado tree and sighed noisily.

When I walked into the kitchen, sweat streaming down my face, Mike was transferring food from restaurant containers onto dinner plates.

"A guy named Brady called you," he said.

"How did he sound?"

"He sounded drunk."

"Do you mind answering the phone tonight in case he calls back? I don't want to talk to him until he's had a chance to cool off."

"You want *me* to take the heat for you? What did you do to the guy?"

"*I* didn't do anything. He fucked up, Lana fired him."

"Now we're a trash mouth?"

"If you don't want to be helpful, I'll leave the phone on the machine."

"I'll answer when I can reach a phone, but I'm going to be under Casey's sink for a while." He held up a serving spoon full of brown chunks. "What is this stuff?"

I looked at the plates on the table and tried to remember what I had ordered because whatever it was looked neither appetizing nor familiar. Mike handed me a glass of cold white wine and after I sipped it I decided I was hungry enough and tired enough that it didn't matter what I ate.

He said, "Thanks for the wine, Mike."

I said, "Thanks, Mike."

"Here's your kiss, Mike."

"Here's your kiss, Mike." I went over to him, pulled

out his shirt, put my wet hand inside on his warm back, and nuzzled his scratchy neck. "Do I have time for a shower before we eat?"

"The water's off," he said.

Casey's sink, he'd said. There was always some fundamental under repair. I washed my face and hands with bottled water and sat down at the table.

We ate what turned out to be eggplant something— definitely not what I had ordered. I washed it down with water and white wine while I told Mike the day's saga. He nodded in appropriate places, but he was unusually quiet. Hector's funeral had to be heavy on his mind. I knew he was feeling mortal and reached out for his hand.

He said, "I talked to Casey. I thought that when she got her schedule she'd come back down to earth. But she's still pretty excited."

"I miss her."

"She'll be fine."

"I know she will. But maybe I won't."

He winked at me, this funny thing he does that is no more than cocking his head and raising his cheek a little, bringing together some of his crow's-feet. I melted. I don't know how he does that to me, or how he knows to do it. A quick little gesture, no more than a tic, and it conveys volumes. I wanted to jump him, and would have if he'd so much as crooked a finger at me.

After dinner, such as it was, we cleared the table and stacked the dishes in the sink to wait until we had running water again.

On our way out of the kitchen, I asked, "Are you still taking me to see Anthony Louis tonight?"

"If you want. Let me finish with the plumbing first."

"It's late."

He kissed my shoulder. "Anthony Louis isn't going anywhere. Besides, he only comes out after dark, with the other vampires."

"Speaking of vampires, will Gloria Marcuse be at the funeral?"

"If she is, I just might have to shoot her."

"Do that. I'll get it on film," I said.

Mike went upstairs to work on pipes, I went into my workroom to get ready for a conversation with a cop killer.

In 1974, Anthony Louis was a lunatic. I wondered what nine years of hard time in San Quentin and nearly ten years of borderline homelessness had done for him. Mike had found him through the probation department, which came up with an address at a half-way house east of downtown.

First item of business, I called Guido.

"We're on for Anthony tonight," I said. "I have a feeling we may only get one shot at him."

"What do I need?"

"I don't know, except the quarters will probably be small and dark. Mike's coming with us, and he's packing."

Guido said, "Ah" and sounded suddenly eager.

I worked with Guido years ago on a series of foreign news assignments that got us shot at now and then, and deported more than once. After an incident in the jungles of Salvador, I decided growing old had certain attractions, so I moved on to other jobs. Guido stayed in the trenches for a long time. He got to be an adrenaline junkie, kept rewriting his epitaph and sending it to me with his Christmas cards. Eventually, something got to him, too. He turned one too many corners and found himself looking into the light once too often, I suspect. So, he came home, accepted a good job teaching at the UCLA film school; he is attached to my contract as a consultant, his students as interns. Now he has a steady income, respectability, responsibility, a cat. But like any junkie, he longs for that rush. If I suggest there could be gunplay, he is my whore; he told me he would be at my house within the hour.

Waiting for Guido, I pulled out the old police files on Anthony Louis.

Louis was questioned in the Frady murder because during the mid-seventies he lured five policemen into ambush situations, killing three of them and critically wounding a fourth. Cops weren't the only object of his ire. He also attacked students at a couple of exclusive local colleges, killing two of them and hacking a third with a machete.

From the beginning, the police looked for anything that might tie Louis to Frady's death. There was no obvious or personal link between them, so the detectives looked for a possible political answer. They investigated potential connections between Anthony Louis and subversive elements that preached against the police, from Black Muslims to more traditional Communists, and found little.

Louis's family was examined, found clean of the common varieties of abuse; they were poor, but lived a stable life. I don't know whether the justice system ever found a motive for the crimes Louis was convicted of. I doubt that Louis himself ever understood what he did, or that the voices that resided behind his inner ear ever took time to explain things.

There is an assumption that when a cop is killed, his colleagues hit the streets like pit bulls, abandoning the fine points of the law in their zeal. In fact, the opposite is true. The investigation will be unrelenting, thorough to the point of obsession, and careful. The last thing they want is for the guilty man to get off on a technicality because of a lapse in their procedure. The Frady detectives worked every angle trying to tie Anthony Louis to their case. They never disproved him as a possibility; they also never turned up the hard evidence needed for an indictment.

I stretched out on the floor with the files and began to read the strange and quirky eloquence of detective-speak in the reports.

Anthony Arthur Louis, born Los Angeles, February 22, 1952. Mother, Ophelia Kinsey, a single woman, bore five children, and reared them in the Aliso Village projects. Mrs. Kinsey is a welfare recipient and the dominant member of the family. The mother bears no apparent animosity toward the police. The family's single encounter with the police occurred in 1968 when the third son, Martin Kinsey, was accidentally shot to death by a neighbor. Mrs. Kinsey described her eldest son, Anthony, as a serious, quiet boy.

Above average in intelligence, Anthony Louis graduated from public high school in 1970 with a 3.2 grade point average. He applied for admittance as a scholarship student at several local colleges, but was not accepted. Louis was accepted by Reed College in Portland, Oregon, on a Rockefeller Foundation grant to aid disadvantaged students. He attended from September 1970 until May 1972, when he withdrew. The notation on his transcript was "Not Academically Motivated."

Reed College has no subversive reputation, other than the fact that the only American buried inside the Kremlin Wall is an alumnus. In-depth interviews with fellow students and several of his teachers failed to reveal any affiliation by Louis with any subversive group, including the Black Muslims. He was described as being a loner, with no known close friends.

In common with any number of rage killers, from Lee Harvey Oswald to the guy who opened fire at a McDonald's and killed a dozen or so kids, Anthony Louis was a friendless loner.

After he failed out of college in 1972, Louis returned to Los Angeles and seemed to fade away. His mother rarely saw him. He moved frequently. Between July 1972 and July 1974 he held five low-pay, low-skill jobs. Coworkers described him as quiet and withdrawn except when angered. Twice he lost jobs because of violent and unprovoked confrontations with his supervisors. "Clean the grease trap" earned his boss a spit in the eye. After July, he couldn't find a job of any kind. There was a pattern developing: he resented authority figures.

By July of 1974, I figured, Louis had built up at least four years of disappointment and simmering resentment. It was just about that time that he hooked up with a childhood friend named Robert Watkins, who pressured him to convert to the Muslim doctrine. Louis carried the Black Muslim newspaper, *Muham-*

mad Speaks, to his mother's house. "I raised him a Christian Baptist," Ophelia Kinsey told police. "What's he think he's doin', truckin' with Muhammad?"

Louis may have flirted with conversion, but the message never took hold; he smoked, he drank, he ate barbecued pork. I suspect he liked the inferred power that came with his identification with the group.

On March 19, 1975, his Muslim friend Robert Watkins was arrested, and later convicted for the unprovoked execution-style shooting of a hitchhiker, a kid named Garry Miller, in the city's Harbor Division.

In San Francisco the infamous Zebra killer, the angel of death, was assassinating white people and taunting the police with boastful letters. When Los Angeles was hit by a similar series of crimes, there was fear that the Zebra killer was at large in the city, or that he had spawned a copycat. Between December 12, 1973, and November 27, 1974, in Los Angeles and its suburbs, there were seven assassinations and assassination attempts on law-enforcement personnel, and four street homicides and assaults on civilians that bore a similar signature. The total body count was five dead and three critically injured.

The LAPD created a suspect profile: "With the exception of two female college students, the victims were all white males, the attacks occurred at night, the attacker was a black male who used the martial arts, firearms, or a machete."

On July 14, 1974, a female student was taking a Sunday walk alone near her school, Occidental College—the school Mike's son now attends, a school very like Reed College in Oregon. It was a peaceful neighborhood, a quiet summer evening. The assailant came from nowhere, hacked the student brutally with a machete, and ran off. She fought back and managed to get his eyeglasses off and gouge his eyes, thus leaving her mark and seeing his face. From the emergency room, she gave police a good description.

The campus went on alert. Fear among the student body over the assault on their peace turned to outrage when the police routinely stopped, questioned, and searched every black male student, even those who did not remotely resemble the description.

Five days later, when LAPD officers James Van Pelt and Kirk Harper took a distress call near the campus, they were already on the lookout. When they stopped a suspicious looking young man, they were prepared to face some anger. But not for an all-out offensive. The young man, of medium height and build, karate-kicked Officer Harper, dropped him to the ground, and, in the ensuing scuffle, managed to get his hands on Officer Van Pelt's .38. The assailant fired all six shots, critically injuring Van Pelt before he got away. With the revolver in his possession.

September 3, 1974, two University of Southern California students, strolling together off-campus, were gunned down. There were no witnesses, but the slugs the coroner dug from their corpses came from a .38.

A distress call came into the Lennox substation of the L.A. County Sheriff on October 6. Two deputies, Garrity and Earl, responded after a warning that the call sounded similar to the call that had led Van Pelt and Harper into ambush. Because of that warning, maybe the deputies used more force than the manual called for when they approached a man of medium height and build who was lurking at the scene. The man became combative, tried his karate, but this time he was overpowered. Anthony Arthur Louis was booked at the Lennox substation, and released on bail put up by his mother.

Two weeks later, late on a Monday evening, a uniformed California State police officer working security at the State Building downtown was shot dead with a .38 revolver. Passersby saw a lone man run from the scene, and gave a good description: medium height, medium build.

There was another attack on a civilian in mid-November. A man backing his car out of his driveway, going to church on a Sunday evening, was shot in the face with a .38 bullet. He survived to tell about the attack. "Some dude walks up and asks me the time, then, pow. My whole world explodes."

November 27, 1974, the day before Thanksgiving. Two uniformed Inglewood police officers stopped a young black man for questioning, a practice that had become even more common and more controversial over the last year. They approached the suspect both cautiously and aggressively. When the suspect reached for a .38 revolver he carried in a shoulder holster, the officers subdued him using a compliance hold. Interpretation: they choked him out.

The suspect was identified as Anthony Arthur Louis. The .38 taken from him when he was arrested was registered to LAPD officer James Van Pelt. Bullets test-fired from the revolver matched bullets taken from the state police officer's chest, taken out of the churchgoer's face, and taken from the corpses of the USC students. Experts matched Louis's voice to the taped ambush calls. The pair of eyeglasses that the Occidental student pulled from the face of her attacker belonged to Anthony Arthur Louis.

I heard Mike upstairs swearing at the plumbing and lost my concentration. There was an ungodly racket of metal banging against metal, then quiet, then Mike started singing an old Hank Williams song about a cigar store Indian. I took this to mean that I might get a bath soon.

Guido arrived late, around nine. When I opened the front door for him he said, "You look like hell."

"And you look like a gangster. What is this, early Halloween?"

"Just want to fit in." He wore black sweats, a black shirt and a black cap. And he carried a bottle of single-malt scotch.

I took the bottle from him. "Something you want to tell me?"

"Like?"

"Like, you boozing again?"

"I brought that for you, Maggie. Thought you might need a drink. Loosen you up."

"You think I'm uptight?"

"I think you're so tight you're gonna break if you don't take the pressure off. Have a drink."

I opened the bottle, took a slug, gasped, wiped my eyes, put the top back on. "Thanks, Guido."

"Any time. So, what's the program?"

"Mike's in the middle of some plumbing. As soon as he's finished, we'll go."

"The dancer, Michelle, get her squared away?" he asked.

I said, "Yes. She'll meet you at nine. Fuss over her a little, will you?"

"Why?"

"She'll respond better for you. It's been a long time since anyone was nice to her."

We sat on the workroom floor among the reports and shared the scotch. Guido glanced through my reading notes on Anthony Louis.

"How many murders on this guy's ticket?" Guido asked.

"One cop killing was all they got through trial."

"He didn't get the death penalty?"

"There was no death penalty in 1974, no life without possibility of parole. Mitigating circumstances—he's nuts—got the charge knocked to second-degree murder. He also went down on two assault-with-intent charges. He drew five to life, and two six months to twenty years sentences, to run concurrently. After nine years at San Quentin, in high-power, they kicked him." I passed Guido the bottle. "You're not worried, are you?"

"Who? Me?" Guido took a drink. "You said Mike's packing."

"He is. Just keep any pencils or other sharp objects away from our subject."

"Why?"

"I told you, you'll see."

He frowned. "Tell me what you want from me."

"His face," I said. "Try to light his face."

"Because he's pretty?"

"You'll see. But it's his face I want."

We talked for a few more minutes about lighting and the equipment Guido had in the back of his Jeep.

It was nearly nine-thirty when we got up to check on Mike.

Mike had his head and shoulders inside the cupboard under the sink in Casey's bathroom.

"Find the problem?" I asked.

He handed out a long, sodden wad of Casey's hair. "I cleared the trap but these old pipes are a bitch to get back together."

"Want a hand?" Guido asked.

The snort conveyed more than no thanks. He slid out and sat up, his hands black with plumber's putty, his face smeared. He smiled. "Hey, Guido."

"Hey, yourself." Guido passed Mike the bottle. "Sorry about Hector, Mike."

"Me, too." He waved the scotch away.

"The family gave me permission to film the funeral," Guido said. "You have any problems with that?"

Mike looked up at me.

"We don't have any footage of Frady's funeral," I said. "We'd like to use Hector's."

"I don't have any problem with that." Mike slid back down under the sink. "Turn on the water, will you? Let's see if anything leaks."

"We have running water?" I asked, watching with wonder as Guido opened the taps.

"Turned it on a half hour ago." Mike sounded as if he were in a deep cave, or maybe he sounded like the ogre under the bridge.

I asked, "Do I have time for a shower?"

Both of them looked me over. Mike was the first to speak. "Don't bother," he said. "Where you're going, you don't need to smell good. You sure as hell don't want to look good."

CHAPTER

8

The room was barely ten feet square, roughly the size of a prison cell. It was dark except for the spotlight Guido had attached near the ceiling.

Anthony Louis sat at the head of his narrow bed, caught in the white beam of light. When he looked straight ahead, he seemed ordinary, almost handsome. But if he turned his head in the least, letting the light find the right side of his face, he became a monster. Set deep in a crosshatched field of scars, his right eye was a small, shiny red bulb, like the rhinestone eye of a toy-store dragon.

Louis raised his hand to shield his good eye from the light.

I asked him, "Are you comfortable, Mr. Louis?"

"Comfortable enough." He smoothed back his hair and fixed the collar of his striped shirt, preening for the red eye under Guido's camera lens—a twin to his own. "Maybe some big-time Hollywood producer will see me and realize that I am the star he has been looking for. Sign me up for a million dollars."

Mike sniffed. "What would you do with a million dollars, Louis?"

"What do you think? I would blow this festering hellhole."

Down the hall there was a shouting match, sounded like three or four men arguing. I heard, "Keep the fuck out of my stuff."

The halfway house was old, and smelled old—mildew and dirt and too many inhabitants. Twelve men lived in space designed for a family of four. The Probation Department contracted rooms from a private company that bought up old houses and divided them into as many tiny bedrooms as the codes would permit, to warehouse felons not quite ready for independence. Weekly counseling sessions and two meals a day were included in the deal.

I had asked Mike to start the questioning because I liked the police-style interrogation Hector had been doing for us. Besides, Mike and Anthony had a history together and I thought it would be more interesting to let them play out another scene in their personal drama. More production value as it were.

"So," Mike said, thinking, arms folded across his chest, leaning against the wall, relaxed. The composition was beautiful, Louis sitting in the beam of light that caught Mike, standing, at the belt. Mike's face was in half-shadow, keeping him anonymous, making him an intimidating presence even though his posture and tone were casual. The metal band on his pistol grip reflected some light when he turned to Louis and began to question him.

"I hear you're a pretty smart guy, Louis."

"If I'm so smart, what am I doing here?" Louis, nervous, chuckled.

"You tell me. You went to some fancy college up in Oregon or something. Beautiful country up there."

"Maybe it would be if it ever stopped raining. I never saw so much rain. Didn't have a raincoat. I was wet the whole time."

"What did you study up there?"

"Propaganda of the white infidel."

"Was that propaganda one A or one B?"

Louis laughed, glanced up at Mike, showed the hideous eye. "I took the full course, brother. The full course."

"Nineteen seventy-two," Mike said. "Long-haired chicks in miniskirts. Doesn't get much better than that. You make any friends up in Oregon?"

Louis's smile collapsed, as if he had been stung. "I wasn't there to make friends."

"What were you there for?"

"To soothe liberal guilt about the neglected black brother."

Mike asked, "What happened to your eye?"

"I was in a fight." Louis self-consciously raised his hand to shield the side of his face as he turned away. "Pig did it. Sucked my eye right out of my skull. Chewed it up."

"You say a police officer did all that? I heard you put the eye out yourself. With a pencil. That's what you told the shrinks at County. Why'd you do it?"

Louis exhaled noisily.

"Takes a lot of something to put out your own eye,"

Mike said evenly. "Must have hurt like hell. What can you see out of it?"

"The truth. I can see more truth out of my blind eye than you'll ever see out of your two good ones."

"Could be." Mike was still relaxed. "You have a thing with pencils, don't you, Louis? Didn't you threaten your public defender or someone with a pencil?"

"My parole officer."

"You tried to escape from County Jail. Put a pencil to her throat and used her as a shield, tried to get out the sally port."

Louis turned away from Mike, but the camera could still see his smug smile. "Something like that. Pencil was the only weapon available. I got a year for it."

"Who were those guys who testified for you at that trial? Who were your character witnesses?"

"Ray Boudreaux and Harold Taylor."

"What were they in for?"

"Offing pigs. One in L.A., one in San Francisco, and two in New York."

"Did they go down for murder?" Mike asked.

"I don't know." Louis shrugged.

"You know they did. How smart was that? You're on trial for shooting an officer of the law, and the guys who speak up for you are the most famous cop killers in the country. Couldn't you have found maybe some old priest, or even your bookie to testify to your good character?"

"Maybe I didn't think killing a pig was a crime."

"Uh-huh." Mike shifted his shoulder against the wall, loosened his folded arms. His right hand dropped maybe two inches closer to the gun on his belt. "You and Boudreaux and Taylor did something else with pencils, didn't you? Some martial arts thing?"

"I taught them how to come off the wall. You know, how to overpower the screws when they come in to shake down your cell. How to come off the wall, get their guns away. Boudreaux and Taylor, they'd hold pencils the way the screws hold their guns, you know?" He made a gun with thumb and forefinger. "I'd take the gun away from them. Just practice, you know?"

"You tried it for real, though, didn't you?"

"Would have worked, except they were three little pigs that time. I didn't see the third one until he was on me."

"Did you use your karate to take Officer Van Pelt's firearm?"

Louis furrowed his brow. "Was that the pig at Occidental?"

"Yes."

"Textbook example."

"Before Officer Van Pelt, did you use your karate on Officer Roy Frady? Did you get his gun, too?"

Louis was taken aback, threw up his hands defensively. "I don't know anything about that one."

"If killing a pig isn't a crime, what are you worried about?"

"I didn't do it. Know nothing about it."

"You told your buddies in County Jail that you did. You told more than one person in module twenty-five hundred with you that you killed Roy Frady. You gave chapter and verse about how you overpowered Officer Frady with your karate, how you took his gun, handcuffed him, drove him in his stick-shift car over to Eighty-ninth Street and shot him six times."

"You going to believe a bunch of cons?"

"If I hear the right story, I am," Mike said. He never raised his voice. "How'd you know Frady had a stick-shift car?"

"It's more Fascist-macho to drive a stick shift." Louis shrugged. "Get better mileage with a stick shift."

"Did being a cop killer give you more status in the high-power module at County Jail?"

"Yes. We were the elite." Louis started to preen again, but looked at Mike's face and toned down, seeing something up in that shadowy region of the room that I could not. "But listen to me. A lot of pigs were going down; I served time on one of them. Frady you can't pin on me. The snitch you used ratted on me just to get himself transferred out of Soledad and into Chino, down to minimum security."

"How come you get all hot when I bring up Frady?"

"Frady's a different game, man. I had nothing to do with Frady."

"What makes Frady different?"

"I don't know anything about it."

"Where were you in May of 1974?" Mike asked.

"You expect me to remember?"

"Where were you the night of the SLA shooting?"

Louis sat up, smiling again. "You can't pin that one on me. SWAT pigs are responsible for that fuckup."

Mike smiled back. "Where were you that night?"

"Working in Inglewood, flipping hamburgers. We heard about it on the radio. I remember because a customer came in and said we could see the fire from the parking lot."

"How far away in miles?"

"Three, maybe four."

"You were sent up for a shooting you did in Inglewood. Were you living in Inglewood?"

"No. I just worked there for a while. I had a place near the coliseum," Louis said. "On Figueroa."

"That's up by USC." Mike said this as a matter of record, didn't wait for a response. "Drive the freeway to work?"

"Never owned a car."

"How'd you get to Inglewood?"

"I took the bus down Figueroa and transferred at Manchester."

"What time did you get off work?"

"Can't remember. That was a long time ago. I know it was late, though. I didn't like waiting around in that neighborhood for the connecting bus."

"The Figueroa bus took you within two blocks of the SLA's first hideout. You were telling people you were a Muslim convert. Anyone maybe walk you over to Eighty-fourth Street so you could meet the revolutionaries, see their guns? The landlord was a Muslim. I understand there was a regular parade through that house."

Louis shook his head, showed scorn in his attitude. "Amateurs. Bunch of white freaks."

"You ever stop in at the corner liquor store for a beer while you waited for the bus, maybe buy some smokes?"

"I might have. I don't remember. I don't remember a lot of things."

"You on medication, Louis?"

"Yes."

"You taking it regular?"

"More or less."

"What happens if you miss a few doses?"

Louis looked at me for the first time. He tapped his head. "I get me some company. They can set up a powerful racket inside here."

"Why'd you put your eye out, Louis?"

"I don't always like what I see."

"The young woman you attacked with a machete, she gouged your eye, didn't she?"

"She fought pretty good."

"You feel bad about what you did to her? Maybe finish the job she started on your eye?"

He covered his eye. "She did it. She won't leave me alone. Bitch yells at me all the time. Night and day. Won't leave me alone."

I stood against the door, next to Guido, so that I could watch the scene in his monitor. Louis dropped his head to his chest. Mike turned to me expectantly. Guido grinned like a shark in tourist season.

I said, "It's a wrap."

CHAPTER

9

I slipped Anthony Louis's tape into the bedroom VCR and watched a few minutes of it while I puttered around between the bedroom and the adjoining bathroom. Mike came in with his toolbox, glanced at the TV, and grimaced.

"I like the way the interview plays," I said. "I like the way you sound and I love the content. Will you do more segments for me?"

"I don't mind. It's tough to look at myself on TV like that, though. I suppose you get used to it."

"You do," I said. "After a while, it's just like seeing yourself in a mirror that makes you look fat."

"Well, I don't always like seeing myself in a mirror, either."

That gave me an idea. When he went downstairs to put the tools away, I stuck a secondary inlet plug into the back of the VCR, but watched a little more of Louis before I completed the switch. Louis would have been a good documentary subject all by himself, but the sad truth was that by the time the Frady film was edited, Louis would be reduced to a few pithy bites. It's always tough to cut good footage, no matter how useless it is for the final cut.

I heard Mike coming back up the stairs. I took Louis out of the VCR and put in a fresh tape, completed the switch, then went into the bathroom to run our bathwater.

Around the turn of the century, when the house was built, bathrooms with built-in tubs were still symbols for the privileged class. Our bathroom must have been designed for a robber baron, because it was absolutely grand. The claw-footed tub in the middle of the room was big enough for the entire family, and, the best part, the room was heated by a small fireplace with a granite mantel.

I poured some bubble bath into the running water, started a fire, laid out towels. Mike came in, stripped off his dirty work clothes, dropped them into the hamper, and made a full turn for my benefit.

I ran my hand down his long back. "Rash is gone."

"That's all you have to say?"

"I love you?"

"That's a question?"

I planted a kiss on his sweaty shoulder. "I wonder whether the long-haired Oregon chicks who sat next to Anthony Louis in English one A ever knew he was a coed killer."

"Maybe I should go out and come in again."

"Maybe you should. I love the way your backside moves when you walk."

"Uh-huh." He tugged off my shirt, kissed my belly, unzipped my jeans. "I'd rather watch your front side."

Mike turned off the lights, leaving the room illuminated by only the fire.

It was pretty, but I said, "I want to see you." And he turned the lights right back on.

Bubbles crested the top of the tub when we stepped into the water.

Later, snuggling in bed, I found the TV remote, rewound the tape in the VCR, and pushed Start.

"I'm already having nightmares," Mike sighed. "I don't want Anthony Louis's face to be the last thing I see before I go to sleep."

"Me, either. Just watch." A few seconds of snow on the screen cleared to reveal the bathroom. I had placed the mini-cam atop the shower door and focused it downward onto the tub. On tape, foreshortened from above, I poured bubble bath into the running water. Mike came in, stripped, did a pirouette. Turned off the lights. Turned them back on.

"Now I get it," he said.

"Aren't you darling?" I said as on the screen we started getting more interesting. "This is the best way to get used to seeing yourself on film—in the raw."

On the screen, Mike had his face buried between my breasts. In the flesh, Mike was shocked. Scandalized. He blushed. He never took his eyes from the screen. "You taped us?"

"Look at that; it's like a miracle. You kiss my breast and your lever rises." I reversed the tape and ran it again. "Isn't that the sweetest thing you ever saw?"

"We're not really going to watch this, are we?"

"I am." I snuggled my back in closer against him, pulled his arm around me. "We don't have a family album. I thought it was time to start one."

"This is the first time, though, right? You haven't been taping us right along?"

I looked back at him. "Relax, baby. You can erase the tape later. But if you're uncomfortable watching it now, I'll turn it off."

On the screen, my back to the camera, I rose out of the water, straddled Mike's lap, and slid down onto him. As he bucked under me, bubbles and water poured over the side of the tub. Mike's eyes glazed over, both on tape and in the flesh.

"Want me to turn it off?" I asked.

When he didn't say anything, I wrapped my top leg over his and nudged him. "Mike? Do you want me to turn it off?"

He picked up the remote and rewound the part where my bubble-streaked abdomen arched back in ecstasy, and he played it again.

The funeral was scheduled for eleven. I went in to the studio around eight, intending to stay only briefly.

The interviews we had accumulated so far were, like the Anthony Louis tape, done piecemeal in a variety of locations, under different conditions. I was worried about how the inconsistent lighting and quality would look when we patched them together to make the final cut.

I took a rough tape in to Bobby, a staff editor. Bobby was an old friend, a social guy in a job that required hours of solitude. He was always looking for an excuse to have company sit and gossip with him. He also knew more about editing videotape than anyone in Hollywood, one of those valuable network resources Gaylord Smith had talked about.

"You wanted noir, you got it," Bobby said. "The trick will be in the transitions. I'd like to sit down with you and play around." He paused, he grinned. "With your footage, that is."

"I don't have time right now," I said. "Maybe this afternoon."

"Nope. I'm leaving for a conference in Vegas. Only be gone a couple days. How about Friday?"

I shook my head. "I'm flying up to Berkeley to see my sister on Friday. Make it Monday?"

"Emily?" He half rose from his seat. "You're going to see Emily? I didn't realize she was still alive."

"Alive is a relative term," I said. I popped out the tape and rose to leave. I didn't want to talk about Emily with Bobby—he wasn't that good a friend. And at that moment, with Hector lying in a coffin waiting for his ride to the church, Emily was too perilous a topic to get into.

"I remember Emily Duchamps." Bobby grabbed my hand and held me back. He was in the thrall of strong memories. "She was so powerful, so charismatic. She'd show up on a press conference about Vietnam or some other federal screw-up, and God, she'd light up the screen, set my head spinning." He dropped his gaze, like a kid during prayers. "I can't believe she's still alive."

Genuine concern, or conversational gambit? I didn't know. Maybe he was genuinely surprised and wanted to commiserate, and maybe he just wanted me to stay and talk. I didn't have time for either, nor fortitude for either. We made an appointment for Monday morning, we shook hands, and I left.

I tried to get out of the building, but I ran into one

problem after another, three of them relating to Brady's firing alone. With no cushion of time left, I ran out to the parking lot.

"Maggie! Have a moment?"

I turned and saw Thea D'Angelo loping behind me. Big and ungainly, she reminded me of the kid in grade school who always gets picked last for teams; tries hardest, does the worst. Inwardly, I groaned. But guilt left over from being the kid who did the team picking made me slow down enough for her to catch up.

I said, "Thea, sorry, I don't have time right now. I'm late for a funeral."

"The funeral of that police officer?" is what she said instead of catch you later. "I read about it. He was a friend of your boyfriend, wasn't he? I'm really sorry. Tell Officer Flint I'm really sorry."

"Sure. Thanks, Thea, I will." I started away but she tugged on my arm. And she tugged too hard. I looked from her hand to her earnest, sweaty face. I said, "I'm late."

She let go, embarrassed. "I'm sorry. Really sorry."

That was four sorrys in a row. Feeling like a schmuck, I stopped. "What is it you want to tell me?"

For a moment she went blank, and then she blushed again. "I have a question about calculating overtime on location shoots. I have the list of scheduled interviews and I want to get spreadsheets set up."

"Well, Thea." I said it slowly, as if speaking to a dense child. "You need to address that sort of question to Lana or to the union. Now, please excuse me."

Too needy, was my assessment when I left her, her thick shoulders rounded with chagrin, fighting back tears as she stood in the middle of the parking lot.

"Maggie," she called after me.

I sighed and turned around. "Yes?"

"Jack, the reporter? He says you're hard to keep up with, so I made him a copy of the shooting schedule. I hope that's okay."

"It's fine, Thea. Thanks for being helpful."

When I finally got back into my car, if traffic had been with me I would have had just enough time to say a word or two to Mike before the funeral; he had been awfully nervous when he left the house. But traffic was dense all the way down La Brea.

I felt frantic. At that moment, I hated L.A. and its never-ending dense-pack of cars. I blew a Stop sign, sailed through on the tall ends of three yellow lights in a row, and then, when I turned onto Wilshire, I hit a solid, gridlocked mass. Add together subway construction under Wilshire, hundreds of black-and-white police units from as far away as San Diego and Santa Barbara, then the press, a motorcycle contingent, family, friends, and the morbidly curious. The result was urban paralysis. I gave up six blocks away from the Scottish Rite Temple, parked in a bank's lot, and walked. I longed to be at home in San Francisco, where moving from one place to another is usually a pleasure.

The walk gave me time to settle down. I was hot by the time I got to the temple, but composed.

Police take care of their own, and they make sure none of the brotherhood goes down unheralded. Hector's services had all the pomp and circumstance of a state funeral. Because the old Scottish Rite Temple, the traditional venue for police funerals, was slated to be closed forever after Hector's services there was an added element of poignance to the proceedings, and a few extra reporters. Along the curb on Lucerne, I counted five news vans. Ours was among them.

I almost collided with Guido, who was running toward the vans.

"What's the rush?" I asked, grabbing his shoulders.

"Michelle was a no-show. We waited for her, now I'm late," he panted. "Not a good day, Maggie. Not a good day. That bar owner, Sal, is one scary guy."

"What happened?"

"He threatened to sue us for breach of contract. He said he'd lose a lot of publicity if we didn't film his place."

"I'll talk to him," I said. "With or without Michelle, the bar is a good interior."

Guido checked his watch. "Later," he said, and ran on toward the vans.

I crossed the street and entered the temple on the Lucerne Street side. Inside, the ornate hall was filled with honor guards, huge flowers, waving flags, a deputation of city brass, the chief, row upon row of men and women in uniform, Bach booming from the pipe organ, and television cameras to make sure none of it was lost.

I felt suffocated, wondered what any of it had to do with Hector.

Mike sat up front with the brass, facing the congregation, watching over Hector in his box. He seemed to be preoccupied, nearly distraught. He kept glancing through the notes he had written for the eulogy, over and over as if nothing was sticking. I decided right then to save myself a lot of grief and die before Mike did.

The family filed in from a side door. Hector's two teenage daughters looked to be in shock and in need of help, but the adults who should have attended to them were so intent on gaining chief-mourner status and claiming front row center seats that everyone seemed to have forgotten where they were, and why. Ex-wife and children, estranged wife, elderly mother already half-smashed at eleven o'clock in the morning, all argued. The issue seemed to be who was entitled to the big prize. That is, to whom would the police chief present the flag that was draped over the coffin?

Doug Senecal, handsome in his uniform with sergeant stripes on the sleeve, was doing duty as a pallbearer. It was Doug who thought of Hector's girls, who stepped away from the dais to hug them, to make sure they were seated close to their father and had funeral cards. He lingered near them like the alpha wolf watching over the young in his pack, found the younger girl tissue when she began to cry, reminded her older sister to hold her.

Watching Doug, I teared up and couldn't clearly see where I was going. Mary Helen Frady came and got me, sat me next to her about halfway back in the auditorium.

"How's Mike holding up?" she asked.

"He's trying to be a tough guy. He really loved Hector."

"Hector would be proud to know all the old gunslingers from Seventy-seventh are here. Those guys are the meanest, hardest sons of bitches going. They're all in the back crying like babies."

I leaned in to whisper, "Did Gloria Marcuse come?"

"She's back there with the honor guard." Mary Helen glanced over her shoulder. "The bitch. Later, we'll get smashed and I'll tell you how she slept her way to the top. She's still going down on the captain."

I'd heard the stories. "Who else is here?"

"I think I saw Barry Ridgeway. If it's him, he looks like shit. I'll introduce you to some wives at the cemetery."

Doug came over and knelt down beside me. "Need you up front," he said.

"I'm fine here. I can see Mike and I can get out in a hurry when it's over."

Doug leaned in closer to me. There was some gray at his temples I hadn't noticed before. "We have a situation, Maggie. Hec's wives got into some big hair-pulling scene at the little girl's junior high graduation last year. Looks like they're warming up for a repeat. I need you to sit between them."

"I don't even know them."

"Yeah." He took my elbow and impelled me up. "So maybe they'll behave better in front of a stranger."

"Where's your wife?"

"She's keeping Hec's mom from falling off her chair. Mom's loaded."

Mary Helen said, "Good luck," as I gathered my bag and got up.

For Mike, I went with Doug, holding on to his muscular arm as he worked forward through the crush of people.

Among the second-string mourners in the second row—Hector's various sets of in-laws, stepchildren and could-have-been stepchildren—were young Michael

Flint and both of Mike's former wives. I had never had a problem with exes. They were both long gone before I came onto the scene, but it was weird to see them sitting together with Hector's peripheral family.

As Doug seated me directly in front of the two ex-Mrs. Mike Flints, Mike's second wife, Charlene, the slick and perfect decorator, leaned into number one, Leslie, the schoolteacher saint—Michael's mother—and muttered loudly enough for me to hear, "Why is *she* in front? She hardly knew Hector."

I wanted to turn around and ask Charlene if she thought that knowing Hector in the biblical sense entitled her to something special, other than the certificate of divorce Mike had already awarded her for the caper. But Michael was there and I didn't want to embarrass him.

Michael had heard Charlene's remark and reacted the way I would expect Mike Flint's offspring to react: he laughed. Michael rose and leaned over me from behind, gave me a hug and a noisy kiss. "How are you?"

"I'm all right. How does your dad seem to you?"

"Sad. I'm glad you came up front where he can see you."

I reached up and pressed my hand against his cheek. "And you, too."

Michael's gesture toward me at that sticky moment was very sweet, and eased the awkwardness all around. Yet I noticed that, as he squeezed my hand, he glanced over at his former stepmother, Charlene, to make sure she was watching, then grinned at her malevolent leer. In many ways, Michael is a chip off the old block.

The organ music stopped and the police chaplain stood up and called the congregation to prayer. Michael went back to his seat as both of Hector's wives began to weep.

When Mike came forward to deliver his eulogy, I watched him trying to hang on to his composure. Clutching his reading glasses, he looked from me to Michael and gave us each a wink.

I knew he was afraid he would break down before he finished his planned remarks. I winked back at him, and, down low where you'd have to be looking for it to see it, flashed him an obscene gesture that made him smile a little. The only way I got through hearing Mike's wavering baritone talk about Hector the good cop, loving father, true and constant friend, was to think about Mike in the bathtub the night before.

Mike rode to the cemetery in a black-and-white unit behind the hearse. Mary Helen offered me a ride. We were somewhere in the middle of the mile-long cortege, hoping her car wouldn't overheat during the long delays.

"How are you?" I asked her. "Does all this fuss bring back Roy's funeral?"

"I don't remember much about Roy's funeral, I was so stoned on Valium." She slipped Garth Brooks into the tape player. "Want to know what I remember about Roy's funeral?"

"What?"

"No gas. Roy died during the oil crisis. Can you imagine this country in such a mess you can't even get a tank of gas to get to your husband's funeral? You were assigned a day you could line up at the pumps, and then you waited a couple of hours for your eight- or ten-gallon allotment. Remember that? The day before the funeral was my day. But where was I going to find two or three hours to wait in line at a service station? The kids needed dress shoes and there were all the funeral plans. I ran on empty for two days." She threw back her head and laughed, reached out for my arm. "I was so afraid I'd run out and have to spend the night at my in-laws that I promised God we'd start talkin' regular again, if he'd just get me through the day."

"Are you talking to God?"

"No. And I'm not talking to Valium anymore, either."

At the cemetery in the Hollywood Hills, Mike and Doug and four of the other old gunslingers carried the coffin up a terraced slope to the grave site. Doug was behind Mike, and twice I saw Doug reach up to touch Mike's shoulder. When they set down the coffin, the six pallbearers embraced, and it was the most heart-wrenching moment of the day.

Mike found me and Mary Helen, hugged her, wrapped his arms around me. The day was hot and his dark wool uniform felt damp.

I whispered, "You did well. I'm proud of you, Mike."

"Left out a few things," he said. "I'm just glad it's over. What's your schedule this afternoon?"

"Work. What's yours?"

"I told Hec's mom I'd put in an appearance at lunch at her place. I'd like your company."

"Okay."

The graveside services were concluded with a lone bagpiper playing "Fleurs of the Forest," a tradition at police funerals ever since the murder of Officer Ian Campbell in an onion field thirty years ago, and finally with a helicopter fly-over. I leaned against Mike through it all. He was fine until the coffin began its descent into the grave, and then he was leaning against me, breathing in short gasps.

Mike stayed near the open grave, talking with old friends, while the crowd dispersed and traffic cleared. Barry Ridgeway, wearing new-looking slacks and a blazer, drew me to the side.

"How are you?" I asked.

He turned his back on the uniformed crowd. "I don't mind telling you, I feel damned awkward. Most of these people I never saw before, and the rest of them seem to think I shouldn't be here."

"Why? Hector was your friend."

"Old beefs die hard." He smoothed the short hair at his temples. "When your partner dies, you're supposed to do something about it. But what could I do that the whole goddamn police force couldn't do?"

"You mean Frady?"

He started to say something, but Mary Helen walked up before he got started, and he clammed right up. She studied him hard before she seemed to figure out who he was.

"Ridgeway?" she said. "It's been a long time. You look different."

He gave her a crooked smile. "This is the way an old cowboy looks when he's had the shit kicked out of him. But you look just fine."

"I'm all right." Mary Helen had frown lines between her eyes when she slipped her hand through my elbow. "You two know each other?"

"We met yesterday," I said. "I'm going to interview Barry."

She thought about that, looking hard at his brand-new blazer. "I'd like to be there when you do. There are a few questions I'd like you to answer. You wouldn't mind if I came along, would you, Ridgeway?"

He paled so suddenly I thought he might pass right out. But he managed to smile when he said, "I don't mind a bit."

When he walked down the hill toward the road, he never looked back.

I said to Mary Helen, "You're a devil. I have a feeling that you were a match for your devil-boy husband."

She nodded proud acknowledgment of a compliment. "You've started me thinking," she said. "There are so many questions I have about Roy that no one would ever answer for me. Before I get any older, I want some truth out of guys like Ridgeway. I know they never told half of what they know."

She took me around, then, introducing me to the old-timers, pressing each one of them to schedule an interview with me. I had only one card left in my bag when she marched me up to Gloria Marcuse, Hector's last girlfriend.

"Lieutenant," Mary Helen said, "the press wants your reaction to Detective Melendez's untimely death." Then she walked away and left me.

"Hello, Maggie." Gloria was tall, hard-bodied, her face lined from the sun—the mask of an athlete. I had never seen her before in her midnight blue uniform. With a sleeve full of hash marks, she was intimidating. The few times I had met her, we got along all right.

Mike described her as one-way, looked out for herself only. That's about the nicest thing I ever heard anyone say about her, except that she made Hector happy in bed. I was not ready to write her off; her eyes were puffy from crying, and she seemed genuinely grief-stricken.

With apparent distaste, she said, "What did she mean, 'the press'?"

"Don't pay any attention to her," I said. "My condolences on your loss."

She said, "Thanks."

"How are you doing?"

"You're the first person to ask. I appreciate it. Some of the people here seem to think I shouldn't have come. When Hec died, I was in the process of moving out, but that doesn't mean I didn't love him. God, what a shock this has been."

In the process? I thought about that.

Guido walked up with a Steadycam on his shoulder and aimed it at the two of us.

"You don't want to talk to me." Gloria touched the back of her hair and looked away from the camera. "I never met Roy Frady. Sorry I can't help you there."

I said, "Hector has a big part in my Frady film. He did a lot of on-camera interviews. Talk to me about Hector. For background, tell me about living with a cop."

"I *am* a cop. The question, can two cops live together? The answer, not easily. For one thing, I outrank Hector. For another, why is it that what's okay for him somehow isn't okay for me?"

"For instance?"

"He goes end of watch, goes out and gets loaded,

screws around, and I'm supposed to understand because his job is so fucking stressful." She started to cry, chin quivering, nose running. "But when I go end of watch, if I don't come straight home, he loses it. I couldn't take it anymore."

"I understand you have a new relationship, with another cop."

"Well." Her shoulders went back, she wiped her eyes and nose on the back of her hand. "We don't work together; he's County Sheriff. And he doesn't screw around."

I said, "Mazel tov."

"Yeah." She sniffled, laughed gently, wistfully. "I'm too old for this shit. Time to hang it up."

I wanted to ask exactly which shit she was too old for, but didn't. Without saying good-bye, she turned and quickly walked down the hill toward the cars. She was openly sobbing when she got there.

Mike and I rode with Mary Helen to Hector's mother's house in Van Nuys. They talked about the old days and family picnics, first houses, first babies, and first divorces. Mike was more reticent than Mary Helen. She talked openly about smelling other women's perfume on Roy's clothing when she did the laundry, about demanding sex with him when he came in late as a sort of check on his activities, about him not coming home for days at a time. Mike laughed now and then, but he kept his part of the conversation on softball games and camping trips, as if reinforcing some ideal of Roy Frady, family man. Or reinforcing the image of Mike Flint, family man. I just listened.

The crowd at Mrs. Melendez's was enormous, barely containable in the big backyard of her Valley tract house. Mike was concerned about fights breaking out: too much family history on a collision course around a tub full of beer. The various factions seemed to lay different territorial claims and, once their plates were served from the buffet, they avoided one another.

Mike walked me around, introducing me to people. After a while he attached himself to a group of old-timers from Seventy-seventh Street and swapped stories with them.

Doug came over with a beer in each hand. He drank one in a long gulp and handed Mike the empty. "Hey, Mike, this remind you of my wedding?"

"Which wedding, Senecal? You had four."

"The last one. He ever tell you about it, Maggie?"

I said, "Why, no." And settled in for the duration.

"Got married in the backyard of my in-laws' house up in Whittier. Real nice place, big rose garden. My wife's father is a sheriff. He didn't want any problems, so he only served wine and beer—no hard stuff. That wasn't good enough for Hector, so he goes down to the store and buys some Cuervo Gold, and sets up shooters. The guys get loaded, go out front and start shooting off their guns, knocking out streetlights— can't do that shit anymore without taking a beef. My wife's brother doesn't want trouble with the neighbors, so he goes out to stop them—he's a sheriff, too—gets in this brawl with Hector, gives him a black eye. Hector knocks him cold."

Doug opened his second beer. "Quite a party, huh, Flint?"

"Quite a party." Mike crushed the beer can. "Hec-

tor could be a mean drunk. I had to drive him home
before he took out the whole neighborhood."

"Hec drank all the time." Doug opened his second
beer. "Till a couple years ago, he even drank on the
job. You wouldn't know, though, unless you smelled
it on him. He was a functioning alky. After work he'd
hit the bars and get really loaded and really ugly. Mike
was the only one who could control him."

Doug sipped his beer. "Like that time in Ensenada.
Remember, Mike? Jeez, Hec was so gone, he was
crazy. Had his two-inch out, trying to fight everyone
in the bar. We were afraid they'd call the *policia,* and
we didn't want to mess with the Mexican police."

Mike scowled. "I didn't want anything to do with
him. I was having a good time. Hell, it was Easter
week and the place was full of horny female school-
teachers from San Diego. I didn't want to get in a
fight. But they kept coming to get me, telling me Hec
was in trouble. I just told them to leave me out of it.
Then they said the police were coming, and I didn't
want him to have to deal with that.

"So, I go into the bar and Hec can hardly stand up,
he's waving his gun, acting like a goddamn lunatic,
threatening everyone. So, I just walk over to him and
say, 'What's up?' The damn fool hands me his gun,
he says, 'Hiya Mike,' happy as can be. Kisses me right
on the mouth. I took him up to bed and had to stay
with him till he fell asleep."

I said, "He kissed you and took you to bed? What
else did he do?"

"Snored," Mike said, eyes narrowed. "He just
snored."

"Makes me think of that sergeant with Gardena PD,

gave us such a hard time." Senecal was off on another tale, egging on Mike, as usual. "What was the deal you and Hector pulled?"

"Sergeant Lukash? That was me and Frady."

"Yeah, you and Frady." Doug looked at me. "Lukash was such a by-the-book hardnose, Gardena PD could hardly function during his watch. He was weird, too. His people didn't want to be in the shower when he was around; lot of soap dropping."

I said, "He was gay?"

Doug said, "He was repressed."

Mike said, "Spell that, Senecal."

"P-E-R-V-E-R-T," Doug said. "So, what was the deal with the drive-in?"

"So," Mike said, again, to me, but for everyone's enlightenment. I was probably the only one who hadn't heard the story five times already. "We were working the harbor strip, morning watch. Usually it was pretty quiet down there, mostly industrial, no one around at oh-dark-thirty. Just one car deployed per watch. We were maybe twenty minutes or more from LAPD backup if anything went down. So, if we needed help, we'd call in Gardena PD or Inglewood PD, whoever was closer. I liked calling in Gardena. Those guys were fun, always ready for a fight. If I had a choice, that's who I'd call.

"There was this drive-in there on Vermont, about Vermont and One hundred and third, right on the L.A.-Gardena city line. The theater was in Gardena, out of our territory, and we weren't supposed to go in there unless we got a help call. But one night, around midwatch, me and Frady got bored—I told you it was quiet down there. So we drove through the drive-in, watched the bouncing cars, drove out. No big deal, but the manager didn't like it. He called Lukash. Lukash filed a formal beef—he didn't have our shop number, so the whole watch took heat. Our sergeant knew it was probably us who did it, but he wasn't about to give that to Lukash.

"The next night, end of watch, sun isn't up yet, colder than hell, me and Frady and these two guys from Gardena who hated Lukash's guts, we all meet up over at the drive-in. Four, five o'clock in the morning, no one's around.

"There's this big marquee over the ticket booths, and when they take down the letters to change the movies, they just leave them lying up there on the roof. So we climb up, change the marquee to read, 'Sgt. Lukash Is a Cocksucker.' Sign it Gardena PD.

"Lukash goes ballistic. Calls in SID to dust for prints. Tries to isolate tire marks. He's so hot to find us, he blows a big-time bookie sting out at Hollywood Park because all his backup is at the drive-in. Couple of his undercover people nearly got hit."

I was the only one not finding the story hilarious. "Did he find your prints?"

"Hell no." Mike gave me a superior leer. "It was cold. We all had gloves on. The thing is, Lukash got a thirty-day suspension, got reassigned to day patrol. Couldn't take the razzing when he got back, went out on stress disability."

"When?" I asked.

Mike shrugged, Doug shrugged, a couple of the others did, too.

I asked, "How long before Frady died did this happen?"

"Frady died in May?" Mike thought for a moment. "I'm thinking this was after Christmas. January, February of that year."

I said, "Hmm."

"Lukash?" Mike frowned, thought about it, looked at Doug. "Where is the son of a bitch now?"

"I would know?" Senecal took a third beer out of his pocket, popped it open, and took a long drink. Then he handed the can to Mike. "Hold this for me. If Rebecca comes by and sees me drinking, I'm back in the doghouse for sure."

Hector's old gray-haired mother was smashed. She came stumbling across the lawn in stocking feet wailing, "My boy, my boy." She either tripped or she flung herself, but somehow she ended up draped all over Mike. Tears and snot running down her lined face, she appealed to him. "Mikey, what am I gonna do? It was murder, Mikey. Plain old murder. And now my boy's gone. What's gonna happen to me?"

"You'll be okay, Mrs. Melendez. Let's go in and sit down." Mike gestured for Doug, and the two of them carted her back into the house between them. I followed, straightened her dress for her when they deposited her on a living room sofa.

When Mike stood back, I said, "I think it's time to leave."

"Me, too. Some of the guys used to work Seventy-seventh thought we'd go up to the academy, raise a glass to Hec. Want to come?"

"Sounds like a private wake. I'll come by for one drink, but I won't stay," I said. "Do you mind if I send Guido to the academy to shoot a few frames?"

"Sure. We'll show him how real men drink. Maybe we'll introduce him to some sweet young thing."

"Fine. Just promise me you won't drive yourself home shit-faced."

He kissed the side of my neck. "I'll get a ride from some sweetie."

"As long as she isn't drunk."

He frowned. "That's it? As long as she isn't drunk?"

"What do you want? A lecture on monogamy?"

"Now and then."

I patted his abdomen, felt him pull it in. "Did you have fun last night, Mike?"

"Definitely. Both the premier and the rerun."

"Weigh last night against what Sweetie has to offer you, then decide which you want. Remember that you can't have both."

CHAPTER

10

The bartender at the academy started pouring Bacardi and Coke, Hector's drink, as soon as the crowd walked in the door. Tall glasses, twenty deep, covered the bar. Within half an hour, there were a hundred officers in the Embers Room drinking rum and Coke. Within an hour, there were a hundred officers well on their way to oblivion.

I came back from the ladies' room at one point to hear Mike telling a crowd of about eight old-timers, "He'd given up booze. When we went into his apartment after he died, Hec's dinner was still on the table. All he had to drink was a glass of water."

"He had dinner on the table?" I asked. "I thought he was out running."

Mike looked aside at me. "Maybe it was his lunch. The point is, he was drinking water."

I took a Bacardi and Coke off the bar and drank it to Hector, who was finally straight when he died.

Doug put an empty glass on the bar and reached

for a full one. He reached for me, too, pulled me against him, smooched my ear and went on with the story he had been telling his knot of listeners before I walked over. "So the case gets to court. Mike's on the stand explaining to the public defender why we went down in there. He says, 'My partner and I saw a light coming from the vacant building, we know no one should be over there, so we went to investigate. We saw the defendant on top of the girl and observed that they were engaged in sexual intercourse. She asked for our help, so my partner and I then arrested the man and booked him for rape.'

"So the PD asks were we aware the girl's a deaf-mute? Mike says we found that out later. The PD says, if the girl can't speak, how did Mike and I decide this wasn't consensual sex between adults? Mike says, 'I trained my flashlight on her and she mouthed, Help me.' The PD says, 'Are you trained in lip-reading, Officer Flint?' Mike says, 'No. But I can read help me.' The PD says, 'How did you acquire this skill? Did you watch Ingmar Bergman movies without subtitles or something to practice lipreading?' And Mike, swear to God, doesn't miss a beat, doesn't crack a smile. He says, 'No sir, I don't read Swedish.' "

To the sounds of general laughter, I walked over to Mike and put my arm through his. "It's time for me to go."

His lips were icy against mine, smelled of rum. "You can stay," he said.

"I know. But I have a lot of work to do, and I'll just be in the way after one more drink. Take care of yourself." I nuzzled the soft place at the side of his neck that belongs to me, and we walked toward the door together hand in hand. "Call a taxi, or call me."

Doug followed us, draped an arm around me, and held me back. "You can't go, sweet thing. Olga heard Mike'll be here and she's on her way. If you go, who knows what will happen."

Olga was a "police regular" I found bouncing on Mike's lap one night, a year or so ago. It had been her idea, not his. He just neglected to dump her off. And someone, thinking he was awfully damn funny, gave her Mike's home number.

I said, "Mike's a grown-up. He can choose for himself, me or Olga."

"Ooo, hooh," Doug sang. "Sounds like the three-strike rule hangs over our boy."

"Got that right," I said, grabbing a handful of Mike's shirtfront. "One more strike and he's a free agent."

The afternoon was hot and smoggy. I burned off the rum by walking down to Chinatown, maybe a mile away, and all downhill. On North Broadway, I picked up the Wilshire bus and rode out to where I had left my car. I paid the parking lot attendant a fee roughly equivalent to a night's stay in a pretty good midwestern hotel, turned west out of the lot, and kept driving until I reached the ocean in Santa Monica.

Hector had lived in a high-rise across from the beach, in an apartment he had rented with Gloria. When I parked in front, I had no plan. I didn't know the area very well, and couldn't think of anywhere else to go at the moment except back to work. The truth is, something Gloria Marcuse had said bothered me.

I was able to get through the secured front door of Hector's building by catching it before it latched shut after a UPS man. I went to the manager's first-floor apartment and knocked on the door.

"Do you remember me?" I asked.

The manager's name was either Sarah or Sandra, I couldn't remember. Hector had introduced us a couple of times when we had been over barbecuing around the pool. I had never seen her in a dress before, or in anything except a bikini or a unitard. Sarah or Sandra was a professional bodybuilder and all the time we stood in the hall outside her apartment, even though she wore a silk dress with lace at the neck, she was doing arm curls with five-pound weights.

"Maggie?" She tested my name. "I saw you at the funeral."

"Sorry I missed you. It was a big crowd."

"No shit." Even her jaws were muscular. "What can I do for you?"

"I'm not sure. Gloria was at the funeral, too."

"I saw the bitch."

"She said she was in the process of moving out. I thought she was gone months ago."

Sarah/Sandra stopped flexing her arms. "She was gone. She was back. Like a yo-yo. Drove Hector crazy."

"He let her come back?"

"She always showed up in the middle of the night. The way I see it, either the new guy was beating on her, or he wasn't giving it to her the way Hector did and she had to have it."

"Hector never said anything about her coming back."

"He was embarrassed. It looked like she was using him. He was still paying the rent, you know, and she had that other guy."

"Hector told you about the project we were working on. Some of my files are in his apartment. Any way I can get them?"

She shrugged, thought for a moment. "I shouldn't let you in, but why not? You're a friend, and it's not as if I don't know where to find you. Hector's mom came by last night to look around. She said she's coming by tomorrow to pack his stuff. If anything belongs to you, maybe you should get it before she comes, save a lot of hassle. I'll have to come up with you, though."

"I'll feel better if you do."

She pulled her door closed and led the way toward the elevator, bringing her hand weights with her, pumped her arms all the way up to the fifth floor. "I told Mrs. Melendez there's no hurry. The rent is paid until the end of the month."

She unlocked the door of Hector's apartment, stopped pumping, and muttered, "Holy shit."

I stepped past her into a nearly bare apartment. I asked, "The furniture was here last night?"

"Oh, yeah. How'd Gloria get all the stuff moved out? And when? I saw her at the funeral."

"You think it was Gloria?" I asked.

"Who else? She had a key."

"She also had a helper." I picked up a stray throw pillow that had been left behind. "Or she had a couple of helpers. And a truck."

"Should I call the cops?"

"You're the manager, that's up to you. You might call Hector's mom and see what she wants you to do."

When Gloria moved out a few months ago, Hector bought new living room furniture, because she took their new furniture with her, and left him with two sets of payments. He had told me he could barely afford the rent on his own, and the extra payments were killing him.

Hector's personal gallery of family pictures and framed department commendations was intact. A borrowed small-screen TV sat on the floor. His new computer was gone. Next to its former place on a kitchen counter, his boxes of disks and about a dozen unlabeled videotapes were still lined up on their shelf as they had been the last time I was in Hector's apartment, maybe three days before he died.

The bedroom furniture came from a secondhand store, and apparently wasn't worth taking. The bed was unmade and both of the pillows still had head dents. His secondhand dresser was full of clothes, mostly underwear and running things. I opened the dresser drawers because the room had the particular perfume common to cop bedrooms: eau de gun oil. Fresh gun oil.

Sandra/Sarah stood by, still muttering about the sleaziness of looting a man's apartment during his funeral. I opened the top dresser drawer and moved the balled athletic socks around. I found two boxes of 9-mm ammunition, set them on top, and kept looking.

"Hector had friends over the day he died?" I said.

"Couple of people I didn't know. She was here part of the time. I saw her in the morning. The shooting happened around three in the afternoon. I don't know if any of them were still around that late."

The gun oil smell was strongest in the small walk-in closet.

Hector always dressed well for work. His expensive suits and dress shoes were gone. His casual clothes, some old things like a few frayed shirts, a worn bathrobe, and some sneakers had been left. The shelf over the racks was crammed with extra blankets and a sleeping bag. I felt around under the blankets. First I found a soft, zippered gun case, then felt around some more and found a hard case large enough and heavy enough for two more handguns. There was also a shoe box with gun-cleaning supplies. But there was no empty gun case, and no .38 shells; Hector hadn't carried a gun upstairs.

"Those things give me the creeps," Sarah/Sandra said as I stacked the guns on the dresser. "How did you know they were there?"

"I live with a cop. All their socks smell like gunpowder, their extra blankets smell like gun oil. Haven't you noticed?"

She turned up her nose. "What are you going to do with all that?"

"I don't think guns should be left here. Anyone could come in and pick them up. Unless you have a better idea, I'll turn them over to Mike. He'll know what to do."

"I should have you sign a receipt. But, hell, if anyone says anything, I'll tell them to call the cops."

She didn't offer to help me carry either ammo or guns into the other room. I said, "Tell me what Hector did on his last day."

"It was like a normal Sunday. You guys used to come over, you know how he'd do. He'd put in his laundry, watch the games, then he'd go run on the beach. If anyone was over they'd run with him or they'd have a swim. I didn't see him go out, and I didn't see him come back in. Does it matter?"

"I think it does. Can you ask people in the building?"

"Sure, but didn't the police ask all their questions already?"

"No," I said. "Because there was no reason to. It seemed clear what happened. What questions were there to ask?"

She walked around, looking at the places furniture had been. "What are you? Nancy Drew?"

"I'm a friend." I looked through the labeled disks. "Were you in the building when the shooting happened?"

"I was down in my place—I told the police all this. I didn't know anything until Mrs. Altunas—that's the mother of the guy who killed Hector—until she came down."

I found a disk labeled Frady.

"Is that your stuff?" She looked over my shoulder.

"Probably." I put the disk in my pocket, stacked the videotapes. "These are, too."

She found a grocery sack in the broom closet and held it open for me. "Got it all?"

"I hope so. Just one thing, could you show me the apartment where it happened?"

She balked.

"Please?"

"Okay. I'll show you which one, but I won't go in. I don't want to talk to Mrs. Altunas today."

I agreed. Mike had told me Mrs. Altunas had had her son cremated and there would be no services. With Hector's funeral all over the news, the mother would be having one hell of a bad day. I just needed to see for myself the route that Hector had taken, to see how it would look on film.

We got back into the elevator and went up four floors.

"Who all went upstairs when Mrs. Altunas said her son was going to jump?" I asked.

"Just Hector, I guess. Mrs. Altunas asked him to go stop her son, and then she came down to my apartment to call the police."

"She went all the way down to you?"

"Yeah."

"Why didn't she call from Hector's place? Or from the neighbor's?"

The manager seemed very uncomfortable. "Okay, here's what happened. Mrs. Altunas didn't want to call the cops. See, she was scared her son would be committed again if she called the cops. All she wanted when she came down was some company. She told me Hector was going to talk to her boy, calm him down, get him to take his pills. No one called the cops until there were gunshots."

"Hector went up alone?"

"I don't know." Something bothered her that she didn't want to talk about. "The whole building could have gone in with him. I just don't know. I was all the way downstairs. It wasn't me who heard the gun."

Mrs. Altunas lived in apartment 915, so her apartment faced the back alley, and not the beach, as Hector's did. I went down with Sarah/Sandra, thanked her, declined her invitation to come in for coffee, and promised that I'd let her know anything I found out. She, in turn, promised to put a new lock on Hector's door.

I felt like a ghoul. I had spent so much time trying to attach motives to everyone who crossed paths with Roy Frady that I began to think my judgment was warped where Hector was concerned. Out of my paranoia I could construct at least three scenarios for his death that had nothing to do with a guy who forgot to take his meds and wanted to jump.

I wanted to talk to Mike, but I didn't want to call him at the academy because he would take heat from his pals. The guys might think I was checking on him. So, I drove back to the studio to work.

Jack Newquist had pulled a chair up to Fergie's desk and was sitting there reading the new edition of *Filmmaker* while she worked. He jumped to his feet when he looked up and saw me.

"Here you are," he said. "You're hard to keep up with. I lost you at the cemetery."

"You should have stuck with Guido," I said. "How's your article coming?"

"Good," he said. "Great. It's been an education. Can I hang with you for a while?"

"You'd have more fun up in the studio because I'll be taking care of junk work for a while. But if you want to sit inside and make like a mouse, go ahead."

Jack found a stool in the back corner of my office and perched there.

Fergie said her ankle wasn't hurting much and

handed me a sheaf of telephone messages. The first message began, "You fucking ball breaker," and ended, "Love, Brady." The second was from Darl Incledon, who was trying to track down Frady's gun. "Still at it," Fergie had written. Lyle, my former housemate, now caretaker of my house in San Francisco, had also called. "Tenants not only bailed on rent, but left a mess. Now what?"

Fergie said, "Now what?"

"Mike wants me to sell the house."

"Shall I call some area realtors and get appraisals going?" Fergie leaned on her aluminum crutches, her injured ankle dangling behind, waiting for instructions.

"I want you to keep off your feet." I picked up a stack of three-ring binders and set them on her desk. "Police files on Roy Frady. Two hundred forty-five interviews, six hundred suspects from tips. Find a comfortable place and go through them again. See what you come up with."

I went into my cubicle and made calls. It didn't take long to forget that Jack was in the corner watching me.

Brady was first on my list. I asked him to come in and talk to me. Then I warned security that he was coming and asked them to escort him up and to wait in the hall until he was ready to leave.

I talked to Lyle. When I moved south to be with Mike, the third floor of my painted lady had been converted into an apartment for Lyle so that he would be comfortable and be able to watch over the property; he was an old friend displaced by the Loma Prieta quake and had become family to me and Casey. I didn't want Lyle to be displaced a second time, and it worked out for both of us to have him there to watch over things.

Lyle is such a fuss, I couldn't imagine tenants getting away with anything that would cause significant damage. On the phone, I asked him, "How bad is it?"

"Lot of holes in the walls where they bolted furniture—quake protection. Leaky water bed upstairs was the problem, though. Floor's a mess, leaked through to the living room ceiling. Jesus, Maggie, I feel terrible."

"It's not your fault," I said. "You couldn't very well go on patrol."

"I told them, no water bed."

"Did they leave a forwarding address?"

"No such luck."

"I'm coming up Friday. We'll see what we need to do. Mike wants me to sell."

"I just bet." Lyle was still a little touchy about Mike taking me away. Lyle, Casey, and I had been very comfortable together.

Lyle offered to call in a contractor to assess the damage by Friday.

My daughter was on her way to dinner when I called her.

"Every part of my body is sore," she said. "I've never worked so hard in my life."

"Do you need anything?"

"A massage. And dinner. I gotta go, Mom. I'll call you later. I love you. Bye."

"Bye." I imagined her long-legged sprint carrying her across the room, even if I could not see the room.

My mother was happy I was coming up Friday.

I took Hector's tapes out of the grocery sack and

piled them on my small office sofa, put the one on top into the VCR, and started it.

The tape was a copy Guido had made for Hector, some of about ten hours of interviews they had done; Hector talking to people from the old days, camera work by Guido. I had only seen clips.

Jack edged closer. "What's that?"

"JoAnn Chin, RN," I said as the woman appeared on the screen. "One of our interviews."

"Hmm," he said, and watched from his stool.

JoAnn was in her middle years, somewhere between forty and fifty, but fighting the inevitable. She was still very pretty. Her short-cropped hair was dyed too dark to look natural, and she wore the gauzy-drapy sort of clothes that fooled no one into believing a svelte figure was hidden underneath. Guido's voice asked her to take off the New Age crystals dangling from her ears because they made noise in the mike clipped to her bodice.

Guido pulled back, bringing Hector into the frame. He was laughing with JoAnn when the assistant director held up the board: JoAnn Chin, October 20, Morningside Hospital.

I found it difficult to take my eyes off Hector: two days before he died he had not an apparent care in the world. I missed the question he asked, tuned in on her answer.

"The night I met Roy Frady, I was working the reception desk in the emergency room. He came in all cut and bloody from a street brawl. What I remember was, he was laughing. He was so full of himself. His partner—I don't remember his name right now, tall guy with glasses, had a cut on the bridge of his nose from the fight—his partner kept trying to calm him down.

"They had arrested three or four kids, brought half of them to the ER with them for treatment. A lot of cuts and bruises all around.

"Roy was so pumped with adrenaline he didn't want novocaine when we sutured him. I thought, what kind of maniac is this? He almost passed out before we finished, and that's when I decided I liked him."

HECTOR: When did the two of you get together?

JOANN: The first time? He was waiting for me after my shift that night. I think he was still pumped. He had these beautiful brown eyes, and, well, who could resist him?

HECTOR: How long did you know him before you moved in together?

JOANN: Around two years. I wouldn't even call it an affair most of that time: I had a boyfriend, he had a wife and kids. It was just [she thinks about it, then smiles] sex.

HECTOR: The relationship wasn't serious?

JOANN: Nothing was serious for Roy, except his job. He'd come into the ER on his lunch break— usually around midnight. We'd go find a quiet place and get it on; in a hospital in the middle of the night, there are plenty of places to go. A couple of times we went out to my car. One time, we did it in Alphy's Coffee Shop. I just sat on his lap in a corner booth and he did me. I loved it. I think he ordered pancakes.

HECTOR: Right there in the restaurant?

JOANN: It was such a quickie, no one noticed. Usually, though, we really got into it. His partner had an old pickup with a camper shell. A couple of times, the partner would show up with a date and the four of us would go roll around in that camper. Probably wore out its shocks.

HECTOR: You don't mind talking about some awfully personal moments.

JOANN: Moments? More like hours. Roy had a gift. But, no, I not only don't mind talking about it, I'm proud of it. Look at me. All my life I was a good girl. I did everything I was supposed to do. Until I met Roy. Every time we fucked, I secretly wished we'd get caught just so everyone would know JoAnn Chin was no Goody Twoshoes. That she could turn on a hot dog like Roy Frady.

HECTOR (*with a skeptical frown*): You said you had a boyfriend. Wasn't he also a cop?

JOANN (*nodding*): I dated a lot of cops—who else do you meet working in an emergency room?

HECTOR: Did your boyfriend know about you and Frady?

JOANN: It took him a couple of years, but he finally figured it out. We were already splitting up by then. He was a loser with too many problems— drinking, gambling, wife and kids. He was in trouble at work. It was tough to live with. I think Roy and I helped each other. I know he helped me over a rough time.

There was a knock on my door. I stopped the tape and turned to see Fergie supporting herself on the door frame.

"Policeman here to see you, Maggie." She hopped aside to let a brown suit pass her.

I went through an inventory of reasons a policeman would come by: Sarah/Sandra called to report the looting of Hec's apartment; someone had learned I was using classified police files and Mike would be fired, without pension; Mr. Edwards at the five-and-dime on Telegraph Avenue had finally gotten around to reporting that I boosted a Snickers bar from his store in 1968.

The policeman glanced at Jack as he handed me his card with its big, embossed detective shield: Larry Rascon, Hollenbeck Division, LAPD.

Fergie, nosy, reluctant to leave, asked, "Can I get anyone coffee?"

I looked at the detective, who did not say no. "Sure, if you can manage it," I said. "And maybe a doughnut. This is a workingman."

Rascon smiled as he patted his hard midsection. "You can skip the doughnut."

"Come in, have a seat, Detective." I stacked the tapes on the floor to make room for him; the inner office was very small, only about twice what the county would call a two-man cell. "What can I do for you?"

He looked at Jack.

"Jack Newquist," I said. "He's researching an article."

"Reporter?" Rascon smiled, offered his hand to Jack, but the handshake became a gentle tug and Jack was on his feet. "You'll excuse us?"

"Uh, sure." With a glance at me, Jack was out the door.

Rascon sat down. "Are you acquainted with a Michelle Tarbett?"

"Yes. I have spoken with her."

"She had your card in her possession."

"I gave it to her yesterday. We scheduled a taping session with her this morning at nine. She didn't show." I studied his face, but he wasn't giving away anything. "I don't like the way you used the past tense just now."

Rascon sat forward. "Ms. Tarbett was found dead last night. We're following up any possible leads, and looking for any information that might prove helpful."

"Dead how?"

"Stabbed. Looks like an ice pick." He pulled out his pocket notebook. "What was this interview you scheduled? She apply for a job?"

"Hardly. She was going to talk about an old friend—an old boyfriend—on videotape. She had an appointment this morning at the Hot-Cha Club on Florence Avenue. I knew she was nervous about being on camera. When she didn't show, I thought she was just scared."

"Who was the friend?" He had his head down, pen poised to write.

"Roy Frady."

He started to write. Then he stopped, pen held over the notebook. It took him a moment to make the connection, but when he did he seemed almost angry. He let out a noisy "Hmm," the way men do when they think they're being played for fools. "Who did you say?"

"I'm filming a documentary about Roy Frady. He used to stop at the Hot-Cha Club on his way to work, get half in the bag, have sex with Michelle, straighten his tie, report for roll call. I wanted Michelle to talk about him."

His smile was crooked, unsure. "Say, what?"

"I think I stated all that very clearly." I rewound JoAnn Chin for a few seconds, pushed Play, not knowing what part of the tape was up. "I'll show you the sort of thing I wanted from Michelle. Here's another of Frady's friends."

JoAnn's face emerged from the snow: "Roy had a gift. But, no, I not only don't mind talking about it, I'm proud of it. Look at me. All my life I was a good girl. I did everything I was supposed to do. Until I met Roy. Every time we fucked, I secretly wished we'd get caught just so everyone would know JoAnn Chin was no Goody Two-shoes. That she could turn on a hot dog like Roy Frady."

I was just a little embarrassed: why did it have to be that exact segment that popped up? I stopped the tape. "Answer your questions?"

"Yeah." He looked around at the clutter in my small space. "What the hell happened to standards? This is network TV?"

Fergie hopped in on one foot, slopping coffee over the tops of two mugs. Rascon stood up and took the cups from her. He said, "Thanks."

I stood up, gave her my chair, and handed her the coffee she had brought me. "Fergie, Michelle Tarbett was killed last night."

"Oh," was all she could say. She set the cup down, sloshing coffee on my Thursday scheduler. Her freckles stood out against a sudden pallor. "Oh, my God. Does Guido know?"

"Detective Rascon, my camera guru Guido Patrini was a little late for the scheduled taping with Tarbett this morning because he had to take Miss Ferguson to the emergency room to get her ankle rechecked. But Tarbett never got to the club."

"Hmm." He looked at Fergie's bandages, and then back at me. He said, "Why Roy Frady?"

"Did you know him?"

"No. He was before my time. But I've heard stories. The detectives working that case always hold it pretty close. Won't give much away."

"What do they say?"

"Not much. Frady's a sort of legend, worked Seventy-seventh with the best of them. He worked with Hector Melendez, the officer buried today."

"Did you know Hector?" I asked.

"Only by reputation. I know he worked with Frady and this senior detective named Flint. Flint's the real legend. He's older than dirt, but he's still working Major Crimes."

"How old do you think Flint is?" I asked. Fergie raised her mug to cover her smirk.

"Don't know. His hair is totally white but I still see him running up at the academy. The guys point him out, they say, 'There goes Flint.' "

"And then they tell you a story, don't they?"

He started to laugh. Rascon covered his mouth with his hand and laughed behind it. He took a "hoo-haw" breath, then said, "Flint was driving down Broadway. There's a grassy median there, and there's this guy all dressed in black leather, kind of strutting, walking a dog on a short chain. The guy starts giving Flint and his partner the death stare. So Flint hangs a U, comes back the other way. Gets abreast of the guy with the dog, and he says, 'What kind of monkey is that?' And the guy says, 'This ain't no monkey. This is an AKC-registered Doberman pinscher.' Flint says, 'I know that. I wasn't talking to you. I was talking to the Doberman.' "

I short-stopped his gales of laughter. "The rest of the story goes like this," I said. "Flint and his partner, Doug Senecal, had three suspects in the backseat of their car, shop eighteen A ninety-seven. Three teen-agers, and the charge was possession for sale.

"Flint hid a running tape recorder under the front seat, read the suspects their rights, told them to sit still and not say a word. Then he and Senecal got out of the car, closed the doors. They're leaning against the outside of the car, fooling with this guy who's out walking his dog, while the punks in his backseat are getting their stories straight, spilling their guts, on tape.

"The point of that story is this: Flint didn't realize how sensitive the tape was. So while he got three full confessions, he also taped enough of his BS line about the monkey to get himself a three-day suspension if anyone heard it. He threw the cassette out onto the street and ran over it on his way back to the station."

Poor Rascon defined dumbfounded. "How do you know that?"

"I hear things."

I hit Play again, and JoAnn Chin said, "Every time we fucked, I secretly wished we'd get caught just so everyone would know . . ."

CHAPTER

11

Detective Rascon hadn't found the bottom of his coffee mug before security escorted in Brady. Brady stopped just inside the open doorway like a schoolboy caught sticking a tack on his teacher's chair.

I said, "Come on in, Brady. Meet Detective Rascon."

"Detective?" Brady froze in the doorway, one leg crossed over the other, the way that schoolboy would if he suddenly needed a bathroom pass in a hurry.

"Come in. Have a seat," I said. "Give me your pitch."

Rascon never suggested he should leave. I think that the first qualification for promotion to detective is a love for other people's business. Rascon seemed well qualified. I liked having him there, the kill switch on what could easily become an unpleasant confrontation with Brady.

Brady sidled in, propped one bun on the edge of my cluttered desk. He appealed to me with Acting 1A-level pathos. "You gotta help me, Maggie."

"Correct me if I'm wrong," I said, "but isn't that what I asked you to do before you blew the power yesterday, help me?"

"I didn't blow it."

"Someone did. Maintenance decided the generator was sabotaged. The overload had to be intentional. Most of us wouldn't know how to rig an overload."

"I didn't do it." His voice sounded whiny. "I'm telling you. It wasn't me screwed it up."

I turned to Rascon. "You see, we have standards. Union rules disallow use of the F word among the crew."

Brady snickered, relaxed his posture.

"I didn't fire you, Brady," I said. "That decision was out of my hands. If you want to appeal, you need to go higher than me. You need to go to the union. I'll be happy to say, on your behalf, that when you put your mind to it, you're the best gaffer in the business. But you better hope no one asks me how often you're inclined to put your mind to it."

"I like working for you," Brady said.

"That and a nickel . . . ," I replied.

"I got a family to support, Maggie. We weren't hardly getting by as it was. I gotta work." He had slipped from whiny to nearly weepy. He tossed in an appeal: "Will you back me up when I file a grievance?"

"I'll back you up as a technician."

Brady's face grew red up into his sparse hairline. He threw Rascon a sidelong glance. "Sometimes the pressure just gets too much."

"I know how that can be," Rascon said.

Brady, on the edge, turned to me. "Why do you need a detective?"

"Mishaps need to be looked into," I said. "Another thing, don't call my house anymore. If you call again, Mike might have to go over to your house and shoot you."

"Shoot him?" Rascon furrowed his thick eyebrows. "Who's Mike?"

"Mike Flint."

"So you know Flint?"

"Everyone knows Flint," I said. I asked Brady, "Do you have anything else you need to get off your chest?"

He looked from me, to Rascon, to Fergie. It seemed to me that reality finally settled in upon Brady. Maybe he had thought that in a face-off with me he could shout me down, or wear me down, or buy my sympathy. We weren't alone, so he never had a chance to get fully into his what'll-my-wife-and-kids-do routine. Shoulders sagging with the weight of his situation, he turned his watery blue eyes on me. "I want my job back."

"My advice is, get yourself a haircut and a new shirt and take yourself over to the union, get down on your knees and ask them how many Hail Marys you need to say to gain forgiveness."

"That's it?"

"That's all I have to offer."

"Yeah." He stood up, extended his hand. "Thanks for seeing me.

"Take care of yourself. Take care of that family."

Brady, looking thoroughly dejected, turned on his

way out to add, "Monica dumped me for some other guy."

"Love is a hurtin' thing," I said, quoting Mike.

Brady slouched out, sandwiched between two security guards. Fergie followed, mumbling about work she had to do. When we were alone, Rascon asked, "What was that all about?"

"Brady shut down half a day's shooting, cost us a fortune because he wanted to get to his kid's soccer game. A film crew is a team. He's the kid who stole the game ball at halftime and ran home with it."

"Some people don't have a handle on the limits of their personal entitlements," Rascon said. "We call those people criminals."

"Or cops," I said. I picked up the VCR remote. "This interview I showed you a piece of is a nurse, JoAnn Chin." I hit the tape replay: "I secretly wished we'd get caught just so everyone would know JoAnn Chin was no Goody Two-shoes. That she could turn on a hot dog like Roy Frady."

Rascon, blushing, said, "You showed me that."

I said, watching JoAnn's smiling face go by in fast-forward, "She said, 'I secretly wished we'd get caught.' They did get caught. Listen to her." I pushed Play.

JoAnn: "My boyfriend was a jealous man and a nasty drunk. The drinking got bad to the point he was going to lose his job, so he kicked the booze for a while—maybe for a couple of weeks, but no more than that. When he was sober, he needed something to keep him busy. So, he started spying on me. I know he had been hearing things. One night, he caught me leaving work with Roy. After that, I moved out on my own, and things between me and Roy got more regular."

I turned the tape off. "She forgot to say that when the boyfriend, a cop named Barry Ridgeway, caught her with Roy, he drew his gun on them. Frady beat the crap out of Ridgeway, but he also protected him— the old code of silence—because he knew that Ridgeway's wife and kids would lose all their benefits if firearms charges were filed against dear old dad. Besides, Ridgeway was drunk when it happened."

"Does that make this Ridgeway a suspect in Frady's murder?" Rascon asked.

"A couple of the investigators put him at the top of the list. He went to jail after the killing on a drunk charge. One of his cellmates, looking for a deal, said that Ridgeway copped to it one night after he'd consumed a pint of pruno. But there was never any substantiation."

I handed Rascon a list with sixty names on it. "At some point, every person on that list claimed to have shot Roy Frady or heard someone confess to it. Most of them were gang bangers or cons looking for status among their peers or snitches looking for favors. Some of them were drunks or petty criminals who just ran out of conversation and needed something to talk about. Barry Ridgeway is on the list. And so is Michelle Tarbett."

"Michelle Tarbett said she killed Frady?" He folded the list to fit his pocket. "When did she do that?"

It would have been easiest to just show Rascon the police files in my bottom drawer, but I couldn't do that without getting Mike into trouble, because I wasn't supposed to have them. So I just told it as I remembered.

"Michelle was dancing in a topless club over on Florence. After work, she did some moonlighting with customers to pay off her dealer—she had a hundred-dollar-a-day heroin habit. The dealer pimped for her, and he didn't like her giving it away." I slipped the list from his hand. "She was giving it to Roy Frady."

I walked to the door, handed the list to Fergie, and asked her to run a copy for Detective Rascon.

"Who's supposed to have shot Frady, her or the pimp?" Rascon asked.

"Probably neither one. The story Michelle told her cellmates when she was in Sybil Brand on a possession charge was that her dealer kidnapped Roy and took him to a burned-out house, beat him up, then forced her to shoot him. Nine shots to the groin."

Rascon crossed his legs. "Does the story fit?"

"No. There were legions of stories on the street about Frady's killing, the shots in the groin was one of them. In fact, he took six shots to the head, and he wasn't beaten."

"If she lied, why did you want to talk to her?"

"Besides background? There were a couple of elements in her story that hit close enough to the mark that it's possible she really did know something. She may not have killed Frady, but she had good information from someone who possibly was there."

Like a traffic cop, he waved for me to proceed.

I said, "Frady's car was abandoned out by Ascot Raceway, and wiped down with an oily rag."

"Car thieves do that all the time to obliterate prints."

"A couple of facts from the Frady case were deleted from all written reports as veracity checks. The oily rag was one of them."

Fergie came in and handed Rascon the copied list. He took it and smiled at her in an absentminded way, as if lost in thought. He said, "When you talked to Michelle, what did she say about her life? Is there a pimp in the picture still? Or a dealer?"

"I think she's independent—she made her own appointments. She wouldn't have told me if I asked, though. She pretends she's legit," I said.

"Who made the initial contact?"

"Hector Melendez."

Rascon seemed bothered. "Can I talk to your sources?"

"Call Detective Mike Flint and Sergeant Doug Senecal, both of them LAPD. They knew her twenty years ago. I had qualms about including Michelle because her story adds a certain scumminess to Roy Frady that I'm not very comfortable with. It's one thing to diddle with a nurse, but another to hang out with a part-time call girl. My project is not about his love affairs."

He rose. "Cop and the call girl, sounds like a story to me."

"You'd get along great around here." I got up and walked with him to the door. "Maybe you have a future in TV."

"Is that sarcasm I hear?"

I laughed. "Management keeps telling me I'm too academic, too PBS. But I'm learning. By the time I leave here, I may have even learned to love the laugh track."

"I hope not," he said, offering his hand. "Thanks for your time. You have my card. Call me if you hear anything I should know."

I caught him glancing at my chest. He was in no hurry to get out the door. He said, "Mind if I call you? I think we'd have a lot to talk about. Maybe over dinner?"

"Sure thing," I said. "If you don't mind Mike Flint tagging along."

He focused higher, gave me a new appraisal. "I wondered about that."

CHAPTER

12

Fergie waited for Rascon to get into the elevator before she announced, "Guido called. We're both starving. Did you eat today at all?"

The clock on the wall said 8:30 and I could not remember whether I had eaten or not. Suddenly I was ravenous. Jack was coming down the hall from the vending machines with a bag of chips and a Dr Pepper with a look of expectation on his face. I had told him we could talk for a while.

"Call Guido back," I said to Fergie. "Ask him to meet us."

While Fergie talked to Guido, I went over to Jack. "Something's come up and I have to go now. Tomorrow we'll be shooting in the studio all day, so just come up any time."

Jack did not seem disappointed to be set loose.

I went inside, cleared up a few things, and locked the tapes away in a cupboard. I was glancing over the next day's schedule when there was a tap at the door.

I looked up to see Thea, her face tear-streaked, her hair wilder than ever, blocking my exit.

I didn't want to know, but I asked, "What is it, Thea?"

"I heard about that woman. It's just awful. I had her spreadsheet all ready, and then ... I can't believe it."

"Yes, it is awful."

Thea took a big breath and smiled wanly as I slung my bag over my shoulder. "I'm always catching you on the run, Maggie. Of course, you're always on the run, so I guess that's the only way to catch you."

I stopped and looked at her. "Was there something else, Thea?"

"Oh." A sigh. "No. I just thought maybe I'd start an office collection. We used to do that at my old job when someone died, or got married."

"Had you met Michelle?"

She shook her head. "But I'll volunteer to be in charge."

She seemed so emotionally fragile that I was afraid that after the second or third knucklehead on the staff declined to contribute, in his or her own crude manner, that she would come apart; it was tough enough to get the staff to kick in for people they knew. Thea seemed so desperate to be needed that I lied.

"The production will send flowers, Thea. Maybe you'd like to take around a card and have it signed."

She liked the idea. While she was standing there, I asked Fergie to order flowers to be sent to Michelle's sister Flora. Thea lumbered away and caught up with Jack at the elevator. I saw their heads bent together in rapt discussion before the car arrived. By the time the door shut behind them, Thea seemed wonder-fully cheered.

I wheeled Fergie out to the lot on a freight dolly and drove us to Le Mistral on Ventura Boulevard, where we met Guido.

"How was the wake?" I asked Guido as we were being led to a quiet corner table.

He dipped his head close to mine lest he offend the subdued elegance of the room. "Wild, and probably still going strong. I'll show you the footage later."

At the table, Fergie delivered the bomb to Guido about Michelle Tarbett.

"She's dead?" Guido was incredulous. "How could she be dead?"

"Ice pick in the neck." Fergie savored his reaction. "Quick and dirty."

Guido asked, "Was it a rough customer?"

The waiter hovered over water glasses. I leaned into Guido. "She serviced old men in retirement homes."

"She told me she ran a registry," he said. "Now I'm sorry I never met her. She could be her own movie, 'Senior Sex.'"

"You're the second one to say that," I said.

"I can't believe she was a call girl." Fergie, age twenty-one, curled her lip. "She was so old."

I asked her, "When you talked to Michelle about Frady, what did she say?"

"She sounded hot for him." Fergie seemed to ex-pect us to share her disdain for geriatric passion. "She said Frady was always nice to her."

"Who found her number for us?" I asked.

"Hector." Fergie motioned for us to come closer. "You know what she told him? She tried to go straight, work in an office. But she missed all the attention, and went back into the life. Isn't that sad?"

"Pathetic." Guido turned his attention to food.

The restaurant was full, but quiet. We ate a beautiful meal, followed by coffee and brandy. When I folded my napkin on the table, I must have sighed.

Guido grabbed my knee. "What's the matter?"

"To quote Brady, overload."

"Too tired to see some footage from the Embers Room?"

"Does Mike disgrace himself?"

"Royally. See for yourself."

Guido's house in the Hollywood Hills wasn't far away. Fergie rode with him and I followed. The night was so dark that once we left the streetlights on Highland and headed into the depths of his canyon, I could only see that which fell into the range of my headlights and Guido's taillights in front of me. If Guido had gone over the side, I would have gone over right behind him.

Fergie made herself comfortable on Guido's living room sofa, looked as if she knew where things were. I sat on the floor in front of her and rewound two hours' worth of videotape while Guido made drinks: Bacardi and Coke again.

When I waved away the offered drink, he insisted. "I'll drive you home."

"I followed your weaving lights up the hill," I said. "If I need a ride, I'll call a cab."

Guido started the tape. At first I looked at it from a technical perspective. The content was good, but there wasn't enough light in the bar for good definition. Guido said it could be enhanced. We watched men drink. For a brief time, the wake was a private party, and then it was cocktail hour and the bar filled up with the usual crowd, which included legions of too-young women wearing too-short skirts and too much makeup: trashy, flashy, big-busted youngsters. Mike's crowd, in the bag by that time, greeted the women the way starving artists go after gallery opening hors d'oeuvre trays.

Guido swept the room with his camera, focused on a couple of very emotional reminiscences between old friends. Got a lot of leg shots. The screen went black, then there was a tremendous amount of background laughter and hooting, and Mike appeared, drunker than I had ever seen him, with a young Chicana, wearing a short, flippy skirt, balanced on his lap.

Mike waved to the camera. "Hi, honey, wish you were here." That waving hand then dove down toward the girl's cleavage, and the camera was gone. I hated what I saw. It left a skid mark as it dumped acid down into that black hole in my chest. And I was embarrassed.

"Thanks, Guido." I stood up, reached for my bag. "That's what friends are for. Gotta go now."

"It was funnier at five o'clock." He seemed genuinely chagrined. He pulled me down onto his lap, crushed me against his hard chest, made me feel even worse. "I was drunker at five o'clock. Don't go. I'm sorry. It looks bad, but it was nothing. Just fooling around. I'm sorry."

I have too much history holding up one side of a triangle to have found the humor in the stunt. I was thinking that a lot of things weren't as funny to me as they used to be; that black hole, again.

Fergie, blushing furiously, turned off the tape and switched to the eleven o'clock network news. In silence, with Guido, repentant, clutching me tight, rubbing my back as I rested my head on his shoulder, we watched the coverage of Hector's funeral. A bite of Mike's eulogy, the only part where he teared up and almost couldn't go on. The chief's generic fallen warrior remarks. The impressive cortege of black and whites, sobbing mourners, the rifle volley, bagpipes, and the helicopter flyover finish.

"I wish I'd been there," Fergie said. The toes of her good foot burrowed under Guido's leg.

Guido was massaging both my neck and her ankle when I pulled free of his grip and started to stand. I felt uncomfortable, like a third wheel. "It really is time for me to go, children."

I glimpsed the TV, and stopped, stunned by what I saw. The human interest story fed from San Francisco to network affiliates across the nation, with both archival footage and live shots filmed in front of my sister Emily's nursing home, was, "Two years after an assassin's bullet left Dr. Emily Duchamps in a coma, her family faces the decision of life or death. Dr. Duchamps, the renowned social activist, lingers in a twilight between this world and the next. Sources say that her family has asked the medical staff at this Berkeley nursing facility to remove her from the life support that has sustained her since the shooting incident in a Los Angeles alley two long years ago. Her family and doctors have refused comment."

Guido chimed in first. "I forgot she was still alive."

Fergie looked at me. "Take her *off* life support?"

I was too busy dialing the phone to answer. The

studio switchboard ran to ground Bob, the editor in whom I had confided that morning, the most obvious source of the story. I had the attack advantage—I caught him asleep in a hotel room in Las Vegas. Tired, plain old up-to-here, I let it all out on old Bob.

"To begin, *Bob*," I snapped, "you got the story wrong. You damn well better get your butt working on a correction before the right-to-lifers start picketing my sister's bedside. The next thing you need to think about is this: it's none of your business. If I spoke to you in confidence, one colleague to another, I sure as hell didn't expect to hear my family problems echoed back to me on the goddamn national news. Where's your heart?" I covered the mouthpiece and appealed to Guido. "I need vocabulary."

"Hair ball, ass wipe, douche bag, putrescent vomitus."

I stuck with the traditional, "Fucking idiot."

"I'm sorry." Bob sounded sorry. "I simply went downstairs and said, 'Emily Duchamps is alive and living in Berkeley.' I didn't expect the news board to assign someone to the story, but they did."

"There is no story," I said.

"Look, I'm sorry, really sorry if you're upset and I'm the cause of it. But there is a story. You're a newsman, you know how it goes down."

"Emily Duchamps is not, has never been, never will be on life support. You go file a correction before the end of the broadcast, or I fry your ass." I hung up.

Guido pulled me back down, held me in his wire-arm grip. "Sorry, kid. Once you put a loved one on life support, you have to do some big-time maneuvering to get them off again. You're in a tough one, all right."

"Emily is not on life support," I said. I said it very slowly.

"Well, then," Guido said, "you have nothing to worry about."

Guido asked me to stay. Fergie, it was clear from her body language, wanted him to herself. I wasn't very good company. So, I drove myself home.

The house was dark. Bowser was sleeping with Michael in his cottage at the bottom of the yard. When I crossed from the garage, Bowser pressed his nose against the glass to give me a token yelp.

I went upstairs, showered, and climbed into bed, alone. It was after midnight. I expected Mike to come home at any time. For an entire year, we hadn't spent a single night apart. We didn't always get in and get out of bed at the same time, but we always met there at some time during the night. Pulling up the cold sheets that night, I missed him as I never had. And I admit that, knowing where he was and what his history was, I felt the raw, gnawing pain of jealous uncertainty.

New anxiety sprang from old grievance, a defense mechanism; once bitten, twice shy. My ex-husband was a cheater. I didn't like it, and I could not live with it. Not then, not ever again.

I read for an hour, watching the clock. The bar closed at one. Half an hour later, no Mike. I turned off the light, rolled over, and tried to sleep. At about two, I gave up on sleep and turned on the TV—*Rear Window,* fragmented by commercials and cut in places that ruined the seamless story.

Knowing better, I switched on the VCR and started the tape. The people making love in the bathtub didn't even look familiar.

I turned off the TV and called Guido. "Can you talk?"

"Now?" He sounded sleepy. "Something happen?"

I heard Fergie's voice in the background. I said, "It'll keep," and hung up.

I was still awake, lying in the dark, when Mike came home at 4:30. He fumbled with the bolt on the front door, ran into something in the entry, then either fell on the stairs or missed the turn at the landing and hit the wall. All during his procession through the house, he hummed "Fleurs of the Forest" in imitation of a bagpipe.

While I listened to him come closer, I was both enormously relieved that he had survived and I was angry. All the nights I had lain awake waiting for my ex to show up made me a veteran of middle-of-the-night rage. That history also confused the situation: whom was I mad at, Mike or Scotty?

I felt physical pain, an elephant sitting on my chest, listening to Mike stumble around the bedroom shedding his clothes. He opened the balcony windows and stood in front of them for a few minutes taking deep breaths, his slender nakedness silhouetted against the blue-gray night sky. I wanted to go over and hold him, to feel his skin against mine. Instead, I rolled over, turned away from him.

Mike got into bed, pressed himself against my back, his face between my shoulder blades, his knee wedged between my thighs. When he draped his arm over me, I took his hand and kissed it.

Maybe the light scent of the season's last roses blooming in the garden below the open window drifted into the room. Or maybe his hand smelled vaguely of perfumed cunt.

CHAPTER
13

I was in my workroom at home, getting materials organized for the day, when I answered the first call.

"Is Mike there?" The female voice sounded young, full of sugar.

"Mike can't come to the phone." Mike was still sleeping. "Can I give him a message?"

"Tell him Olga called."

"Does he have your number?"

"Oh, yes." She giggled. "Mike has my number."

I hated her, whoever she actually was. And the guys who put her up to it.

The volume of the VCR was too low to get through the sudden ringing in my ears. I turned it up so I could hear the raspy voice of Frady's former gang unit sergeant. His name was Houlihan.

"Roy Frady was one of the best officers to work CRASH detail. He went out and developed a network of reliable snitches." Houlihan took a hit from the oxygen tank next to his chair; he had emphysema so advanced that Hector and Guido had gone to his home for the interview. "Nothing gang-related went down in South Bureau without Frady knowing about it."

Hector asked, "What made Frady so effective?"

"Girls." Houlihan coughed. "Frady was good with the girls. Back then, the girls didn't count for much in gangs. Still don't. The boys would strut and brag about their crimes and their caper plans just like the girls weren't even there. When the girls heard something, they'd go straight to Frady with it. 'Bam Bam's picking up a load of bud tonight.' 'Sugar Bear and Undertaker took out that liquor store on Manchester.' They'd tell him anything."

"What did the women get from Frady in exchange?"

Houlihan thought about it. "He was probably the only man in their lives who didn't beat them daily. Maybe all he had to do was buy them a soda and listen to them."

Hector paused for effect; by that time he was an experienced interviewer watching for Guido's cues from behind the camera. "Did you ever go back to the snitches and ask them if they heard anyone talk about killing Frady?"

Houlihan nodded, his red face somber. "Every one of them tried to deliver the killer. Little girl named Tina snitched off that Sugar Bear I mentioned, told us the Bear's car had been used—sure enough, Sugar Bear drove a Buick that fit the description the witnesses gave—and that he had used his own nine-millimeter Smith and Wesson to take out Frady. And then he was going all over town bragging about it.

The Bear was the only actual arrest made in the case. As I recall, his polygraph showed guilty knowledge of the crime, but all that the investigators got from him was one more version of street rumors. Couldn't make the charges stick, and he kicked."

I turned off the tape. Sugar Bear was a dead end, literally. Six months after Frady's killing, the Bear died in a shoot-out with rival gang members. More than half of the gang members on my list were dead, most of them by violent means, and most of them before the age of twenty-five.

Frady's murder didn't look like a gang killing. It was too organized. Even in 1974, drive-by shooting was the MO of L.A. gang bangers. Handcuffs, kidnapping, moving his car and wiping it down were not their style. Not that they all didn't want credit on the street for taking out a policeman, or that they weren't creative in the manner they claimed credit. It's just that they didn't do it.

The next level of claimants was the small-time drug dealers. Seventy-seventh Street narcotics dicks heard through a "previously reliable source" that a kid in old County Jail was saying he had arranged for Frady to be killed by his associates while he was in custody so that he would have an alibi. He told the snitch that Frady had arrested him several times, and he was tired of being harassed. Frady was cutting into his business and making him look like a fool to his customers. He said his crime partners used a girlfriend as a decoy, had her lure in Frady by telling him that her friend needed help in the alley behind Eighty-ninth Street.

The source said Frady fell for it because the decoy was beautiful. She got into Frady's Pinto and took him to the alley, where he was captured, handcuffed, forced to crawl on all fours like an animal and beg for his life. He was shot and dumped. They dropped the murder weapon into the flood-control channel.

Frady never crawled anywhere. Never wrinkled his crease.

If people on the street knew anything that was useful, it had been buried under the sheer volume of fabrication and false confessions. For the film, I was putting together a montage of a dozen or so versions: he crawled, he was beaten, he took it in the groin, he took it in the head, he took it standing up and lying down, he had his pants around his knees, he was emasculated, he was set on fire, he was in uniform, he was robbed, he wasn't robbed. He was shot with his own gun.

I went upstairs to dress for work. Mike was still sleeping it off. He lay naked and uncovered on his back in the middle of the bed with his arms out and his legs spread, his morning erection like a leaning pole. He snored like a foghorn.

On the bathroom mirror, where he would be sure to notice it, I left his phone message—"Olga called"—written in shaving cream letters ten inches high. I finished the message by going back to the bed and adding a shaving cream flag to his pole. He didn't move.

I drove down into South Central before going in to the studio. I wanted to know why Sal Ypolito didn't just go away.

First, Sal gave us permission to film in his club, then he tried to back out. So, when we didn't use his place after all, I thought, given the circumstances, that he would be happy. He could keep the money, and we wouldn't inconvenience him. But I had a letter from his attorney, delivered by courier, claiming high-dollar damages for lost publicity because we weren't going to showcase the glorious Hot-Cha Club in the movies. The stunt was too bogus to ignore.

I arrived at the Hot-Cha Club before opening, just about the time we would have been filming with Michelle the day before. Sal had told us he was always there early to sign for food and liquor deliveries and to oversee setting up for the day.

When I walked through the kitchen entrance, Sal was mopping the floor. Without looking up, he said, "Be right with you."

"I can wait," I said, and he nearly lost his grip on the mop handle when he heard my voice. He glanced up, drilled his cigar deeper into the corner of his mouth, and turned his attention back to the floor, swabbing in wide arcs, working his way toward me, or toward the open door behind me. He put the muscles of his thick shoulders into the job like an old deckhand.

"What do you want?" he asked, making it a challenge.

"I want to know what you're trying to pull, Sal. This letter I got from your attorney is a real treat. Who is he, anyway, your brother-in-law?"

"Nah." The ugly cigar twitched in lieu of a smile as he rinsed his mop in a bucket and slapped it back onto the floor. "The shyster's my cousin."

"What did he tell you? TV studios have all that money, and he was going to get you some?"

"It was worth a shot." He did not seem at all embarrassed. "I was expecting F. Lee Bailey to come by, not you."

"I'm all that's coming. The legal department got a good laugh out of your caper. For that, they thank you."

"Entertainment's my game."

"Hope you're as happy when your cousin sends you his bill."

At that, he did not smile. Sal squeezed out his mop and propped it against the back wall. Then he rolled the bucket out the back door and dumped out the dirty water on the lot.

I followed him out, shielding my eyes against the brightness after the dimly lit kitchen.

He wiped his hands on his towel apron and leveled his gaze on my chest. "You came all the way down here to tell me what?"

"Just want to make sure your feelings aren't hurt, Sal. Maybe you thought you were going to be a star, and now the dream's gone."

"Uh-huh." He turned the bucket upside down next to the door. "That smart mouth can get you in trouble, sweetheart. I got work to do. What do you want?"

"I want to talk about Michelle."

"What's to say? It's too bad, but the surprise is it didn't happen to her a long time ago. Michelle's the type, she's never satisfied. Know what I mean? She's always pushing the envelope. She starts dancing, next thing, she thinks she needs to own a club. Turns a trick, wants to run a call-girl service. Gets hooked on H, and she's looking at fucking real estate in Colombia. She can't hardly feed herself, but she thinks someday she's gonna run the whole damn farm. People like that? I stay away."

"Why?"

"There are rules." He sat down on the overturned bucket. "The things Michelle was nosing into, it don't make sense not to follow the rules."

"You're talking about rules set by pimps and pushers and mob-connected club owners?"

He stabbed a finger up toward me. "Don't say mob to me. I got nothing to do with no mob. Every guy with a wop last name ain't into the mob."

"Every guy who owns a club isn't you, either. Michelle said something to me about wanting to open a club. How far did she get with it?"

"Nowhere. She hooked up with this cop—he'd put up the money and she'd front for him. That was the deal. But they wasn't going nowhere. He was a class-A drunk, but his real problem was the ponies. Gambling locks into a guy worse than booze—I won't never place a bet on nothing. The two of them put together some earnest money, but he couldn't keep it in his pocket long enough to sign a deal."

"Are you talking about Barry Ridgeway?" I asked.

"Yeah. Ridgeway. I hear he's around again. You want to talk about the mob? Talk to Barry. Word I get is he borrowed from some Vegas connection to make his down payment on a place up by the airport, and lost it on a long shot at Hollywood Park."

"When?"

He shrugged elaborately as he struggled back to his feet. "I don't know dates. Barry got sent up for DUI. It was before that. Ask him."

"I will."

He pushed the bucket against the wall. "Look, I'll see you around, okay? I got work to do."

"Thanks for talking to me."

"I figured you had your money's worth coming." He unplugged the cigar stump and flicked it into water running toward the gutter. "Just don't tell my cousin I said so."

"No problem," I said. I almost liked the little troll. "One more thing. Was Michelle still working for you when she partnered with Ridgeway?"

"Yeah." He looked as if he'd sucked on something bitter. "I bounced her ass when the Vegas boys came into my club looking for their first payment from her. I don't want the mob nowhere near my place. It ain't good for business."

That was Sal's parting bit of wisdom.

My mother called just as I walked into my studio office. She sounded more cheerful than she had for a very long time.

"Emily has attracted a lovely demonstration this time, Margot." Mother is the only person who ever uses my given name. "The usual fringe element of right-to-lifers called the press and is out there praying. But no one is paying the least bit of attention to them. It's the others who have turned this into an event. I've decided to go into business. I'll buy an hour on public-access cable and sell segments of it to people who have a message to deliver. My first guest will be the man who's out front right now carrying a placard proclaiming that Emily was stolen by aliens years ago. When I spoke with him, he told me all the fuss was merely preparing the public for her reentry."

"You spoke with him?"

"Wouldn't you?" Mother laughed. She asked, "Are you staying over Friday night, and is Mike coming?"

"If I stay over, I'll stay with Lyle at my house. I need to see how much damage the tenants did. And I don't know about Mike."

We said good-bye.

Guido came in, put a single rose in my hand, and kissed my cheek.

"What's the occasion?" I asked.

"I love you. You're my best friend in the world, and yesterday I acted like a jerk to you not once, but twice. I shouldn't have let you hang up. I should have called you back. I should have come over."

"Don't beat yourself up," I said. "You were occupied. Besides, I haven't been much fun to be around lately."

"Did Mike get home okay?" he asked.

"He got home."

"Maggie, honey, things aren't going so great for you guys, are they?"

"When we're together, we're perfect." I didn't want to talk about it with Guido. I put the rose into my empty coffee cup and smiled at him. "What did you do to Fergie? I need her."

He grinned. "You want a play-by-play?"

"No. I want Fergie."

"We overslept. She's on her way." If a man can purr like a cat, Guido was purring.

I said, "We have a full schedule of in-studio interviews booked today. Are you with me?"

He bowed. "I'm yours."

We went downstairs to our assigned soundstage. The vast area had been divided into three sets: a living room complete with silk flowers and a paint-and-canvas garden outside the false window, a stark police inter-rogation room, and a graffiti-covered wall. Interview-ees were to be placed in the set that most closely defined their background. I had fought long and hard with Lana for a plain blue backdrop, and I had lost.

Long ago, I slipped away from the bonds of just-the-facts-ma'am journalism. Documentaries have a point of view about a subject; that's their reason for being. But offering opinion is still a long, long way from the gross story manipulation that occurs when actors interpret scenes and pretend they are showing real events. My first glance at the sets Lana had or-dered made me feel I was headed on a downhill slope toward scripts and actors.

Jack arrived, poured himself coffee, and walked over to me.

"How's it going, Jack?" I said.

"Great."

"Great? I don't see much of you and you don't ask a lot of questions. Are you getting what you need for your article?"

"Oh, sure."

I asked him, "What is the focus of your article?"

"Haven't found it yet. But I will. I usually just hang out, and it comes to me."

"How long have you been a journalist?"

Again he shrugged. "I covered a couple of your sister's peace marches."

"A long time," I said. I took him into the control booth and introduced him to the staff and hoped they would keep him busy.

The first interview was with Otis Furlong, the cousin

of the man who rented the SLA the shack on Eighty-fourth Street. The landlord wanted nothing to do with me, but Otis had been more than willing.

Otis had put some thought into his attire. He had even called to find out what the requirements were. I told him, "Stay away from bright white and diagonal weaves or prints. I recommend solid primary colors."

He wore denim overalls over a black T-shirt, a baseball cap over his jheri curls. I asked Otis which of the sets he preferred, and he chose the graffiti wall. We sat side by side on tall stools.

I asked him, "Did you meet the six people who moved into your cousin's house in May of 1974?"

"Oh, sure," he said, assertive about it. "I see them that very next day after they move in. My cousin say, 'Hey, Otis, let's go over there and talk to those crazy people move into my place. You never see so many guns. Let's get some weed from them.'"

MAGGIE: Did you see guns?

OTIS: Yes I did. At first, I thought they was toy guns, they was so many. But this crazy white dude, he tells me, "Go on and pick it up. It's the finest money can buy." Later I see the dude's picture in the newspaper. By then, he wasn't nothin' but ashes and a belt buckle.

MAGGIE: Was that Willy Wolfe?

OTIS (*only shrugs*): We go inside there that first time, and the big dude, the one call hisself Cinque, he pushes up this scrawny white chick to us and he say, "You know who this is? This is Tania." Now, we see the girl's pictures all over the TV from some bank robbery or other. That little thing he was pushing on us didn't look nothin' like the real girl, and my cousin? He say so. He say, "Her hair's too short." So Cinque, he tells the girl, "Go put on your wig." Then we see right off, it's the same one. The one was kidnapped.

MAGGIE: Patricia Hearst?

OTIS: That's the one.

MAGGIE: Did you see what went on in that house?

OTIS: I hear more than I see. It wasn't but a real small little place. They was inside there all day, running around with their guns up, like boot camp or something.

MAGGIE: Did they have visitors?

OTIS: Some, mostly at night. No one stay very long because those people talk so crazy all the time, naggin' all the time like some cemetery plot salesman on commission. Only what they sellin' is the revolution that's comin' and how they're only part of this great big army and we better join up. But I say, so if you're so big-time, how come you livin' in a house ain't even got no lights, got no telephone?

MAGGIE: What did they say?

OTIS: Nothin' but nonsense.

MAGGIE: Death to the Fascist insect?

OTIS (laughing): Like that.

MAGGIE: Did anyone ever mention Officer Roy Frady?

OTIS: I know the gentleman. I know when he die, and all. His people come askin' me questions, but I don't have nothin' much to tell them. Except what Cinque tell me one night I go over there to get me some weed.

MAGGIE: What did he tell you?

OTIS: He arguin' with a couple of them. They all been drinkin' all day long, smokin' weed. Look like they been dukin' it out some. He come over to me—he's a big dude, too—gets in my face, and he say, "It ain't no crime to kill the pig."

Otis was happy with his performance. Jack had been hanging around behind the cameramen during the interview. When the lights went down and Otis had his mike unclipped, the two of them went off toward the soda machine together.

I had time to powder the glow off my face and get some water before Mary Helen Frady was brought to me.

Mary Helen came dressed in a bright pink flowered skirt and jacket. I thought that filming her in her Japanese garden in Lakewood would be more interesting, but she wanted to see the studio. The garden would probably have been cut, anyway.

Mary Helen was seated in the living room set and a mike was clipped to her collar. We spoke for over an hour on camera, no new information, but new insights into the life Roy Frady had turned his back on.

Toward the middle of the second hour, I found myself watching the clock. Fergie, who should have known better, had scheduled Frady's last girlfriend, JoAnn Chin, right after Mary Helen.

People frequently show up early and hang around late out of curiosity because they are intrigued by the Hollywood trappings and are so happy about getting

their allotted fifteen minutes of fame—even if it turns
out to be fifteen seconds in the finished film. Most of
them have never been around a studio or a filming
site. Their excitement is fun to have around, so I don't
mind quiet spectators. My concern was that Mary Hel-
en's presence would inhibit JoAnn.

Twenty minutes before JoAnn was expected, I
wrapped up Mary Helen's interview and collared an
intern to take her on a tour.

Twenty minutes after JoAnn was expected, I began
to worry. I was on the telephone, hoping she would
answer, when Mike walked in.

He caught me off guard. I felt a hot rush I couldn't
sort out—dread, anger, relief in equal parts.

Mike had dressed carefully in a crisp dress shirt and
a red silk tie with a perfect knot, and pressed slacks;
his suit coat was slung over his shoulder. All the nice
clothes, even his fresh shave, couldn't cover the rav-
ages of what had to be a bodacious hangover.

I waited for JoAnn's machine to kick on, and left
a message to call. A long message, while Mike waited,
leaning against a far wall.

I walked over to Fergie and went through a check-
list with her, viewed a bit of the Mary Helen tape with
Guido, talked to Holly, the new gaffer—none of it
was necessary, all of it was stalling the inevitable
encounter.

Mike shifted his coat to his other hand as if it
weighed tons, and wiped his brow. I decided he had
suffered nearly enough and walked over to him.

"Good morning," I said. "You survive."

He looked absolutely miserable. "Can we go
somewhere?"

"Bad time. You can see we're in the middle of shooting. You just missed Mary Helen. If you stay around, you'll catch both JoAnn Chin and Barry Ridgeway."

"I'll pass." He tossed his coat over the back of a canvas chair. "Guido bawled me out this morning. You're really mad, aren't you?"

"Should I be?"

"The Olga thing was just good old boys fooling around. You know how we are."

"Yes, I do."

"You could have stayed with me at the academy last night." He was still defensive, but getting over it. "I asked you to."

"Are you suggesting that the mischief you got into is my fault because I declined to chaperon you?"

"No." He winced. "I don't want to argue. My head hurts."

"I don't want to argue, either."

"But?"

"No buts. Did I ever tell you how I left my husband when he cheated on me?"

"You think I cheated on you?" He was aghast. "It was a stupid joke."

"Stupid and cruel. I don't understand the kick you and your good old boys get out of trying to make me feel jealous."

"I don't do that." Righteously indignant.

I walked out of the soundstage and down the hall to the elevator because I didn't want to cry. Not in front of Mike, and not in front of my crew.

He followed me, looking as miserable as I felt.

"Maybe I do that," he said. I heard this as an apology. But I wasn't ready to accept it.

I went down to the security office on the first floor and asked Tommy for the grocery bag I had checked with the night man.

Mike, being Mike, took the bag to carry for me. And Mike, being Mike, peeked inside. His pallor colored. "What the hell?"

"Hector's guns."

"How'd you get them?"

"I went over to Hector's yesterday after the funeral to retrieve the Frady project tapes Guido had given him," I said. "What's the manager's name, Sarah or Sandra?"

"Brooke. And you didn't go over there for your tapes. You went over there to snoop."

"Mike, someone looted Hector's apartment during the funeral. Cleaned out his good clothes, took his new furniture and his computer."

"Why didn't you call me?"

"Yesterday afternoon?" I opened my office door and held it for him. "What would you have done?"

"Did you at least call the police?"

"That's Brooke's job. I took the guns because I thought they shouldn't be left lying around. Anyone could have taken them."

"Obviously." He pulled out the gun cases and laid them on my cluttered desk. "The cases are locked. Did you think to take the keys?"

"I drove over there because something about Hector's murder bothers me."

"Yeah?" He scowled. "Something bothers me, too. It's this: Hector's dead."

"But the picture is all wrong, Mike. Gloria and some other people were with Hector Sunday afternoon. You're a cop. If someone came and asked your friend to go talk her son out of killing himself, would you say, go ahead, I'll wait here, keep your beer chilled till you get back? Any cop would go up right behind him. So would any nosy friend."

"I didn't know Gloria was there."

"I don't know if she was there at that exact time. But Brooke said Hector had friends over. You told me the Santa Monica PD report said he had just come up from the beach with some friends. And he was unarmed. The mother said there was no gun in her apartment."

Mike groaned. "I need caffeine." He dropped down onto the sofa and covered his eyes with his hand. I went down the hall and fetched two Cokes from the machine. During the two minutes I was gone, Mike didn't move. I thought he might have gone to sleep. I opened the hand he had resting on his lap and put the cold can into it.

"Thanks," he said, still unmoving. "Have any aspirin?"

He opened his eyes when he heard the aspirin rattling out of the bottle, swallowed four with soda, then held the cold can to his forehead. "I haven't been thinking clearly the last few days. I didn't like the investigation, but I held back because I thought . . . I don't know what I thought."

"You thought you were in denial and therefore insinuating strange and unusual possibilities into a case that was perfectly straightforward."

Finally, he smiled. "Trust me, Miss Graduated from Berkeley, I never insinuated possibilities in my life."

"Yes, you did. And another thing, do you remember Michelle Tarbett?"

He furrowed his brow and seemed to be in pain as he rifled through his mental files.

I said, "Worked at the Hot-Cha Club."

"Jeez." He groaned from a deeper place. "How did you ever connect with Michelle?"

"Yesterday she had an appointment to meet Guido for an interview, but she didn't make it. Took an ice pick in the jugular Tuesday night." I waited for that to sink in. "Do you know Larry Rascon?"

"Name's familiar. Works Newton?"

"Works Hollenbeck. He's investigating."

"Hookers get murdered by their clients all the time." Mike rolled his head toward me. "Are you insinuating strange and unusual possibilities into a case that could be perfectly straightforward?"

"Yes, Detective, I am."

"I'll look into it." He grinned. He still looked like hell, but he seemed to be in recovery. "The good news is, you're talking to me."

"About Hector and Michelle, maybe."

He patted the sofa beside him. "Come here."

"What good would it do me?" I laughed, and stayed behind my desk. "Look at you. You're such a worthless piece of shit today you can't even stand up to get a little nooky."

The effort hurt, but he got to his feet, stopped a moment for his head to get used to the new altitude, and walked across the office toward me. He took me into his arms, held tight, and leaned heavily.

"I'm a two-time loser," he said. With his lips behind my ear, I felt his baritone as much as I heard it—I felt it all the way down my spine. "But I'm learning. Stick with me, Maggie. I know this time I'll get it right."

"What are you learning?" I asked.

He rubbed his head. "Twenty-five-year-old rookies and twenty-five-year veterans can't play the same games. I feel like I'm dying."

"You don't look so hot, either." I pressed my cheek into the hollow of his neck and breathed him in. "You smell good though."

He was perking up. So was I.

The phone rang. I said, "Did you give Olga this number?" as I picked it up.

"I might have."

Fergie called from the soundstage. "JoAnn Chin had some kind of accident. There's a cop on his way up to see you."

CHAPTER

14

The walls of JoAnn Chin's room at County General Hospital hadn't been patched since the big quake of 1994. I wondered how safe she felt looking up into a network of plaster cracks, trapped as she was by the apparatus that held her right arm in traction.

"You didn't see the man who attacked you?" Mike asked for the third time.

"No." JoAnn's lips were so split and swollen she could hardly form words, so what she uttered sounded like, "nuh." Her face was a red-and-purple mass crisscrossed by stitches. Both of her eyes were black and her nose was taped. Veteran nurses shuddered when they came to tend her, and she saw their revulsion. From all accounts, JoAnn's beauty had always been her stock-in-trade. Behind her shattered face she expressed a deep chagrin that went beyond both her pain and fear.

Mike examined her visible injuries as if she were a courtroom exhibit. "You must have had an impression of the man. Big, small, young, old, white, black?"

"Nothing."

"What did he smell like?" I asked. "Did he smell like booze or sweat or food?"

"Like aftershave."

I turned to Mike. "A well-groomed assassin."

He frowned, gave me a nudge. I wasn't supposed to be there because this was a preliminary police interview. Mike glanced at his notes, and I wondered whether he would write my name on the "persons present at the interview" line.

He went over JoAnn's story a third time. "You were getting out of your car in the garage at your residence this morning at around one-thirty. You were seized from behind, you put up a struggle using a tire iron you kept in the vehicle for defense purposes. Your assailant took the tire iron from you and used it to beat you. Correct?"

"Uh-huh." Tears ran down JoAnn's face, washing rivulets through the iodine stains around her stitches.

"How did you get away from him?" Mike asked.

She had to say it twice before we understood, "Kneed his groin."

"During all of the commotion, you never got a look at him?"

"I covered my face with my arms."

"If your face was covered, how did it get so smashed up?"

She moved the fingers of her shattered arm. "Couldn't cover my face anymore when he broke my arm. There was so much blood, I couldn't open my eyes." Sobbing, she was even more difficult to understand. The gist of her mumbling from that point was that she was worried about how scarred up her face would be when she healed. She was also afraid the man would come back to finish his work. I took her uninjured hand in mine for a quick squeeze, but she wouldn't let go.

I thought that Mike was being hard on her. They may never have been friends, but he had known JoAnn when she was dating Roy Frady, and before that when she was dating Barry Ridgeway. It's possible that she didn't recognize Mike after twenty years, with his hair turned white and without the little cookie-duster mustache he used to wear. But he knew exactly who she was, and he didn't even bring up their old acquaintance. He never offered a single word of reassurance.

Larry Rascon came in and called Mike into the corridor for a conference. JoAnn still clung to my hand. I asked her, "Would you like some water?"

I held the glass for her. After a sip, she lay back as if exhausted. Finally, her sedative seemed to be taking effect. Mike glanced in, winked at me, went back to his discussion with Rascon. JoAnn saw the wink. She said, "He's making a play for you. Stay away from the asshole. You'll only get hurt." Asshole was the clearest word I had heard from her yet.

"Mike's okay," I said.

"He's dangerous. He'll lead you on, make you fall in love with him. Nail you to the mattress when it's convenient for him. But he'll never divorce his wife." Her eyelids drooped. She yawned, and flinched when it stretched her jaw. "He'll never split his pension. He'll never divorce her."

"Do you feel like talking about Roy Frady?"

"I was." JoAnn touched her cheek as she closed

her eyes. "No cameras." She let go of my hand and seemed to have fallen asleep.

I joined Mike and Rascon in the hall outside her room.

"She's asleep," I said.

Mike asked, "Did she tell you anything?"

"She warned me to stay away from you."

Mike took my hand. "Good advice."

"But too late." I leaned against him. "Tell me something. Frady and Mary Helen were separated for a long time. Why didn't one of them file for divorce?"

"There was no hurry. Divorce is expensive."

"When the press interviewed JoAnn, she said she and Roy were planning to get married as soon as his divorce was final. Roy must have said something to you about his plans. Did she lie to the reporters, or did Roy lie to her?"

Mike glanced in at JoAnn before he walked me away from her open door. Rascon, like a good detective, came along.

"The thing is this," Mike said. "Roy couldn't even afford a place of his own. When he split with Mary Helen, he had to move in with his parents. It wasn't working out. JoAnn had an apartment, so he more or less moved in with her." He half turned from Rascon. "Trust me, JoAnn wasn't the type of girl Roy would ever marry."

I said, "She's beautiful. She's smart. What's wrong with her?"

"She slept with half the guys in the division and she talked about every one of them. Because of her, we all knew Ridgeway was hung like a cashew and Frady was good with his tongue. JoAnn was not the girl you took home to your mother or asked to baby-sit your kids. Get it?"

"He used her, and she's still bitter," I said. "That's what she was talking about."

"That was twenty years ago. I have a feeling Roy wasn't the last man to use JoAnn."

"I don't know what to do now, Mike," I said. "If you count Hector, my little film project has three major casualties. I'm afraid to go on with it, because I don't want anyone else to get hurt. But I hate being jerked around."

"You think there's a tie-in?"

"I don't believe in coincidences." I put my hand over the gun on his belt. "And neither do you."

Rascon cleared his throat to remind us he was there. "Are you taking this case downtown, Detective?"

"Probably. It looks like a serial crime situation, and the crimes occurred in several divisions. Miss Chin lives in Highland Park, putting her, if I'm not mistaken, out of the Hollenbeck area, where you came aboard. And we have to liaison with Santa Monica PD."

Rascon was not happy to be reminded. "Chin's a quarter mile inside Northeast."

"Boundaries aren't the deciding factor," Mike said. "Major Crimes will take over for one simple reason: I want the case, and that's where I work."

Rascon shrugged in resignation. He was a young, eager detective. He had told me earlier that this was one of the first cases he had worked that was more interesting than drive-bys, bar brawls, and lethal domestic disputes. Mike, after watching Rascon's reaction, reached out and caught the elbow of the younger man's jacket and tugged it.

"You're a good detective, Rascon. You've done good initial fieldwork. We're going to need liaison with Hollenbeck. How would you feel if I asked your lieutenant and my captain if it would be okay to lend you to Majors for a while?"

Rascon's grin was slow coming on, snuck up on him at the point of bursting, so he had to tap his cheek to bring it in check: tough detectives do not let out war whoops in hospital corridors. Emotions under control, he said, "I wouldn't mind."

"First thing I want to do is bring Anthony Louis downtown and get a search warrant for his premises." Mike reached for his pocket notebook. "I'll give you an address so you can get started on it."

Rascon raised a hand to stay him. "I've got it. Anthony and I go way back."

"Let's make our calls and get formal approval, get the warrant going, call in uniform backup. If you know Anthony, you know he's one unpredictable son of a bitch. And I want medical personnel on standby in case there are any recent injuries on his person. I want every little nick examined." They were already headed for the elevators, and Mike was in charge and getting bossy. "Maggie, I don't want you interviewing anyone until we get a handle on things, or can arrange protection. We need a list of everyone you've contacted."

"I can give you my list right now. But I don't know who all Hector talked to on his own. I'll go through the tapes and the disk I lifted from his apartment, but I have no idea what's on them."

"Take a look at them," he said.

I asked, "How difficult would it be to get a warrant to search Gloria's place?"

"Because she took Hector's things? It would be tough to pull off. You can't break into your own house, and her name was on the lease." He made a note, though. "What do you think she has?"

"Guido's video camera. And the tape that possibly was in it."

Mike grinned, gave me a wet kiss in the middle of my forehead. "I love the way your mind works. I love all the rest of you, but I especially love your devious mind. Gloria's new boyfriend showed up at work today wearing Roy's leather jacket—the one his mother gave him for Christmas. I've been trying to figure out a way to get into her place all day. I doubt we'll get a warrant, but we'll get inside one way or another."

"Just don't hurt her when you boot the door."

Rascon, the bright boy, said, "Gloria Marcuse? I heard about the jacket and I wasn't real surprised. I have a few scores to settle with the"—he glanced at me—"with her."

I led them into the elevator. "You two sound like a marriage made in heaven. But I'm warning you, Detective Rascon, watch out. It'll be a honeymoon you won't ever forget."

CHAPTER

15

Lana did not rant. Lana did not rave. I sat on the edge of my chair in front of her desk with both feet planted and ready for a fast exit—out the door and out of my contract. But all she did was sit back in her big leather chair and grin at me.

"I'm sorry," I said. "I know we're already over budget and behind schedule. But I cannot risk the safety of anyone whose participation with the project might put them in jeopardy. The police want us to shut down for twenty-four hours."

"This for real?" was all she said, but she said it three times in a row.

"The police are afraid that there is some connection between my film and the attacks on Michelle Tarbett, JoAnn Chin, and maybe even Hector Melendez. And so am I. I don't have hard evidence. If I err, I prefer to err on the side of caution. The police will provide protection, but they need twenty-four hours to put it in place."

Lana picked up her desk telephone and pushed one of her speed dial buttons.

"I'm sorry," I said. "We'll lose time and money. But this is the way it has to be."

She waved away my apology, brightened even more when there was a voice at the other end of her receiver. "It's Lana, Gaylord. Listen to this. Someone is killing off the people who help Maggie MacGowen research her Roy Frady film. No lie. Two deaths, one victim in intensive care. Police are asking us to help with their investigation." She made a Miss-America-is-waiting-for-her-roses-and-tiara smile as she picked up her desk clock. "It's two o'clock here. I can get something on the satellite in thirty minutes, in time for East Coast news at six. We'll have a full story ready for five o'clock in Chicago, four on the West Coast, expanded coverage for the elevens."

I was on my feet; there was no way to stop this from happening.

"Wait, Maggie," Lana said. Then she repeated for Gaylord, "Two deaths, one intensive care. And we had an incident of sabotage on a location shoot. Shut us down for half a day. Call publicity. Maybe we can get a *People* feature, *Time* and *Newsweek* will follow. We already have *Rolling Stone* on site, but their publication schedule doesn't work for us and the assigned reporter defines the word 'nobody.' Call Larry King. We'll step up the filming schedule, take advantage of the public interest."

At the door, I paused. "I have to go, Lana. The police have given me an assignment. You can reach me at home."

She protested, gently. "Have Thea work up some figures."

I said, "Sure," knowing what she wanted was a banner line: "Network, at a loss of X dollars, shuts down production plagued by, et cetera." Thea was the last person I wanted to see—would we be sending flowers to JoAnn next?—and I delegated the task to Fergie.

I found Guido in the editing room, and filled him in. He was, in his way, as excited as Lana. Except, he had the decency to also be repulsed and alarmed.

"Hector told me you lent him a video camera," I said. "Did he give it back?"

Guido curled his lip. "I forgot about it. It's network property. You didn't happen to see it when you burglarized the joint?"

"No." I know I sounded impatient. "I picked up some tapes at Hector's. Most of them have your label on them. I'd like for you to go over them to see whether there's anything there that you didn't give him, or if anything is missing. And I need help compiling a list of everyone who has participated or who has been contacted, and the walls around here have eyes. Can you come home with me?"

"Sure." He shut off the dialogue loop. "What will you be doing?"

"Going through Hector's computer files."

He was on his feet, the old war correspondent rising to an occasion. "Who's catering?"

"Chateau Jacques in the Box."

We drove through on the way.

Because Mike had set up both my computer and Hector's, I had no problem opening his files. I had intended to get right into them. The problem was Guido.

Guido had three VCRs running simultaneously, was eating tacos, juggling remotes. When you come home at the end of the day, there are chores to be dealt with: take the messages off the machine, feed and placate the dog, change into sweats. Guido wanted attention, so I never got to any of it. Every time I started to do something on my own, Guido called me over to look at whatever he had on the screen—usually something he himself had taped. I was happy to have him in the house, because the truth is, I was a little bit afraid to be alone. Guido kept me from getting into Hector's files, but I managed to feed the dog and retrieve messages.

Casey needed money, my mom wanted my flight information, Brady was sorry. I had a mystery call, a man who gave no name, only a number, and asked me to call. The voice seemed familiar and held no apparent menace. That was the first call I returned.

"This is Maggie MacGowen," I said after the same voice had said hello after the sixth ring. "I'm returning your call."

"Margot Eugenie Duchamps MacGowen? Date of birth, September twenty-sixth at University of California Medical Center, San Francisco, California?"

"At nine-ten A.M. Who are you?"

"We spoke the other day. This is Special Agent Chuck Kellenberger."

"FBI," I said for Guido's enlightenment. "What can I do for you?"

"Maybe we can do something for each other. I understand you're going to Berkeley tomorrow."

"You're a scary guy, Kellenberger. Don't you know the cold war is over, communism is dead, and you don't need to follow ordinary citizens around anymore?"

He laughed. "Detective Flint told me you were going."

"He told you my name and my birthday, too?"

"No. That information I took from your jacket. Look, MacGowen, while you're up north, you might want to drop in on an old friend of mine. Name's Carlos O'Leary. He might have something interesting to tell you."

"Is he an FBI agent?"

"Not hardly." He told me where to find O'Leary, by the banyan tree in People's Park. "Be patient. O'Leary's a little gun-shy."

"Give me an opening gambit."

"O'Leary was a card-carrying member of the Symbionese Liberation Army."

Immediately after we said good-bye, I left a message on Mike's voice mail to call me.

Guido and I watched the five o'clock news, and it was just about what I had expected: sensational lead-in, little substance in the story. The facts were all right, though. I would have preferred that the story not be broken so soon, and so far from my control.

Around six, Michael came home from the library. I hadn't seen him since the funeral.

"Any leftovers?" Michael asked, looking at the ends of tacos on the table.

"Sorry." I wadded up fast-food wrappers and stuffed them back into their greasy bag. "Let's go see what we can find for you in the kitchen."

I love Michael. He isn't my son, so I have no qualms about spoiling him. I hooked my arm through his and walked him to the kitchen, grilling him about school.

"I talked to Casey last night," he said. "She sounded happy."

"She's happy. But I miss her."

Michael put his arm around me, as he often does, and it felt so strange. Now and then Mike says to me, "If I'd met you way back before either of us was married, would you have even looked at me?" The answer is, probably not. We were in enormously different phases of our progress toward wherever the hell it is we're headed. Besides, I was still in high school the first time he got married. So, when I look at Michael, I search for some essence of his dad as he was back then. Some clue to what I missed. Or what I was spared.

The comparison between father and son is not a fair one, even though physically the two men are much alike. Michael, honor student at a fine private liberal arts college, would have turned my head. Mike, representative of the running dogs of capitalism, i.e., uniformed cop, probably would not. Except, I always liked bad boys.

I looked inside the refrigerator, found eggs, zucchini, and mushrooms, and offered to make an omelette. As soon as the butter started melting and I tossed in diced garlic, Guido joined us. Peering over my shoulder, he said, "Make me one of those, too. Okay?"

"Take out three more eggs," I said.

"Where's the Anthony Louis tape?" he asked, walking to the refrigerator. "I haven't seen it since we shot it."

I had to think for a moment before I remembered. "It's upstairs in my room. I forgot to bring it down."

He asked for permission to retrieve it, and left me and Michael alone again.

"Where's Dad?" Michael asked, grinding coffee beans.

I said, "He's protecting and serving. I don't know when he'll be home."

"I saw something about your sister on the news last night. It didn't make any sense to me. What happened?"

"Nothing, really. I'm going up to Berkeley tomorrow to see her." I tossed eggshells into the disposer, wiped my hands on a towel. "What's your schedule tomorrow, Michael?"

He thought. "Classes till eleven. Peer counseling at noon. Teach a math tutorial at the high school till three. Then I pick up Sly at his group home and coach his soccer team."

Sly was a street kid Mike and I brought home not long after we got together. Sly helped us find a murderer, and Michael kept him. Or Sly hooked Michael. I'm not sure which way it worked, but they remained a team. Sly had just celebrated his eleventh birthday in our backyard.

I beat the eggs.

"Do you need some help with something tomorrow, Maggie?" Michael asked.

"No." I poured the eggs on top of the sizzling garlic. "But company would be nice. I'm flying to San Francisco in the morning, and I wondered whether you might be free to come with me. But you're busy."

"Too bad. Another time, though." He was studying me the way Michael studies all of his projects, with intense interest. When Guido came back into the kitchen with a videocassette under his arm, Michael looked at him, too. Then he asked me, "Did you say Dad is working?"

"Watch the eleven o'clock news," Guido said.

"No thanks." Michael took plates out of the cupboard. "I'd rather see Dad in the flesh."

Guido took his omelette, toast, and coffee back to the workroom. I sat with Michael while he ate, and drank coffee while he put his dishes into the dishwasher. When he dried his hands and picked up his books, he said, "Is Dad okay?"

"He's fine. I think that he has taken on a heavy workload to keep his mind off Hector."

Michael frowned. "Hector's funeral was hard to get through—Hector was like an uncle to me. Dad didn't want to tell me how he died."

"He didn't want to worry you."

He smiled in a self-deprecating way. "Tell Dad I can vote now."

"You'll always be his baby," I said. "Do me a favor? While I'm gone, look in on your father for me."

He hugged me good night and I kissed his stubbly cheek. And I ached to see my daughter. The best I could do was leave another message on her machine.

Guido, lulled by food and the boring chore of watching videotapes in fast-forward mode, sat quietly on his side of the room. I was finally able to get to Hector's disk.

Mike often told me that Hector was the best detective he ever worked with; he was smart and methodical. Sometimes he pushed methodical to the point of being anal, and annoyed the more freewheeling Detective Flint. I was happy for Hector's method: he left me a long list of names and addresses, and his calendar of scheduled interviews. I turned on the printer and ran several copies of those two files.

"Maggie, look at this." Guido was running a tape in reverse, showing Hector moving from the sofa in his apartment over to the lens of a camera he had obviously set up on top of his kitchen counter. The field of vision included most of the living room and the hall beyond the doorway. Guido started the tape forward, and I walked across the room and sat down next to him.

Hector, wearing running shorts and a T-shirt, crossed his living room and sat down on his sofa, too. He leaned back, crossed his legs, smiled.

"Hi, Maggie. Hi, Guido. We've been talking to everyone we can dig up about Roy Frady and the good old, bad old days. I thought, hell, I've got nothing but time, I might as well use it. Put in my two cents.

"I'll probably never give you this tape, but if doing this helps get me through the night, I guess I'm ahead. It's Friday night and I'm all alone. I think I miss Gloria, but I can't be sure. Maybe all I miss is having a hedge against being single, because the singles scene looks more like a toxic zone to me all the time.

"Generally, I guess, my life is in the shit can. I can't see my daughters until next weekend, and I really miss them. I'm trying to stay straight—I've been sober for two weeks—and everywhere I normally hang and everyone I normally hang with is gonna get me into trouble.

"Maggie, I called you and Mike a while ago to see if you'd want to get some dinner, maybe go to a movie, but you were out or you weren't taking calls. I started to feel sorry for myself and that gets dangerous. So, well, here goes.

"For twenty years I've been talking about the night Roy died. Every time a couple of us get half in the bag, Roy comes up. It's like Kennedy. You know, where were you the day Kennedy was shot? Everyone who's old enough to remember can tell you exactly. I can tell you what I had on at school that day—chinos and a blue madras shirt—and what I bought for lunch—a tuna sandwich. When something like that happens, something that really hits you where your heart is, you can't help but remember.

"It's the same with Frady. Ask any cop who was on the force at the time, and he can tell you where he was when he heard Roy Frady was murdered.

"I first heard that Roy was dead at around noon the day they found him. On Saturday. I wasn't due to report for roll call until ten, ten-thirty that night—I was working morning watch. But they called us all in around noon. I hadn't been to bed yet; my wife was still at me for coming home drunk at dawn, so I was kind of relieved when the call came.

"In the locker room at Seventy-seventh, everyone was talking about Roy, a lot of rumors going around because they weren't giving out details yet. At first I didn't believe Roy was dead. I thought the guys were screwing with me because I felt like hell, and maybe Frady was late because he was in bad shape, too. I thought that if what they were saying was true, if Frady was dead, he must have had a wreck on his way home from the academy. He had been pretty juiced.

"Then they said he was shot—it was Mike who told me. He was in shock. Right away, I thought Roy must have been caught with another man's woman. In Roy's life, that sort of trouble was pretty normal.

"At roll call, the captain came in and told us Roy had been assassinated. Roy's car was still outstanding and there was a lot of talk that there was a contract out on all cops. Back then, that wasn't such a crazy speculation, because there were radical groups out there claiming they were taking out cops. We had a couple go down in our own division and there was some talk they were assassinated.

"The brass wanted a strong presence on the street. They told us to contact our snitches and find out what the word was.

"The truth of what happened to Roy took a while to sink in. To begin with, I didn't feel so good, and I'd missed a whole day's sleep.

"My first reaction after disbelief was anger. We all got pissed. A lot of talk about radical hit squads taking out police all across the country. I thought that if some misguided bastards wanted war, I was more than happy to join up. I did my time in Vietnam. I knew more about jungle warfare than those draft-dodging commie sons of bitches ever would, and I was more than willing to show them. That's how I felt.

"Frady was my partner. But that rotation he was on assignment to CRASH, so I got teamed with the division problem child, Barry Ridgeway. I got along okay with Ridgeway. Everyone was worried about me and how I was going to handle the Frady thing. But what I was thinking when we went in to roll call was how Ridgeway would take the news about Frady, because there was a history between them.

"When I drove in, I'd seen Ridgeway's car out in the lot, so when he didn't sign in, I went looking for him. We were all on edge. Frady's car was still missing, rumors were getting out of hand about how he had gone down, like everyone was saying he had his dick shot off. So I go out to the lot and I see Ridgeway curled up on the backseat of his car. I thought he was dead at first; he looked dead. I broke the window getting in. He was just drunk. Jesus, he was drunk.

"Ridgeway already had a bad-checks beef hanging over him. We didn't want him to go down on a drunk charge. Any other day I might have left him to take his lumps. But because of Roy, we were all sticking close, you know? Feeling protective of each other. Sort of us against them.

"Mike and Doug and I got Ridgeway into uniform and put him in the back of my unit, let him sleep it off. All day he was back there moaning while I was up front driving. Couple times I pulled over so he could throw up in the gutter. I didn't care. All I had on my mind was finding the assholes who killed Roy. And staying alive.

"We were on the radio constantly, me and Mike and Doug, keeping track of each other. All day, it was, you okay? and where are you now? and meet me here, let me see you. Every time shop eighteen A ninety-seven rolled up, I nearly cried I was so relieved to see those two guys were all right.

"Evidence trickled in. We got an approximate time

of death, a description of a getaway car. Something concrete to look for. Every time I saw one of my informants, I pulled him over, questioned him, told him to get the word out: we're looking for a green Buick. Anyone hear or see anything around half past midnight? We wanted to find them so bad, we got awfully aggressive. I threatened and bribed and promised anything to anyone with good information. I got nothing but more rumors for my efforts.

"We pulled a double shift. By morning watch, Ridgeway was sitting up front, but he was still in a bad way. We stopped at a liquor store for a bottle so he could get through the night. A little hair of the dog.

"Around eleven, we got a call that Harbor Division had spotted Roy's car down by Ascot Raceway. I heard Mike's voice on the radio first thing, claiming the call. He and Doug went straight down there to verify the ID.

"I stayed on patrol another half hour, then I went down to Ascot because I had to see for myself. When I got there, Mike and Doug were parked next to Roy's little gold Pinto.

"It was a piece of crap car, a little station wagon— couldn't afford anything better. Roy hated driving that car, and there we all were, standing over it like it's a shrine or something. None of us had seen Roy at the crime scene; all we had to hang on to was that fucking Pinto—sorry Maggie, I need a bleeper, I guess.

"Whoever dropped the car wiped it down. Oil or something, had a film of some kind all over it. Ridgeway went back to sleep and we three just stood out there in the cold and damp and talked about Roy and some of our capers. Talked about his kids and

how they'd handle knowing their father was dead—
they were two and four, something like that. How
rough it would be growing up without a father.

"We all said we'd try to stay close to them, look
over them. But Mary Helen had different ideas. We
talked about her, too. She was a good-looking woman.
We thought she'd connect with some guy pretty soon,
if she hadn't already; she and Roy had been separated
for a while.

"We talked about our own families and how they'd
get along without us. Mike's wife was pregnant with
Michael. They weren't getting along real well—they
never did—but he wanted that kid real bad. He always
said he wasn't ready to get married, but with the kid
coming, he was in for the long haul.

"I had the feeling my wife wasn't ever going to let
me inside the house again.

"We stayed out there all night. SID didn't come to
check out the car until end of watch—seven, eight
o'clock the next morning. By the time the sun came
up that Sunday morning, the three of us who were
still alive had told each other things we had never told
anyone. I have never felt closer to two human beings
than I felt to Mike and Doug that night."

Hector got up off the couch, walked into the lens,
and the screen went black.

"Is there more?" I asked.

"I don't know," Guido said. "He taped this at the
end of another interview. I'll have to go through all
of the tapes and see."

Mike came home before nine. I walked out to meet
him in the entry. He looked tired. He had his collar
open and his tie loose, and held his suit coat draped

over his right hand. In his left hand he carried the stack of unsorted mail that had been accumulating for a few days on the front table.

When I kissed him, his cheek felt clammy and he smelled funny. Medicinal.

"Guido found a tape Hector made. You should see it." I reached for his coat to hang it up for him. But he moved it out of my reach.

"What's on the tape?" he asked.

"Hector talking about the day after Frady died." I snatched the coat away. The tough guy had a two-inch square of gauze across the palm of his hand, all taped down with a Big Bird Band-Aid. My stomach did a roll, but all I said was, " 'Splain this to me, Lucy."

He looked sheepish. "Anthony Louis didn't want to come in. Had to take a knife away from him."

"Stitches?"

"Two."

"Did you cry?"

"Hardly a whimper. All in a day's work."

"Did you find anything in Anthony's room?"

"Not yet. We don't have the warrant, yet. Tell you what though, assault on a police officer gets him out of circulation for a while. I hope the DA requests no bail and makes it stick at least until we get a better handle on Anthony's involvement."

"How's Rascon?"

Mike smiled. "I'm going to like working with the boy. He gave Anthony some pretty impressive dummy bumps pulling him off me."

I peeled up the edge of the gauze, saw some neat black macramé in the center of his palm. "Looks clean."

"It's no big deal."

"You think this will get you out of washing dishes, think again."

He laughed, pulled me close. "If I can wash dishes, guess I can take a bubble bath."

"My thinking exactly." I kissed the underside of his chin.

Guido interrupted. "Darl something-or-other is on the phone, Maggie. Says she found your gun."

CHAPTER

16

Las Vegas is trying hard to become a real city. Beyond the hard-core gaming dens downtown, out past the glitter domes and pleasure palaces of the strip, lies creeping urban sprawl that would put any good-size burg to shame. It seemed somehow fitting that counterculture fugitives would choose the edge of this brave new world to hide out, cool off. Disarm.

A fairly new neighborhood minimall now covers Les Allsworthy's junkyard, possibly burying forever the story about how Roy Frady's revolver turned up during the winter of 1976. The motel where Patty Hearst and Bill and Emily Harris lay low on their way to a safe house on the East Coast has been consumed by the expansion of the county hospital. The motel managers, the parents of the man who aided and abetted the fugitives, long ago walked into the light.

I stood in the parking lot atop the leveled junkyard, held in the eye of Guido's video lens, and read aloud the Las Vegas PD report Darl Incledon had found.

"Mrs. Anita Allsworthy reported that while sorting through the belongings of her deceased husband, Lester Allsworthy, she discovered a thirty-eight-caliber Smith and Wesson Airweight revolver, serial number three two eight four one four. Mrs. Allsworthy stated that she did not know how her late husband came into possession of the weapon. LVPD accepted custody and gave Mrs. Allsworthy a property receipt.

"Property Section performed a routine check of the serial number, and ascertained that the weapon was registered as the personal property of LAPD officer Roy Frady, and had been reported stolen."

The last notation on the report showed that Frady's two-inch had been turned over to the FBI the day after it was identified. After telling the camera all that, I stepped out of the frame so that Guido could film background.

The air temp was 103 degrees, and we hadn't even had breakfast yet.

Guido and I had begged space on a weekend gambler's special flight from L.A.—the earliest plane leaving LAX for Vegas—and had been met at the airport by Darl Incledon just after dawn.

I was thinking about stretching out under the puny cottonwood on the easement when Darl drove up with sodas from the drive-through burger stand around the corner. I walked over and met her at the curb.

"I called Mrs. Allsworthy," Darl said, extracting herself from the rental Geo. "She'll see you, but she says she only barely remembers turning in the gun. It's been a long time."

"We'll go see if we can prod her memory with a little cash; I don't have time to fool around with her."

I accepted a jumbo Coke from Darl. "I'm booked on a noon flight to Oakland. I have an appointment there that I don't want to miss."

Darl, looking fresh in a white piqué dress, reached up and smoothed the collar of my blue shirt. "We get up on the wrong side of the bed today?"

"We got up on the wrong side of the sunrise," I said. I held the cold cup to the side of my face. "Did you have trouble getting the report?"

"Piece of cake." She preened, justifiably. "I've done a lot of work in this city—all the construction going on, there's a lot of equipment moving in and out. I just mined some of my local police contacts, called in a debt, bought a few drinks. Wouldn't have taken as long as it did, except the report's so old it was in storage. Too bad there isn't more to it."

"Too bad," I agreed. "Were you able to find out how the FBI got into the picture?"

She shook her head. "When you brought that up, I called and asked my man. There's nothing in the report. He suggested that the FBI had a flag on the gun and when the inquiry was made, the Feds swept in and took possession—interstate crime. There are no names and no receipt. All the notation says is that the gun was handed over to the local federal field office."

"The FBI agent who gave me the tip about the gun also said that it was a dead end." I shook the ice in the cup. "It has been my experience that sometimes when you come to a dead end, there's still some usable road on the other side."

"God, it's fun to work with you again." Darl laughed, her dark eyes sparkling. "If I stopped at half the dead ends I run into, I'd never get anywhere. Hell with 'em, huh?"

Guido joined us. "Can we eat now?"

I looked at my watch and said, "Not yet."

The only shade around Mrs. Anita Allsworthy's single-wide trailer was provided by the rotting canvas cabana attached to the side. We had to stay outside, she said, because her place inside was a mess. I didn't try to argue with her, even though there was a swamp cooler hanging from her window. If the yard was more presentable than the house, then I didn't want to go in, air-cooled or not. From the appearance of her tiny yard, she had brought more than a little of her dead husband's junk with her: cannibalized appliances, torn and broken pieces of furniture, boxes and boxes of old magazines, waist-high stacks of trash right up to the lot line.

Guido took off his white T-shirt and soaked it under the leaky garden hose. Then he draped the shirt over his head and shoulders before he picked up the camera. The desert landscape beyond the cabana shimmered with silvery heat, and he fussed about what the temperature was doing to the surface of his videotape while Mrs. Allsworthy and I cleared some space and set up two folding chairs.

I sat next to Mrs. Allsworthy with a cup of ice held clamped between my thighs, dodging the arrows of bright light that pierced the holey cabana, arrows that shifted with the breeze. When we arrived, the thermometer on the side of her trailer said the shade was 108 degrees. Fifteen minutes later, when we began talking, it was 110 and climbing.

"When my husband died, I had to sell the business."

Mrs. Allsworthy picked at the hairnet covering her tight, white curls. "I guess that gun had been in his things for some time. I don't know how he got it."

"Why did you take the gun to the police?" I asked, full profile to Guido's camera.

Enunciating clearly, looking directly into the camera, Mrs. Allsworthy said, "I turned in the gun because it's the law." But she sounded as if she were reading from a script memorized for some old school recital: "For I cannot tell a lie, Father." The answer was too correct for me to buy, and I had come too far to be nice about it.

I guessed her age to be eighty-something, but didn't ask. When we knocked on her door at eight, she was already dressed for the day and was watering her cactus garden; her industry was a measure, I thought, of her general state of being. She was pleasant enough when talking about her grandchildren, but questions about her husband made her shy and defensive.

I tried again. "Guido and I stopped at the site of your junkyard. When did they build the mall?"

"It's been some time." She looked out across the desert as if Lester's place might still be out there to give her some answers. "Ten years? Maybe a dozen. That mall is a darn sight prettier than Lester's junkyard ever was."

I said, "Tell me about your husband's business."

"It was just like any other junkyard." She dabbed at her powdered cheeks with a paper napkin. "Sold spare parts and what-have-you."

"How did he acquire his stock?" I asked.

"His stock?" She laughed. "You mean, his junk."

"Whatever."

"He'd go out and find it on the street. Or people would bring him things to trade or to sell. Finding the junk wasn't the problem; finding someone to buy it was."

"Did he regularly buy and sell firearms?"

"No," she said, putting up her guard. "Lester kept a few guns for his own protection. But he wasn't a dealer. He didn't have a license for that. Couldn't afford one."

I sat closer to her, saw Guido tighten the focus. "How did Lester come into possession of Roy Frady's gun?"

"I couldn't say." She gazed off across the desert. "Of course, that little gun wasn't the only one I turned in that day. There was a Luger and a couple shotguns, too."

Mrs. Allsworthy also said she didn't remember whether she had ever met the motel managers that hid Patty Hearst. But twenty years is a long time to remember.

Darl drove Guido and me over to the Federal Building. Like nearly everything east of downtown, the building was newer than my story. I got nowhere with the field agent who agreed to speak with me, or with the media liaison I was shunted to. Even Darl batted zero with the Feds. Racketeering, fixed games, and money laundering were one thing. An old story about a dead L.A. cop was nothing. She promised to stay at it.

I left Las Vegas with what I thought was some interesting footage, and a puzzle with too many missing pieces. More than anything else, I was sick of being lied to.

CHAPTER

17

I flew into Oakland and took the BART to Berkeley.

Like Las Vegas, the town of Berkeley is always a street circus, but the shows are radically different. While Vegas is glitz and glitter, Berkeley is a more or less harmonious mix of leftover hippie street vendors, suit-and-tie yuppies who commute across the bridge into San Francisco, and legions of students all sharing available space.

Shattuck Avenue, Telegraph Avenue, Bancroft Way, the main streets around the campus, were abuzz with activity when I arrived on that very warm Friday; Cal was only a couple of weeks into its fall quarter. I walked among the crowd, happy, hearing a street refrain as familiar and beloved as my father's off-key lullabies.

My favorite group at the beginning of the school year is always the freshmen. They arrive during the week before classes, honor-grad paragons of their communities, the hope of the future delivered to the

Big U in family station wagons with their names sewn
into their underwear—just like summer camp. By the
time they go home for Thanksgiving, their new clothes
are all the same dull red-gray because who has time
to sort the wash? Their hair untrimmed, with heads
full of half-learned curriculum to fuel their half-baked
opinions, they are cocked to deliver a full-on assault
on everything their parents hold dear. By the end of
May, after their third round of finals, they will be either academic washouts or reborn paragons.

The air was warm, but compared to the desert I had
just left, it was balmy. I stopped at Fruity Rudy's for
a fresh fruit slush, just to have an excuse to linger and
watch the parade pass by. The cup was overfull. I took
off my linen jacket and carried it over my shoulder,
holding the rapidly melting slush out front to keep it
from dripping all over my shirt. After two long sips,
I gave up, tossed the mess into the trash, and
walked on.

My sister's nursing home was on the northwest side
of campus, less than half a mile from the house where
I grew up. I walked up Shattuck, intending to take the
shortest route across campus, maybe stop in at the
physics department and say hello to old friends. But
I had lots of time, so I made a detour and walked up
Benevenue at the southern edge of campus, stopped
in front of 2603, the house from which Patty Hearst
was kidnapped.

The cedar siding dated the fourplex where Patty had
lived, but it was still *nice*. Still far beyond the budget
of the vast majority of students, and probably young
faculty as well.

I could understand how Patty's comfort might foster

resentment among the disadvantaged, or, for the loosely wrapped, maybe stir up rage. Except that, Patty's kidnappers were neither poor nor crazy. They were, like her, pampered children of the upper middle class. Honor-roll students. College grads.

The neighborhood was very quiet. When Patty Hearst fought her kidnappers and screamed out in the night, the neighbors were no more helpful than the neighbors around 122 West Eighty-ninth Street had been the night Roy Frady died. Similar method of operation in both cases, both marked with similar cynical brazenness: go ahead and scream because no one's going to help you.

I felt a chill just imagining her terror. As I walked onto campus, I stayed to the path, stayed with the crowd. I kept checking behind me.

Campus was cooler than town. The ancient redwoods that shade the grounds were like a deep green canopy high overhead. Among them, oaks and sycamores were beginning to turn pale yellow and soft orange against the green. Bright leaves littered the ground. Even in that very quiet and peaceful place, I still felt spooked.

I walked up Strawberry Creek, which bisects the heart of the massive school, breathing in the scented woods, and came out on Grizzly Peak, where my parents live. The nursing home was straight down the hill.

Mother had told me about the pickets. I expected a few signs, maybe a news van. I was surprised to see a crowd that numbered probably a hundred souls. I steeled myself, wondered whether it was too late to find a disguise of some sort, but walked straight into the fray.

The purpose of any picket is to get media attention. The organizers of this demonstration were notorious opportunists, and were very skillful manipulators of the press. The press knows this, but is not deterred.

There were two news vans in place when I rounded the corner, and a third arrived before I was halfway up the block.

A woman with a born-again bouffant-do waved a Save Emily sign in my face. If a camera hadn't been poised for just such an encounter, I would have decked her. At that point I seemed to be unrecognized as a member of the evil Duchamps family that wanted to pull Em's plug, so I decided to wait until I was on my way out before I hit anyone. Otherwise, I might never get inside.

I refused to make eye contact with the picketers who chanted at me as I walked toward the front door. When an old man reached out and tapped my shoulder, I turned, ready to glare him down.

"Hi, honey," he said. The sign he waved exhorted, Save the Fishdarter. It took me a second, I was so caught off guard, to recognize this rabble-rouser as August Perlmutter, professor of nuclear physics, emeritus, and my father's longtime office mate.

Standing next to him, in a soft pink faculty wife twinset, was Mrs. Perlmutter, my mother's best friend. Her sign proclaimed, The Aliens Are Among Us. It's Time for NASA to Tell the Truth. Mrs. Perlmutter's tennies matched her sweaters. She winked at me and marched on down the easement waving her sign, cutting off a Save Emily picket as a camera focused in on it.

I walked a few steps behind her, greeted in very

private ways by Mother and Dad's trio sonata group, their bridge partners, their colleagues, former students, and neighbors. Each of them seemed to have given up all reason: Nixon Was Right. Legalize Cannabis. Ché Guevara Died for Your Sins.

Celibacy Is the Only Answer, was held aloft by Freda Walsh, age eighty-two. As I passed her, she jiggled her picket and said, sotto voce, "Don't believe it, sweetie."

In all, I estimate that the Save Em'ers were outnumbered four to one. And outmaneuvered at every turn. No newsgathering organization, confronted with this gathering of apparent flakes, would take anyone there seriously. The counterdemonstration was the sweetest expression of friendship I had ever seen.

I laughed all the way up the steps and down the sterile hospital corridor. My mood changed to one of concern as soon as I walked into Emily's room and saw my parents. Both of them were gray with fatigue.

"Who organized the demonstration?" I asked, kissing both in turn.

"Your mother," Dad said. "The woman watches too much football: the best defense is a good offense."

"I suppose someone is having a potluck as soon as the newspeople go away," I said.

"At the Perlmutters." Mother smiled. "We invited the news folks to come, too. Just a light lunch."

I said, "Oh, Mom," because there was nothing else to say.

When I came in, I had interrupted my father's pacing in the narrow space between the end of my sister Emily's bed and the door. When I was seated on the end of Em's bed and out of his way, he started up again.

Dad is six foot five, all legs and loose-hinged arms, so there was a fair amount of shin and elbow banging, as there always is with Dad, as he maneuvered from one side of the room to the other.

Dad said, "The issue is, Now what? What instructions are we prepared to give the hospital in case Emily goes into crisis?"

"What have you two discussed so far?" I asked.

"Only this," Dad said. "The final decision has to be yours, Maggie. Ultimately, you will be left with the consequences. Your mother and I both have already exceeded our allotted three score and ten. If we authorize mechanical intervention to bring Emily out of a crisis, then we must be prepared for Emily to live, on support, for another thirty or forty years—entirely within the range of possibility considering her age and overall health. She could so easily outlive your mother and me, darling Margot, that you will be left, alone, saddled with the ramifications."

"Mother?" I said, appealing for some help. My mother was giving my sister Emily her weekly manicure and scarcely glanced up.

"I get it," I said. "You two are arguing over this and you want me to be the swing vote."

"We aren't arguing." Mother flexed Emily's long fingers, massaged them with lotion. "How can we argue when we aren't speaking?"

I looked from the black scowl on my father's lined face to the imperious cool on my mother's. Compromise, the great strength of their fifty-year relationship, had failed them where the issue was the survival, however elemental, of my sister Emily. Mother and Dad had presented me with a dilemma worthy of Solomon, and abandoned me.

I couldn't expect much help from other family members, either. After a failed two-day furlough to visit Em, my uncle Max was back at the Betty Ford Center, drying out, screwing aging, alcoholic movie stars. My nephew Marc was off on a postgraduate tramp around the globe—he wouldn't reach his next contact point for two weeks. I still had the counsel of my daughter and Mike, and in her way, my sister Emily.

When I was a little girl in a fix, I would go climb under the covers with my big sister and talk things over with her. That's what I was remembering when I sat down on the end of her hard hospital bed.

"So, Emily," I said, nostalgic for her wisdom. "You're the doctor in the family. It's your life we're deciding here. Give me some input."

Emily said nothing, as she had said nothing for over two years.

I took hold of her top leg as the therapist had taught us, firmly pulled it a few degrees straighter, massaged the calf muscles that were as stiff and stringy as beef jerky, pulled some more. It seemed to me that every time I put her through this drill, there was less flesh, more resistance. Never a response.

Emily was fed and drained by tubes, artificially kept in chemical equilibrium. For two years she had managed to take care of the crucial functions all by herself, to breathe, to keep her heart beating. My entire family had agreed after the shooting, as soon as we realized that Emily was not ever going to recover any mental function, that no artificial life-support would be employed, no resuscitation would be offered.

So, for two years, Emily had hung in, lying in nearly the same position in a variety of hospital and nursing home beds, her body slowly coiling in on itself, her continuing health rapidly bankrupting the family.

The weird thing was that two years ago all of us agreed that there would be no heroic intervention if Emily stopped functioning on her own. Brilliant Emily without a functional brain was, for us, a corpse. Then, oddly, over time, we had grown accustomed to Emily as she had become. We loved her, talked to her, adjusted family routines around her. In some ways, in fact, we needed her. But did that mean that the decision about heroics had changed for any, or all, of us?

I saw threads of red in the drainage bag attached to the side of Emily's bed, a sign of infection.

"I'm very clear," I said. "I know what Emily would say. But I want some assurance from you that, whatever happens, I have your support."

My mother smiled up at me and I was expecting some platitude about their faith in my judgment. What she said was, "Did Daddy tell you he's considering a consulting job in France? Some god-awful industrial suburb south of Paris. I can take the rapide into the city, but, well, it isn't nice there."

I grabbed the back of my father's belt to make him stop pacing. "How long would you be out of the country?"

"Two years. Maybe three. We're going over next week to talk to the people."

"You're abandoning me," I said, breathless as from

a blow to the solar plexus. "You don't want to be here to argue me out of my decision, whatever it is."

Mother said, "It's best this way."

"What about your house?"

"Lyle will take care of it," she said.

"Damn." They had their escape well planned. Lyle had been my solution when I took off for parts south.

I stretched back across the bed and tried to count ceiling tiles, got to twenty and was no closer to anything that looked like an answer. Emily, seized by a spasm, shot out her foot and caught me sharply in the ribs. I grabbed her foot. "Thanks for the input, Emily."

Emily's doctor came in to let us know that she was as clueless as we were about Emily's prognosis. She was more confusing than helpful. Mother and Dad followed her out and left me alone with Emily. To talk things over with her, I suppose. Emily was not at all forthcoming and I needed help.

I called Mike at the office.

"Major Crimes, Flint here." He sounded fierce, but that is his job.

"MacGowen here," I said, sounding to my own ear like a whipped puppy.

"What's up?"

"How's your hand?"

"Throbs a little. Flight okay?"

"No flames upon landing." I told him about Mother's counterdemonstration and he laughed.

"How is Emily?"

"She had another seizure. Doctor says she may have a brain lesion, but there isn't much point in doing expensive diagnostics to pinpoint the problem. Em could have a cerebral rupture at any time."

"Any time today, or any time this year?"

"Exactly. There's more to it, too much to go into over the telephone. Mike, get someone to cover for you. Come up. I need you."

Big sigh. "I can't, baby. I've got a line on my torture killer. And I'm waiting for the judge to hand down the warrant to search Anthony Louis's hovel. I'm too close to too many things."

"You're working all night?"

"Probably. I found the dump where my torture murderer has been shackin' and arrested his clothes and shit. Got everything he owns in the trunk of my car. He can't go back home, and he's got nowhere else to go, so it's just a matter of waiting till he gets tired of being on the street, smelling funky and eating at the shelters. I got stakeouts everywhere I figure he might show up looking for a handout. He'll hit one of them and I'll bring him in. Could be tonight. Could be next week. But until I get him, I can't leave Dodge."

There was a long pause, and then he said, "I ran the guns you took from Hector's."

"And?"

"One was his side arm. The other two were throw-aways. I don't know why Hector would keep throw-aways at this stage in his career."

"Maybe he never got around to disposing of them. Maybe they were Gloria's."

"Could be, but she says no."

"Did you talk to Gloria about the video cam?"

"Yeah. But giving it back is an admission that she took it in the first place. She's going slow."

"Guido can get you the serial number. Could we file a civil case?"

"That may be our fallback position. The thing is, all we want is the tape inside the camera, if there is a tape. I don't want to tip Gloria because she might do something to it. Maybe I'll just go get it back the same way she took it to begin with."

"Don't hurt her on your way in."

"I'll try." He chuckled. "What else do you know?"

I told him what a bust the Las Vegas trip had been. Then I said, "I made an appointment with a realtor. I'm meeting him at my house tonight."

"Appointment with a realtor?"

"I thought we should get an appraisal before we make any decisions."

"We?" he said. "Who is this *we*?"

"You and me."

"Uh-huh."

"I'm up to here with solo decisions, Mike. I miss you. I'll deny this if you quote me, but I need you."

"Good to hear." He laughed the way a man laughs when he hears his child has been especially clever. "Look, if there's any way I can get away, I'll do it. If I get enough accomplished tonight, maybe I can fly up in the morning, we can hang out a little, and fly home together tomorrow night. That's the best offer I can make, and it's soft."

"I'll cling to the hope," I said. "Good-bye."

Emily seemed to be asleep. Her breathing was very slow and regular. I shook her by the foot and nothing changed.

It was late afternoon in Houston, a good time to

catch my daughter in her dorm room. When I called, she bubbled over with exciting news.

"I won't be home for Christmas."

I managed to say, and maybe even to sound calm when I said, "Why not?"

"I'm going to dance the part of the Snow Queen in the Houston Ballet *Nutcracker*."

"Congratulations. That does change things. I was just thinking we might have Christmas in Paris with Grandma and Grandpa."

"Why Paris?"

"They're talking about staying there for a while."

A long pause before she said, with pity, "Oh, Mom. You'll be all alone at Christmas."

"I'll be with Mike and Michael. And if you're dancing in Houston, we'll be there with you." I looked over at Emily. No matter how the arrangements were sorted out, Emily was going to have her first Christmas all alone. Rather, we were going to have our first Christmas without Emily. I held on to Em's clawlike hand.

I said, "I'm proud of you, Casey."

Christmas I could handle, but three more months without my daughter's leotards in my laundry? I said, "Tell me about the auditions."

She chattered on, apparently satisfied by my occasional "uh-huhs" and "reallys?" that I was following her dance jargon during the audition play-by-play. But I was completely lost. It was just nice to hear her happy energy.

Em stirred me from my mental wanderings with another hard kick. When I pushed her leg aside, she pushed back. The kick was not a voluntary response;

I saw her eyes roll back in their sockets, the skin of her face grow taut like shrink-wrap over her fine bones.

To my daughter I said, "Emily's having a seizure. Will you hold on just a second?"

With one hand, I snapped up the bed's side rails to keep Em from falling to the floor, then I grabbed the nurse's call button and held it down until I heard running feet approach down the hall. Emily was in the throes of another grand mal.

The nurses came, the doctor followed. Emily bucked and grimaced and frothed from the mouth. During it all, scared to the point of panic, I managed to lie the big mother lie, saying nothing to my daughter instead of sharing my horror. Despite my efforts, Casey was alarmed.

"Talk to me, Mom."

"The doctor is giving Emily something."

"She okay?"

Emily's body still shook, but the muscles were not as rigid; the seizure was passing. And she still breathed, her heart still beat.

"I think she's okay, Casey."

"Grandma told me Aunt Em had been sick. An infection or something?"

"That's part of it."

"Everybody always tells me how I'm just like Emily."

"In many ways you are," I said. In more ways than being six feet tall like her aunt, and having my father's hump on the bridge of her nose, and being smarter than everyone else.

"I hope Grandma's wrong," she said.

"What? You don't want to be like Emily?"

"Not that," Casey said. "Grandma always says that we should be careful what we say around Aunt Emily, because no one can say for sure if Em can hear or feel, or think about things. I hope she can't think at all. Because, if we're so much alike, I know she'd be going insane if she couldn't move or she couldn't say what was on her mind. Excuse me for saying this, I know she's your sister and you love her and all, but I'd rather be dead than frozen like her. Worse than being buried alive."

"Out of the mouths of babes," I said.

"Jeez, Mom, I'm not a baby."

"That's not what I meant," I said. "You are like Emily, Casey. Don't ever stop saying exactly what's on your mind."

She said, "Yeah?"

"Call Mike and Michael and tell them you got the part you wanted. They'll be as proud of you as I am. I'm sure we'll all be in Houston for Christmas."

When Emily's storm passed there were bruises on her alabaster white flesh where she had knocked against the side rails. On her forehead, where the entering bullet had left a daisy-shaped scar, she gave herself a real shiner, as if she had attacked that gruesome spot with concentrated violence. But she still breathed in and out. Her heart rate was normal, even if mine was not.

I spent most of the rest of Friday afternoon in my uncle Max's Oakland law offices, discussing Emily's legal situation with Max's partner, Jackson Allgood.

"We'll have papers ready for signature before we

go home tonight," Jackson said. "Tell me where you'll be and I'll deliver them myself."

"At my house," I said. The hug he gave me was full of emotion; Jackson had had a massive crush on my sister once. In a way, I suspect he still did.

He walked me back to the BART station, holding on to my arm. "Damned hard deciding not to intervene. I admire your decision, but do you think your parents will stick with it?"

"They have a right to back down," I said. "It would be a tremendous relief for me if either of them would express some strong opinion one way or the other. Right now I'm flying on instruments. I know Emily would prefer death to being hooked up. But my parents? Who knows?"

"I don't envy your situation," Jackson said, squeezing my arm.

I leaned against him for a moment. "All my life, I have known that my parents would leap through fire to save their children. My dilemma now is defining what it means to them to be saved. To live, in legal terms? To be saved from further indignities?"

"Shall I draw up a second set of instructions?"

I shook my head. "We have it right."

CHAPTER

18

I drove my father's car across the Bay Bridge into San Francisco at around six that Friday evening.

Mark Twain once said that the coldest winter he ever spent was a summer in San Francisco. The entire Bay Area was under a summerlike siege. Heat in the East Bay and inland valleys drew a dense layer of cold, heavy fog off the sea, leaving the city under a shroud.

I like fog; it softens the edges, lays a blanket of quiet over the land. After the heat of Oakland, the soft, damp coolness of the West Bay was a blessed change. I took the Embarcadero home, during rush hour, in peak tourist season, just so that I could drive along the bay front and hear the foghorns out at sea. It's a beautiful sound, more mournful than trains in the night, as melodic in its way, and as natural to the area as hooting owls are in the woods.

When I parked in front of my restored house in the Marina district, Lyle, my housemate, was sitting on the front stoop watching the gray shadows of commuter ferries fan out from the city, heading toward Sausalito, Tiburon, Vallejo, and points north. The boats are a pretty sight in any weather.

Lyle got up and strolled over to meet me as I walked up the steep hill.

"Benedict Arnold," I said, kissing his cheek, anyway.

"Me? Who's selling my home out from under me? Your mom and dad offer me a new gig, am I going to say no?"

"Who says I'm selling my house?"

"The real estate agent you called is inside with his little forms, going through all the closets, looking for cracks and leaks. I should have tripped him on his way in."

I looked up at the front of the house, saw the marina, the water, the Marin side of the bay reflected back in the tall windows. I would have bought the house for the view alone. Anyone would. Then I saw the agent standing inside on the landing between the second and third floors, looking out at the same scene, maybe figuring a price tag to put on it. I felt sick.

"Lyle, Lyle, crocodile." I grabbed his arm. "What am I going to do?"

"Hell if I know. Except, you're taking me to Masa's for dinner tonight. You owe me that at least."

The agent, a neighbor I'd had a nodding acquaintance with for years, made his way down through the house and out the front door. In common with every second real estate agent, his name was Jerry.

"I haven't seen inside here since the earthquake," Jerry said, holding his folder of forms close to his chest. "You've done a great job with the restoration, Maggie. Absolutely top drawer."

Lyle looked a little green. He had supervised most of the rebuilding and redecorating. If the house was ready to be placed on the market, it was largely his fault. I put my arm through Lyle's and leaned against the shoulder of his bomber jacket.

The agent seemed to be measuring the house with his eyes. "Why do you want to sell, Maggie?"

"I'm living in L.A.," I said. "Keeping up two houses is too expensive. When this house is vacant, it's a killer. But even when Lyle has renters in here, there's a negative cash flow. I can't cover the hemorrhage much longer."

"What a shame." Jerry struck a mournful posture. "This is a bad time to be selling a house; the worst I've known in twenty-five years selling houses in the city. I hear what they're saying about statewide recovery, but the local housing market is still in the toilet, and looks to stay there for another couple of years. You're not going to get anywhere near what this house is worth if you sell now. You'll be lucky if you recoup the mortgage debt. But it's your decision. If you want to list your home, you know I'll bust my butt to sell it. Think over your options, though. If there's any way you can ride out the slump, I advise you to do it."

Lyle, who is my height, beamed into my face. "Listen to the man."

What I heard when I listened to the man was the sound of my evaporating bank account. So I offered Jerry my hand to let him know he should go away. I said, "Thanks for your time. I'll let you know what we decide."

I went straight inside, called Mike, and told him what Jerry had to say about selling. Mike said at least we had more information. Then he said, "You're all over the news tonight, sweetheart. According to what's his name with the comb-over on channel two, the reason you weren't available to comment on the Documentary Deaths is because you were unplugging Emily."

"Life is rich in its variety," I said.

Mike said he was sure he wouldn't be able to fly up. Not Friday night, and not Saturday morning. I said good-bye.

Lyle showed me the water damage to the ceiling. He said, "It isn't as bad as I thought it was. A little cosmetic plaster and paint, you won't notice it."

I was looking at the beige stain when I asked, "How much did those tenants cost us?"

"They skipped on last month's rent. We won't get anything this month while we get the place back in shape. And every month until we find a new tenant, nada. Add some paint, some cleaning, replace broken fixtures."

"Thousands," I said.

"Thousands," he agreed.

Jackson came by at seven with papers and a bouquet of white mums. He was very solemn as I signed the instructions to the hospital staff that they were to continue Emily on intravenous nutrition but were not to intervene mechanically in any way to resuscitate or sustain her. The deed was easier to accomplish than I had anticipated. In fact, I felt a sense of relief.

Jackson left to deliver a set of papers to my parents, and another to the hospital administrator.

When he was gone, Lyle said, "Dinner. Now."

The restaurant Lyle chose had a dress code that my jeans wouldn't pass. I went up to the attic storage room, found a red silk sheath and a string of phony pearls in one of my trunks, and put them on. We took a taxi to Masa's near Union Square for the best Japanese dinner in the city. And for drinks.

We had a lot to talk about. We went from Masa's to Kimball's for some jazz, then on to an after-hours club south of Market Street to hear honest-to-god rock and roll. It was so nice being with Lyle, so comfortable all around, so far away from the telephone, that I didn't want to let go of the evening. We stayed out too long. I drank too much.

I must have broken the string of pearls trying to get out of my dress. When I woke up on the living room couch Saturday morning, the dress looked like a red puddle on the rug, and there were fake pearls everywhere. I wrapped myself in the quilt Lyle had thrown over me at some point, and followed the smell of coffee into the kitchen.

"You obviously didn't have enough to drink," I said, dismayed by Lyle's crisp oxford cloth shirt, the khakis with a crease, the smooth glow on his cheeks. I closed the shutters against the morning sun before I sat at the table. With my head propped on my hands and hair failing over my face to keep the remaining light out of my eyes, I asked, "Were we in a train wreck?"

"You were." Lyle scooped steamed milk onto a big mug of coffee and put it in front of me. "Your whole life flashed in front of you. I take that back. Your whole life droned into my ears."

"Sorry." I hate maudlin drunks. Especially when they're me. "I don't remember, did I resolve anything?"

"Only that you're going to disembowel someone named Olga. Might be a good idea, but promise me you won't use the good kitchen knives." He handed me a warm bagel and a plate of lox. "Who's Olga?"

"A metaphor for all the bimbettes who hang around the police academy bar on payday."

"Ah-ha." He pushed me the cream cheese. " 'Jealousy, thy name is woman.' "

"Wrong," I said, pushing back the cream cheese. " 'Vanity, thy name is woman.' What you want is, 'The venomous clamors of a jealous woman, Poisons more deadly than a mad dog's tooth.' "

"You can't find your way home alone, but you can remember that shit?"

I looked up at him with one eye. "Lyle, Lyle, crocodile."

Lyle sat down across from me and reached for one of my hands. He had been flip and sarcastic and funny all through the night before, but that morning I saw genuine concern, real tenderness on his face. "So, you're in a no-winner, kid. What are you going to do?"

"To which no-winner do you refer? The house? Sell it at a loss, or keep it at a loss? My sister? Actively let her die, or actively keep her in limbo? Mike?" I had to look away. "Oh, shit. What am I going to do about Mike?"

"Okay, so I'll let you use the good knives just this once."

"Thanks," I said.

"Mike called last night." He got up and handed me the telephone messages he had taken off the machine. Beginning at 8:53 P.M. Friday, and in order: Mike Flint loved me. My daughter needed money again, Kellenberger said Carlos O'Leary would be in People's Park. Mike missed me. Jack Newquist felt abandoned. Lana Howard wanted a quote from me for the eleven o'clock news, Guido had information and was considering flying up with it, my parents wanted to reassure me they supported my decision and wanted me for dinner Saturday. At midnight, Mike wanted to know where the hell I was.

It was still early, so I thought I might catch Mike at home. I dialed, and on the third ring, a woman's voice said "Hello."

I said "Is Mike there?" hoping she would say I had misdialed.

"Mike can't come to the phone," she said. "I'll give him a message."

I said no thanks and, too nonplussed to ask her who she was, I hung up.

She could have been a friend of Michael, friend of a friend. I didn't even mention this conversation to Lyle. I swallowed two aspirin with the last of my coffee and left the room.

Saturdays Lyle volunteered at the hospice in the Castro. While I took my shower, he put the Beatles on the kitchen CD and made his usual double batch of Alice B. Toklas brownies to take with him; a voluptuous appetite is the key to good health, according to Lyle.

I came down in time to help with kitchen cleanup. As Lyle carefully put things away in his immaculate cupboards and drawers, I saw his hands linger over the cups and bowls and spoons, as if seeing them for the last time. Saying farewell.

I said, "Don't pack your bags yet. The house isn't even listed."

He smiled wistfully. "Will you still need me, will you still feed me, when I'm sixty-five?"

"Count on it." I meant it, but already we were drifting. I loved Lyle like family; since the earthquake we had lived like family. Would the glue hold once we had gone our separate ways? When Mike retired and moved to the woods, what would be different?

I dropped Lyle at the hospice, then stopped by the network affiliate to send a message down to Lana. My headache was only a dull throb by the time I was back on the Bay Bridge headed east toward Berkeley.

CHAPTER

19

Carlos O'Leary skillfully formed the silver wire in his hands to make an earring loop and snipped off the excess. He didn't look at me when he asked, "Why should I talk to you?"

"Hell, I don't know, Carlos. Why should you talk to me?" I sat on the grass next to him in People's Park in downtown Berkeley. Once the symbol of grassroots political activism, the park was now a haven for the homeless and the aimless, and an illicit drug superstore. It smelled bad—overfull rent-a-cans—and I didn't want to be there anymore. After fifteen minutes, a pair of earrings and some idle chatter were all we had accomplished between us. The sun was directly overhead, and I was too warm and too hung over to wait around any longer for Carlos to tell me something useful.

I turned down Carlos's offer of a hit from his joint, and started to rise. "Half the country wants to talk to me today, Carlos. If you don't, well, fine."

"Hold on. Hold on. Don't get all uptight." He snuffed the end of his joint between two fingers and laid the smoking roach on his tray of crystal beads. He was probably fifty, his face weathered from living outdoors. He was a leftover flower child in purple tie-dye and love beads and Birkenstock sandals, with a beard that looked infested; anywhere but Berkeley, he would have been taken for an escaped lunatic.

Squinting against the sun, he said, "Maybe we're having a communication problem here. I just don't get why a pretty thing like you would want to talk to an old bum like me about ancient history."

"A man named Chuck Kellenberger thought you might have some information about the people in the SLA."

"Kellenberger?"

"Kellenberger," I repeated.

"Oh, yeah. I know him. Feds."

"He said maybe you'd heard the SLA talk about what happened in L.A. before the shoot-out."

"Who? Me? He musta got the wrong Carlos O'Leary."

"Maybe he did. Look, it's been just awfully interesting talking to you. But I have some business to take care of." I stood up and slung my bag over my arm. "See you."

"Don't go away sounding mad, pretty lady." He picked up the earrings he had just made, long crystal dangles, and extended them toward me. "From me to you. Let me wrap them up for you so their karma doesn't spill out in that sack of yours." He twisted the earrings in a scrap of yellow paper and handed them up to me. "Good luck to you."

"Good luck to you." I slipped the earrings into my bag and put a ten into his hand.

Carlos picked up his smoldering roach and relit the charred end, sucking in a long drag as he did so. By the time I reached the sidewalk, he was swaying to the music of some internal symphony. And I was forgotten.

As I said, I grew up in Berkeley. Carlos O'Leary was not my only available resource. The demonstration at Emily's hospital reminded me how well connected I was.

I found my mother's friend Mrs. Perlmutter setting out tulip bulbs in the sun-washed flower bed at the side of her house. In her broad-brimmed straw hat and denim coveralls, kneeling on the ground, she made a beautiful picture. Tendrils of her hair escaped from under her hat to frame her seamed face in a soft, silver cloud.

Mrs. Perlmutter's hearing had been fading for a few years. She apparently didn't hear me when I took out my camera and knelt on the grass about ten feet from her. I had shot two frames before she sensed I was there, and turned.

"Oh. Maggie, dear. It's you." She barely registered surprise, only tucked in a stray curl. "Do you want me to do something? Show some leg?"

"I like you as I see you, Mrs. Perlmutter." I softened the focus when she was full face to the lens and snapped a third frame. Then I put the camera away and walked over to her. "You look beautiful. I'll send you prints."

She reached up a gloved hand to me, gripped me firmly, impelled me down beside her. Then she passed me a spade and a bucket of bonemeal. "I was hoping you would drop by. And here you are, just as in the old days, and with your camera. I once asked your mother if she would let me have one of your school pictures so that I would know what you looked like. All I ever saw of you was the business end of a camera."

I laughed. "Holding a camera in front of my face was as close to being invisible as I could get. It still is."

She smiled fondly up into my face. "You were always a different sort of child, little Margot. Always knew exactly what you wanted."

"Did I?" I dumped about a teaspoonful of bonemeal into the three-inch hole she had gouged from the mulched earth. "It seemed to me, as a kid, that life was a massive, formless landscape that I wandered over without a road guide, perpetually lost."

"And all these years I thought you were one of the few with dead-reckoning." She chuckled softly, and handed me a tulip bulb. "What brings you by now, dear?"

"The Symbionese Liberation Army."

"Yikes." She raised her hands in mock horror. "Haven't even thought about that mob for years. Are they your new project?"

"They're part of it."

"I'm flattered you thought I could help. But how?"

"You just know things." I planted another bulb. "There was a brief resurgence of the SLA in Berkeley after the shoot-out in L.A."

"Brief and violent," she said firmly. "They painted graffiti all over town, Death to the Fascist Insect That

Preys upon the Life of the People. Not very original, were they?"

"Do you know where any of those people are now? Anyone I could talk to?"

"I suppose the ones still in prison would be easy enough to find; whether or not they would talk is, I suppose, a separate issue. Henry Gates might help you there." She tipped back her hat. "You remember the Gateses? He was a federal judge before his stroke."

"How is Judge Gates?" I asked.

She was thinking hard, was already way past Judge Gates. She said, "Sara Jane Moore."

"Sara Jane Moore?" It took a moment for the name to click. "She took a shot at President Ford?"

"You have a good memory, just like your mother," she said. "You should talk to Sara Jane. I'm sure she's still in prison somewhere. She was the liaison between the Hearst family and the SLA during the ransom negotiations, a bookkeeper I think, stayed on with Hearst for quite a while to get through the paperwork. She was not only a confidant of the SLA left in Berkeley, but also a paid FBI and police informant."

"Did I hear you say April Fool?"

"No. Really. Talk to her."

"How do you know this woman?"

"From here and there. She would march with us in Another Mother for Peace demonstrations," she said. "She had some inherited money. I think that's the only reason those SLA kids would even speak with her. The woman was obsessed with Patty Hearst, called her family at all hours, tried to negotiate her release. She spoke of nothing else. Maybe she had a hero complex, I don't know. She so wanted to be the one to bring in Patty that when the FBI did the honors without her, she went off her rocker. She tried to shoot President Ford only a few days after the FBI arrested Patty."

"Could I trust anything she might tell me?"

"Ah. Good point." Her gaze trailed off and she planted another tulip while she thought. And then she looked up at me with her clear blue eyes. "Let's go inside and call Henry."

Using my shoulder for support, Mrs. Perlmutter rose to her feet, wincing when she straightened her knees.

The first thing Judge Gates said about the SLA was, "They got away with murder." I had an expectant chill before he named the victim. "Mrs. Myrna Opsahl. A fine woman, the mother of four. Mrs. Opsahl was gut-shot during a bank robbery in the Sacramento area. Witnesses at the bank said that Emily Harris pulled the trigger. If I remember correctly, the three survivors from Los Angeles, Hearst and the two Harrises and a few new recruits were hiding out over there. They supported themselves by painting houses and robbing banks. I believe they were trying to raise funds to break the Marcus Foster killing suspects out of jail. The bank robbery was well planned—something about garaging stolen cars well in advance, buying disguises. They made off with something like twenty thousand dollars."

"And killed a woman," I said. "What you've told me sounds very consistent with other SLA capers. But it isn't the caper I'm interested in. Mrs. Opsahl may not be the only murder the SLA got away with."

"What do you think I can tell you?" Judge Gates asked.

"Names. Anyone who might have been in contact with them around the time they were in Los Angeles."

"I'll ask around, but I don't hold out much hope that anyone will talk to you. There's no statute of limitations on murder."

"If you hear anything at all, you can reach me through Mrs. Perlmutter."

I must have shown my disappointment when I hung up. Mrs. Perlmutter insisted that I have a glass of tea before leaving her house. With promises to call, we said good-bye.

I crossed town to Emily's nursing home, feeling prickly enough to take on all comers. There were a dozen pickets still working the line—Ashes to Ashes, but in the Lord's Own Time—and a pair of city police watching over them. The demonstrators stayed on the sidewalk out front and said nothing to me as I walked up the street. There was no visible press.

The headline on the local paper in the rack beside the front door said, Duchamps Lingers near Death.

Emily had passed a quiet night. I helped her day nurse bathe her and struggle her into a fresh cotton gown.

All of her life, Emily had been a formidable athlete, a runner, a swimmer like me; there was never an extra ounce to jiggle on her six-foot frame. Now the thin layer of flesh still hanging on her bones was atrophied and flaccid and ugly. There was nothing left of her except a pair of rock-hard breasts riding high on her chest.

When I said Emily didn't have any jiggle, her chest

was included. She had never had anything more than buttons on her rib cage. Then, a few weeks before she was shot, and for reasons I will never know, my unadorned, pragmatic sister had an industrial-size set of saline-filled breasts surgically installed.

While she wasted away to nothing, those artificial, imitation accessories remained unaffected. I imagined her being dug up a few aeons hence and still having them firm and in place. Then, out of nowhere, I was crying.

The ridiculous picture that flashed through my mind was the first time I had accepted that Emily was going to end up in a coffin. Nothing is real to me until I have a picture of it in my mind, and there it was, in full color, with startling clarity: Emily buried in the gown I had just buttoned up, twin mounds filling out the lacy bodice. Emily really and truly was going to die.

I kissed Em's cold cheek. Then I picked up the packet of legal documents with the hospital administrator's signature on the line below mine, his official acknowledgment of the terms and went back outside.

I didn't know quite what to do with myself. My parents were out making preparations for their big trip, and I didn't want to sit around their house alone. They expected me for dinner, a formal send-off. Otherwise, I would have gone to the airport and taken the first flight south.

Ever since my talk with Carlos O'Leary, I had felt oddly edgy. There was so much to be done in L.A. and I was cut off from it. I was bothered by my conversations with Mrs. Perlmutter and Judge Gates, unsure who the real lunatics were. I had just about

decided that everyone involved with the SLA was a
loose cannon and beyond deciphering.

With nothing better to do, I walked into campus,
past the physics buildings, to the Phoebe Apperson
Hearst grove, and sat down on a stone bench beside
an arch dedicated to Patty's great-grandmother. I wondered whether O'Leary's earrings had spilled their
karma in my bag. I took them out to get a better look
at them.

The earrings were actually very pretty, a bit big for
my taste, but interesting. I thought that Casey would
like them, and started to wrap them back up. That's
when I noticed the writing on the wrapper: "M. E.
Duchamps. Come. 1:00. Love, Kellenberger." And
there was an address in Sausalito.

All the time that I sat in the park with O'Leary, he
never touched a writing implement. I was sufficiently
intrigued to drive down to the marina to catch a Sausalito ferry.

It was already after three when the ferry left the
berth. It was nearly four when I found the Sausalito
address: a houseboat moored at the end of a long slip,
with an unobstructed view of the San Francisco skyline across the bay. It was so late, I didn't expect Kellenberger to still be around.

The houseboat was fairly new, a confection of
carved wood and stained glass. I could hear Chopin
inside when I knocked on the door.

A middle-aged man wearing a golf shirt and khaki
shorts stood in the open door and grinned at me.
"Hello, pretty lady. Come in."

"Maybe you should come out, Carlos," I said. His

beard and straggly hair were but an illusion of memory.

Chuck Kellenberger stepped into view behind him. "You're late. But we saved you some lunch, anyway. Come on in."

"Lunch?" I said. "Your invitation was pretty iffy, Kellenberger. What made you think I would come at all? I might not have seen your little note for days. Maybe never."

Kellenberger, dour desk jockey no more, chuckled happily. "I knew you'd find my note. I just didn't think you'd be so slow about it."

"I had things to do," I said. "Wouldn't it have been easier to just call and arrange a meeting at a McDonald's or someplace and skip the dramatics in the park and the coded message?"

"Too risky," Carlos said.

"Risky for whom?" I asked.

"Carlos had to look you over before he would talk to you," Kellenberger said. "He decided you were okay. Trust me, he's more worried about you than you are about him. Right, Carlos?"

I looked from one to the other. "You like to play games."

"It's no game." Carlos handed me a Polaroid of the two of us in the park, and one shot of me full face, but focused on the people behind me. "Recognize anyone?"

I said, "Damn," when I spotted Jack Newquist peering through a juniper hedge. "How did he find me?"

"You weren't trying to hide," Carlos said.

"He's a journalist," I said. "Journalists do a fair amount of skulking around."

"You checked his credentials?" Kellenberger asked.

"No. I didn't."

Carlos stood aside. "Come inside. Let's talk."

I followed Carlos, with Kellenberger following me, down a dark, narrow passageway that led between two bedrooms and a bath and then opened up into a huge, bright, high-ceilinged living space with floor-to-ceiling windows on three sides. The kitchen, dining area, and sitting area were all one big room without partitions to interfere with the magnificent view of San Francisco Bay and the city skyline rising from the fog on the far side. Water lapped under the redwood deck that extended beyond the room.

"Better than a postcard," I said.

"Damn right," Kellenberger agreed. He dropped his bulk onto a curved white sofa, restaking his claim on a half-eaten sandwich he had left on the coffee table. "Bureau takes care of its own—the boat's confiscated drug property."

I looked at Carlos again. "You're an FBI agent? Kellenberger told me you were part of the SLA. Which is it?"

"Both and neither." He went to the refrigerator and brought out a covered plate and a diet Coke. "But close enough on both counts. You like mustard, don't you?"

I said, "Sure," and sat down near Kellenberger.

Kellenberger beamed like a forty-niner squatting in the middle of a mother lode stream. Carlos, more sub-dued, handed me a linen napkin and set the plate, which held a salami sandwich and potato salad, next to me. I opened the soda. "What's going on?"

Kellenberger sat forward. "I need some promises you'll respect Carlos's need for anonymity."

Mentally, I had already calculated the light levels and set the camera angles for filming the room. The houseboat was too photogenic to just give away. So was Carlos. Out of costume he was good-looking, almost handsome.

I said, "You haven't told me anything yet. My guess, based on our earlier conversation, Agent Kellenberger, is that I have something you need. It isn't your custom to hand out information to the media. Let's make a floor offer before we start negotiating the fine points. What did I stumble into?"

Carlos and Kellenberger exchanged glances. It was Carlos who spoke.

"We became interested in your project when Michelle Tarbett was murdered."

"Who is *we*?" I asked.

"Your government, who loves you," Kellenberger offered over a mouthful, losing some lettuce out of the side of his mouth.

Carlos rolled his eyes, but he smiled. "You asked about the SLA. Kellenberger and I worked that case from the beginning, from before there was an SLA."

"How could you be interested in them before there was an SLA? They were nobody."

"They never were anybody. That particular group of little snots sprang out of a misguided prison rights reform movement—that's where most of the kids in the SLA hooked up with each other. They'd go into the prisons and visit hard cases, think they were going to save some old pros from the oppressor. The cons played them like a pipe organ to get sex and privileges. In the end, the two groups used each other.

"They moved from prison reform to terrorism in the name of the oppressed. They didn't look like the oppressed, so they capered in blackface and Afro wigs: Nancy Ling Perry, Patricia Soltysik, Angela Atwood, Camilla Hall, Bill and Emily Harris. White guilt made them do it, and they came off as phony as an old D. W. Griffith movie."

"As phony as a what?" Kellenberger laughed. "How old are you, anyway, Carlos?"

"Blackface," Carlos said. "Griffith always used white actors in blackface."

"Can we go back to *Go*, here?" I asked.

Carlos faced me again. "*Go* was state prison. Donald DeFreeze escaped from Soledad, and a couple of the SLA women took him in. Hid him in their Berkeley house. Used him as a front, turned him into their figurehead, balled him till he was half dead."

"You're blaming the whole thing on women?"

"The leadership was all women. White, middle-class little dears."

"I'm offended by your patronizing language," I said.

Kellenberger laughed. "He can't say 'little dears'?"

"Eat your sandwich," I said. "And here, have mine." I turned to Carlos. "You're saying no one would take a bunch of suburban brats seriously when they started a revolution in the name of the oppressed. So they found a front."

"That's it. They made a house pet out of DeFreeze. They kept him in Akadama plum wine and screwed his brains out to keep him in line. They stole his life history to use in their manifestos, called him General

Field Marshall Cinque, called themselves followers. But, trust me, they were in charge from the get-go. He cooked for them. They planned a revolution."

"This isn't all new information to me," I said.

Carlos shrugged. "There was a year, the lost year, between the shoot-out in L.A. and the day the FBI finally brought in Patty Hearst. Patty and the Harrises and a handful of wannabes spent part of that year bombing the shit out of the Bay Area. They hit General Motors and police cars, took out the power lines, left a bomb in the mayor's office." Something crossed his mind that made him smile. "Did you know that Joe Remiro, the asshole convicted in the Marcus Foster shooting, was a relative of the San Francisco mayor?"

I didn't bother to answer.

Kellenberger picked up the story. "There have been rumors for the last seventeen, eighteen years that the SLA didn't disappear. The name has changed, but some of the old gang is still hanging in. Still making trouble."

"You think the SLA killed Michelle Tarbett?" I asked, skeptical. When no one answered, I said, "Carlos, I would love to have you on camera. But I won't sneak pictures of you or credit you as a source without your permission. So, why don't you tell me whatever it was you brought me here to learn."

"Michelle Tarbett was our mole in the SLA while they were in L.A."

"She was a topless dancer."

"What line of work was Nancy Ling Perry in before she went underground?" Carlos asked, watching me closely, like a professor during an especially tough exam.

"She danced topless," I said. "Clubs in North Beach, San Francisco."

"Got it now?"

I should have made the connection by myself. "Michelle told me an old friend of hers from the city dropped into the Hot-Cha when Frady was there. The night before he died. She introduced them." I watched their faces. "Was the friend Nancy Ling Perry?"

"Give the lady a prize," Carlos exulted. "Michelle knew Nancy was hot—she watched TV. Nancy was an old friend. She needed help. She needed a place to hide out. She needed some weed. Michelle helped her on all counts. And then she snitched her off."

"Nancy was a friend, and she snitched her off?" I asked.

"Frady was her friend, too. They had a deal: he was nice to her and she gave him solid information."

"She told me she was in love with Frady," I said. "She expected the two of them to be a couple."

"She knew better," Kellenberger said.

I felt a little ill, thinking about Michelle. "He used her."

"They used each other. He got information, she got off with someone who wasn't a sleazeball." Kellenberger pushed his plate away. "That's the way it works."

"Did she tell Frady about the SLA?" I asked.

"We don't know what she told Frady, but she called us."

"Why would she call you?"

"We had her on retainer." Kellenberger seemed to

be enjoying himself. I wondered how long it had been since he'd done fieldwork. "We got the police to lay off her solicitation charges, and she fed us information about drug movement. The owner of the Hot-Cha was a major distributor."

"Did you know where the SLA was before the big shoot-out?"

Again, they looked at each other. I saw Kellenberger shake his head, one small movement to the side.

"Can't say or won't say?" I asked.

"Comes to the same thing," Kellenberger said. "No comment on that."

I looked at Carlos. "You're a narc."

"When I need to be." He peered at my plate. "You want some more potato salad?"

I hadn't eaten anything. With the talk of drugs and the situation, I had no interest in food.

"We want to see your videotape of Michelle," Kellenberger said.

"There isn't one."

"According to Michelle, there is."

I thought about that. It was possible that Hector had made an interview on his own. If it was on the tapes I had taken from his apartment, Guido would find it. Or, Michelle had misrepresented our conversation with a microcassette running. The other possibility was that Michelle had lied—fibbed—"I was filmed" rather than "I will be filmed."

I said, "I am not aware of a Michelle videotape. But I don't work alone. I'll check with my staff." I got up and walked over to see the water. "You could have called me and asked to see anything I have, Mr.

Kellenberger. One woman is dead, and another was attacked. I worry that I may be in some way responsible. I have fully cooperated with the LAPD. And you know it. So, I'll ask you one more time. What do you want from me?"

Kellenberger deferred to Carlos, who rose and walked across the room toward me. "The media and law enforcement don't always get along. I don't know why not, when all we both want is the truth."

"Problem is, the truth has many sides, and all you people want is one answer."

He bowed his head in acknowledgment. "This is the truth: we don't know what's going on. We've picked up rumors over the years that the SLA survivors moved from robbing banks to running drugs to money laundering—a natural evolution; getting rid of cash is always a problem for the drug trade. Most of our information comes from jailhouse snitches who want favors in exchange for talk. They aren't reliable." He cocked his head to the side, smiled at me. "Do you know why Cinque escaped from prison?"

"Because opportunity presented?"

"He went out and made an opportunity," Carlos said. "Cinque was a snitch. The asshole of the main line. For a candy bar, he'd snitch off his mother. Brought down his partner, sent up his cellmate. Everyone knew it. It got to the point he wasn't safe inside anymore."

"Half of the jail population is snitches," I said. "So what?"

Carlos turned to Kellenberger, who sat forward to say, "It's okay. Tell her."

"Cinque was our mole in the SLA up to the point

Patty Hearst was kidnapped. He'd let us know where they were buying their weed, hooked us into the campus drug line. He told us when radicals were stockpiling explosives or arms, and when they were planning to make a move."

I said, "He was an escaped con, and you didn't bring him in?"

"Why would we?" Carlos held up his hands, shrugged. "He was nothing but a petty crook, held up ma 'n' pa and stiffed hookers. He was far more useful to us on the outside."

"More useful? He shot the Oakland superintendent of schools, kidnapped an heiress, robbed a bank, and shot a couple of bystanders," I said, exaggerating outrage. "What did you write on that report? 'Oops'?"

Kellenberger laughed. "More like 'Oh shit' than 'Oops.' "

"I told you," Carlos said, reaching toward me, "Cinque was a pawn. He didn't shoot Marcus Foster. He might have been there, but Nancy Ling Perry was the shooter. Cinque was along for the kidnapping and the bank robbery, for the same reason Patty was, for the cameras. He didn't plan anything. The guy just wasn't that bright."

I said, "If you know so much about him, what kind of underwear did he wear?"

"Boxers. Size thirty-six." Kellenberger stretched, grinned lazily at me. "Willy Wolfe and Bill Harris wore boxers, too. Thirty-fours and thirty-twos. They were skinny little guys, didn't eat very well on the run."

"You couldn't just tell me that when I came to your office?"

Kellenberger frowned. "I didn't know who you were."

"Sure you did." I felt angry enough with Kellenberger to give a share of my ire to Carlos. I walked back to the sofa to get my bag. "I need to catch the five o'clock ferry. The LAPD has access to my research. If you need anything, call them."

"I'll drive you to the ferry," Carlos said.

"I'd rather walk." I glanced at my untouched plate. "Thanks for lunch."

Carlos came out with me, walked down the gangway with me. "You aren't really angry. You know how this works."

"I know how it works. Doesn't mean I have to like it."

"It isn't over, Maggie." We were past the end of the gangway and out on the sidewalk, walking toward the ferry terminal around the point. "We can't spill our guts just because it's been twenty years and you really, really want to know something. There would be a lot more Michelle Tarbetts if we did."

"You think I'm responsible for her?" I asked. "And JoAnn Chin?"

"I don't know about Chin. Or about Detective Melendez, either." He took my arm and moved me into the parking lot when passengers from a newly arrived ferry glutted the walk. "Michelle gave information both ways. I don't think you're responsible. You may have stirred up some old trouble, but don't beat yourself up about it. Just be careful."

"I try." I fished in my bag for my return ticket. "Someone just brought up Sara Jane Moore to me. Where does she fit in?"

He shook his head. "Community punching bag. Everyone wanted something from her. No one gave her what she wanted."

"Which was?"

"Love."

I looked off across the water. "Can't blame her for that, can we?"

He was quiet for a moment, then said, "I'm sorry about your sister. I remember Emily. I ran a file on her."

"She had nothing to do with drugs."

"But she had a lot to do with radical politics. There was a connection, you know. Swapping drugs for guns."

"Emily wasn't involved with guns, either."

"Her friends were."

I found my dock and took a place at the end of the line of waiting passengers. Uninvited, Carlos waited with me. He said, "Until I saw the news, I didn't realize Emily was still alive." He looked at me out of the corner of his dark eyes, smiled a very appealing smile. "When I saw that picket line, I thought someone must be slipping something funny into the water over at the Cal Faculty Club. You don't often see a Nobel laureate claiming the aliens are among us."

"Friend of the family," I said.

He nodded, smiling wider. "I saw Emily's influence on that caper, the way they turned it around. That sense of humor. She'd tweak us, make us look like fools now and then in her speeches and demonstrations. A sense of humor is what set her apart from the rest of the radical fringe. Made the public like her. Hell, even I liked her. I wanted her in jail, but I liked her."

"I love her very much."

He seemed contemplative, took a deep breath as he turned away. The sun was low, just resting on the middle supports of the Golden Gate Bridge, a bright red gum ball suspended in the hovering fogbank.

"I remember you." Carlos turned and looked directly at me. "You've changed. Last time I saw you, you were a scaggy little tomboy with braces on your teeth."

"Did you do surveillance on my sister?"

"No," he said. "On your father. He had government research grants. We kept close tabs on him because of your sister's subversive activities."

"Gives me the chills," I said. "I don't like to be spied on."

"That routine at the park today was an attempt to see whether you recognized me."

I looked at him more closely. "Should I?"

"Not if I did my job right."

"You watched me, too?"

"Your boarding school uniform was a blue plaid jumper and a white blouse." Then he blushed furiously. "I know when and to whom you lost your virginity."

I punched his shoulder with a tight fist. "Jesus Christ."

He laughed, rubbed his shoulder. "You snoop doing your job. I snoop doing mine."

"I don't look into little girls' windows."

"You would if you needed to. And I didn't look in your window. Your parents were out of town and you snuck home in the middle of the week, met one of your father's graduate students, stayed inside for two hours, then you locked up and went back to school. It wasn't hard to figure that one out."

It was my turn to laugh. "You misread the evidence, Agent O'Leary. I remember that day. The boy was my father's teaching assistant. Dad, the absentminded professor, went to a conference and left his speech behind. He had me come home to let the TA in so he could read the speech over the phone to a hotel stenographer. That's all that happened."

"Ohhh. Then it must have been that other time."

I pulled back my fist again and he flinched.

"You plan to help us?" he asked.

"I'll help you," I said. "If I find anything useful, I'll get it to you. But I need some information in return."

"I wondered when you'd get around to it." He looked deep into my eyes, took my hand that was still balled into a fist. "Want to talk about Roy Frady?"

"Yes," I said, and pulled my hand free. "What did your moles say about him?"

"Everyone in L.A. with a favor to ask tried to barter with information on Roy Frady."

"What did Michelle say happened that night in the Hot-Cha?"

He shrugged. "Michelle was working. Nancy came by. She was telling Michelle she needed a place to live when Frady dropped by for a drink. Michelle asked him if he knew of any places that were available."

"You're not going to tell me that Frady sent her over to the house on Eighty-fourth Street."

"Don't know what Frady said. Michelle's boss told her to go do her bumps and grinds, so she left the two of them talking and went back to work. Nancy was a good-looking woman, so Michelle watched them to make sure they didn't go off together. Frady had one drink and left. Nancy waited for Michelle to finish her set, and the two of them went out for breakfast. And that was the last time Michelle saw Nancy."

If Frady ran into Nancy the next night . . . If Frady made a date to meet Nancy the next night . . .

The ferry was ready to board and the line surged forward. Carlos offered his hand, which had a slip of paper in the palm. "Call me," he said.

I put the number in my bag as we followed the people ahead. I was lost in thought for a moment and slowed down so suddenly that the man behind me stepped on the back of my shoe. "Sorry," I said, and hurried along with the line.

We were moving so fast it was difficult to talk. I grabbed Carlos by his arm and kept him close as we approached the gangway. I said, "The LAPD never heard any of this. Michelle was questioned several times, and never mentioned Nancy Ling Perry. Why should I believe you?"

"Because it's true."

I stepped onto the gangway and had to let him go. "Show me evidence."

He dropped back, stepped to the side. He had to shout: "I think you already have it."

CHAPTER

20

Always know where your shoes are.
Always know where your Molotov cocktails are.

—Symbionese Liberation Army,
"Defense Plan," January 1974

I called Guido from a pay phone in the Berkeley Marina ferry terminal.

"Where the hell have you been all day?" he demanded. "I've left messages with Lyle and your mom and Mike and no one knows where you've been."

"You sound like a mom. I've been talking to the FBI." I told him what Carlos had said about Michelle and Nancy Ling Perry. And about Jack Newquist showing up in Berkeley.

"Come home," he said. "I have a lot to show you."

"Maybe I can get a late flight. Right now I have to see my parents."

He nagged a little more before I got him off the line. Then I called Mike at Parker Center and no one knew where he was. I left a message on the machine at home and a message on Michael's machine in the guesthouse. I dialed Mike's voice mail and told the recorder I would be at my parents' house.

Mom and Dad were unloading groceries from the

trunk of Mother's car when I pulled Dad's car into its space in the garage.

"There you are," Dad said, handing me a bag with eggs and milk inside. "Next time you come up, sweetheart, bring a secretary."

"Who called?"

"Mike. Guido. Lyle. Special Agent Kellenberger. Lana Howard. Uncle Max." He combed his hand through his sparse white hair. "That's all I remember. I wrote them down."

The trunk was full of their marketing, too much food for people planning to leave town in a few days. I picked up a second bag. "They have awfully nice food in France."

Mother said, "We aren't going, not even to take a look around. Daddy called and told the consortium he isn't interested."

"Just like that?" I asked, puzzled by the quick turnaround.

"I'm sorry we even considered leaving." Mother held the back door for me. "It was cowardice, pure and simple. I was afraid that if we were here when the time came for Emily, we wouldn't have the courage to let her go. I don't know how to explain it, but signing the documents clarified everything. It may not be easy, but I have no qualms that we will do the right thing. Thank you for taking care of the legal end, darling. Now you're stuck with us."

"Good. You can come to Houston with us for Christmas and see Casey in the *Nutcracker*."

In several trips, we carried the groceries inside and put them away. Dad handed me my list of messages, all of them needing urgent response. I tore off the page and stuffed it into my pocket.

The kitchen clock said 5:50. If there was room on the 6:30 flight from Oakland, I could be at home within two hours. My father was getting a saucepan out of the cupboard. I said, "Mom, Dad, could we do dinner another time?"

They both smiled at me as if I had said something clever. Mother said, "Of course. We aren't going anywhere. Next time, bring Mike."

Dad drove me down to the Oakland airport. On the way, I told him what Carlos had said about surveillance.

"You met one of *them*?" he said, bemused. "All through your sister's antiwar period, they were like ticks on my butt. Several of us had tails. Became a competitive thing: what, you aren't under surveillance? Project must not amount to much." He patted my knee. "It was worse in the fifties. People had to leave the country."

"You left the country," I said. "Is that why? Were you a subversive physicist?"

He laughed. "That's an oxymoron. We went because it was easier to work without McCarthy and J. Edgar in the closet."

"That's a pun."

He hugged me at the departure gate and waited for the plane to take off. I felt very young, and very safe, having my dad watch over me from the terminal window.

At 7:35 I was on the ground in L.A. At 7:45 I was in the shuttle that would take me to the external lot where I had parked my car. I called Guido from the car and asked him to meet me at my house. I still hadn't connected with Mike.

At 8:35, Guido and I, over the remains of his bottle of single-malt scotch, began to swap information.

"There is a Michelle video," he told me, and went to the stack of tapes on my workroom floor. "Not her exactly, but Hector talking about her. He took the list of people he had contacted for us and went through them, gave a little rundown."

He found the tape, put it in the player, and forwarded to the preset stop. Hector came on, wearing running shorts and a two-day beard.

"Michelle Tarbett," Hector said, reading from a sheet of paper. "Heart-of-gold whore, nice ass, face like a train wreck. I never understood what Frady saw in her. She did drugs, she did tricks, she was a breakdown ready to happen. He kept saying she was okay. I know he got information from her because Frady's thing was street news. That's what made him so effective on CRASH, hooking into the pipeline. But he could pat her on the bum, buy her a drink, and get the same information. He didn't have to bleep her.

"The big turn-on with Michelle, if you ask me, was the danger factor. She had a boss who was into the mob. She had a pimp plugged into big-time drug distribution. No one wanted her to fool with Frady, and that's why she did it. He could take on the bad guys for her. Besides that, she was a sweet kid. Michelle worked a pretty tough client list. White woman in the ghetto—big pay, big grief."

The phone in Hector's apartment rang and he walked off to answer it, leaving the tape running, focused on an empty sofa. After the call, he must have forgotten about the tape. I heard what sounded like a refrigerator opening and closing, the fizz of a can being opened, before Guido turned off the machine.

"When was the tape made?" I asked.

"Mike said those are the shorts he was wearing in the morgue. My guess is, last Sunday."

"What time?"

He shrugged. "Draw me a diagram of the apartment's orientation. Then we'll chart the shadows in the room. I think we can get within an hour or so."

"You're a genius, Guido."

"That's what I keep telling you." He took the remote from me. "How's Emily?"

"Status quo." I took out the tape and slid it into its box. "Is there a JoAnn tape?"

"No. He goes after Mary Helen, but I think he was talking more about his own ex-wife or ex-girlfriend. Mike took that one."

"Where the hell is Mike?"

"Haven't seen him since this morning when he dropped off some tapes he wants me to work on. He was all bothered about not knowing exactly where you were, so he came by the studio looking for you."

"He knew I was up north."

"He knew you *were* up north. He just didn't know exactly where you were at the moment."

"Go on."

"He collared me about that stupid tape we made at the academy. He wanted me to reassure him you knew it was a prank."

"And you said?"

"I let him suffer."

"Do you know where he is now?" I asked.

"Haven't a clue."

I wasn't sure how I felt about all that. I didn't mind making Mike squirm now and then, but I didn't need or want my friends to help me do it. I read some undercurrents in what Guido told me. Guido had felt pushed out from the day Mike walked into my life. Guido made it clear way back in the beginning that he didn't think that Mike was exactly suitable for me. Or even housebreakable.

I got up and packed the tapes into a carton for Guido to take with him. I said, "You were busy today."

"Kept my nose to the grindstone." He handed me an empty cassette box. "Every time I wander, I get buttonholed by that number cruncher, Thea. How many penalty hours do I estimate and what budget line do I want to assign lost equipment? All that stuff is bullshit. I tell her to be creative and get scarce. But she is omnipresent."

"Thea's job is the details. She's good at it."

"She's a pain in the butt."

"That, too." I closed the carton and handed it to him. "How's JoAnn today?"

He frowned. "She'll recover. She's still pissed about how she looks, but she's okay."

"I need to see her. Want to come with me?"

"Uh." He demurred. "I told Fergie I'd give her a hand. Those crutches make doing things around the house difficult."

"Has Mike seen all the tapes?"

"I made copies for him. But I don't know if he's gotten to them."

I stood up and stretched, yawned until my eyes ran. "Anything else I need to know?"

He shook his head. "Tomorrow's Sunday. We're filming background along Manchester, and then we're going down to Long Beach for the same."

"Do you need me?"

"No. I'm sending my interns out to do it—class project. They don't even need me." Guido rose and picked up his leather jacket. "I'll be busy putting together my costume for tomorrow night."

"Oh my God," I groaned. "I forgot all about it. Lana's Halloween party. I don't have a costume. I don't want to go."

"It's mandatory," he said. "Go as a foreign correspondent. You can assemble that, can't you?"

We were walking toward the front door. "I'll think of something to wear. But how am I going to talk Mike into a costume?"

Guido put his hand on the front door. "You make your bed, you lie in it."

That was a dig I didn't acknowledge. I gave him the Polaroids from Berkeley and asked him to fool around with them. Then I kissed him good-bye and went back to the workroom for my car keys.

In her semiprivate hospital room, JoAnn was propped up on lacy pillows, her hair pulled back in a red ribbon. When she heard me come in, she snatched her reading glasses off her taped nose and tucked them under the covers.

I handed her a stack of magazines I had bought on the way over. "How are you feeling?"

"I hurt. But they're giving me good drugs. I might stay around for a while just for the drugs." She seemed a little loopy. "Doctor says I'll have black eyes for a couple of weeks, so I don't know when we can film your thingy."

"Don't worry about it." I pulled up a chair, sat close to the high bed. "Can we talk, though?"

"Oh, sure." She primped. "I saw you on the news. Too bad about your sister. I think I remember her name. What did she do?"

"She was a doctor."

JoAnn's grotesque face pulled into a pout. "I thought she got shot."

"She did."

"Boy, they'll shoot anybody nowadays. When Roy got it, well, it was pretty unusual. But now . . ."

I hoped she was loopy because she was beginning to sound like an airhead. "Tell me about Roy."

"He was a wild one. But I loved him."

"I read all the police reports, and I don't remember anyone asking what you did when he never came home the night he was shot. Telephone records show he called you, and he told his friends he had a date with you at ten-thirty or eleven. What did you do when he didn't show?"

"Nothing." She reached for the magazines and thumbed through the top one. "All he said was, he would try to come by. I was in pain. I took a sleeping pill and I didn't know he wasn't there until the police woke me up the next morning."

"You'd had surgery," I said.

She picked at the bodice of her gown over her ample bosom. "Roy gave me these babies. They were still ugly when he died; they were brand-new. I always bruised pretty easy." She touched her discolored cheek. "Roy said he would try to come by that night, and I told him he didn't have to because I didn't want him to see me looking like that. He had vacation coming, starting the next day, so we were going to have a lot of time together, trying on lingerie and stuff when I felt up to it."

What she said didn't quite square with the Frady lore. "You weren't expecting him?"

"Sort of."

"He told his friends he had a date. He called you. Everyone thought the date was with you."

She closed her magazine. "You're going with a cop. Does he always come straight home?"

I didn't bother to answer. "What did Roy say about his plans? Was he going to stop somewhere, or see anyone?"

"He was drunk," JoAnn said, as if that explained a lot. "He told me how happy he was to be back at Seventy-seventh with the boys. He told me he loved me, and he told me what he had planned for my new chest. He liked to talk dirty. That's what we talked about, sex. He was really getting into it, so I thought he'd be right home. I was supposed to wait up, but, like I said, I fell asleep. He knew the best he could expect from me that night was a blow job—he couldn't touch me, I hurt too much."

"Kind of like now," I said.

"Wasn't this bad. God, I'm glad he can't see me now."

"A lot of people miss him," I said.

"I guess the way I said that sounded bad. I'd like to see Roy, sure. But I wouldn't want him to be turned off by how I look. The way their women look is important to cops."

"Did you know Michelle Tarbett?"

"I knew of her. I dated a couple of the guys in the division before Roy. They used to talk about her."

"What did they say?"

"She was a pro." She drew in a breath, coughed, touched her taped ribs. "Damn."

"You know she's dead?"

JoAnn grimaced. "If I hadn't got in one good shot ... Look, I'm tired. It hurts to talk."

"Maybe tomorrow you'll feel better," I said.

"I doubt it." She closed her eyes and turned away from me.

I went home to an empty house. There were no new messages, and I couldn't locate Mike. I began to worry about him for all the usual reasons. I was worried about where he might be, and who might be with him. It was too late to call Casey, so, for someone to talk to, I dialed my parents. All I reached was their machine, meaning they had probably gone to the Perlmutters for their usual Saturday night bridge game. Everything was back to normal.

I took Bowser for a short walk, combed some burrs out of his fur when we got home, played catch with him for a while. He followed me around as I locked up. We left a light burning in the kitchen for Mike and went upstairs. Looking bored, Bowser waited for me to take a quick shower, and then jumped up on the bed when I folded back the quilt.

Mike's voice mail pager beeped. He had left it on his nightstand with his extra reading glasses and a plumber's wrench. I picked it up, watched his office number scroll out on the tiny screen, signifying that someone at Parker Center wanted to talk to him. When I pushed message retrieval, I got a readout of fifteen numbers, the device's limit, and calculated that half that fifteen had come from me.

I read for a while, and at eleven I turned on the news and watched the updates on my own life: Emily was hanging in, there were no developments in the Documentary Deaths, though there was some talk about a movie deal in the works—a movie about a movie. Then I turned the set off, rolled over, and fell asleep with Bowser in my arms.

I thought I heard Mike come in, but it might have been a dream. Cool air brushed my face, I felt the opposite side of the bed sag down—probably Bowser moving. I didn't look at the clock or turn over. I only remember feeling tremendous relief that Mike was home. And then Bowser started to bark.

I snapped on the light to see why; Bowser is not a barker. Bowser bounded to the floor and started pacing by the door, urging me to come with him. I had never seen him so agitated, keeping track of me, watching the stair landing, alternately barking and growling.

There was a strong breeze coming up the stairs, and the faraway hum of the freeway. I had never before heard the freeway from inside the house. I went to the closet and got Mike's .357 Magnum revolver off the shelf, found a box of the right ammunition among his socks, and, with shaking hands, loaded six rounds.

The house was cold and all I had on was underpants and one of Mike's T-shirts. I whipped the lap quilt off the end of the bed and wrapped it around my shoulders. With the gun in one hand and a portable phone and the edges of the quilt in the other, I whispered to Bowser, "Go get 'em, old man."

Bowser took off for the stairs, nails clicking on the hardwood as he tried to get traction. I followed more slowly, listening for sounds that did not belong in my night house.

Bowser never barked at family. But, if Michael had come into the house for something and had brought a friend, maybe that would set off Bowser. As I walked down the stairs, I dialed Michael's cottage, just to see whether he was there. In the distance, I heard his phone ringing, four rings; then the machine kicked on. I rang off, and called out his name. But there was no response out of the dark beyond the end of the stairs.

Bowser paced along the bottom step, waiting for me to tell him to go ahead. I gave him the signal, and followed at a distance as he ran across the entry.

The front door stood open. There was enough light from the street to see that the dead bolt had been cut right out. It lay on the floor, peppered with sawdust. Bowser sniffed the bolt, put his nose to the floor near the threshold, and, like a vacuum cleaner hosing up dust, followed the trail of foreign scent across the entry all the way to the door of my workroom.

The workroom door was closed, and I had left it open. A sliver of light showed underneath. I dialed 911.

"Someone came into my house," I told the person on the other end, a woman. "They might still be here. I'm all alone, I'm holding a gun, and I'm scared. Could you hurry?"

"Stay on the line. Do you see anyone?"

"No." I told her what I could see—the broken lock, the sliver of light. Bowser stood at the workroom door and barked.

She asked me to confirm the address and she asked for my name.

When I said my name, she came back with, "*That* Maggie MacGowen?"

"Afraid so."

"How's your sister, honey?"

"She's okay. Thanks for asking. Can you hurry?"

"They're on the way. Just stay on the line with me."

In the workroom there was a low *whoomp*. A flash of bright orange outlined the door and lit the yard outside. I immediately smelled smoke and gasoline. Bowser went insane, barking and scratching at the door.

"There's a fire," I yelled at the sweet voice in the phone. I dropped the quilt and ran toward the kitchen to get the extinguisher out of the pantry, carrying the gun and the phone in the same hand.

The operator was still calm. "You said the door's closed?"

"Yes."

"Don't open the door," she implored. "I've alerted the fire department, they're on the way. Go outside and wait for them."

"This is an old house. It could go in two minutes. I have an extinguisher."

"If you open that door, you'll feed the flames. Can you hear sirens?"

I held the phone away from my ear and listened. "I hear them."

"Go outside and flag them down."

Fire or not, I wasn't going to flag down the police in my underwear. I grabbed the quilt from the floor on my way out.

I could see the flashing red lights in the treetops on the next street.

"Maggie!"

I put the phone back to my ear. "What?"

"Hold the dog. Don't let him get in the way."

Bowser was still inside the house. I screamed at him. "Bowser, come here old man!"

He started for me, but wouldn't leave that door. I went in to get him. The entry was thick with smoke billowing under the workroom door. It was hard to see, harder still to breathe, and getting worse. My hands were full, so I tried to herd Bowser by nudging him with my bare foot. He wouldn't come with me. I would not leave the gun to perhaps explode in the fire, so I told the operator my dilemma and dropped the phone, grabbed Bowser's collar, and dragged him out.

I was backing out the door when I felt arms around my middle, pulling me, then lifting me. I thought it was the police or the firemen rescuing me, or thinking they were, so I cooperated. Very quickly, the quilt was pulled down over my face and rolled tight around me like a shroud. I tried to get free, but the quilt was so tight I couldn't move my arms. My lungs already burned from inhaling smoke, and I could not get enough air. I couldn't see the flashing lights, but I knew the police and the fire department had to be right there. I felt safe long after I should have.

Like an old rolled-up parlor rug, I was slung over

someone's shoulder and carted off at a run. I felt Bowser leap against me and whoever was holding me. Then I heard the dog yelp in pain.

Shock turned to anger, and I began to struggle in earnest. It isn't easy to carry a full-grown woman over a distance, especially if she doesn't want to go. I had worked some space free to move my arms when I was dumped over a narrow ledge into some kind of box. I was on my back with the quilt edge pinned under me.

My abductor tried to fold my legs in with the rest of me, but I kicked at him, bucked against his efforts, and managed to get my left hand out and free to scratch at him. Because he was too much in control of the situation, I kept the gun in my right hand tight at my side when I started to scream. I didn't want him to turn the gun on me. The quilt still covered my face, so the sound I made was probably too muffled to carry.

I hoped that my captor would give up and run away, and I wouldn't have to use the gun. There was a lot of confusion around the front of my house and I knew the neighbors, being suburban neighbors, would be out in the street gawking. But he kept up the fight and no one came to help me.

I got my face free and saw I was in the trunk of a small car parked on the side street about halfway to our alley. As long as he didn't have my legs tucked in, we weren't going anywhere, so I kicked. I hurt him once in the head hard enough for him to cry out. But then he grabbed me around the knees and pinned my legs between the car and his body. It hurt like hell.

My captor loomed over me, a dark, featureless

shadow. Like the outline of a man on a shooting range target.

He was too strong for me. He had my legs pinned in his grip. Before he could fold them into the trunk, I slipped the quilt away from my right hand. Lying on my back with the creep directly in front of me, I brought up the revolver, aimed at his ten ring, and fired.

The sound of that big Magnum exploding inside the trunk of a car stunned me, deafened me. The flash dazzled my eyes. I sat right up, struggled out, and got ready to fire a second round, but the man was gone by the time I had my feet on the pavement and found my equilibrium. I knew I had hit him. I had blood spattered all over my front. But I couldn't find him. Bowser, instead of giving chase, was all over me, making it difficult to move.

I heard the police running toward me, saw some of the gawking neighbors point me out. The first officer to spot me saw the Magnum and drew his weapon. I set the gun on the pavement and backed away from it. In my underwear and blood-spattered and torn T-shirt, I sat down on the curb to wait.

CHAPTER
21

"Why did you have a loaded firearm in your possession, Miss MacGowen?" The South Pasadena police sergeant, Avery Wong, was a very soft-spoken, genteel-looking man. He had already informed me that the events at my house that night—burglary, arson, assault, attempted kidnapping, a shooting—constituted 83 percent of the violent crime reported in the peaceful city of South Pasadena so far that year. He never raised his voice, and he never let up.

I knew Wong was only doing his job, but his calm was getting to me. I was tired, I was scared. I had no idea where Mike and Michael were, and, after what had happened to me, I was beginning to feel panicky about not knowing.

For the third time, I said, "I loaded the gun and took it downstairs with me because I was alone in the house, and I heard something."

"What did you hear?"

"My dog bark."

"Dogs bark all the time. Is it your habit to walk around the house with a loaded weapon?"

"My dog does not bark all the time, not with as much agitation as he exhibited. And, no, I don't walk around with a loaded weapon."

"Why did you carry the weapon outside the residence?"

"I had it in my hand when the fire started. My only thought was that if I dropped the gun, it might get hot and shoot one of the firefighters. So, I just didn't put it down."

Sergeant Wong laid a computer printout on the desk between us. "This is not the first shooting you have been involved in.

"No, it isn't," I said. "Sometimes the work I do gets me into trouble. The other shooting was declared justifiable, self-defense. May I have some water?"

"Certainly." Wong gestured to the officer sitting by the door, who then left, I hoped, to get me a drink. My nose and my throat burned from breathing smoke. It was nearly three, and the adrenaline letdown had left me exhausted. While Wong was polite and patient, I got the sense that he wasn't convinced I had been a victim, rather than a gun-toting arsonist.

Wong asked, "You're sure you shot someone?"

"Well, Sergeant." I leaned my elbows on his desk and leveled my gaze on him. "I fired the weapon—your people heard it. My shirt is covered with blood—your investigators took it from me. Except for some bumps and bruises on my backside, I am not injured. I'll leave the conclusions to you."

He almost smiled. "It would be more convenient if we had a shooting victim. We don't doubt you shot someone or some animal. He left a bloody trail that was easy enough to follow. We just can't find him."

I sat up. "Where did the trail go?"

"Dead-ends at your driveway."

"He didn't climb into my car, did he? He seems to like trunks."

He froze his expression. "Was there a car in the drive?"

"My car." I had a whole new set of bad feelings. "Did he steal my car?"

"There is no car there now."

"Oh, great." I dropped my head to my hands and studied the backs of my eyelids.

"We need DMV information. License, registered owner, make, model, year."

I gave him what he asked for. Then he asked, "Are you alone a great deal?"

"Not very often."

"Are there problems at home?"

"Sergeant Wong," I said, "later with the psycho-analysis, all right? I've had a rough day, and I really can't take any more. I want to go see what shape my house is in. I need to find my significant other. I need a place to sleep. If you want character references, I can give you plenty. Tonight, please, just take my word for this: I didn't set my house on fire and I didn't fake a kidnapping to get attention."

"Why would anyone kidnap you?"

I was about to say, Have you ever heard of Patty Hearst? when I heard the door behind me open. I turned around, hoping it was a cop with a cup of water.

Mike, black circles around his eyes, jaw set in hard

knots, walked in. He snapped, "Where the hell have you been?"

I was so relieved to see him that I started to tear up, but I bit it back, thinking, Damn him. I snapped back at him. "What happened to, Hi honey, have a nice day? And where the hell have *you* been? How am I supposed to make contact with you if you're never around and you don't leave phone numbers and your pager is at home in the bedroom, from which, by the way, you have been markedly absent? I was set on fire and kidnapped, and where the hell were you?"

He came over and put his arms around me. "Hi honey, how was your day?"

I nestled my sooty face into the hollow of his neck that I like so much and said, "Fuck you," while he patted my back.

"Did you see a doctor?"

"I don't need one. Have you seen the house?"

"Unfortunately. Your workroom is a total loss, and the fire department wasn't real conservative about where they aimed the hoses. But it could be worse and we can fix it."

"Where's Michael?"

"He's at home." Mike held me away to get a better look at me. "You need a bath, cupcake. You smell like the bottom of a barbecue after a neighborhood picnic."

"Where were you, Mike?"

"Following you around." He smiled sheepishly. "Michael told me how you invited him to go up to San Francisco with you. He felt bad that he didn't cancel everything and go. We talked about catching the UCLA game tonight. Then I said, 'Why don't we fly up and get Maggie, have dinner with your parents, spend Sunday in the wine country?' So we did. Or we tried to. We never connected with you. Talked into a lot of machines, but no one ever got back to us."

"How could anyone get back to you? No one knew where you were."

"I think we were flying up about the same time you were flying down. No one was at home in Berkeley, so I thought you'd all probably gone out. Didn't think to call home because I didn't expect you to be there. Michael and I went to dinner in Chinatown, hung out. Went over and saw Lyle, but he didn't know where you were. We took the BART over to Berkeley, and finally, your folks showed up around midnight. You'd been home for hours by then."

"Don't surprise me any more," I said. "And don't forget your pager again."

Sergeant Wong had been taking notes through all this. He looked at Mike. "What is your relationship to Miss MacGowen?"

Mike looked at me significantly. "What am I?"

"Absentee landlord?"

He held me tight again. "I'm sorry."

"Me, too," I said into his chest. "Pay the waiter and take me home."

Mike fished out his police ID and one of his business cards and handed them to Sergeant Wong.

Wong looked from the photo on the ID to Mike. "LAPD?"

"Yes. Look, Sergeant, I know you have to take care of business. But I wouldn't mind a little professional courtesy. I promise you'll have access to Miss MacGowen. But right now, I don't think she can be very useful to you."

Wong gave him back the the ID. "I need to know where to reach Miss MacGowen."

Mike asked, "Maggie, where are we going?"

"A hotel."

Mike promised Wong, "As soon as we get settled, I'll call you."

We stopped at the house to pack a few essentials and to look at the damage. Firemen were still there, watching for embers in the blackened hole that had been my workroom. While we were upstairs, a team of arson investigators arrived.

I'd had so much input during the day that I could hardly react to the apparent loss of a good portion of my life's work. The only issue that raised any sort of feeling was whether Michael could spend the rest of the night in his cottage, alone except for the investigators in the main house and a very sleepy dog.

"Bowser won't make it in a hotel," Michael said. "He stinks. And I can't leave a hero alone."

"Then we'll all bunk with you," Mike said. But Michael's cottage was a single room with a daybed.

"No one will get any sleep," I said. "Let's go to Guido's."

Mike shook his head. "He'll keep us up all night rehashing everything."

Michael had a brainstorm. "I'll take Bowser over to my mom's and stay with him. She has a big yard. It'll be okay."

"Your mom will take in my dog?" I asked, skeptical.

He looked askance, and then he started to chuckle.

He put an arm around me. "She'll take in your dog, Maggie. But I think you'd better go to the hotel."

There was no need to ask the county Scientific Investigation team and the arson squad to lock up when they left. Anyone could drive a truck through the hole in the wall. The South Pasadena police promised that when everyone had finished we would be put on a regular patrol watch. My thought was, Why bother? Anything of real value was either ashes already, or was driving the two cars backing out of the drive, namely, Mike and Michael.

Mike and I checked into the Biltmore downtown. Mike had a pristine change of clothes in the carry-on he had taken to San Francisco. But when I opened my bag, everything that had come from the house smelled like smoke. I called the desk and explained my problem, and a valet came and took my things, promising to have them washed first thing in the morning, even though it was Sunday.

I didn't need clothes to take a hot bath and, finally, slide between clean sheets with Mike.

As he reached over me to turn off the light, I said, "By the way, he stole my car."

CHAPTER
22

Room service brought the Sunday papers with breakfast.

Mike handed me the front page of the *Times*. "New record for you, kid. Three features on the front page, and a background article, Who Is This Troublemaker? on page two."

With a sense of dread, I unfolded the paper. There were articles on Emily and on the murder of Michelle Tarbett, and a late news brief on the fire at our house the night before. There was, indeed, a short biographical article about a woman with my name, but she bore little resemblance to the person I saw in the mirror every morning. This other woman had probably had more adventures than she needed.

Guido was quoted about some caper we had been involved in during an assignment in El Salvador years ago. Almost everything in the article was ancient history distorted by the waterfall of retelling. All of this blather was innocuous until the reporter brought up the previous shooting I had been involved in. By the end of the piece, I sounded like a gun moll.

I tossed the paper onto the floor, stretched out alongside Mike, and wrapped my arm around him. "Tell me what you did all day yesterday."

"I arrested my torture killer."

"Good boy." I kissed his belly. "How?"

"He was tired of being on the street. I knew he was hanging out by the shelters down on skid row, but those people down there don't talk to cops. So I put the word out that he was killing homeless people, and they started calling in, telling me where they'd seen him. He went into the Weingart Center for lunch, and I got a call, 'Come on down.' Went over there, parked outside, and waited for him. Sure enough, out he came, looking like a beaten stepchild. So, I asked him, 'You ready to come in?' He hopped into the backseat and that was it."

"Did you make that up?"

"Nope. Didn't have to. You call that good police work. Took about two hours of talking to him downtown, and we got our confession."

"No rubber hose?"

"I was kind of hoping he'd get froggy with me so I could give him a little medicine. But he rolled over for me. Gave me chapter and verse. At that point, he'd do anything for a shower and a place to sleep."

"You're a genius. But did you get the warrant to search Anthony Louis's room?"

"Huh-uh." He yawned. "Judge says I don't have probable cause. I didn't push it. I declined to file charges, and Anthony kicked yesterday."

"That beast is out of jail?" I was not happily surprised. I raised up to see his face. "But Mike, he cut you."

He flexed his stitched hand but shrugged off my concern, ever the tough guy. "We put a tail on him. I want to see what he does. If he's up to something, I'd rather have him go down big-time than get warehoused for three months on a crappy assault beef," he said. "Besides, Anthony isn't organized enough to have done anything but a slash-and-run caper. This one isn't on his ticket."

"Whatever you say." I rested my head on his chest. "But if he touches you again, he'll have me to deal with."

He pulled up my chin and kissed my face. "How is Annie Oakley today?"

"I don't know. It's all so unreal. I shot a man, and it's as if he evaporated. Bam, and he's gone."

"In your car."

In my car. I wished I knew where he went in my car. And what his plans had been for me in the trunk of his car. I felt the shakes coming on again, starting somewhere behind my solar plexus as a little tremor, and growing stronger as they worked outward. I wrapped my leg over Mike, pressed into him to hold off the aftershocks.

"Make love to me," I said.

"I just did. You have to wait awhile. I'm an old man." He held me, started patting my back. "How about I just do this. When Michael was little and he couldn't sleep, I'd pat his back like this until he settled down."

We lay there quietly for a few minutes, the soft pat-pat on my back in rhythm with my heartbeat, fast at first, gradually slower. I let out a long sigh, feeling fairly certain that I had things in check if not under control. I was still angry at the man who had invaded our house, but it was contained anger at the moment.

"I think he was an opportunist," I said. "How could he know I would come outside? What if he was lurking around to make sure that his fire caught properly, and then he grabbed me as an afterthought? Maybe he didn't even know I was in the house. Or maybe he didn't count on Bowser being such a fine fellow."

"I thought about that."

"Is that how Frady went down? Crime of opportunity?"

"Like how?" He stopped patting.

"Don't stop unless you're ready for passion."

His "heh-heh" rumbled through his chest under my ear. And he started patting again.

I said, "The night the SLA came into town, Michelle introduced Frady to Nancy Ling Perry. What if, the next night, he stopped for a six-pack on his way to JoAnn's house and ran into Nancy at the liquor store?"

"Which liquor store?"

"Probably the one on Manchester and Main. It wasn't the closest store to the SLA hideout, but it was the best-stocked store in the area. The FBI told me Cinque liked to drink Akadama plum wine, and every little store wouldn't carry something like that. Nancy and a couple of the others—"

"Who?" he interrupted.

"I don't know. There were three or four people in the green Buick that drove away from the murder scene. The neighbors who saw the car said the occu-

pants were black. It was late. It was dark. The SLA
capered in blackface and Afro wigs all the time, like
the night they killed Marcus Foster."

A little impatiently, Mike said, "Okay. So Nancy
goes out to buy plum wine."

"I think she went out to do a number of errands,"
I said, curling his chest hair. "She had found the house
for them. They moved in late at night and lay low all
day, met the neighbors, settled in. They never went
out until after dark. So, that night, Friday, there were
things to be done. Like the laundry. Like putting in
supplies. Like buying wine for Cinque to keep him
happy.

"Frady drops by his usual store for a six-pack,
maybe he's hoping to see some of the guys because
he's a little drunk and he's feeling emotional about
being assigned back to Seventy-seventh Street patrol.
Nancy happens to be there, he recognizes her as the
dancer Michelle introduced to him. She has a friend
with her, another good-looking woman. They all talk,
they flirt, he's high, they're available. He gets into
their car to fool around, or maybe to go get some
drinks. Or maybe he even follows in his own car, I
don't know.

"Nancy knows Frady is a cop, and she has a different idea about what makes a good time. She pulls a
gun on him—or they both do—takes his two-inch,
cuffs him with a pair of cheap, imported cuffs she has
in her bag with her nine-millimeter—cuffs she bought
in a gun shop before the Hibernia Bank robbery. She
cuffs him in front, not in back, because she doesn't
know any better.

"Nancy has the laundry in her car—boxer shorts in

three sizes—fresh from the Laundromat. She grabs a pair, pulls them down over his head so he can't see where she's taking him, ties his own shirt over that to hold them in place.

"My best guess is, she takes him to the house on Eighty-fourth Street to show him off. The SLA often said that next to Patty Hearst the best hostage would be a cop. Now they have one. But the group isn't happy with this gift she brings them. They're so hot that they can't keep him. Besides, the house is too small and Frady would be much more difficult to control than a one-hundred-ten-pound teenager had been.

"They want to throw Frady back, but it's too late. Frady wasn't so drunk he hadn't recognized them by that point. The group was tired and didn't want to run again for a while. Besides, they were planning to go deep into hiding, and they didn't have all their gear together yet.

"Frady was a mistake. They tossed him into a borrowed or stolen car, drove him to a burned-out house around the corner from the liquor store. Quickly, cleanly, Frady was executed, and they drove away. Laughing. If the SLA had lived longer, if they had gotten out of the area, maybe they would have taken credit for killing a cop."

"But they died," Mike said. "On May seventeen, 1974, a SWAT sharpshooter severed Nancy Ling Perry's spine with a bullet when she came running out of the burning house up on Fifty-sixth Street. She was trying to bug out while her buddies burned up inside."

"Right."

"They're all dead."

"Not all of them," I said. "Three of the nine weren't

in the house when it burned. They went back to
Berkeley and holed up with the SLA second string—
they must have bragged about shooting a cop. Kellenberger told me about the fringies yesterday, a trig-
ger-happy little band. They killed a woman in a
Sacramento bank heist. It's a terrible story. The dying
woman's husband was the emergency room doctor she
was taken to. And do you know what Emily Harris
said afterward? 'Fuck her, she was a bourgeois doctor's wife.' Nice kids, huh?"

"Hold on a minute." Mike was not patting anymore.
"You tell a good story. But it doesn't explain what's
been happening this week. You have an alternate
scenario?"

"Sure." I stroked his long back. "Roy was always
plugged into the neighborhood: gangs, drugs, prosti-
tutes. Maybe he simply plugged into the wrong information highway and got run over."

"And maybe you did, too."

"Hector was on that road ahead of me. It feels like
déjà vu, Mike. I think we should go down to Ascot
Raceway and see if my car's there."

"Yeah, sure." His tone was the least bit patronizing.
"Look, sweetie, it's nice to have a big case to solve.
But most cases don't amount to much more than
piddly little crap. What do JoAnn and Michelle have
in common besides impending middle age?"

"Roy Frady's dick."

"Bingo." He sat up, threw off the top sheet. "Wars
have been fought over less."

I wasn't ready for him to leave my side. I reached
for him, but he slipped away from me. I pleaded pa-

thetically, "Don't go," but he was already halfway across the room.

"We need to stop by the house," was the last thing he said before his peachlike butt disappeared behind the bathroom door.

The street in front of our house was filled with a dismaying variety of media trucks. We skirted around them, talked our way through the police barrier tape, and approached the house from the alley.

Guido must have arrived right after dawn. He had the entire film crew camped out in the backyard and was directing Monica where to set up lights to show off the worst of the damage to the best of its advantage. Ever the pro, he finished his instructions before he bothered to say so much as hello.

Mike, looking glum, waved at Guido and then went over to talk to one of the investigators, who was drinking coffee with the crew.

I wended my way through the mass of light and camera cables to see what Guido had in his viewfinder.

"Can't let you out of my sight," he said, giving me a hug. "I turn my back and, kaboom. What a mess, Mag. Have you inventoried your loss?"

I shook my head as I surveyed the blackened mess. Gray water ran in snaky runnels into the shrubbery. I kept thinking that I should be more upset. The repairs would be a gross inconvenience, but what else? It was, after all, just a house.

"We're all right." I looked in at the ruined shelves and cupboards and tried to re-create in my mind's eye everything they had held. "All of my footage of Casey growing up is in storage in San Francisco, or my parents have it. You told me you gave copies of all the

Hector tapes to Mike, so they're safe. Everything related to the Frady project was duplicated somewhere. The equipment is insured. My calendar and Rolodex are duplicated at the studio. I have my purse.

"Other than that, I had a lot of outtake footage from other film projects, but it has no real value. I could never use it, I just hated to throw it away. A few personal mementos are gone, but right now I can't even think what they were. We haven't lived here long enough to have much squirreled away." I looked at Guido. "You spent as much time in there as I did, Guido. What's gone?"

He smiled at me like a fond old uncle, reached over and squeezed my hand. "We lost at least three fingers left in the bottom of a pretty good bottle of scotch."

"There you go." I squeezed his hand in return. "Everything is replaceable or expendable."

"Keep saying it, maybe you'll believe it." He gave me a thumbs-up and a quick hug, and went back to work. Guido asked the county arson investigators to walk around amid the rubble for the camera. Very happily, they complied.

Lana came through the back gate with a potted palm in her arms.

I crossed the yard to her. "What's this? Reforestation?"

"I wanted to bring you something. But it's Sunday." She set the palm at my feet. "This is all I could find."

"Thanks, Lana."

She laughed self-consciously. "It seemed like a good idea an hour ago. But I think I should have brought a load of drywall instead."

"And a construction crew to install it."

"We could justify that," she said. "We'll get Thea to find a place in the budget."

We walked around to the side of the house so that she could see the extent of the damage. Lana, always so calm, teared up as she looked at it. "What a mess, Maggie. I don't come out of news, so I'm not used to this sort of thing."

"Who is?"

Her riposte had a sly edge. "According to the *Times,* you are."

"That report has as much fact as a movie of the week."

"Movie of the week? Not a bad idea." With a scary light in her eyes, she watched an investigator bend over to pick up something to display for Guido's camera. "Mind if I stay around?"

"Be my guest. And go have some coffee. You're paying for the caterer."

Lana frowned for just a fleeting moment. "On what budget line will we put the caterer?"

"Ask Thea."

Lana gave me a very phony sorority-rush smile. "That Thea is so efficient. She is absolutely overqualified for the job she has. I completely understand why you requested her."

"But I didn't," I said. "Remember? You did."

"Did I?" Lana looked askance at me. "Maybe so. I need to talk to Guido about getting footage on the satellite uplink for four o'clock. Let's do lunch."

"Tomorrow," I said. "Tell Fergie to remind me."

I went across the yard to the caterer's canopy and found the coffeepot and poured myself a cup before I joined Mike on the grass. We sat with our knees

touching, because every time I lost physical contact
with him, I felt the panic begin to rise.

"They're having a ball," Mike said, watching the
investigators pose and posture like actors. "Their
kids'll love seeing them on TV."

"What have they found?" I asked.

"It looks like the fire was started by a small incendi-
ary time bomb. Simple but elegant, they say. The uni-
formity of the burning says something inflammable
was spread around the room, probably gasoline. Elec-
tronic timer set off a spark, ignited the gas, and poof."

"How long was this person inside the house?"

"After he drilled the dead bolt, he only needed as
long as it takes to place the device, pour out the gas,
and shut the door. A minute, maybe less. From the
time Bowser started barking, how long did it take you
to get downstairs?"

"Probably five minutes. I had to load the gun. Trust
me, I was in no hurry to get down there."

"Five minutes is more than enough time. In five
minutes, he could have been a long way into somewhere else. I don't like it that he stuck around."

"An artist needs to see his work," I said.

Mike looked away, watched the investigators laughing with Guido, blew out the little puff of air that
precedes something that's difficult to say. He put his
hand on my knee. "They're bringing in Brady for
questioning."

I shifted from stunned surprise to acceptance in the
time it took for me to turn around and watch Monica
intercept the come-on from the younger of the investigators. "Maybe that's a good idea," I said.

Detective Rascon came in the back gate, smiled at

the circus in the yard, and looked around until he spotted us. For an unflappable detective, I thought he seemed excited. Mike and I walked over to meet him.

Rascon didn't take time for, Gee, I'm sorry about the house or, Ain't it swell you're in one piece. He went straight to, "We found the car, right where you said to look, Mike."

I nudged Mike, and he blushed, wouldn't meet my eyes. I said, "Where?" almost sure I knew the answer.

Mike took Rascon's elbow and started to lead him away from me, saying, "Police business."

"Nice try." I took Rascon's other arm and walked with them. "So, Larry, where did you find my car?"

He looked from me to Mike, confused.

"Was it down in the South Bay where Ascot Raceway used to be?" I asked him.

"Yes." Rascon seemed only more confused.

"Only a genius would think to look there." I leaned past Rascon so I could needle Mike. I said, "Most cases don't amount to much more than piddly little crap. But now and then you hit a big one. When did you call Larry with this brainstorm?"

"When you were in the shower."

"Guess we better go take a look, don't you think, boys?"

CHAPTER
23

"That was me," Mike said, meaning the young uniformed officer guarding my car. "And that was Frady's car."

"Doug told me the three of you stayed up all night out here," I said. "Watching Frady's car and waiting for SID to come and check it out. He said he never felt closer to anyone than he did to you and Hector that night."

Mike's eyes were all misty, so he had to turn away to shrug off the tide of emotion that obviously came over him remembering. He sighed as he said, "Yeah. Me and Doug and Hector."

"Where was Ridgeway?" I asked. "Wasn't he riding with Hector that rotation?"

Mike thought for a moment. "He was here, drunk off his ass. First and only thing he did was vomit in the gutter. Then he climbed into the backseat to sleep it off again. We had to cover for him when the sergeant came by."

I pulled out my camera. "Walk over and stand with the uniform beside my car."

The request didn't seem to appeal to him. But instead of arguing with me he said, "Say please."

"Please. And don't fool around; just walk normally, do what you would do at a crime scene."

He was self-conscious, walked as if he had a stiff back instead of his usual easy, athletic stroll. He had been treating me like a delicate flower all morning and it occurred to me that the reason he was being so cooperative was some fear that I would come apart on him. To get things on the track back to normal, I was tempted to run out and tackle him, start some roughhousing. Instead, I raised the Nikon.

I shot about a frame a second, finishing the roll in the time it took Mike to cross to the car, look in the window, step back, and engage the uniformed officer in conversation. Laid in sequence, the pictures would give a semblance of movement. A good noir, real quality.

I reloaded the camera and crossed 186th Street to get a better look at what had happened to my car.

Doug told me that Frady's car had been wiped down with an oily rag to obliterate prints. My car had been wiped down, too. But not with oil. There was a fine brown film all over the inside of the windows.

The two days my car had spent in a public lot while I was in San Francisco gave it a layer of gray city grime that was still largely undisturbed. When I picked up the car the night before, I had not bothered to look it over for new dings, so I could not say for certain that the front left headlight hadn't already been cracked at the time the car was stolen. But I think I would have noticed the fourteen-inch scrape along the driver's-side door. Considering the possibilities, the exterior damage was minimal. The interior was beyond redemption.

Blood, enough of it to be wet and dark red after eight hours, soaked the back of the lamb's wool seat cover on the driver's side and pooled in the middle of the seat. There was a trail of blood, distinct right-shoe prints alongside long slashes, as if the thief had dragged his left foot. The slashes, dotted with spatters, led from the car, around the front in a wide arc, and up onto the curb, and then disappeared in the patchy lawn planted along the easement.

Rascon had been talking with the sergeant sent out from Seventy-seventh Street. He walked over next to Mike.

"He was hurt," Mike said. "But where is he?"

"We'll find him." Rascon was cocky. I raised the Nikon and focused tight on his face. "Seventy-seventh Street is canvassing the neighborhood. So far, no one has come forward with information, but it's still early. The problem is, there's so much vacant land here that it's real possible no one saw or heard anything. This is a favorite dump spot for stolen cars for just that reason."

Everything in the car, from fast-food wrappers to stray videotapes, was as I had left it. Almost everything was as I had left it. I turned to Rascon. "The phone was used."

He looked over my shoulder. "We'll put in a request for phone records. See anything else?"

"I have to think about it," I said. "What do you know about the car he tried to get me into?"

"It was reported stolen yesterday in Inglewood."

Mike's pager beeped. He took it off his belt and held it at arm's length so he could see the readout. "The office," he said.

I followed him back across the street and leaned against the doorframe of his car while he called in. He said, "Uh-huh," three or four times before he hung up.

"Gloria says we can come over," he told me. "I don't think you should be there."

"Why?"

"She filed a countercharge against you for taking things out of *her* apartment."

Bullshit maneuver, I thought, and I must have shown some of the disgust I felt for her. Mike said, "You can help us out by finding a serial number for the camera. I forgot to ask Guido."

"I'll call him."

SID arrived to take over the examination of my car. They would probably keep it for weeks, and I needed wheels right away.

I put my hand through Mike's arm. "Would you drop me by the car-rental zone at the airport? I have places to go."

"No need," Mike said. "Take mine. I'll use a city car until you get yours back."

"Get my car *back*?" The thought of ever again getting into that bloody vehicle made me feel queasy. I hoped that somehow the insurance company could be persuaded to total it. I put out my hand and said, "Keys?"

"Now?"

"I have things to do, cupcake."

He closed his keys into his fist and held them high, out of my reach. "Where are you headed?"

"To the studio. You said you wanted a serial number."

"Make sure that's where you go." He dropped the keys onto my palm. "Call me. Every time you move, call me."

"Count on it." I kissed his face.

"Rendezvous point is the Biltmore. Six o'clock."

"Fine. Unless you want to go back to the hotel with me right now."

His cheeks glowed.

"Hold that thought," I said.

When I drove away, Mike was flagging down a tow truck.

At the studio, after a hassle about not having a parking sticker on the car I drove into the lot, I went up to my office and paged Guido.

"Where can I find an identification number for the camera you lent to Hector?" I asked without preliminaries when he returned the call.

"Business office keeps an inventory log. Thea gave me a copy. Look in the cabinet behind my desk. My keys are under the cactus plant."

I went upstairs and had security let me into the filming studio assigned to us. The room was a large open space with exposed girders under a high ceiling. When we were working, the area was full of noise and people and activity. So much activity that Guido, always our point man, found it difficult to get anything done. Out of self-defense, he had partitioned off a little no-man's-land for himself using an assemblage of mismatched cupboards and shelves—anything he could commandeer—and planted his cluttered desk in the middle of it.

The cupboard keys were where he said they would be, under a spiny cactus. I unlocked the cabinet directly behind his desk and swung the tall doors wide.

There were nudie posters on the insides of the doors. At first I didn't bother to look at them, wasn't interested in them, dismissed them as part of the general visual clutter that papered Guido's work area. My only thought was that I was glad he had the sense to keep them out of plain sight lest they offend some litigious female staffer. My attention was focused on the stacks of papers and bound reports on the shelves—the neat documents Thea bombarded us with, and that we rarely read.

I rifled the stacks, and on the bottom, of course, I found the equipment log. I was closing the doors when I glanced at the posters and, after a double take, realized what they were. Even then I resisted the truth, wouldn't let it register. I turned on the desk lamp, opened the doors, and looked again from a remove of about four feet.

Thirty-six-inch by fourteen-inch color stills taken off a videotape, retouched in soft peach-tone pastels, mounted on display board, and laminated: me in the bathtub, my abdomen arched back at the moment of ecstasy, and me, a full frontal shot, rising out of the water with bubbles like silver lace sliding down my breasts and thighs. Mike had been expunged from the scene. I was so stunned that the posters existed that I couldn't think what to do about it. Guido?

The telephone on his desk rang and I picked it up. "Maggie!" It was Guido. "The reports you want probably aren't upstairs. Don't bother looking. I'll be right there."

"Too late. I've seen them."

"Oh, shit," like a sob. "No."

"Can you explain this?"

"No."

"Try, Guido."

"I took the wrong tape out of your bedroom the other night. The box said Anthony Louis, but . . ."

My chest was tight and my ears rang. I had to sit down. That damn tape should have been locked up. So Guido had watched me and Mike fuck—no big deal. How many of us would turn off a tape of our friends going at it? But for him to have made prints with such care, and mounted them, was another matter altogether.

I managed to say, "Why?"

"Oh, God. Why?" He cleared his throat. "It's not what you think, kid. I shouldn't have watched the tape, but I was curious, you know? Fascinated even. It's a pretty tape. I was going to slip it back into your room, but I thought Mike would like to have some stills, some wallet-size even. Christmas card pictures. Wallpaper."

I had been staring at the posters. It was a shock at first to see myself in the raw, in full color. But I had to admit that Guido had done a nice job, with a loving attention to detail. I asked him, "When were you planning to give them to Mike?"

"Christmas?"

"I have to think about this for a while, Guido. We've been friends for a long time. Has something changed?"

"No." He laughed softly. "I'm normal; I always wanted to see you naked."

"Who else has seen them?"

"Oh God," he repeated.

"The boys on the crew?"

"No. Only Thea. I caught her in my office looking at them."

"Was she alone?"

"No. She was giving a tour to that old cop she always has in tow."

"Ridgeway?"

"Yes."

"She was giving him a tour of your cupboards?"

"Yeah. She said she was showing him what she does, showing him what happens to her reports."

Now I felt truly sick—poor Mike if Ridgeway talked to all the old-timers. I didn't bother with good-bye, I just dropped the telephone. I snatched my pictures off the doors, sandwiched them facedown inside the big logbook, and fled to the sanctuary of my own office.

I locked the posters away in my bottom drawer. My first priority was getting out of the building, taking the posters away. So I flipped open the log and scanned the index with so much impatience that I probably only added time to the task.

Every piece of equipment we were using was listed and tracked from shoot to shoot. I found the line for the camera that Guido had signed out to Hector. The entry did not make sense. I turned a few more pages, trying to find an explanation for what had to be an error. According to the log, Hector returned the camera on Thursday. A good trick, since he died on Sunday. Someone probably got the numbers screwed up or checked the wrong box, I thought.

In other circumstances, I would have called Guido for clarification. I settled on Thea as the second-best solution. Her home number wasn't in my Rolodex. Since it was Sunday and there was no one in personnel, I set Tom in security to the task of finding her.

I dialed Mike's pager and then, steamed and confused, too restless to concentrate, I paced my office floor—pacing is a family trait.

I started with Guido. What was I going to do about Guido and how were we ever going to get back to the old status quo? I had known him for a long, long time, and this poster gaffe, squirrelly as it was, wasn't the first problem we had bumbled through. Wouldn't be the last, either, I was sure. In a day or two, everything would settle down and we'd go back to insulting each other and loving each other and working together, as usual. That thought brought me full circle to Ridgeway.

You call an old friend you haven't seen for twenty years, and what's the second thing you say after, "How have you been?"

Certainly Ridgeway's problems—drinking, gambling, women—cast a shadow over relations between Ridgeway and his old LAPD colleagues. But time bridges old rifts, and the fact that anyone makes the effort to look you up makes you shovel aside the old garbage, at least initially. You had been close once, and that's what you first remember. So this is what you say: "Let's get together." My place or yours, maybe some favorite old haunt. And if you agree to a meeting with a terrier like Hector, even if you're only filling airspace when you say it, he would make a firm date. Because Hector always meant what he said. "Come on over, old buddy. Let's go for a run. Barbecue some steaks. Talk about the old days."

And the old days were Roy Frady days.

I paged Mike again, adding a three, as in code three, come with lights and sirens.

I was scrolling through Hector's files when Mike finally called.

"I'm at Gloria's," he said. "What's up?"

"Who answered the phone at our house yesterday?"

"Yesterday? What time?"

"Around nine."

I gave him time to mull the question. He said, "No one. Michael and I were both out of the house by seven-thirty."

"There was a woman in our house."

"You probably dialed the wrong number."

"I don't think so."

"Still." His tone was dismissive and he went right into the next piece of news. "Gloria finally admits she was at Hector's on Sunday. Says she saw the camera but she didn't pick it up. She says we should ask the people who came over as she was leaving. She describes them as a dumpy woman and a tall, good-looking older man."

"Ridgeway," I said. "And Thea."

"Ridgeway's a possibility. Who's Thea?"

"Our bean counter. I'm sure you've met her; big, frumpy gal with wild hair."

"I think I have. Wild hair?"

"Very," I said. I thought back to the day I had walked Ridgeway down to the Eighty-ninth Street shoot, remembered Thea's unrequited enthusiasm over him. I asked, "Did they arrive together?"

"No. The woman knocked just when Gloria was leaving, had some papers for Hector. The man arrived a few minutes later, got out of the elevator just before Gloria got in. She saw him ring Hector's bell, then the elevator doors closed and she went down. She didn't actually see him go inside."

"Ask her if she saw that man at Hector's funeral," I said. "Ridgeway was there."

"I'll ask. Do you have any pictures?"

"Probably. The lab sent up a couple of rolls I haven't had time to go through yet." I found the packets among the accumulation in my In basket and went through them. There were several shots with the ever-present Thea in the background. And one of Ridgeway at the Eighty-ninth Street shoot. I told Mike, "I have pictures, but they aren't very good. Guido must have them both on video."

"Will you call him?" Mike asked.

I said, "No. Be easier if you page him yourself."

"Stay put there awhile," he said. "I'll be by to pick up those pictures." He gave me the number at Gloria's, and I hung up without mentioning Guido's artwork.

When I was looking through my basket for the photographs, I found a tape sent down from the film archives of some of the old news footage of Sara Jane Moore I had ordered the afternoon before. I had forgotten about her until Mrs. Perlmutter's friend Judge Gates brought her up. I was curious about her, as I was about anyone who knew the SLA.

While I waited for Mike, I put the first tape in the

player and let it run as background noise—the building was too quiet. Looking up now and then to watch Sara Jane, I worked on a calendar, laying the week's sequence of events just the way I would lay out storyboards for filming. And around this thin frame I wrapped a lot of supposition.

I glanced up to see Sara Jane Moore standing next to Randolph Hearst, Patty's father, at a news conference. He was tall and elegant, and she, in contrast, was a sad, frumpy, overweight woman who seemed both bewildered and just tickled to death to be where she was, on-screen with Mr. Hearst.

Sara Jane, on the fringes of the radical community, an FBI informant, had been hired to help the Hearst family distribute food to the poor as part of the SLA's ransom demands: PIN, People in Need, a $2 million rip-off.

Cut to the food distribution center in Oakland, and Sara Jane is crying, perplexed by all the activity when delivery trucks begin off-loading food into the arms of a greedy crowd. Then she is swallowed up as the distribution turns into a riot. Hams and turkeys fly through the air like missiles, $2 million worth of edible missiles. Cadillacs draw up to the warehouse and fill their trunks with groceries. Pinkerton guards hired to keep order fill their own cars with groceries. An embarrassing fiasco for all, devastating to Sara Jane.

The next indexed footage shows Moore being wrestled to the ground after taking a shot at President Ford in the middle of a San Francisco crowd. Motivated by chagrin, Kellenberger had said, that the FBI had brought in Patty without her. I thought of the line from the barroom song, "More to be pitied than scorned," and turned off the tape.

I called Tom in security.

"I found the number you wanted," he said. "You need the address, too?"

I told him I did, and he gave me a number and an address in Culver City for Thea. Before I could call her, I had to steel myself a little; I was embarrassed she had seen me in a very private way. A way I would never have willingly shared with Thea because she would have been too keenly interested. My face felt hot, but I dialed.

Thea's voice seemed thick when she answered, as if she had a cold, or had been weeping.

"I need you to interpret an equipment log entry for me," I said.

"Did I do something wrong?"

"It isn't a matter of right or wrong. I think someone just checked the wrong box."

"I'm sorry." She began to snotter and I was afraid she was going to cry.

"Do you have a fax?" I asked. "I would like for you to look at the entry."

But she had no fax and her car wasn't running, and there was no way for her to get to the studio.

I found her response odd, because Thea was usually too eager to do little favors, too needy of random praise to miss an opportunity. I started the Sara Jane Moore tape again and watched the woman lumber across the screen toward Randolph Hearst with a sad, expectant smile on her doughy face. She reminded me of Bowser when he's hoping for a head scratch. She reminded me of Thea.

I said, "Maybe you can just solve this one for me over the telephone. I'm trying to track a company camera that Hector Melendez had at his house. When you were there Sunday, did he mention it to you, or did you see him put it away maybe?"

"Sunday night?" Her answer came fast. "No."

I said, "I'll think of something," and hung up.

What I had thought of was going down to the Culver City address to see what had made her suddenly so unhelpful. When Mike walked in, I explained why, and he drove us in his valetudinarious city car.

Thea's building was two doors in from busy Venice Boulevard, a sixties-era green stucco two-story in a long row of similar sixties-era buildings—apartments for swinging singles, thirty years ago. The swimming pool that had once doubtless been the centerpiece of the tenants' social life had long ago been drained and fenced off, posted against vandals and trespassers. Thea lived on the second floor, with a view over the empty pool.

When Mike knocked, I saw the living room drapes sway to the side. I knew that Thea would be surprised to see me, and was afraid she would be flustered to incoherence by Mike. He had to knock a second time and call her name before she decided to open the door, and then it was only a crack.

"Maggie?" Thea peeked out. "Officer Flint?"

"I thought, Why should Thea come all the way out to the studio when it's my problem?" I said. "We were in the neighborhood and took a chance you would be in."

She hesitated before she said, "It's Sunday."

"I know, but I couldn't wait until tomorrow. No

one knows this stuff better than you do." I held up the
log. "Do you mind taking a look? It'll really help out."

She was nonplussed. Thea, being Thea, couldn't say
no to being indispensable. She let us inside.

The apartment was decorated with television memo-
rabilia, some of it kitschy, a lot of it pricey; Thea
was a fan. Surrounded by Brady Bunch posters and
Partridge Family franchised junk—from lunch boxes
to LPs—she looked like a big kid. She had dressed in
a gauzy skirt and an oversize T-shirt, and her wild hair
was pulled back into a froth of a ponytail, heightening
the youthful illusion.

Mike sniffed the air, crossed the room on the pre-
text of looking at something on a shelf next to the
hall door. "Nice place."

"Have a seat," Thea said, guiding him toward the
sofa. "Can I get you something?"

I said, "No," holding out the log to her. "If you'll
take a look at this, we'll get out of your way."

She sat, clinging to the edge of the sofa, her skirt
sweeping the floor, looking as if she were waiting for
me to drop a bomb on her. I handed her the log and
flipped it to the page I had marked. I said, "Look at
this entry and tell me where that camera is now." And
remembered to add, "Please."

Thea blushed such a deep and furious red that I was
afraid she was having a stroke. I repeated, "Where can
I find this camera?"

"I'm so embarrassed," she croaked. She leaned in
close to me to keep Mike from hearing. "Am I going
to get into trouble?"

"It depends, I suppose, on what you've done. You
want to tell me about it?"

"We're friends," she said, meaning she and I. "I can trust you."

"Of course you can."

"He said it would be okay. He said because of the funeral and all that it would be easier this way, to just sign the equipment back in." She looked up, unhappy to see Mike looking over her shoulder. "It is company property. I was afraid it would end up on the lost-and-damaged log if I didn't take charge, and then there would be so many papers to get filled out and signed. I didn't want to upset anyone. I never thought anyone would notice. I mean, it's not like anyone ever reads my reports."

"Where's the camera, Thea?"

"In the equipment locker. He gave it to me and I put it away where it's supposed to go."

"Who is he?" Mike asked.

I chimed in, "Barry Ridgeway?" watching her face.

Thea was thinking hard as she shifted her gaze from me to Mike, and then off into a corner, where I suspect she hoped she could find an alternate scenario. Finally, she nodded, mute, as if any word she uttered would get her into trouble.

Mike was letting me do the talking. I asked, "How well do you know Barry?"

She broke out in strawberry-colored blotches. "We've been dating."

"For how long?"

"Since Monday. I met him at Hector's house last Sunday."

I sat on the low table in front of her. "Until today, you never mentioned that you were at Hector's on

Sunday. Do you realize that you're one of the last people to see him alive?"

"But Maggie." She was suddenly exasperated. "You never talk to me at all. When would I tell you anything? What would I say? Here's your overtime report, and by the way, I saw Hector for two minutes on Sunday?"

"Why were you at Hector's?"

"Why am I ever anywhere? He needed some information, so I took it to him."

"What information?"

"The weekly filming schedule." Her flash of anger was quickly spent. "He said he needed the lineup so he could arrange time off from work to do the interviews."

"Barry Ridgeway arrived while you were there," I said. "Did he see the schedule?"

"I don't know." She dropped her chin to her chest and spoke to the floor. "He said he only had eyes for me. He walked me to the elevator. That's when he asked me out."

I felt sick. The shooting schedule included a contact number for every person listed. How easy it would have been for anyone with a copy of it to call Michelle or JoAnn. You call an old friend you haven't seen for twenty years, and what's the second thing you say after, "How have you been?"

Mike had wandered off toward the small kitchen. "Did Ridgeway go back inside?"

She nodded. "They were going out for dinner."

I touched Thea's soft shoulder. "I don't have a number for Barry. How can I reach him?"

"I'll give you his number." She reached for a pencil

off the desk and her Rolodex "But he hasn't answered all day. I don't know where he is."

There was more. There had to be. Just returning a camera wouldn't be enough to make her hand shake so badly that she could hardly write. I said, "Where were you yesterday?"

She gulped, looking ridiculously bug-eyed when she glanced from me to Mike to the pencil in her hand. Mike, in the kitchen alcove, opened the dishwasher and looked inside.

"Someone answered the phone at my house yesterday," I said. "Was it you, Thea?"

An embarrassed giggle: "I felt so stupid when I did that. It was an automatic thing. You know, the phone rings, you pick it up."

"There's nothing automatic, however, about breaking into someone's house."

"He said it would be all right." She burst into sobs that made her body shake all over. "He said it was just to spare everyone's feelings."

"What was?"

"I made a mistake," she said. "When I signed in the camera I took out the tape that was inside and shelved it with the other project tapes. I numbered it, logged it, put it away where it was supposed to go. But he told me that the tape showed Hector getting shot and the other guy killing himself and if it got out to 'Hard Copy' or something it would traumatize Hector's kids and the other guy's mother, so it would be a kindness to just let him have it back and he'd get it to his police friends."

"Did you get the tape back?" I asked her.

"I couldn't find it," she said, still emotional. "You and Guido keep moving the tapes around."

Mike was going through the kitchen trash.

I asked, "Do you know what happened at my house last night?"

She gave me a bug-eyed stare again.

"Someone set a fire," I said.

"It wasn't me, honest, Maggie. You know I wouldn't hurt anyone. All I did was watch videotapes in fast-forward all day."

I said, "Thea, did it occur to you that if there is a tape of Hector's death then there had to be a third person in the room when the shootings happened?"

"I'm not stupid, Maggie." Finally, a flash of defiance from her.

"Did Ridgeway make promises to you?"

"Go to hell!" She was steamed. "Do you think that just because some idiot buys me dinner and fucks me that I would lose my mind and go set a house on fire? Well, think again. He didn't use me, Maggie. He loves me. People like you never believe people like me can have lovers. Well, for your information, my man doesn't need naked pictures to get a hard-on for me."

Mike, who had wandered back in, missed the infer-ence. But I saw the quick appraisal Mike gave her, comparing her, I suspected, to his memory of Ridgeway's other women. Maybe I read him wrong, because he said, "You could do a whole lot better for yourself than an old con like Barry Ridgeway. And con is exactly the right word for the guy. Do you know where he is?"

"He was here last night." With pride she said, "I made us dinner and then we made love."

I thought of JoAnn Chin, and what she said about Frady during her interview: "Every time we fucked, I secretly wished we'd get caught just so everyone would know . . ."

Mike asked, "What time did he leave?"

"Around midnight. Maybe later."

He said, "Uh-huh," in a way that was a challenge.

"Midnight," she repeated, firmly this time.

Mike stood, walked across the small room in five long strides. Before he went through the hall door, he said, "Mind if I use the rest room?"

"Sorry." New blotches rose up her neck. "The toilet doesn't work. I'm waiting for the plumber."

"On Sunday?" He sniffed the air again. "Let me take a look. You don't want to pay Sunday rates."

"No!" Thea screamed, following him, with me behind.

Mike went straight for the laundry hamper and spooled out sheets printed with Batman scenes in deep reds and blues. The print masked the dark stains, but not the smell. I caught it every time Mike moved the sheets—the distinctive rustiness of blood.

"I smelled it the minute I walked in," Mike said, holding up a stiff brown patch.

"I'm on my period," Thea offered.

Without acknowledging what she said, Mike opened the cupboard under the sink and pulled out a trash can full of bloody dressings. Setting the can back, he turned to her. "How bad was it?"

"I don't know what you're talking about."

"Show me the bedroom," Mike said, but it wasn't a request. He had already brushed past us and turned down the short hallway. We followed and found him stripping back the bedding to expose a brown-stained mattress. The source had vacated.

He asked Thea, "You want to tell me again what time he left?"

She clamped her lips tight and shook her head, bouncing her ponytail, looking ridiculously awkward.

"Don't make it hard on yourself," he said. "Ridgeway knows how this goes down. Trust me, when we bring him in, he's going to dump everything he can on you to make us go easy on him. Better for you to get the first shots in."

"I know I don't have to say anything without a lawyer," Thea said. "Don't harass me."

"Have it your way," he said.

Thea was too scared to cry. She stood as if numb when Mike used the bedside phone to call for uniformed backup and to request a Scientific Investigation unit. There were no tears even when he snapped handcuffs off his belt and hooked her up.

When she turned to me, I asked her, "How far will you go for this man who loves you?"

"What do you mean?"

"Will you go to prison for him?"

With an air of martyred pride, she said, "Depends."

CHAPTER

24

"You need a little extra money, you give me a call." Sal Ypolito wiped barbecue sauce off his chin. "We could use you on Saturday nights when the place really cooks."

He was talking to Mike, not me, offering him a part-time security job.

The Hot-Cha Club's sparse Sunday afternoon crowd seemed bored. So did the dancers. More interest was being given to the Rams game playing on the TV behind the bar than to the naked behinds up on the stage.

Mike seemed transfixed by a set of bounceless, augmented breasts swinging ever closer, like a pendulum, over his head. His answer to Sal's offer was slow in coming.

"I don't do part-time work anymore, Sal. Save the offer for one of the young guys with a mortgage and a couple of kids. I'm too old to work more than one job."

I said, "What's this too-old shit?"

He winked at me. "I need to save my strength for my domestic duties."

"See that you do," I said, and squeezed the top of his thigh under the table, felt the extent of the effect the dancer was having on the boy. I turned back to Sal.

"You've had some time to think about Mike's question. You come up with an answer?"

"Yeah, sure. Why not? It's not like I did nothin' myself. I think sometimes, maybe if I say somethin' about what happened that other time, maybe things coulda' been different. So, what the hell, huh? You say nothin's gonna come back on me."

"So?" I said.

"So." He shrugged. "I seen them in here last week. I didn't recognize either one of them right off. Then they started talking to me and I knew it was Melendez and Ridgeway. Ordered Coke, the both of them. Jeesh, times have changed. Coke, can you believe that? Next it will be Ovaltine.

"Like I said, Ridgeway used to work security for me. He was a good bouncer, but he was also a lush, so I never knew if he was starting a fight or breaking one up. Then he had this deal going with Michelle, talkin' about opening their own club. I never could figure that, I mean she musta' had some hold on him because he was a smart guy and she was a bimbo." Sal looked at me. "Sorry. Don't speak ill of the dead—but it's the truth."

I said, "She wasn't a businesswoman?"

"You could say that. Never got the big picture, you know? After a while, I couldn't trust her—always stealin' piddly little shit like napkins and glasses, like that was how she was going to stock her bar. Costs thousands to stock a good place and she's nickel-and-diming my paper supplies. Don't make me repeat myself."

He leaned into Mike. "Every time Ridgeway came in, she'd dance raunchy for him like there was no one else in the place. I was going to let her go, 'cuz I didn't want to get shut down. I mean, there are limits to what the girls can do up there. But then he gets sent to prison and she settles back down." Sal took another mouthful of chicken and talked around it. "She stayed on with me as long as she kept her figure. Never opened no club."

"The night Frady died," I said, "did Ridgeway come into the bar?"

Sal nodded, chewing fast. "Ridgeway came in late, real drunk. I told Michelle to go take him home. I didn't want no fights."

"He called you last night," Mike said. In his shirt pocket he had the list of three calls made from my car after it was stolen. "You talked for two minutes."

"Last night?" Sal thought about it. "I never talked to him. What time?"

"Three-forty-two."

Sal's eyebrows went up. "That was him? Some guy gets my machine last night after closing, starts screamin', 'Sal, Sal, pick up!' Never gave no name. I didn't know it was him. What did he think, I sleep here?"

"He wasn't thinking. He was hurt."

"What happened to him?"

I said, "I shot him."

Sal backed up and gave me a horrified mug. "I knew better than to mess with you. But . . ."

"Call me if you hear from Ridgeway, Sal." Mike dropped some bills on the bar as he started to rise.

Sal wadded up the money and stuffed it back into Mike's pocket. "On the house, Officer. Just like the old days. Drop by for lunch anytime. I serve a nice buffet."

Then he looked at me. "No firearms allowed on the premises."

Outside again, when I reached for the car door, Mike gripped my arm. He had a deep furrow between his white brows. "No cop killed Frady."

"Whatever you say," I said. "But what about Hector? Did a cop kill him?"

"I don't know." When Mike drove out of the lot, he avoided looking at my side of the car.

Mike called in: the stakeout on Ridgeway's apartment said there was no mail in his box, but the morning paper was still on his doorstep. The neighbors hadn't seen him all day, and his car was gone. Mike had already asked for an APB on Thea's missing VW bug. He added Ridgeway's car to the list.

Three calls had been made from my car: to Thea, to Sal, and to Michelle's sister Flora.

Freeway traffic was light all the way to Boyle Heights in East L.A., where Michelle Tarbett had lived. The surface streets were jammed with Sunday cruisers, the sidewalks full of family groups parading in their Sunday finery. All the little girls wore bright-colored ruffled dresses and shiny black shoes, and danced the way girls in ruffly dresses must, looking like so many flowers blowing along the sidewalks.

Mike smiled as he watched them. When I touched his arm he said, "Little home wreckers."

"They're only babies," I said.

"They're home wreckers in training," he said. "And ain't they cute?"

They were cute. Much cuter than their young, worn-out-looking mothers.

From the street when we parked, we could see Michelle's sister Flora inside her living room, sewing on a frothy white garment. When I knocked, she glanced up only long enough to see who I was, and then her head bent back to the clouds of lace spilling over her arms.

"May we come in and talk to you?" I asked.

"I don't mind." She bit off an end of thread the same way I had seen Michelle do it. "I got the flowers you sent. Real pretty ones. Looked nice at the services yesterday."

"I'm sorry about Michelle," Mike said, standing over Flora, watching her swift hands.

"Yeah." Her chin rose a bare inch. "Me, too."

"I know the police spoke with you, and you're probably tired of all their questions. But I want to make sure we didn't miss anything. Do you feel up to some questions?"

"I don't mind," she said again. She glanced at me as she reached for her thread and rethreaded her needle. "You was talking to Michelle about that cop killing that they never caught the guy. I don't want it like that for her, you know? It isn't right for the bastard to get away with something like that."

"I agree," I said. I carried the chair from Michelle's battered old desk and set it down next to Flora.

"When I was here, Michelle received a number of calls. She wrote them all down in an appointment book. But when the police came to question you, you told them there was no book. What happened to it?"

"I know how she earned her money," Flora said, almost scolding. "And I know what that book meant. It should have been buried right beside her. Put to rest. My sister is dead. I don't want no police dragging her through the mud."

"Where's the book?" Mike asked.

"Yesterday before the funeral, I said the rosary for Michelle and threw that damn thing in the garbage. That's where it belongs—in the garbage."

"Where's your garbage?" Mike asked.

"Out in back," she said. "It's still out there. But I ain't going to touch it."

"Mind if I look?" he asked, but he was out the back door before she had time to respond.

Flora shrugged. "What bit him?"

"He's just the energetic type," I said. I touched the lace edge of the garment and she opened it out for me, laid it across her lap so that I could see it, a very ornate baby dress of silk organza and re-embroidered lace with seed pearls, like a wedding dress.

"It's beautiful," I said. "Is it for a christening?"

"No." She made the sign of the cross. "For a funeral. The priest asked me yesterday, right after Michelle's funeral, could I make something for a little baby Mr. Rojas found in the dumpster behind his market. I tell Father, I don't mind. I have lots of leftover stuff around here, plenty to make a tiny baby a burial robe. I figure, if I couldn't make the mother a dress for her wedding, at least I can do this for her baby. You know?"

"I know," I said, and she bent over her work again.

"What made you change your mind about giving up Michelle's appointment book?"

"I'm a little scared," she said. "I got some phone call last night from one of her men, wanted me to come over, like I'm going to take over the business for her. It makes me think maybe the police should tell those dicks-for-brains where they should jump off. Know what I mean?"

I nodded. "Did he give you a name?"

"Not until I told him I was going to hang up. You know how late it was? Scared me, phone rings in the middle of the night. I met him a couple of times when Michelle and him had some kind of deal going on. That was a long time ago. I barely remembered who he was when he started calling Michelle again."

"A week ago?" I asked.

She nodded. "Michelle kept telling him they had nothing to talk about. The past is past."

"Maybe she changed her mind," I said.

Mike came in with the appointment book, smelling of coffee grounds and dead flowers. He gave me a thumbs-up and walked across the room toward the front door. He said, "Thank you, Flora. I'll keep you posted."

She nodded her head but didn't look up. I saw her dab at two fat tears before they could fall on the snowy fabric in her hands.

"I'm sorry," I said again, because I couldn't think of anything else.

"All she wanted was something better." Flora

caught my hand as I picked up the chair to put it back. "Maybe she has it now."

"I hope so."

"Yeah."

We left her bent over the baby dress.

Back in the car, I asked, "What did you find?"

"Ridgeway's phone number penciled in for ten o'clock Tuesday night, and the address of a coffee shop east of downtown. She was found in her car a couple of miles from there."

"Did they have sex first?" I asked.

"No. Whoever did her didn't even get into the car, just reached in through the open window and stabbed her."

"Maybe he was kissing her when it happened."

"Maybe, but who cares?"

"It would have been important to Michelle."

"If you say so." He took the First Street exit toward downtown and pulled into the first parking space past the end of the off-ramp. We were in one of the scarier parts of the city, at the edge of Aliso Village, the dean of the city's crumbling federal housing projects. The neighborhood where Anthony Louis grew up—a jumping place.

"Now what?" I asked.

"You tell me. You've made up your mind about Ridgeway, but I'm not there yet. Where is he?"

"If this were a movie of the week, he'd be in a patrol car in the Seventy-seventh Street lot, sleeping it off."

Mike called Seventy-seventh Street and asked to have the lot checked. While we waited for a call back, he asked me, "Why would Ridgeway go after Michelle and JoAnn?"

"Because there's no statute of limitations on murder. Just when Ridgeway is beginning to feel safe again, Hector comes along and starts digging around about Roy Frady. JoAnn and Michelle can somehow connect Ridgeway to Frady that night."

Through clenched teeth, Mike said, "Ridgeway didn't kill Frady."

"You keep saying that." I crossed my arms over my chest, slouched down in the seat, and looked out the window, too tired to risk getting into anything with Mike. He was tired, too. I said, "I don't want to be in this place anymore. You driving on, or shall I catch the next bus?"

He started the engine. "Are you mad?"

"Hell no." I flipped the radio dial from his hokey "There's a tear in my beer" country music to "The Mozart Hour" on NPR and turned up the volume.

"You're mad!" he shouted over the music.

"Do you want the truth about what happened or do you just want to be right?"

He snapped off the radio when his telephone buzzed. The conversation comprised no more than a dozen words: Barry Ridgeway was not cooping at Seventy-seventh Street.

We crossed the bridge over the Los Angeles River, a thin black stream in the middle of the concrete channel, and passed into Little Tokyo.

"If you're talking," Mike said, "I'm listening."

"Okay. Jump in anytime," I said. "If I were going to dramatize my version of events, this is how it would play." I leaned into him. "May ten, 1974, ten-thirty p.m. Roy Frady, coming off his high, swings off the freeway to get a six-pack. He runs into his old pal Barry Ridgeway again. They're both drunk. Ridgeway has one of his babes in tow, Michelle, and he's all over her. But maybe it still burns Ridgeway that Frady is sleeping with his former girlfriend, maybe it makes him feel better when he sees Frady take off with one of Michelle's friends, knows he's going to cheat on old JoAnn. A little payback on its way.

"If it were my script, I would have Ridgeway call JoAnn and tell her that her guy is out screwing a dancer named Nancy, and not to wait up for him. JoAnn has never mentioned any such call; it's too bad that reality doesn't always make the best drama."

"Then what?" Mike asked.

"That's it. Frady never goes home and Ridgeway is afraid to confess that he may have been the last man to see his old partner alive. He knows he'll be a suspect. It's possible that he was so drunk that the exact sequence of events is unclear to him. I think that when he sees Frady's car and realizes what it means, he gets sick. He stays drunk for the better part of a week, and when he gets sober enough to sort things out, the SLA is ashes and the obituary of the girl he set up with Frady is all over the papers—Nancy Ling Perry of the Symbionese Liberation Army. It's too late to start talking at that point. Besides, he's into a loan deal with the mob and he can't bear the close scrutiny that would follow if he talked."

"Why doesn't Michelle come forward?"

"Two reasons: she hopes things work out between her and Ridgeway, and she's in on the mob loan. She's going to be Ridgeway's partner in this club, remember? Would an optimist like Michelle toss away a shot at something better than dancing for Sal and servicing his clients just to snitch off a killer who's already dead? Of course not."

Mike had a crooked smile. "That's how you figure it?"

"That's how I'd play it. One hundred minutes long, one hundred pages of script, a plot hook slapped at the end of every fifteen minutes to bring the audience back after the commercial breaks."

He picked up my hand and kissed it. "When you write this potboiler, where will Ridgeway be when he's found?"

"I've been thinking. It appears at first that he has a bizarre need for symmetry. That's why he left my car where he did. On second look, I decided that he simply has no imagination and he just couldn't come up with something new when he was shedding blood on my upholstery. So, I wonder, where would a street-wise guy go if he had a bullet in him?"

"And?"

"Remember that bullshit story you told me about arresting the torture killer down on skid row?"

"Yes."

"Where does a desperate man go for shelter?"

CHAPTER
25

We missed church services and dinner at Victory Outreach down on Manchester. The dormitory was closed until 9:30, so men who held tickets for beds that night were passing the time by watching television in the dayroom downstairs or finishing the chores that earned them their cots and showers.

Two cars from Seventy-seventh Street had come in with us. When we paraded through the dayroom—four uniforms, Mike, Rascon, and I—a couple of the men slithered out. The others not only stayed but seemed to regard us as the evening's entertainment. They drew in uncomfortably close.

"Who you lookin' fo'?" "I didn't do nothin', honest (followed by laughter)." "Leave the sweet one down here, boys."

At that last remark, I pushed right up against Mike and held on to his elbow: fifty newly scrubbed, semi-sober, gap-toothed, homeless bachelors were not my choice of companion.

"We missed Barry this morning." The director was a thin, soft-spoken, white-haired man with wire-rim glasses. A holy-looking man. "He usually escorts the women's shelter residents to Sunday mass. I was afraid he had fallen victim to Saturday night temptations."

"Has he called you?" Mike asked.

"No. Sorry." The director selected a key from his ring. Then he turned to me.

"You'll have to wait down here. No women are allowed in the men's dormitory."

"But the dorm's empty," I said. "Everyone is down here."

He raised his hands to show the policy was not his to break. "Something happens to our residents when a woman passes through their sleeping quarters. I can't explain it—a scent left behind, perhaps, that sets off their buttons. I only know that it leads to fights."

Mike gave me a look that said, Please don't push it; but if I was going to be the source of contention in an empty dormitory, what could happen in a fully populated dayroom? I didn't want to find that out, so as Mike went up with the director and the uniforms, I hurried back out toward the reception area. On the way, I gathered in half a dozen admirers, two of whom got into a shoving match when I said I wouldn't mind a drink of water and they each wanted to show me where to find it.

I asked the little gnome who tucked himself up close to me, "What happens if you come in after curfew?"

"Nothing." He had no teeth at all in his smile. "They lock up at eleven. If you ain't inside by then, you ain't gettin' in."

"What if you're sick and you want to come in during the day?"

"Call the paramedics. They lock us out of the dorm from eight in the morning until nine-thirty at night. This ain't a hotel, you know, girlie. You can't just come and go. And they don't make exceptions for nobody."

"If you were going to sneak someone in, how would you do it?"

His face went all mushy and he pressed in closer to me. "If it was you, honey, I'd find us a way. But we could have us a whole lot more fun over behind Jimmy's, where we could be alone. Upstairs, every asshole would expect a piece of your sweetness."

"What if I was a man?"

He winked. "I ain't interested in that kind of stuff."

My gnome was shoved aside by a younger man. "You'd have to get to the guy with the key. I've tried talking my way in before, and it never did me no good."

"Anyone else have a key?"

"Nope. Just him." He gestured toward the stairs the director had taken.

"Is there another door in?"

He pointed toward the dining room. "It's locked just as tight."

I said, "Thanks," and moved off toward the office, where the staff was having coffee. If Ridgeway had gone up either set of stairs, someone would have seen him, and everyone would have heard about it. Unless there was a hole in the time line I had worked out, and if in fact it was Ridgeway whom I had shot, then he could not have arrived at Victory until about the time the others were going down for seven o'clock breakfast. My best guess was that he had stayed at Thea's until I called, and then he had bolted. Knowing what I did about Ridgeway, if he was being sheltered by his friends at Victory Outreach, he would not be found in the men's dormitory.

I shook my escorts and walked through the office to the back passageway that led to the supply room where I had first met Ridgeway. The supply room door was closed, but not locked, so I went in.

Rows of setups—a sheet, a towel, toiletries, and a New Testament—were neatly stowed on shelves. The counters and floors were still damp from their evening cleaning. Bags of dirty laundry were lined up next to the back door—a door that I knew led out to the alley.

Ridgeway sure as hell wasn't folded into a laundry bag. Anything else that might be found inside them was Mike's department. I followed a draft to its source, the back door, and found that the door was ajar, as if someone had neglected to give it a last tug to drop the latch. Careless about locks in that neighborhood?

I pushed the door open and peered into the dark alley, saw no one there, and closed the door firmly. When I turned, there was a woman in the room behind me. She held a tearful child by the hand and carried a plastic diaper pail. We startled each other. And she failed to ask me the usual question.

I asked her, "Where did you come from?"

She pointed toward the ceiling as she brushed past me. "Gotta get these in to soak," she said, dumping soiled diapers into a stationary tub. She poured out soap flakes and ran hot water. "We're running low. I think someone's triple diapering, 'cause they sure went fast. We just washed the whole lot of them yesterday."

The woman watched me more closely than she watched the tub. And when I left the supply room and went back out to the passageway, she came with me. I found a door propped open with a child's wooden building block, and opened it. The door led to a narrow stairway that ended at a second door, this one also propped open. When I started up the stairs, the woman tried to get in front of me.

"Residents only," she said. "You can't go up there."

"Sure I can." There was no way she could stop me; I was taller than she and didn't have a child tugging on me. But she followed as closely as she could, scolding all the way up the stairs and into the women's shelter.

The rigid rules downstairs about staying out of the bedrooms did not prevail upstairs. Six or eight women and their children lived like a big family, sharing a kitchen and television room, with each family apparently assigned private sleeping quarters.

It was bedtime for the younger children, homework time for the older ones, popcorn and cocoa time for the mothers. Through the open door of a bedroom on the far side of the dining alcove, I could see a baby sleeping in his crib, a mother reading to a toddler tucked into a bed next to it. The activity in the common areas did not seem to bother them, or anyone.

A girl about age ten was the first to speak to me, the first to ask the usual question. "You from the county?"

"No," I said, watching the diaper lady hurry away to caucus with the women sitting at the dining table.

The girl looked me over carefully, shrugged, and went back to her board game on the floor. While the kids, perhaps accustomed to strangers moving through their quarters, paid me no attention, their mothers were obviously concerned.

I invaded, began peeking into open doors. When I reached for a closed door, an older woman, too old to belong to any of these small children, came up behind me. She wore a rosary on her belt, looked like a nun in plain clothes. "Can I help you?"

"I'm looking for a sick friend," I said. "He'll be in big trouble if he doesn't get help soon."

"He?" She had slipped between me and the door. "Men aren't allowed on this floor."

"That's why I'm checking beds. I heard a rumor." I reached past her and turned the knob.

Mike had said he could smell blood as soon as he walked into Thea's house. What I smelled when I opened the door was baby and the sharp, acrid sweat that accompanies cold fear.

As I reached for the light, the door slammed into me, hitting me on the side of the face hard enough to make me reel backward. Barry Ridgeway streaked past me. For a wounded man he ran pretty well. I started after him, but two of the women tried to hold me back. I broke free, vaulted a low coffee table, sprang at Ridgeway's back before he reached the exit, and dropped him facedown into the middle of the kids' game. They squealed with both terror and delight as their dice and playing pieces went flying. I hung on and wrapped my arms and legs around his middle.

Ridgeway was a big man, trained in street brawling. He rolled up, brought me with him, had his fist hauled back and ready to fly at my head when I said, "You're okay."

"What the ... ?" was all he said, keeping the fist in check as he seemed to realize who I was.

"I didn't shoot you?"

He relaxed his fist and I untangled my legs and slid to my feet. I kept patting his chest, finding nothing but solid, intact flesh.

He demanded, "What the hell are you doing here?"

"More than a few people want to ask you the same question."

He pulled down his shirttail and smoothed back his hair. "I suppose you brought your film crew?"

"No. Just six cops. Where were you last night?"

"Here," he said, looking a little dopey. "I needed to lay low."

"Why?"

"Because for the last week, every time I made a date to see an old friend, they ended up dead. Hector, Michelle, JoAnn—I got calls, they went down. So when I got a call from some guy said he was your pal Guido, said you wanted to see me at your house, I figured it was a setup. Lana told me you were out of town. I thought I would lay low up here until I could get enough money together to get out of town."

By that point, I had made three complete circuits around him, and he was all there. I peered up into his ruddy face. "Do you really date Thea D'Angelo?"

"Date her?" He smoothed his hair again, seemed thoroughly perplexed. "We had a dinner meeting about scheduling an interview in the studio, but I sure as hell wouldn't call it a date."

"Were you at Hector's on Sunday?"

"Yeah." His eyes suddenly filled. "I got there just about the time they took his body away. We were going to talk about Roy. For twenty years I wanted to talk to Hec about that night. I finally get there, and it's too late."

"What did you want to tell him?"

"That I was sorry. If I hadn't been drunk off my ass, things might have been different."

"How?"

"I never told anyone before." He put his hand up to still the quivering at the corner of his mouth. "It's none too easy to talk about now."

"Three people are dead, and one is still in the hospital. If you do talk, could anything worse happen?"

He gave me a sardonic grin. "If you don't have a film crew maybe you're bugged."

"I don't need to be bugged, because I have a whole roomful of witnesses."

The women had formed a circle around us and stood listening with rapt stillness. Ridgeway's circuit of their faces stopped when the woman with the rosary held the beads out to him. She said, "Confession is good for the soul."

I said, "She's right. What might have been different?"

"Frady might have made his twenty-five years," he said. "It was because of me he went down to Manchester and Main that night. We'd been talking up at the academy about how JoAnn didn't mean enough to either of us for her to be the cause of bad feelings between us. We were going to bury the hatchet, meet like it was a normal end of watch—a fresh start—have a beer in the usual place."

He fingered the rosary beads, as if each one repre-
sented a step along his path that night twenty years
ago. "I left the academy before Frady did. I stopped
for more drinks on the way, picked up a girl—
Michelle—fooled around till I was late. But Roy
waited; he was a better man than me, more serious
about patching things up.

"When I got to the lot there on the corner, he was
talking to a couple of chicks. If I had been on time,
if I had been sober, I would have gone with him, or
he would have come with me. But I was so far gone,
Roy just told me to go sleep it off and we could talk
later. Last I saw him, he was getting into his car with
the girls."

"Getting into his own car?"

He nodded.

"Did you recognize the girls?"

"Michelle knew one of them."

"A friend she used to dance with?" I said.

He must have prayed too hard; he broke the beads.
He studied the two ends with a guilty look on his
face, squashed as if he had committed yet another
unforgivable transgression.

If Ridgeway was telling the truth, then Mike's version of that night had been closer than mine in some
important details. I steeled myself, knowing I was
going to hear about it for a long time. But I took
Ridgeway by the arm and steered him toward the
stairs. I said, "Now that you've told your story once,
it won't be hard for you to tell it a second time."

CHAPTER

26

The sun was just rising behind the Oakland hills on the far side of the bay when the paramedics arrived. The blue-black water of the bay flashed fire red and then faded to deep green, all within the minute it took for the emergency crew to grab their gear and run down the gangplank to the houseboat.

Kellenberger lay on the polished floor of the houseboat, his bandages soaked through and reeking. His head was turned to the side and his eyes were open to watch the sunrise. He said, "How beautiful."

"Yes it is," I said. I sat on the floor beside him.

Even as the paramedics knelt to tend him, he kept his eyes on the bay. "How is your sister?"

"She had another seizure last night."

"I always liked her. She was the enemy, but I liked her."

"Am I the enemy, too, Kellenberger?"

"No, honey. Sorry you got in the way."

"That's all you have to say to me? Sorry?"

"You understand."

"No, I don't," I said. The blanket I tucked up under his chin didn't keep him from shivering. "Did Carlos O'Leary drive you up here?"

"There is no Carlos O'Leary."

When the first paramedic pulled away Thea's dressing to see what he had to work with, the wound began to bleed again. His partner was taking vitals. They exchanged a look, a solemn shake of the head, just the way a movie doctor would tell John Wayne that Gabby Hayes wasn't going to make it. Kellenberger would appreciate the image, I thought. As a matter of form, the medics started an IV and prepped the patient to be moved.

"Why did you grab me?" I asked him. "What were you going to do with me?"

"I don't know. You weren't supposed to be there, remember? I didn't want you to die in the fire, that's all. You kept going in after that damn dog."

Mike was outside on the deck talking with Jack, my erstwhile *Rolling Stone* man. All the subterfuge around my first visit to the houseboat became clear when Jack showed us his ID. Special Agent John Newquist, FBI, was assigned to keep an eye on an agent under a cloud, Charles Kellenberger, and to figure out why he was so interested in me. The Bureau didn't like the answer Kellenberger gave when they questioned his request for informant money. Desk jockeys don't need informants, travel money, and sudden time off.

"I don't get it, Kellenberger," I said.

"Sure you do." In full sunlight, he had no color. I had never seen a living human as bloodlessly pale. "It was me or them."

Three people were dead because Kellenberger had a twenty-year-old secret to protect. The stakes were his name, his career, the image of the Bureau. His pension.

I was nudged aside so that the paramedics could move Kellenberger from the floor to a stretcher. He reached for my hand. "Will you ride with me, honey? I don't want to die alone."

I said, "Sure," because at that point it didn't matter to me that I had shot him in self-defense. The bottom line was, I had shot him, and that fact pained me deeply. I took his cold hand and walked beside him to the ambulance. Mike and Newquist met us there.

I said to Newquist, "You should get a different cover. You make a lousy journalist. You're not hungry enough." I handed him the Polaroids Kellenberger took of him lurking at People's Park. "And you stick out."

"We had to come up with something in a hurry. That cover was the best we could do. You're not easy to tag." He pulled out a set of handcuffs and snapped one cuff on Kellenberger's wrist, the other on the stretcher frame.

"Is that necessary?" I asked.

"It's procedure," he said. And then he stopped me from getting into the ambulance behind the stretcher.

"Can I have more time with him?" I asked.

Newquist checked with the paramedics, got the same hopeless-prospects frown, and told me to go ahead.

Alone for five minutes, I crouched beside Kellenberger. "Was it you at Hector's Sunday afternoon?"

"Yeah." His breathing was shallow. "Bad move. Didn't think it through. Been out of the field for too long. I guess you could say I panicked. That Melendez—all the shit he got ahold of through the goddamn Freedom of Information Act—he had us hammered."

"What did he find out?"

"Frady. Maybe the LAPD and the FBI didn't get along back then, but it never was okay to let an officer go down."

"You knew Frady was going to be shot?"

"No way" sounded like a chest gurgle. "All we knew was, the girl he thought he was going to get lucky with was in the SLA. Those knotheads talked all the time about kidnapping a cop, so that's all we thought they were up to. We thought we could go in and take him back, and take Patty Hearst back, any time we wanted to. We had information coming from that house."

"Nancy Ling Perry talked to Michelle Tarbett."

"You got it. People underground need an outside person. Nancy picked Michelle. Tried to recruit her for the revolution. Michelle was a source for us on a lot of things. Her boss was into the mob and we liked to keep an eye on him."

"Hector figured it out, too," I said.

"He was getting awful damn close. Problem was this: after the fact, we neglected to inform LAPD that we had information relating to Frady's whereabouts and companions the night he died. We weren't ready to go in on the SLA, and we didn't want the LAPD fucking things up."

"If you had been more cooperative, there might never have been a shoot-out."

"What if, what if, what if. You can't rewrite history."

"Isn't that exactly what you've been trying to do?" I said. "What happened at Hector's on Sunday?"

He looked at the tube running into his cuffed hand. "If I live, I'll deny I ever said a word of this."

"Hope you get that chance."

"Yeah." He pulled out the IV and held it up to show me. "Insurance."

"I made a promise, keep yours."

"Sunday night. I was talking to Melendez when the old woman called for help. I went up with him, two for the price of one. Hector was a pro; he didn't need help. He calmed the kid right down, got him to take his meds. Ten minutes, he was home free. But I saw an opportunity to save my butt and I took it, that's all."

"Why were you carrying a throwaway gun unless you intended to use it?"

"Contingency planning."

"Three people," I said. "How valuable do you think your butt is?"

"Don't beat yourself up worrying about it. They all played their parts. Except the kid who went down with Hector. He didn't want to die, he just wanted to get locked up. I feel real bad about him."

"I bet you do. Did you use Thea as your mole to

find out what we were doing, what we had found out?"

He chuckled. "She was happy to help any little way she could."

"One more thing, Kellenberger. Did you fuck Thea?"

He gave me a wan yet gallant grin. "Sure. We both needed it."

The paramedics came to the door, bounded in when they saw the dangling IV line. I was ordered, "Out."

"Good-bye, Kellenberger," I said, releasing his hand. "Any last words?"

"Yeah." He winked at me. "Go ahead and tell Thea I loved her. Why not, huh?"

"In lieu of payment? Was that how you kept Michelle in line?"

He smiled, patted his round belly. "I wasn't always fat and bald, honey."

I got out, went straight over to Mike, and put my head against his shoulder. "Goddamn," I said.

The ambulance doors closed and it drove away, without lights and sirens. Jack was the first to speak.

"How did you know to look here?" he asked.

"I didn't," I said. "The houseboat was just one more possibility. Once it was clear that Ridgeway wasn't our man, then we had to look at everyone else who had some connection, go through a process of elimination. In the end, Kellenberger was the only one left. That's when I thought about this place. He brought me here last week to find out how much I knew."

"Every step of the way, he was setting up

Ridgeway," Mike said. "And doing a pretty good job of it."

I nudged Mike in the ribs. "Say it. Get it over with. Say I told you so."

"Not me." There was an evil little light in his eyes. "I wouldn't stoop that low."

I said, "Uh-huh," and started walking toward the lot where we had left my father's car.

He called after me: "But I told you from day one, no cop killed Frady."

CHAPTER
27

Christmas Eve, Casey, the Snow Queen, jetéd across the *Nutcracker* stage. Her long, skinny arms and legs had acquired solid, round, mature muscle during the two months she had been in Houston.

My mother began to weep as soon as my daughter appeared, stage left. It was difficult for me not to follow suit, but I wanted to seem composed for Casey, whether I was or not. She had warned me: the Snow Queen's mother should not bawl, gush, or give her more than one bouquet of flowers during curtain calls. Decorum, please; there were professional dance company scouts in the audience.

My father, his eyes brimming, leaned in close to me to whisper, "My God, she looks so much like Emily. I never realized."

He was right. Tall and graceful and bursting with cocky athleticism, Casey was truly cast in the image of her late aunt Emily. Emily left us no children of her own, and so I took comfort in seeing the resemblance passed to the next generation through my own daughter. I missed Emily.

Casey executed a leap that made her audience gasp. Mike slipped his hand under my elbow. When I looked up at him, he gave me his wink, no more than a gathering together of his crow's-feet. He said, "She should try out for the Olympics."

Emily had passed away the week after Thanksgiving. There had been no seizure, no stroke, no medical dramatics of any kind. One night, shortly after midnight, Emily simply ceased to breathe. She had been alone in her room, so no one could say exactly what her last moments were like. But the nurse who discovered Emily during regular rounds told us that the sheets were still folded neatly right up under her chin: no pain, no struggle.

Christmas in Houston had turned out to be a blessing for us all, a break from traditions that would have been painful to go through because Emily was no longer a part of our celebration. Surrounded by my family and our closest friends, dazzled by my nearly grown daughter, I could not remember ever feeling happier. Even my ex-husband and his next wife—a Houston native—sitting in the row behind us did not spoil my sense of contentment.

The Frady film was in final editing, and I was more than pleased with the shape it was taking. Two crimes: the straightforward terrorist murder of Roy Frady, and Kellenberger's tangled cover-up. The contrasts were both stark and full of irony: one death spawned four.

On the editing room floor there was, figuratively, a piece of discarded tape, a sequence of Kellenberger walking into Hector's apartment the night Hector died, and a voice-over, Emily Harris reading the eulogy to her dead comrades, chanting, "Death to the Fascist insect that preys upon the lives of the people." Guido had put it together as a joke. And I had excised it because some things aren't funny.

The Snow Queen was called back for two bows; a dozen friends and relatives can make plenty of noise. And when it was over, and the kisses and gifts had been delivered, and the white tutu was replaced with red sweats, Casey was still so high that she needed the tethering of her grandfather's long arms to guide her into one of the two limos hired to ferry her entourage of admirers back to the hotel.

Wearing a tiara that Michael braided out of ribbons taken from her bouquets, Casey presided over an elegant post-theater supper set up in the sitting room of the suite shared by my parents and the Perlmutters: a Houston blowout was their holiday gift to each other. There was cake and champagne, and another round of accolades for our ballerina. And then Casey crashed.

When she was tucked into bed in her room, with R.E.M. playing on her CD as antidote to two months of "Dance of the Sugarplum Fairies," Mike and I retired to our own room next door.

I slipped a tape into the VCR.

Mike, nuzzling my neck, unzipping the back of my dress, said, "I'd rather do it than watch it."

"Gift from Lana; Guido brought it with him." I pushed Play. "It's a roughcut of the dramatization we filmed. I want you to see it, see if I got it right."

"Okay." He pulled me down on the bed with him and wrapped himself around me as the screen filled with the interior of the Hot-Cha Club. He kissed the back of my neck. "You won. It's black-and-white."

"I lost. It's a dramatized recreation."

This section of the film begins at around eleven o'clock on May 10. Sal Ypolito narrates as the actors portraying Barry and Michelle play out their scene: a raunchy dance, several drinks, they're asked to leave. "I couldn't have that kind of activity in my place. I run a class establishment. It ain't right to speak ill of the dead, but that Michelle didn't know when to stop unless someone told her. So I told her, take the drunk cop home."

The narrative is picked up by Barry Ridgeway as the actors appear outside the liquor store at the corner of Manchester and Main. "I'd had too much to drink—but that was par for the course for me in those days. When Michelle and I left the Hot-Cha, we went over to the corner where I was supposed to meet Roy. I didn't expect him to be there so late, but he was. Maybe he was waiting for me, or maybe he was waiting to get lucky. When I got there, he was swapping tongue with these two good-looking women. One of them was a friend of Michelle, a dancer named Nancy. Her friend started coming on to me, said I should dump Michelle and make it a double date with them. Michelle got pretty hot. So we left. I saw Roy get into his car with the two women and head north on Main Street, up toward the station. That was the last I saw him."

The actors portraying Michelle and Barry try to have sex in her car, but he's too drunk, so she takes him to his car in the Seventy-seventh Street Division parking lot, wrestles him into the backseat. And then she calls her FBI contact, Charles Kellenberger, and tells him that the SLA has picked up a cop. Kellenberger tells her to keep her mouth shut and to keep pumping her mole in the SLA. Then he makes a date with her. Fade out.

My voice comes on and explains that what happens next is only my best guess. Frady, blindfolded and handcuffed, his shoelaces tied together, is paraded in front of the nine residents of 833 West Eighty-fourth Street. Nancy hands the officer's gun to one of the others, who tucks it into his belt. The group debates whether they should keep Frady as a hostage, but there are too many liabilities. So they bundle the young cop into the trunk of a car stolen for the purpose—a low-rider's green Buick Riviera. Frady is driven away by three people. The Nancy actress, wearing an Afro wig, drives.

Frady's own car is taken down the freeway, with an SLA van following. The car is dumped and wiped clean. This scene is shot in deep shadow that masks the drivers because, though I have my own ideas, I cannot know who of the nine, or how many of the nine, they were.

Cut to an approximation of the burned-out house on West Eighty-ninth Street. Frady is marched into the ruins by his SLA captors and made to kneel. Mike narrates: "Roy Frady was shot execution style with a semiautomatic pistol. There were numerous wounds to his head and body. No witnesses have come forward. Sometime between midnight and one A.M., neighbors heard a single shot, followed by five or six more in a burst." Frady falls forward; I declined to have the sound of gunfire added to the loop. But when the shooters leave Frady alone, in the background we hear a car drive off, and laughter.

The sun rises on Frady's car, and the voice-over is Mike and Doug in conversation about what it was like to hear that their friend was dead, and then to find his little economy station wagon. Ridgeway joins them.

"I had a hangover," Ridgeway says. "But that wasn't what made me so sick. It was seeing Roy's car. I was already under Internal Affairs investigation for bad checks, so I was really scared about saying that I might know something. I said nothing. Twenty years is a long time to keep a secret like that."

I turned off the sound. "What do you think?"

"I think the guy who plays Frady spent too much time in the gym. Frady wasn't a big guy."

"I did it for Mary Helen and her kids. A goodly portion of the audience will think this is real." I kicked off my shoes. "Whatever real is."

There was snow on the screen and an image trying to form. I turned the player off because I did not trust Guido. I didn't want to find a little homemade goody edited in—naked bodies in the bathtub, for instance. Guido still had not returned my tape. I thought he was afraid that doing so would remind me of his gaffe. We were working together as if everything between us was status quo. But it wasn't quite. I never went over to his house anymore. I never used him as a convenient shoulder, either. And he respected that space.

"I've only used actors where the real players are dead, except for Ridgeway," I said. "I'm still not sure about the dramatization, but Lana is wild for it. She wants to call the film 'The Bitter Web,' as in 'What a bitter web we weave, when first we practice to deceive.' "

"What do you want to call it?"

"I think a variation on 'Ode to an Athlete Dying Young.' "

Mike shook his head. " 'Requiescat in Pace.' You've made Roy Frady's eulogy."

"The title decision will be made by the marketing people, so there's no sense getting committed to one. Gaylord is already looking for a writer to do the treatment for the movie-of-the-week version of the making of our movie. The working title is 'Film Fatale.' "

"It's your story, why don't you write it?"

"I wouldn't touch it with a fork."

"Who's going to play you?"

"Good question."

He peeled my dress off over my head. "Will her period be late, too?"

AFTERWORD

Kill Mike Edwards

—Graffiti, Nickerson Gardens Federal Housing Project,
May 1974

This is fact: sometime after midnight on May 10, 1974, Officer Michael Lee Edwards, who worked out of the Seventy-seventh Street Division of the LAPD, was shot dead in a burned-out triplex at 122½ West Eighty-ninth Street in the city's Southeast section. His murder has never been solved.

This also is fact: the night before Michael Lee died, and less than a mile from the murder house, the nine core members of the Symbionese Liberation Army, including their prize captive, Patricia Hearst, moved into a shack at 833 West Eighty-fourth Street. They lived in that tiny unit, without telephone or power, for one week. On May 17, 1974, six of them moved to another hideout, and it was there that they died in a shoot-out with the police.

The rest of the story you have just read is fiction. As far as I know.

Don't miss the new mystery featuring
Maggie MacGowen,
coming soon from Dutton in 1997.

Chapter 1

Honey Thi Nguyen pushed our little boat away from a muddy hump rising out of the water using one long bamboo oar. The water ran slow and shallow close to the bank, so we regularly ran aground. No matter, Honey said when I groused, it was better to get stuck now and then than to be spotted out in the open, rowing in the center of the river.

A heavy canopy of jackfruit and banana leaves provided good cover as we moved downstream through the night. Honey stood in the stern behind me, rowing with a strong and steady cross-arm movement, while I sat in the bow and steered with short paddles. Sitting, I was nearly as tall as she was standing up.

Honey spoke to me in French, though her English was flawless and my college French was beyond rusty; another form of cover, she said, in an area where Americans were still rare. She teased me incessantly, affectionately: "I thought you did not believe in such mumbo jumbo as astrology, Maggie MacGowen."

"I don't," I said.

"If you don't believe, then why do you say that if Khanh Nguyen had consulted her astrologer, she would still be alive?"

"Because Khanh's astrologer, Mr. Chan, talks too much." I managed to maneuver us around a marooned clump of water palms. "Mumbo jumbo? Is that the proper vocabulary you learned at the Sorbonne?"

"No. That is the vocabulary I learned from the GI who couldn't pronounce my name and first called me Honey."

It was February, near the end of Vietnam's dry season, and the water was low, leaving normally submerged plants and a variety of junk exposed. Because the night was nearly moonless, obstructions were often difficult to see until we were in danger of collision. Twice, Honey had to use her oars to pole us along over sandbars. Both of us were tired, and both of us looked forward to reaching the confluence with the Han River above Da Nang where the going would be easier: deeper water, more anonymity.

My blistered hands stung. "It's late, Honey. There's no one around to see us. Can't we move into the middle of the river for a while and let the current do more of the work?"

"It is not safe." Her oars made no more sound cutting through the water than the riff of a breeze through the leaves overhead. "You were telling me about Khanh's astrologer."

"Mr. Chan is an old man and very lonely," I said, ducking as a palm swept my face. "Almost no one comes to see him, probably because he talks so much. Every morning, Khanh had to set aside at least thirty minutes for his chatter before he got around to reading her forecast."

"Thirty minutes is a very long time to talk on the telephone," Honey said. "Even before the Americans left, when I still worked at the museum in Da Nang, I never talked for so long on the telephone. Every day, you say?"

"Every day, except last Friday."

There was a gap in the leaf canopy where a village dock jutted from the bank, an exposed stretch of water maybe twenty yards long. Before venturing into the open, we stopped to scan the cluster of mud and bamboo huts at the end of the dock for light or activity, and then, when all seemed still, we sprinted across the breech, pulling furiously against the water until we were again sheltered by the jackfruit leaves.

My arms ached. Behind me, Honey panted. As we slid again into the black silence of the shadows, Honey rested her oars and let our momentum push us along for a moment. I could not see her moon-shaped face well enouch in the dark to read an expression, but I heard her chuckle.

"Where did you learn to row like that?" I asked.

"After the war, when the Hanoi government reassigned my profession from assistant museum curator to rice paddy laborer. Rowing is not all that I learned to do."

"You must be tired," I said. "Would you like to trade places?"

"You are too tall, Maggie. That hat may hide your hair, but if you stood up, your height would give you away. Anyone could see that you don't belong here. Word travels fast along the river, as fast as any telephone. They would be waiting for us when we reach Da Nang."

"If we had driven, we would be there by now," I said.

"Faster is not always safer."

I deferred to her. Honey had survived a lifetime in the combat zone, while I, a documentary filmmaker and reformed news hen, had been only an occasional visitor to the front, and always as nothing more than an observer, a photographer stealing images to sell. I went to El Salvador, observed the inglorious invasion of Granada, and spent four days with Desert Storm, always carrying press credentials that offered me some protection. But this trip to Vietnam had nothing to do with my job, and I had no shield other than this eighty-two pound tyrant wearing rubber sandals.

I opened our basket of provisions and handed Honey a Coke bottle filled with lemonade and a rice cake wrapped in a square of banana leaf. While she rested and ate, I checked to make sure our cargo was staying dry. The cargo was small: six cereal box-sized metal ammo cases stenciled with *U.S. Army* and covered by a musty, leftover camouflage tarp.

Our boat was something like the old skiff my father used to take my sister and brother and me fishing in off the Berkeley Marina when we were kids—nearly flat-bottomed, with a square stern and a pointed bow—but this boat was smaller. It seemed to me that everything in Vietnam was scaled small. Or that I, at five feet seven inches, was scaled too large.

Honey ran her hands through the water, cooling them. I felt responsible for her discomfort and for the very real peril I had put her in. Conditions in Vietnam had eased considerably during the last couple of years, but one never knew when the hammer might fall again. Honey didn't need ten more years of forced labor on her résumé, and I wanted to go home.

I said, "It won't be light for hours. Why don't you lie down for a while. I'll watch over things."

"We don't know what's ahead. We can't waste time and darkness by sleeping." Honey handed back the lemonade and picked up her oars. "Tell me the rest of the story about my cousin Khanh and I will forget to be tired."

Honey poled off from the bottom, slipping us again into moving water. I steered around a dark eddy that I thought was an animal of some kind swimming upstream, but it turned out to be an exposed stump. When we were past, I resumed the story.

"As I was saying, Khanh was very rushed last Friday morning. Normally, she would have driven to my house, but Sam, her husband, had a dead car battery that morning. They own a big restaurant in San Francisco, you know. With Tet coming, Sam needed to make deliveries and buy supplies. He took Khanh's car and left her to use the bus.

"Sean, her elder son, called to say he had managed to get a standby seat on an early flight, and would arrive home Friday afternoon instead of Saturday. All of Khanh's children were coming home for Tet and she was suddenly short of time to finish her preparations.

"Around eight on Friday morning Khanh called me and asked if it was all right for her to drop by my house, but only for a minute. There was so much to be done that morning, she said, she didn't even have time to call Mr. Chan."

"Getting ready for Tet," Honey said, "if Mr. Chan had told Khanh Nguyen that Friday was not an auspicious day to leave the house, she would have gone out anyway."

"The point is this, if Khanh had taken time to call Mr. Chan, she would have missed the nine o'clock bus. She would not have been at the intersection of Van Ness Avenue and Lombard Street in San Francisco at precisely nine-thirty a.m. to be hit in the head by a bullet."

"A random act, you say?" Honey swatted at a swarm of mosquitoes.

"Poor Khanh happened to be in the right place at exactly the wrong time."

For a long moment, Honey was silent. Only the rhythmic push of the boat assured me she was there at all. When she spoke, her voice was softer than before, and did not carry its usual teasing undertone. "Do you believe in karma, Maggie MacGowen?"

"I don't know." Dark seemed to envelope us; the leaves overhead were now so dense I could not see the water.

"If Sam's car did not break," she said. "If Sean did not get a seat on an early plane, if Khanh did not change her morning routine on Friday, then would you be here with me now?"

"Probably not."

"Probably not also means perhaps."

I turned in my seat to look at her, but saw only a dark shape. "Being here is my fate, you say?"

"Fate? Maybe it is mischief. You have to be careful during Tet not to offend the spirits of the ancestors. They can slip over into this world so easily." Honey thumped the covered ammo boxes with the toe of her sandal. "Consider what we carry."

"Knock it off." I caught her shoe and tugged it. "It's scary enough out here without angry ancestors for company."

"Do you still pray for Khanh Nguyen?" she asked.

"I sat vigil with Sam," I said. "I went to her funeral."

"That is not enough, Maggie MacGowen; she has been dead now only five days. We believe that Khanh will walk with us until she has been dead for forty-nine days. All that time we will pray to the ancestors to accept her into the next world. Because she died with such violence, and so close to Tet, we must be especially diligent with prayers and offerings. Otherwise, the ancestors may not accept her. Her spirit could be trapped in this world forever. She could do much mischief to our families."

"I'll pray." I pulled harder on the oars, aiming for a brighter patch of water, abandoning any notion of resting again before we reached Da Nang.

What I did or did not believe about the soul's afterlife seemed at that moment to be less important than what Khanh had believed. Last Friday, when she was shot in San Francisco, Khanh was half a block from my house, where all of those I hold most dear were eating breakfast. Khanh had been a friend for many years. A good friend. Just the same, I did not want her spirit, angry or otherwise, trapped so close to my front door.

SUPER SLEUTHS